CW01642554

THE CRUELLEST MONTH

The Life and Times of Ann Brown

Part 2

Sam Young

Sam Young

First published 2025 by Maeday Press

ISBN: 978-1-0686431-1-8

I am grateful to the MS Society UK for permission to use their logo.

Editiorial & typesetting: Averill Buchanan

Cover design: More Visual, Leicester

For my Ma, who continues to inspire.

For Mae. Wife. Friend. Inspiration.

With thanks to Wendy for everything.

For everyone living with MS, their carers and families.

All the proceeds from the sale of this novel
are going to MS research.

Thank you to the MS Society UK, which is working hard to find better treatments and, hopefully one day, a cure.

MS Society

Thank you to everyone who buys this book. I hope you enjoy reading it.

April is the cruellest month …

T.S. Eliot, *The Wasteland*

CHAPTER 1

In the smoky gloom, it looked like nothing much had changed in the Starr Ballroom. Ann was early. The band was still setting up. A few girls she knew were sitting at the tables lining the sides of the dance floor. It seemed smaller somehow. Doreen Johnston, Harry's sister, caught her eye and Ann went over.

'Hi, Ann,' Doreen said. 'What's the craic? Long time no see. Sit down.' She shuffled over to make space. 'How's Walter? And the wean – Daisy, isn't it? And your ma?'

Ann felt sick. She smiled, trying to stay calm. This was a mistake. 'They're all grand, thanks, Doreen. It's good to be back. You're looking very pretty. How's Harry doing?' Better to get Doreen talking about herself and everyday things, then she'd be all right, Ann told herself.

'He's doing okay, I think. It's hard to tell. He doesn't talk to me much. He's still at Nestle's, but I think he misses Joe more than he lets on.'

'No girlfriend?'

'Girls appear and disappear. Nothing serious.'

'Still playing football?'

'Yes, yes. He goes out with Nigel in his wee car now and again. Have you heard from Joe at all? And what about Walter? How's he doing? What is it – a year now? More. Must be hard for you.'

Ann wasn't sure if she could talk about Walter. Talking about Joe was easier. 'Joe has learned to write since he joined the navy, but he's obviously not good at it yet. He's only sent one letter. We're not even sure where he is. But no news is good news, so he must be all right or we would have heard something. Are you on your own?'

'No, John's up at the bar and Sadie and Billy are coming. You're welcome to join us if you want. Oliver's back tonight, so it should be good.'

John appeared from the back of the scrum at the bar and carried down two glasses of brown lemonade.

'Ann Brown, as I live and breathe!' He set the drinks down and gave her a hug. 'Long time no see. You look gorgeous.' He suddenly caught himself on and looked guiltily at Doreen. 'How's Walter? Can't believe where the time's gone. We really miss him at work. Any chance he might be back soon?'

They were genuinely concerned about Walter. Ann knew she couldn't keep dodging their questions. It was time to stop hiding and confront things.

'Walter's just okay. He's not making any real progress … not quickly anyway. He can get up out of his wheelchair now, but only for a wee while. He's a long way from being able to go back to work.' *He'll never be back at work.* The thought hit her like a punch in the guts.

'Well, that sounds good,' Doreen said. 'Maybe he'll come on faster now. It must be so hard for you, what with the wee baby and all. I don't think I could do it.'

'I can't give up on him. I know Daisy isn't his, but she needs a da and Walter will be a great da.' Ann had her fingers crossed behind her back as she said this. She hoped they couldn't see her blush.

'You're a hero,' John said before he took a large swig of his lemonade and burped.

Doreen shook her head.

'Oh, there's Oliver. I must go and say hello,' Ann said, escaping before they could quiz her any more.

'Come here!' Oliver gave her a big bear hug. 'You look a million dollars.' Charlie, the giant drummer, appeared on the stage. 'What time do you call this?' Oliver said, tapping the face of his watch. He turned back to Ann. 'Sorry, what were we talking about?'

She laughed. 'Nothing, Oliver. You're busy. Good luck tonight. Showtime, eh?'

'Oh yeah, thanks. Hope you enjoy it.' He flashed her a grin and was immediately back in band leader mode.

By this time there were no spare seats, so Ann went up to the bar. The male crowd parted like the Red Sea, surprised to see a lady in their territory. There were lots of familiar faces.

'Ann Brown! Great to see you. How are you?'

'Hi, Ann. How's Walter?'

'Where have you been?'

'How was Belfast?'

'How's Walter?'

'How's the wean? What's her name again?'

'Do you want a drink?'

She smiled and mumbled answers in the general direction of the crowd, said yes to the last question. Big Alec was still behind the bar.

'Ann Brown! Long time no see. You look great. Cider?'

‘I’ll get that,’ Robbie said. He was another of Walter’s friends – an actual baker in the Model Bakery.

Alec poured the bottle and slid the full glass across to Ann. ‘There you go, love. Get that into you and you’ll be flyin’.’

‘Thanks, Alec. Thanks, Robbie. Cheers.’

They clinked glasses. Ann took a long drink and breathed a deep sigh. She had missed all this, and the cider would help.

The band started the first set and Robbie asked if he could have the pleasure. She said yes.

* * *

Ann opened the front door. Ma and Fred quickly separated, looking a little sheepish as she came into the living room.

‘You’re early, love,’ Ma said, patting her hair.

‘No need to stop on my account.’

‘Don’t be so cheeky! How was it?’

‘It was good – no, it was great, but I got tired. I didn’t want to stay for the last dance in case someone asked to walk me home, but it was good.’

‘And you saw lots of your friends?’ Ma slumped into her chair. Fred turned the radio down and sat in his chair on the other side of the hearth.

‘Yes, a lot of old faces. Big Alec’s still behind the bar. Iris was there – I think she’s going to get married soon – and I was talking to Doreen Johnston for a while at the start.’

‘How’s Harry?’ Ma asked.

‘She thinks he misses Joe, but he’s okay. No steady girlfriend, still at Nestle’s, still playing football and running around with Nigel.’

‘He’s a good boy. How was the dancing?’

‘Oliver was better than ever. It was good. It was just one big long excuse-me, which is why I’m so knackered. I never got a rest. Some of the dancers were quite good, but not a patch on Walter.'

Ma exchanged a glance with Fred. 'I'm glad it was good and you enjoyed yourself.'

'I did. It was great to dance again and I didn't get pregnant, which is a big plus.'

Fred laughed out loud, an old man's whiskey-and-fags chuckle.

'Ann!' Ma spluttered. 'That's an awful thing to say.'

'But it's true.'

'It's still awful.' Ma pursed her lips, trying to look cross. 'Poor Walter.'

'Poor Walter my arse,' Ann retorted. 'Poor me, stuck with a useless gobshite who can hardly stand up.' She looked down at her feet. 'I miss him.' She was determined not to cry.

Fred stood up and put on his duncher, pulling it down tight and straightening it at the peak. He gave Ann a peck on the cheek.

'It's good you got up the courage to go back,' he said. 'You need to live a bit and enjoy yourself. You're still young.'

'Thanks, Fred. There's no need to leave just yet. I'm off to bed. Don't forget, Ma – church in the morning.'

'Yes, dear,' Ma said, and they all grinned.

Daisy was fast asleep in her cot in Ann's bedroom upstairs. Ann kissed her daughter's head. 'I'm not cheating on Daddy. Honestly, I'm not,' she said in a low voice. 'I needed to dance and have a bit of craic. It was very strange without him. He'll understand, I know he will. You can tell him all about it next week.'

She heard the radio being turned off downstairs as she snuggled under the blankets.

'Sorry, Walter,' she whispered at the ceiling.

CHAPTER 2

Ann was woken by the cries of her little blond alarm clock. She didn't sleep that well any more, unlike Daisy, who slept ... well, like a baby. She picked her up out of the ancient wooden cot and wrinkled her nose at the smell.

'How come more stuff comes out of you than goes in?' Ann scolded. 'There, there, I know it can't be nice. I'll get you all cleaned up in a minute or two.' She wrapped her up in a blanket and gave her a wee kiss on the forehead. Daisy stopped crying. 'You're as good-natured as your da, aren't you?' she said and put her back in the cot. 'I'll get the kettle on. You wait here.'

She tried to sneak down the stairs, but she knew Ma would be awake at the first creak of the first step. She took the big blackened kettle out to the tap and filled it. The running water made her want to have a wee. I need new slippers, she thought as she sat shivering in the outside privy, and this toilet seat is about to fall apart.

Back in the kitchen, she poured some warm water into her jug and went upstairs to get washed and dressed. She listened at Ma's door for a moment, knowing that Ma was listening back.

'Kettle's boiled, Ma. Would you like some porridge?'

'No, best not, love. Plays havoc with my bowels. A piece of toast will do going out.'

'Are you sure you're going to be okay going on your own?'

'It won't be the first time. I'll be grand.'

'When was the last time you went to church by yourself?'

'It's been a while, but I'll be grand. I'll be down in a minute.'

'Okay, I'll make the toast when you come down. Daisy needs changed, so I'll do that first.'

'Did she sleep all right?'

'Like Walter at the pictures.'

Ann washed Daisy in the tin bath, and left the dirty nappy to soak in a bucket of cold water and Persil. It would get washed out later.

When Ma came down, they had tea and toast. Ma rarely said much that wasn't necessary, but Ann knew she wasn't looking forward to going to church, which was sad. It had always been a place where she'd found comfort and stability.

'Are you sure you're okay?' Ann asked for the umpteenth time.

'Yes, stop going on about it. I'll be fine.'

'Is Mrs Bann calling here?'

'No. I'll knock her door and we'll go up the town together.'

'Six of one, I suppose, whichever way you go. You still have to go up the hill.'

'We'll hold each other up. Walking sticks on the outside. We'll be grand.'

They sat on for half an hour or so.

'I'd better go,' Ma said eventually.

'It's very early.'

‘Well, I want to get in before everyone else, and Betty is even slower than me.’

Ann knew there was no point in debating it any further. ‘I’ll have the soup ready when you get back.’

‘That’ll be lovely, and please don’t worry. I have to go and it’ll be fine.’

Ma bent down over the source of all their worries and gave her a wee kiss on the cheek. ‘You look after your mummy now, won’t you? And be a good girl.’

Daisy flashed her killer smile and gurgled.

‘See, Ma! She’s just like her da.’

* * *

Betty Bann tried to make small talk as they staggered and puffed their way up Courthouse Hill. ‘They think butter and sugar will come off rationing soon. Doesn’t look like there’ll be a flood this year. What do you think?’ Her old friend usually had an opinion on most things. She mightn’t say much, but what she did say was always simple common sense. But Kathleen wasn’t herself this morning. She seemed on edge. There was a lot of gossip about her new wean, or was it Ann’s. It certainly seemed odd, but Betty decided it was best to say nothing.

They leaned in against each other and wheezed on as John Street merged with James Street. They could see Reverend Goodman standing outside the main entrance of the church, ready to meet and greet. Betty felt Kathleen tense up.

‘Damn, I think he’s seen us,’ Kathleen said. ‘Now we’ll have to go up and say hello. We can’t just walk past. No, hold on a minute …’

A young couple came round from the back of the church and engaged the minister in conversation.

'Who are they?' Betty asked.

'No idea. Must be new. It doesn't matter. Come on, hurry up and we can slip in round the side.'

With imperceptible acceleration they went round the corner to the left of the church and in through the gate on Fairmount Road.

'No steps, Betty.'

'Indeed, Kathleen.'

They were out of breath as they entered the old church and were first in.

'You go on now, Betty. I'll be alright from here,' Kathleen said, and Betty knew she had been dismissed. She shuffled on down to her pew, six rows from the back in the middle of the main body of the church. She would soon be joined by children and grandchildren. She normally got a lift in her son's car, but Kathleen needed her company that morning.

Ma made her way round to her pew in the transept – third row back on the right-hand side facing the pulpit. She went all the way in to the wall, where she always sat. The empty bench seemed huge.

The Johnstons arrived and said polite hellos as they moved sideways along the pew in front, sitting in the same order they always sat in. The whole family still together. It wasn't lost on Ma.

Harry always sat at the outside, as Joe had done, but while his sisters sorted themselves out, he stepped into Ma's pew.

'Hello, Mrs Brown.' He held out his hand.

'Good morning, Harry.' She gently took his hand. 'You look very smart.'

'Thank you.' He was blushing ever so slightly. 'I feel like I'm trespassing here.' He smiled. 'We could squeeze up a bit, if you'd like to join us.'

Ma's voice trembled a little at the innocent generosity. 'Thank you, Harry, but I'm happy to sit here, where I've always sat. I'm all right. Honestly, I'm fine.'

Harry didn't think she was. Her handshake was feeble and she looked old and small, but he decided to let it drop. 'Any word from Joe?' he asked.

'No, just that one letter. No idea where he is or what he's doing.'

'Well, maybe no news is good news. I'm sure they'd have told you if they'd made him walk the plank or anything.'

'Oh Harry, could they really make him walk the plank? I've got enough to worry about.'

Harry could see no hint of a smile to let him know she knew he was joking. She was genuinely upset.

'No, they won't, Mrs Brown. Sorry, it was just a wee joke. That was just something pirates did in old movies. I don't think they do it in the navy. Sorry if I upset you.'

'It's all right, Harry. I'm sure Joe is safe and well and will be home soon.'

'I hope so, Mrs Brown. You're sure you're all right?'

'Yes I am, honestly. Thank you.'

Ma paid no attention to the hats and fashion as the church filled up. The service started, she stood up, mumbled the words of the first hymn and sat down again. Harry obviously still thought God was deaf and she couldn't help but smile as she listened to him belting out the hymn, completely out of tune. He's a good boy, she thought, and he's still here.

The sermon started and Ma's mind wandered off for a wee private chat with God:

I know you're really busy, it being Sunday and all, and I know I pray a lot and you don't always listen, but I need you to listen now, coz this is no ordinary prayer. I need a miracle. But you probably already know that because you know everything. So, you know I've always worried about the weans. And it was easy when they were wee because I could worry about them all at the same time, but now I don't know which one to worry about next. I don't even know where Joe is. Harry says they might make him walk the plank if he's naughty and Joe has always been naughty. If that doesn't happen, he'll probably end up getting eaten by a cannonball in the jungle somewhere. You need to keep Joe safe for me. What happens to cannonballs when they die? Can they go to heaven, even if they've eaten some poor innocent cub from Omagh? I know you made them all, but they're not really Christians, are they? I suppose they don't even know that they're not Christians, so how can they get into heaven?

Talking about getting eaten, I'm worried about Hilda. There's big giant polar bears walking about the streets where she lives. Can you go to heaven if your head's inside a polar bear? It doesn't bear thinking about.

Muriel thinks that Al might be in love with her, but he's posh and she's just ordinary and he's probably going to marry somebody posh like him and she'll be left all alone. She'll be upset and will have to come home and that would break her heart because she loves her job and she likes London, but that's only because Al is there to take her places and show her all the sights.

I know these worries are all ifs and buts and maybes, but my real prayer today, my really big worry, the miracle I'm asking for, is for Ann – well, Walter, I suppose, because he's the one who's crocked, but Ann is in a bit of a mess too, as you know. And we both know that Walter caused this mess and the only way out of this mess, that I can see, is if you make Walter better so he can marry Ann and help her look after Daisy and they can all live happily ever after like good Christians. Is it wrong to want Walter better just so he'll make Ann happy? You know that's not what I mean.

I like Walter and want the best for him too. Maybe you can't forgive him, or don't want to make him better, if his broken head was meant as a punishment for what he did, but surely that's not very Christian. He can't repent or ask for forgiveness or anything, not the way he is. Ann has forgiven him and she's the one who's suffering for what he did, so maybe you can forgive him too and do a wee miracle.

Finally, I'll say a wee prayer, like I always do, for the Catholics, and the cannonballs, and for Fred. You know he's a good man and he can't help the way he is, even if nobody knows the way he is except me and you.

I've never asked for a miracle before and I promise I'll never ask again. I'll stop having a wee drink on a Sunday night with Fred and I'll stop wishing I had the money for a new hat. It's fifty years old if it's a day, but it still looks as good as new, so it'll do another while yet.

Please make Walter better. Please God, I'm begging you.

Forever and ever amen.

By some kind of divine timing, the sermon ended just as Ma finished her prayer. She wiped her eyes, unlocked her whitened fingers and, grabbing the back of the pew in front of her, pulled herself up. She wobbled a bit, then steadied herself as some equally wobbly organ-playing led into Hymn 210. As Ma silently sang 'O God, our help in ages past', she asked God again for help right now.

After the benediction, she searched the bobbing hats for Betty. When she caught her eye, Betty pointed at the door they'd come in. Ma nodded and waited for Betty to battle her way against the tide that was flowing towards the main doors.

'Are you waiting for Mrs Bann?' Harry asked her.

'Yes, love. You go on.'

Harry let the rest of his family out. 'I'll wait till she comes, if that's all right.'

'Are you all right, Kathleen?' Betty said when she arrived, puffing from the effort. She didn't dare say anything out loud but her old friend looked very forlorn, as if the weight of the world was on her shoulders. Kathleen liked a good worry and would be worried sick if she had nothing to worry about, but this seemed more serious than usual. Whatever it was, it was causing her a lot of anguish.

'Yes, I just need to go now,' Ma said.

'Have you got your stick?' Betty asked.

'Stick?' Ma looked into the pew. Her stick was lying on the floor.

Harry stepped into the pew – forbidden territory – picked it up and handed it to her with a broad grin on his face.

'Your stick, madam. Regards to Ann, and tell Joe I was asking about him – if you ever hear from him, that is.'

'Thank you, Harry,' Ma said.

He wished them a safe walk home and bounded off.

'He seems like a nice boy,' Betty said as she and Ma stood side by side and locked arms, preparing for the off.

'He is,' Ma replied. 'He's steady and polite. Mrs Johnston must be proud of him.'

'Let's go,' Betty said. 'Hope it's not raining.'

Ma hoped the Reverend Goodman wasn't outside.

'Kathleen? Elizabeth?' It was Reverend Goodman. 'How are you both? It's good to see you back in your pew, Kathleen. We've missed you. If you hadn't been out today, I was going to call in during the week. Have you been all right?'

'Yes, just a wee touch of the lurgy, that's all,' Ma lied. 'There's a lot of it about, but I'm much better now, thank you.'

'Glad to hear it. How's Ann?'

'She's grand. She's at home with wee Daisy.'

'Yes, I've heard about Daisy. A real tragedy, but you and Ann have done a very Christian thing in taking her in like you have. God really does work in mysterious ways.' He clasped his hands together in front of his chest.

'He does indeed. Daisy is a bundle of joy.'

'Has she been christened yet, do you know?'

Ma was flummoxed. 'I don't know. They didn't have much time before her poor ma died.'

'The service was very good today,' Betty said in an effort to change the subject. 'We were just saying how good it was, weren't we, Kathleen?'

Ma was fiddling with her hanky, twisting it into knots. 'Yes, very good,' she said, trying to smile.

Reverend Goodman took the hint. 'I'll let you get on, ladies. It looks like it might come on to rain. Oh, how is Walter, by the way?'

'Still the same. I'm praying for him.'

'Good. I'm sure the Lord will hear your prayers,' he said with a beaming smile. 'God bless you both and safe home.'

'Thank you, Reverend. Let's go, Betty,' Ma said and the two women linked arms again. Leaning into each other, with their sticks as props on the outside, they tottered off.

Back at the house, Ann helped Ma out of her coat before she slumped into her chair. 'How was it?' she asked.

'It was fine,' Ma said, still a little out of breath. 'We managed to avoid most people, but Reverend Goodman cornered us on the way out. He was asking about you and Walter. He said he thought we'd done a very Christian thing in taking Daisy in and he wanted to know if she'd been christened. Has she? We'll have to think about getting that done sometime. What do you think?'

'I agree – it was a very Christian thing we did.'

'I meant what do you think about having Daisy christened?' Ma shook her head. 'It's not very Christian to lie to everybody. And it's not just now we're lying. We'll have to keep lying to everybody for ever.'

'The truth would be even worse, Ma, you know it would. Otherwise, why would we bother to make the whole story up in the first place? Everything will be all right. All we need is Walter to buck himself up a bit and everything will be rosy.'

'I prayed for him today – for all of you. I asked God for a miracle.'

Ann went over and hugged her frail, frightened, amazing Ma. 'I don't even know if there is a god any more, but if there is and he listens to anyone, he'll listen to you,' she said. 'If you don't ask, you don't get. So Walter will get his miracle and we'll all live happily ever after.'

'But what if there is no miracle? Maybe God didn't like me asking.'

'He's not much of a god if you can't ask him for things. It won't be because of you, Ma. It'll just mean he has other miracles to do and maybe Walter isn't on his miracles list because of what he did.'

'I thought of that myself. If God had punished him for what he did, then he'd hardly turn round and do a miracle on him just because I asked him to. Walter made a mistake, that's all. Everyone makes mistakes.'

'It was a bloody big mistake.'

'I know, but surely he deserves some forgiveness. People in glass houses and all that.'

'I hope you're right, Ma. I really do. A miracle is exactly what we need right now. Did he ask how you were?'

'Who?'

'Reverend Goodman.'

'He did. I told him I was grand, but I'm not sure if he believed me.'

'He's no dozer. He'll be round to find out how you really are.'

'Probably. We'll have to get something in.'

'Aye, later in the week. But I'll go and get the spuds on now. It's nearly half twelve.'

As Ann cut the black bits out of the spuds, she wished she had Ma's simple faith that God would fix things and that everything really would be all right.

They would have to think about getting Daisy christened. Someday. But not today.

Back to work tomorrow. She'd have to concentrate. But at least she would be safe in the reality and normality of it all.

CHAPTER 3

The following Friday, Ann was staring into the fire, reflecting on a good week at work. There were still a few flames flickering. Daisy was asleep; Ma was dozing in her chair. Ann was nearly happy.

Patty Paige came on the radio singing 'Tennessee Waltz' and Ann started to hum along. 'I wonder if everywhere in America has a waltz named after it?' she asked herself out loud.

'What?' Ma said, stirring from her sleep.

'Sorry, Ma, just talking to myself. This is a beautiful song and I was wondering if everywhere in America has a waltz named after it. I mean it's important to know these things, isn't it?'

'What are you talking about, love?'

'Well, remember when Muriel first spoke to Al and he was waiting to be put through to Uncle Louis, she told us that he started humming the "Missouri Waltz"? So I was just asking myself if everywhere in America has a waltz named after it.'

'You have little to wonder about if that's what you're wondering about. It would mean an awful lot of waltzes, if it was true.'

'It would, wouldn't it.'

They listened to the end of the song.

'That would be a lovely tune to dance to,' Ann said, looking like she was miles away.

'There's a "St Louis Waltz",' Ma said.

'Named after Uncle Louis?'

'I doubt it. He's no saint and he couldn't waltz to save his life.'

'His name is Louis, but the Americans pronounce it Lewis, so it would be the "St Lewis Waltz" in America.'

'What's wrong with Americans that they can't speak properly,' Ma said as she gave the fire a poke.

'Do you think we'll be able to understand Hilda if we ever get to speak to her again?'

'Don't say that, Ann. Her letters home are proper English.'

'Almost! Like I've said before, Ma, we'll have to get a telephone. Then we could speak to her.'

'We're not made of money, love.' Ma looked flustered.

Ann went over, lifted Ma's left hand and kissed the blue veins. 'I was going to say don't worry about it, but I caught myself on. That's like telling the wind not to blow. What I will say is you're a better ma than I will ever be.'

'Your situation is different, love, very different. You love Daisy and that's all you need to be a great mother. Everything else is just stuff that comes and goes – things to worry about for a while before something else comes along to worry about. There's always something to worry about and that's what keeps us going. You just need to worry a lot more and a lot quicker and keep going.'

'You're a wise old owl, aren't you,' Ann said, grinning.

'Less of the old.'

'But you do look like an owl.'

'Cheeky,' Ma said and she gently slapped Ann's wrist.

'Walter will get his miracle and be on his feet soon,' Ann said, perking up, 'and he loves Daisy as much as I do. They have wee gurgly chats all the time.' She stared into the fire again. 'I think we should buy something new for the house,' she said after a few moments. 'That would cheer us up. What do you think?'

'There's nothing we need, love.'

'We could buy something we don't need.' Ann grinned at Ma, who looked completely confused by this ridiculous idea.

'Something like a new mangle … or a coal bucket,' Ann said. 'Look at it' – she pointed to the bucket sitting next to the fire – 'it's just a load of holes held together with bits of bucket. It might be the first bucket ever made.'

'It still holds all the big bits.'

'Just about. Maybe it's an antique. It might be worth a fortune.'

'It's a coal bucket, love.' Ma was shaking her head and smiling.

They fell into a companionable silence as the fire crackled in the grate.

'Muriel seemed in good form last Sunday,' Ann eventually said, shifting in her seat.

'The line was a bit crackly, but she does seem very happy.'

'Wedding bells soon?'

Ma just smiled.

'What?'

'Don't get me wrong, love. You know I want her to be happy – I want you all to be happy – but he's posh. He could marry anybody he wants, and his family will want him to marry somebody from the same background.'

'Maybe he wants Muriel,' Ann said. 'Maybe he loves her.'

'Maybe. She needs to be careful, is all I'm saying.'

If someone could be either her or Muriel, who would they choose right now? Ann thought wryly. 'I hope the wedding's in Omagh,' she said. 'Imagine all them posh lords and ladies in Omagh. You'll have to get a new hat.'

'That's well down the worry list at the minute.'

They exchanged a knowing smile.

'We must be due a letter from Hilda again soon,' Ann said. 'God knows where she is now. Still up to her oxters in snow, no doubt.'

Ma nodded. 'Daisy's very quiet. She's such a good sleeper.'

'Just like her ma.'

'Ssh, don't say that,' Ma mock scolded. 'Her ma's dead remember, God rest her soul.'

The radio was playing the Andrews Sisters' latest song, 'I Can Dream, Can't I'. Ann was listening intently to the words.

'No harm in dreaming, love,' Ma said, reading her mind.

'You'd nearly think they had me in mind when they wrote that.'

'Except the bit about getting drunk on wine.' Ma gave her a broad grin.

'I don't know what you mean,' Ann said, putting her nose in the air. 'I don't even like wine.'

'That's what I meant, love, that's what I meant. You don't need wine as well as Guinness!'

'You're very cheeky. Time for bed?'

Ma looked up at the clock on the mantlepiece. It had been a retirement gift from one of gentlemen she'd cleaned for.

The other two clocks were still in their boxes under her bed. 'Is that the time?'

'No, I think it's stopped.'

'Seriously? What time is it then?'

'The clock's right, Ma. I'm only winding you up.'

'You'd be better off winding the clock up more often.'

Ann chuckled. 'Yes, Ma.'

* * *

The next week passed without incident, but it rained almost the entire time. Ann hadn't been able to take Walter outside when she called after work. Despite the rain, the general opinion was that there would not be a flood this year. Even Ma was optimistic.

Saturday dawned, cool and still, the yellow and golden tints of autumn breaking through the grey foggy air.

Daisy bawled and filled her nappy. Ann sang quietly as she changed her. She lit the fire and made some tea and toast. Then, with Ma safely ensconced in her chair, she headed off to the shops with a sweet-smelling Daisy.

The shopping trip didn't start well. Mrs Chesney was in the Reform Stores and watched as Ann bought some jars of baby food, baby oil and Vaseline. Ann nodded by way of a hello.

Mrs Chesney gave her a shark-like smile and came over. Sticking her head into the pram, her huge face just inches from Daisy's, she cooed for a second and then asked, 'How is little …'

'… Daisy,' Ann said, helping her out.

'Yes, Daisy. How is little Daisy?'

'She's perfect. Sleeps well, eats well. She does everything that babies usually do with great enthusiasm.'

Mrs Chesney pulled her head out of the pram. 'She's a lovely wee thing. I suppose you'll be getting her christened soon.'

Ann stayed calm on the outside. That's none of your business, she thought. Out loud she said, 'Ma's spoken to Reverend Goodman about it. I think we'll be doing it soon.'

'So she'll be a Brown?'

What a stupid question, Ann thought. She felt like saying *no, we were thinking of calling her Daisy the Cow.* She wanted to say *she's actually Daisy Green.* What she did say was, 'Of course. Ma's adopted her, so she'll be Daisy Brown.'

'That's a lovely name. Tell Kathleen I was asking about her,' Mrs Chesney said and she left the shop like a landslide of lava, oozing out through the door.

Ann paid for her shopping and headed home. It took her a wee while to calm down after talking to Mrs Chesney. She passed on her message to Ma but didn't tell her about the rest of the conversation. Ma worried enough as it was.

In the afternoon, she took Daisy out to see Walter. The walk to the hospital gave her time alone with Daisy.

'We're going out to see Daddy,' she whispered into the pram as they left Campsie and crossed the Crevenagh Road. 'I know I've said this before, but you're very like your da. So how much goes in here' – she touched Daisy on the head – 'is anyone's guess … Okay, I'll say it again, I need you to help me get him better. I've been trying, but I can't do it on my own. He listens to you. I need you to tell him to stop farting about and get his arse out of that wheelchair. You don't have to use those exact words – use whatever words you like, whatever gurgles you think he'll understand. Will you do that for me?'

Daisy smiled up at her. She looked so like Walter that Ann's heart melted all over again.

'Good girl. We can do it. Between us we can do it.'

The receptionist at the hospital knew her well by now. 'Hello, Ann. How is wee Daisy today?'

'She's good. You're very good, aren't you, Daisy.'

'She's getting big. How old is she now?'

'Nearly three months.' Ann tucked Daisy's blanket in around her.

'Time flies, eh? She'll be up dancing soon.'

Does she mean 'like her ma'? Ann wondered. Why did she say 'dancing'. Surely 'walking' or 'crawling' would be more natural things to say. Was she being paranoid?

'That's more than we can say about Walter,' Ann said, trying to smile.

'Oh Ann, don't say that. I'm sure he'll be okay.'

'I hope so. Thanks, Beatrice,' Ann said, and she pushed Daisy down the corridor and into the ward.

Every time she saw Walter, she fell in love all over again. All the sad, dark thoughts, all the problems disappeared, at least for a moment. He looked animated and happy to see them. He gurgled loudly and Daisy gurgled back. Ann set the baby in his lap, wiped his mouth and kissed his lips. She wanted to hug him and take him home.

'What's he saying, Daisy?' she asked. 'Right, Blondie, let's go outside, get some fresh air and you can tell me all about everything.'

Out in the garden, the trees were almost bare. Ann kicked the orange and gold leaves lying on the ground. They swirled and danced in the breeze. Once she was out of sight of the buildings, she put the brakes on the wheelchair and set Daisy on the bench. She lifted a handful of leaves and scattered them over her. Daisy was like a wean with a new toy, giggling and burbling in delight. Ann turned to Walter and put her hand on his.

'I really need you to come home,' she said solemnly. 'Come on, let's try again and get you up. Are you ready?'

Walter was drumming his fingers. She took this as a yes.

With her legs planted each side of the wheelchair, she leaned down, wriggled her hands in behind his back and clasped them together. She could feel his ribs. She pulled him towards her, trying to straighten her legs at the same time. It was like trying to lift a bag of coal. She could feel her face burning red. Then suddenly, he was up and his feet were settled on the grass.

He immediately slumped forward over her shoulder. But Ann was ecstatic. This was the first time they had been 'in hold' since *that night*. The night of the party. She hugged him and started to cry on his neck.

'Can I have this dance?' she spluttered between sobs.

He tapped a mad tattoo on her back and she could feel him beginning to collapse. She couldn't hold him up any longer and he crashed back down into the chair, her arms still wrapped around him. She fell head first into his lap.

'Walter Green, what if somebody sees us! My arse is up in the air. They'll think we're up to all sorts.' She let out a loud sigh. 'But we will soon – get up to all sorts, I mean. I promise.'

Walter made a noise, one he'd never made before, like someone struggling on the toilet. At least it was different from gurgling.

She grabbed both his ears and shook his head as if he was a child. Then she kissed him on the forehead, on the end of his nose and finally on his lips. 'That thought has perked you up a bit, hasn't it? What do you get up to with those nurses when I'm not here? That's what I'd like to know.'

Ann turned round to look at Daisy. The leaves had nearly all blown away and Daisy was currently being entertained by a robin perched on the arm of the bench. She waved at it and it flew off. She started to cry, but stopped as soon as Ann put her in Walter's lap again. She released the brake on the chair. There was definitely a bond between them, Ann thought.

'I knew it would help if you told him to get his bony arse out of that chair, Daisy. Whatever you gurgled seems to have worked.' She pushed Walter and Daisy back towards the hospital. 'Let's get you back into the heat. The last thing I need is for you to catch your death out here … Ma's praying for you. Did I tell you? She prayed for a miracle, but she's been praying for Fred's bunions for years and they're as bad as ever. I don't hold too much store by it … I've never really believed in all that stuff, but maybe this time it worked. I think we had a wee miracle today. You stood up – granted, not for long – and you made a new noise – at the thought of a bit of hanky-panky, admittedly – but it doesn't matter … Does it make me some sort of floozy if I'm promising you *you-know-what* in return for you getting better? I don't care. I'll do anything … I'd have sex with the pope if I thought it would help you get better. Mind you, we'd probably have to move if I did that. We might even have to go to Larne! That's way too high a price. Forget I ever said that. Anyway, here we are, back in the heat.' She pushed him in through the ward door and parked him beside his bed. 'I love you, Walter Green,' she whispered as she lifted Daisy to put her in her pram.

She gave Walter one last peck on the cheek and then it was time to go. She floated home; it was as if the pram was pulling her along. She stopped before crossing the Crevenagh Road and looked around to make sure no one could hear her as she bent over the pram.

'Thanks, Daisy,' she said in a loud whisper. 'Maybe Ma got her miracle.'

Ma was asleep in her chair when Ann got in, but Daisy soon let her know they were back and she woke with a yawn and a cough. Ann set Daisy on Ma's lap and they cooed at each other like long-lost lovers.

'How was he today?' Ma asked as she tickled Daisy.

'He stood up, Ma,' Ann said, taking her coat off. 'It was only for a wee while, but I think he's getting there.'

Ma looked over her glasses at her happy little girl. 'Seriously, love? Sit down and tell me what happened.'

'Daisy had a stern gurgle with him. I told him that you'd been praying for him and had asked God for a miracle. He looked like he was listening, but it's hard to tell. Then I helped him a wee bit and he got up out of the wheelchair. He stood on his two left feet. It was only for a second and then he collapsed back down again. I think he got dizzy or something. Oh, and he made a noise like Joe used to make on the po after a feed of liver and onions. It sounded like he was trying to say something.'

'You'll have to let your Uncle Louis know. Maybe he's turned a corner.'

Ann smiled and a wicked grin lit up her face. 'It was turning a corner that caused his accident. Anyway, I told Beatrice about it and she said she'd tell everybody on Monday when they're back in.'

'That is good news, love. It really is. Maybe God was listening after all.'

'I hope so. Maybe there *is* one after all.'

'Oh Ann, don't say things like that. You have to believe in God. He won't do a miracle if you don't.'

'That's blackmail.'

'But it's true. And what if Walter does get better? We'll have to start thinking about what we do then.'

'Oh God, Ma, there'll be plenty of time for that. One worry at a time.'

'It's never too early to start worrying about things,' Ma said with a smile.

'I know, I know – I should probably start worrying as soon as possible. In fact, I'll make a start right now.' Ann put on a worried face and began to twiddle her thumbs at high speed.

Ma laughed. 'That's good, love. You worry for a while and I'll take over later, when you get tired.'

'Tea?' Ann asked, getting to her feet.

'Did you buy biscuits this morning?'

'They weren't on the list, but I got some digestives.'

'Lovely. Good for worrying, digestives.'

'I was so happy on the way home, I nearly bought a new coal bucket. Crawford and Wilson's had them in the window. Only four bob. They call them scuttles. Then I remembered, shilling ... pocket ... best friend and decided to wait till I get my next certificate. Then we can splash out.'

'We don't need a new coal bucket ... or a scuttle.'

'Yes, Ma.'

They had two digestives each, sandwiched together as usual, with a thick layer of butter. Ma took over the worrying duties when Ann went out to bring in the washing.

'I'll do the ironing in the morning, if that's all right,' Ann said.

'As long as my blouse is ready for church.'

'Your blouse will be ready before you are, Ma. I'll go and get the spuds peeled.'

'And the turnip.'

'Yes, Ma, and the turnip.'

Fred called just after dinner. A biting wind made his face even redder than usual, but he was as happy as ever. He never seemed to be down; neither Ma nor Ann could remember him being in bad form. There must be something in this bachelor life, Ann thought. Nobody to worry about, but then, where's the fun in that.

Ma didn't go up the town as often as she used to. She preferred not to meet people and relied more and more on Fred. Ann did the shopping; Fred did the gossip. Ann tried her best to keep her eyes and ears open, but she didn't have Muriel's predatory instincts. Her reports were sketchy and her attention to detail left a lot to be desired, according to Ma. Fred, on the other hand, knew everybody and everything, and he was able to tell Ma exactly what she wanted to know.

'It'll be interesting to see who gets that job,' Ma was saying to him as Ann came in from the toilet.

'What job's that, Ma?'

'Something in the Courthouse. They've come from all over for the interviews. Fred says there was a stranger in a suit in Andersons the other day and someone heard him say he was from Derry! Imagine!'

'He might have been a salesman,' Ann said.

'Well, he should stay a salesman, is all I can say.'

'Everybody needs a job, Ma.'

'They'll be wanting houses next.'

'Ma! That's a terrible thing to say.'

'We all have to learn to live and let live, Kathleen,' Fred chimed in.

Ma didn't look convinced.

CHAPTER 4

There were four of them celebrating Maud's birthday in Iris's house. Iris's parents had gone to see a show in Belfast. As the evening wore on, their conversation and the shrieks of laughter got louder and louder.

'Are we having another one? For the road?' Iris asked, slurring her words.

'I think we should. It's not every day you're twenty, is it Maudy?' Ann hugged her friend.

'It seems really old. Will I have to wear a cardigan?' Maud pouted.

'You'll have to drink sherry,' Iris said.

'And get married and have weans,' Jean added, but then she remembered about Ann's situation. 'Sorry, Ann, I didn't mean …'

'It's okay.' Ann laughed. 'It's not like I can get married to Walter at the minute and I don't really have a wean. So I'll be able to keep 'er lit for another while yet.' Ann was smiling but her eyes were filled with tears.

'As long as you're okay.' Iris looked blearily concerned.

Ann burst into tears.

'What's wrong, love?' Iris put her arm around her friend's shoulder.

'Nothing … everything.' Ann found a tissue and blew her nose. 'I better go,' she said, staggering a bit as she stood up.

Jean held up an empty bottle. 'None for the road, girls,' she announced and they all giggled.

Ann held onto the furniture as she went round and hugged them all.

'Happy Birthday, Maudy. I'll see you on Monday,' Ann said as she tried to find the left sleeve in her coat with her arm.

'Will you be okay getting home on your own?' Iris asked, helping Ann with her coat.

'I'll have to be, won't I?' She wiped her nose on the back of her hand.

Ann weaved her way home. The giddy happiness of drinking with her friends, of forgetting for a while, had turned to black, self-pitying sorrow. To make things worse it was raining. 'I nearly didn't go into work that day you crashed your van,' she mumbled to herself as she made her way down Bridge Street. 'Then we'd never have met, and you wouldn't be in hospital, and I wouldn't be alone with our wean. I'd have become a proper dancer and married a film star and you'd have become the best bread-van driver in Omagh, or maybe even the world, and we'd be happy … But then there'd be no Daisy. Can't imagine the world without Daisy … It's a bloody mess, Walter, and it's my fault for letting you make me fall in love with you, despite you being blond and stupid and not even close to looking like a film star. You look more like Marilyn Monroe than Clark Gable, for God's sake. Bloody eejit.' She fumbled, trying to button up her coat, which was already buttoned.

I need to toughen up, and YOU need to stand up. For Daisy. We need to get you better … Why are you not getting better? Is it me? Something I said? … Oh God, maybe you feel so bad about what happened that you don't want to get better. Oh God, Walter, I never thought *of that. Maybe you remember everything but don't want to. You can't face the truth, can't face me, can't face Daisy. Listen, we all love you, and I know you love Daisy and I know you love me, so you need to forgive yourself. Get better. We can have a proper chat about it next week. Then you'll understand better and you'll stop feeling so bloody sorry for yourself. Easy for you, just lying there, getting bed baths from pretty nurses. Getting all your food made for you and no dishes to do and the meter never running out … I have to do everything. Look after everybody and I can't even look after myself. I don't have any money and it's Christmas soon – Daisy's first – and she has no da. No ma either, allegedly, but Santa doesn't know that. What should we get her?*

She stopped at the corner of Bridge Street and the Back Market. This was the spot where Walter had been knocked down. She put her hands on the wall and leaned her forehead against it. The cold stone cleared her head a little. She thought she could smell his blood. A man came out of Mary Yarrow's pub and staggered towards her. He looked drunker than she was. She braced herself for an altercation, but he weaved his way on up the way she had just come.

'Ugly bastard,' she muttered to herself. 'I bet your wife is looking forward to you getting home,' she added more loudly.

She kissed the wall and wandered on, her mind a confused, emotional jumble of fragmented memories.

The light was still on downstairs when she got home. The front door banged loudly against the wall when she let herself in, and she made a beeline for the sofa, where she slumped down heavily.

'Are you okay, love?' Ma asked, bemused. She winked at Fred. 'Have a good night? You look a bit worse for wear.'

'It was great craic, Ma. They're all still mad. Then Jean said something – I think it was Jean …' Her hands shot up to her face and she buried her head in her lap. She cried, her chest heaving with big, loud, messy sobs.

Ma sat down beside her and put an arm around her. 'You need to go to bed, love. It'll be all right in the morning. You've had a wee bit too much to drink, that's all. It's understandable, given all that's gone on.'

'Oh Ma, I don't think I can do this any more. It's all too—' and she waved her arms around her head.

'Help her up, Kathleen, and I'll put the kettle on,' Fred said. 'A hot jar will help her sleep.'

'I'm okay, Ma,' Ann said, standing up and steadying herself. 'I need a pee.'

While Ann staggered out to the privy, Fred boiled the kettle and filled the jar.

'I'll be all right on my own,' Ann announced when she came back in. She made her way upstairs and closed her door with a bang.

Ma crept upstairs with the jar, slipped it in beside Ann and lay down beside her on top of the bedclothes. Ann was almost asleep already.

'Sorry, Ma,' she said, giving a loud sniff.

Ma tucked a curl of hair behind Ann's ear. 'It's okay,' she whispered. 'Nobody said it was going to be easy.' She waited until Ann started to snore gently, then got off the bed and kissed her forehead. 'Sleep tight, love.'

CHAPTER 5

At work, the postman always brought more than just a bag full of brown envelopes. It was Ann's turn to meet the puffing round ball and get all the gossip as he dumped his bag on the floor of the office.

'Well, Kevin, what's the craic?' she asked.

He was more out of breath than usual and looked frazzled. 'Have you not heard?' he said, setting three bundles of letters on the desk.

'Heard what? We only hear stuff from you.'

'This morning.' He was panting heavily. 'At the station … Big accident.'

'Sit down, Kevin. Would you like a wee glass of water?'

He nodded. 'I'm punctured.'

Ann brought him the water and he gulped it down. 'So, what's happened?' she tried again.

'There was a crash. A train crashed into some men who were working on the track. Just heard it from Sean. He does the station on a Friday. The Derry train was late because of the thick fog. The permanent way boys were working at the points and they must never have heard the train. Maybe it was going too slow. Anyway, it ran into them. Sean says there was bodies everywhere and people screamin' and cryin'. Terrible. Terrible all together.'

'It sounds horrific!' Ann said, not able to take it all in. 'You sit there for a minute or two. Get your breath back. Do you want more water? Or a cup of tea, maybe.'

'Oh, tea would be lovely. I'm shaking like a leaf, so I am.'

Ann made the tea, told Mrs Crammond, her immediate boss, about the accident and returned to Kevin.

'Do you know the head porter at the station – Peter Green?' she asked him.

'I know Peter all right. Sound man. Son's in the T&F.'

Ann winced at this matter-of-factness. She knew all too well that Walter was in the Tyrone and Fermanagh Hospital – the T&F for short. 'Was he hurt – Peter, I mean?'

'Don't know, love. Don't know who's hurt exactly, but there's loads.'

When Kevin had finished his tea, he thanked Ann and patted his bag. 'Better get on,' he said. 'These boys won't deliver themselves.'

'Thanks, Kevin. Take it easy,' Ann said, opening the door for him.

The accident was the talk of the office, and as the day wore on, Mrs Crammond was able to find out a bit more. Details were still sketchy. Estimates of the number killed ranged from two to ten and a whole clatter of people had been taken to hospital. No names had been released yet.

'I hope Mr Green is okay,' Mrs Crammond said as they sipped their tea later that afternoon. 'They've had enough trouble with Walter.'

Ann just nodded.

Mrs Crammond went on, 'Was your Tommy in today, Alice?'

'No, he was off, thank God. He was going to paint the front door.'

None of the rest of them had anyone working at the station and they tried to settle to their work. Dribs and drabs of fact and fiction came in with each caller. When the clock struck five, Ann buttoned up her green Firestone coat, wrapped her scarf around her head and set off. She went to see Walter every day unless the weather was really bad, but today she went to the County Hospital first. It was on the way.

The scene inside was chaotic but eerily quiet, apart from the moaning of the injured. Dazed patients and family were scattered everywhere, some on the floor. Ann stepped over an old man who seemed to be asleep just in front of the reception desk. The receptionist, a young girl, looked exhausted.

'You must have had an awful day,' Ann said sympathetically.

The girl nodded. 'It's been busy!'

'Has a Peter Green been admitted, do you know? He works at the station.'

The girl flicked her untidy ginger hair from her face and scrolled down a long list with her forefinger. 'Green, Green. Yes, Peter Green. Broken ankle. Ward 3.'

'Can I see him?'

'Visiting's allowed all day. Just go down and see what the nurses say.'

'Thanks. What time do you finish?'

'Soon, thank God. Never seen anything like it. I've only been here a week.'

'You might need a wee drink after all this.'

'I need something. I know that.'

'Look after yourself,' Ann said and went off to find Ward 3.

Mrs Green was sitting beside Peter's bed and looked up when she heard Ann speaking to the nurse. She waved at her to come down.

'Oh Ann, I'm so glad you're here,' she said, bursting into tears and giving Ann a crushing hug. She'd never hugged her before. 'It's a nightmare, so it is.'

It's only a broken ankle, Ann thought. She turned to Peter. 'Are you okay? What happened?'

He shifted uncomfortably in the bed. 'I was helping an auld doll with her case. She was going up to Belfast. The fog was very thick.'

'Thicker than Walter?'

Peter, used to Ann's black humour, gave her a feeble smile, but Mrs Green started bawling again.

'Don't say things like that, Ann.'

'Sorry, Mrs Green. Not much of a joke. Go on, Peter.'

'Well, the Derry train was late due to the fog, and the other train should have gone, but it was still sitting at the platform.'

'Did they crash into each other?'

'No, the Derry train hit the permanent way crew that were on the track. It was going very slowly, but the stationary train was getting up steam, so they didn't hear it until it was on them.' He shook his head. His eyes were wet. 'They didn't stand a chance. There was no crash, just this wailing and screaming all of a sudden. I ran to the end of the platform and was nearly on them before I could see anything. There was bodies all over the place. People staggering about, people trying to get off the train. I went to help a wee lad out of the front carriage. I had him in my arms when my foot got caught in the tracks somehow. I heard a crack and dropped the wee lad. I must have passed out. Then I woke up here.'

Ann tutted. 'That's terrible. Are they keeping you in?'

'The nurse says I'll get home later today after the doctor comes round. I'm one of the lucky ones. So many dead. Loads more injured.'

'Do they know how many?'

'Last I heard it was three dead, but it might be more.'

'We heard all sorts of rumours in the office,' Ann said. 'Somebody said there was dozens killed.'

'There were only five men on the track at the time. One of them had gone to the stores to get something, and Billy Wilson was tidying up at the other end of the station.'

Ann turned to the permanently tearful Mrs Green. 'Are you okay?' she asked.

She had sniffled to a stop, but this started her again. 'I went into a complete tizzy. Nobody knew anything, but they all knew it was bad. I was in Hendly's getting some brandy balls when I heard that two trains had smashed into each other. There were dead bodies everywhere, apparently. I didn't know what to think, or what to do, or where to go.'

She was in full flow again now and Ann felt genuinely sorry for her. She must have been scared out of her wits.

'Well, it's good to know Peter's okay.'

'Yes, oh yes,' she said, sniffling and blowing her nose. 'I hate the thought of going out to see Walter on my own.' She was smiling now.

Peter grinned at Ann. 'That's all she's worried about. Give me a kiss,' he said to Mrs Green. She leaned over and he kissed his fragile, shaking wife.

'What happened to the boy you dropped?' Ann asked. 'I hope you didn't drop him on his head.' She waited for Mrs Green's reaction, but she was smiling.

'Ann! That's an awful thing to say.'

'Oh God,' Peter said. 'I'll have to find out. I hope he's okay.'

'Later, love. Later. You need to get some rest. It's a long way to the T&F on crutches.'

Ann left them sitting there holding hands.

CHAPTER 6

'You won't believe what happened yesterday.' Ann set the piece box on Walter's bed. He was out in his wheelchair.

'Do you get gossip – sorry, news – in here?' she went on, putting Daisy in his lap. 'Anyway, there was a crash at the station yesterday morning. The fog was really thick – even thicker than you are, or so your ma said. The Derry train was late because it had to go so slow and the Belfast train, the one I used to get to see you when you were on your holidays, was still sitting in the station getting up steam and you know how noisy that is. Well, there was a gang of men working on the track and normally, they'd get out of the way of a train. I mean, even you would get out of the way of a train. But they didn't hear it coming and it ran into them. Five killed, nineteen weans left with no da.'

Ann stood behind Walter's chair and disengaged the brake. 'So you think you have problems? At least you're alive – sort of – and Daisy still has her da, sort of.' Ann started to wheel Walter out of the ward. 'I'll get an extra blanket for you. It's freezing outside but it's dry. We'll do your exercises under the rowan tree if that's okay. Your da broke his ankle by the way, which is why he won't be out to see you till he gets the hang of the crutches. He's a hero, your da. He broke his ankle trying to rescue a wee lad from the train, but his foot got caught and he dropped the wean, not on his head you'll be glad to hear, otherwise he'd be in here beside you.'

Ann parked the wheelchair under the skeleton of the tree. She lifted Daisy off his lap and set her on the bench. There were no leaves for her to play with, but the resident robin soon appeared.

'Did you know that robins are magic? I'm talking to Daisy here,' she said, looking round at Walter. 'Well, they are, because usually they live on the front of Christmas cards, but sometimes they escape and become real robins, just like this wee chap.'

She pulled the blanket up over Walter's chest and smoothed it out.

'Like I said, your da won't be able to get out to see you for a while. So yippee, no more smelly sandwiches. I like corned beef, so I'll bring those instead, unless you only like egg and onion? Two taps if you only like egg and onion.'

Walter tapped the back of her hand twice.

'Shite. I hate egg and onion. They make me fart something desperate. What about corned beef and onion, or egg and corned beef? Tap again if you want a change.'

No taps. She swore Walter was laughing at her.

'You're in cantankerous form today, Blondie. Did somebody steal the currant out of your bun? I'll tell you one thing, you won't be able to have smelly sandwiches when we're going up to collect the prize at the Best Dancers in the World competition.'

She thought Walter was trying to raise his hand.

'Do you want up?'

Tap, tap, tap, the code for yes.

‘Okay, let’s try. You keep an eye on him, Daisy. Make sure he’s trying his hardest.’

Ann assumed the position – legs akimbo, arms round his back, hands clasped together. ‘Okay, here we go.’

She pulled and straightened up at the same time. Suddenly, Walter was on his feet.

‘It’s getting easier, isn’t it, Daisy? Can you do a step? Come on, love, do a step. Doesn’t have to be anything fancy. I’m not expecting a fleckerl or anything. Just a step. Either foot will do. Left or right. Do you know which is which?’

Three taps.

‘It’s not funny, Walter Green, and don’t do both at once. That could be a disaster. One will do.’

Walter made his constipated groaning noise. He closed his eyes and slid his left foot forward about three inches. Sweat glistened on his forehead.

Ann’s heart leapt in her chest and she gave a little clap. ‘Oh God, Daisy. Did you see that?’ But Daisy was asleep. ‘You missed it, girl. I hope you’re not going to be as dozy as your da.’ She could barely contain her excitement. ‘I’ll not tell your ma and da, or my ma, for that matter, that it was your left foot you moved. They’ll think the nurses have turned you. Can you do it again?’

Walter made a noise like someone who had stood on a tack in their bare feet, and pulled his foot back to where it had been. He felt very wobbly in her arms and she lowered him back into the wheelchair.

‘Progress, Blondie. You’ll be up dancing in no time, especially if you start eating proper sandwiches.’ She hooked her finger into a curl of his hair and teased it back off his face, then kissed his forehead, which tasted of salty sweat. ‘I love you,’ she whispered. ‘Do you want a wee kiss from Daisy?’

Tap, tap, tap. Then *tap, tap, tap* again.

'Okay, okay, keep your hair on.'

She picked up the now-awake Daisy and held her up to Walter's face. His daughter slobbered over his nose.

'See? Daisy loves you too. She doesn't slobber over just any old body.'

Ann put Daisy in his lap, wiped his face with her hanky and turned the wheelchair to go back inside.

'I'll try and get up during the week as usual, if it's not too wet. I don't love you enough to get soaked to the skin. In the meantime, keep practising your steps – sorry, step. One step at a time and all that shite.' She kissed the tips of her fingers and touched his nose with them. 'See you, love.'

Tap, tap, tap.

When Ann got home, Ma was asleep in her chair. Needle, thread and a button lay in her lap.

'He moved his foot, Ma,' Ann said, waking her mother up. 'He nearly stood up by himself and he moved his foot.'

Ma's lips curled into a slow smile as she asked, 'Which foot?'

'I knew you'd ask that. It doesn't matter which foot it was. I told him to move whatever one he liked.'

'So he moved his left foot.'

'Yes, but it was only an inch or two. You'd need to move your foot further than that to be called a left footer.'

Ma laughed. 'You would, love.' She hauled herself out of the chair and hugged her daughter. 'It's great news and you deserve it. He's lucky to have you.'

'I'm the lucky one. I have Daisy, I have Walter and I have you.' She gave Ma a peck on the cheek. 'I'll put the stew on.'

'The spuds are already in.'

'Lovely. I'm starving.'

CHAPTER 7

The train crash was the talk of the town right up to Christmas. A Disaster Fund was set up to help support the five families affected. St Eugene's Brass and Reed Band played at the funerals. One of the deceased, Dan McCrory, had been a member of the band. A verdict of accidental death was recorded at the inquest.

Grief stunned the town. The mood was subdued as the shops sprinkled their seasonal glitter and Anderson's shop window became a magical magnet for all the children again.

'What do you get a five-month-old wean for Christmas?' Ann asked Ma as she cleaned out the ashes in the fireplace.

'You all got a rattle for your first Christmas.'

'The same rattle, I suppose.'

'You didn't know it was the same rattle.'

'I bet Hilda wanted it back when she saw me rattling it about like a mad thing,' Ann said, smiling.

'I had to take it off Hilda before the new year. The noise would have put your head away.'

'Was I the same?'

'Worse. I took it off you on Boxing Day.' Ma looked far away as she recalled the happy memories.

'You did not! I bet Joe was the worst.'

'He'd broken it by bedtime and then bawled his eyes out. There's the kettle. I'll make some tea.'

As they sat with their tea and a bit of toast, Ann asked, 'So do you think I should get Daisy a rattle?'

'No need. Fred fixed it and I kept it, so now Daisy can have it.'

Ann shook her head and smiled. 'I'm sure she'll love it as much as we all did.'

It was Saturday, the day before Christmas Eve, and three cards dropped through the letter box.

'This must be Hilda's,' Ann said, holding up an envelope covered in stamps.

'And this is Joe's writing.' Ma's eyes sparkled.

Ann lifted the last one. 'I'd recognise Muriel's scrawl anywhere.' She gave it to Ma. 'You open them, Ma.'

Ma sliced open the flap of Hilda's envelope with her finger and pulled out the card. 'Oh look, a picture of a polar bear … again.' She read out what Hilda had written inside: '*All well here. Lots of snow. Wee Jimmy is getting big and he's up walking. Dan has to go to Europe in the spring, so I'll come with him and visit. I'll bring Jimmy. I think we'll be able to fly over, which will be exciting. Hope you are all well. Happy Christmas. Love Hilda, Dan and Jimmy.*'

'That's good news. You'll get to see your wee grandson.'

'And your nephew. Should she be taking a wee wean like that on an aeroplane? Sounds very dangerous.'

'You're right, Ma. I'll tell her not to come.'

'No, no, don't be silly. I can't wait to see them.'

'Just think of all the extra worrying you can do in the meantime,' Ann added.

'There is that. Never had to worry about an aeroplane before.'

They were both grinning now.

'Joe's next.' Ma opened this envelope more carefully. 'Look.' She held the card up so Ann could see the picture.

'How did he get a card with a polar bear on it?' Ann said, laughing.

'Maybe he's in Canada too.'

'What does he say?'

'*Happy Christmas. Thought of Hilda when I saw this card. Hope you are both well. How is your cough, Ma? Any sign of a ring from Walter, Ann? Might get home early next year. Got promoted to Leading Writer. Things are good. Love Joe.*'

'Promotion already. The navy must be in a bad way,' Ann said, taking the card and setting it on the mantlepiece.

'He seems to like it. That's the main thing. But he doesn't say where he is.'

'I suppose it doesn't matter where he is if he's on a ship.'

'True, true.' Ma paused. 'I wonder what a "leading writer" is.'

'It probably means he leads the writing classes.'

'You're very hard on him, Ann. Right last one.' Ma tore open Muriel's envelope. 'Oh look, it's an old church in the snow with a robin. A proper Christmas card. Lovely.' She held it up to show to Ann.

'Very nice. Boring, but nice. What does Muriel have to say for herself?'

As Ma took a deep breath, she launched into a coughing fit. Ann got her a glass of water.

'Are you okay?' She gently patted Ma's back. She could feel every rib.

Eventually the coughing subsided. 'I'm okay now, love.' Ma took another sip of water. 'Muriel says *Happy Christmas to you both. Hope you are well. I've been invited out to Maldonwood Manor again. Al says it will be extra special this year. He won't tell me anything more, but I think there might be somebody famous coming. I'll tell all on Christmas Day. I'll call the phone box at quarter to four.'*

'Oh, I wonder who it could be – an actor maybe, or a singer. What do you think?' Ann's eyes were bright with excitement.

'You know what I think. She'll end up being hurt by all this. Al won't marry a telephonist from Omagh. He'll marry somebody rich. That's just the way it is. She's not Cinderella.'

'Don't be such an old misery guts, Ma. It's a great adventure. She's going to his castle for Christmas. He must have some feelings for her or why would he do it?'

'Maybe he has no one else at the minute and needs a partner for all these fancy balls and things.'

Ann shook her head. Ma was always so pessimistic, but perhaps she had good reason where Muriel was concerned. It might all come to nothing … nothing other than heartbreak for Muriel.

'I'm going to have more tea,' Ann said. 'Then I'm going out to see bubble head.'

'What have you got him?'

'I'm going to give him a hard-boiled egg and an onion. If he wants any more smelly baps, he'll have to make his own.'

Ma was smiling broadly at her incorrigibly optimistic daughter.

Ann laughed at her ma's happy face. 'I've got him some jelly babies. He likes jelly babies and they're easy to eat.'

'Did you tell me about the jelly babies before?'

'I did, but maybe you weren't listening.'

'I don't like the black ones.'

Ann shook her head and didn't ask why.

Once the chores were done, Ann took Daisy out to see Walter and did the shopping on the way home.

'Best Christmas present ever, Ma,' she reported when she got back. 'He moved both feet today. Not at the same time, of course. The nurse said that they're working hard with him and he's responding well. Maybe God listened to your prayer after all.'

'Maybe he did, love. Imagine how many miracles he's asked for every day. It must be easy for some of them to get lost in the crowd. I've never asked for one before, apart from … but that doesn't matter now.' Ma fidgeted with her hanky. 'Anyway, miracle or not, it's great that he seems to be getting better.'

As time had gone on, Ann had become less and less sure that he'd ever be better, but she would never admit her doubts to anyone. 'I'll get him back dancing, Ma, you'll see.'

'I know you will, love. Did you get eggs?'

'Do you know how much they were? Two bob! For half a dozen eggs! Anyway, Tom told me they were this morning's, so they're fresh enough.'

'I'll make the stuffing tomorrow.'

Fred came over after dinner that night and brought a bottle of Bush with him. So they had a wee drink and a chat and listened to Christmas songs on the radio. Bing Crosby came on singing 'Silent Night'. They fell quiet, each lost in their own thoughts, staring at the crackling fire.

CHAPTER 8

Ann got nappies, a Platignum pen and the usual box of Black Magic for Christmas. She got Ma a box of Milk Tray with *two* layers and a pair of sensible black shoes. She couldn't remember Ma ever getting new shoes before. The old pair had been repaired a million times and the last time she took them to Taggart's, they told her it was best to leave miracles to the Lord. Ma didn't go out so much now. These new shoes would last forever.

Fred came over in the afternoon, after Ma and Ann had had their Christmas dinner; they all had a few drinks and left together after the King's Speech. Fred staggered round to his brother's house while Ma and Ann linked arms and went up to the phone box to wait for Muriel's call. Ann pushed the pram and Ma clung on. Ma wore her new shoes. It would take a while to break them in, so she brought her old ones with her in her shopping bag just in case. Ann parked the pram outside the phone box; she could keep an eye on Daisy through the glass. They had hardly squeezed in and closed the door when the phone rang.

'Go on, Ma,' Ann said, nodding and grinning.

Ma picked up the receiver and held it between them. 'Hello? Muriel? Is that you?'

'Happy Christmas, Ma. How are you?'

It was wonderful to hear Muriel's voice. She had a wee English twang to her accent.

'Happy Christmas, love. We're fine here. What about you?'

'Oh Ma, wait till you hear the news. Is Ann there?'

'Happy Christmas, Mu,' Ann shouted into the mouthpiece of the phone. 'You sound very excited. Who was the surprise visitor then? Cary Grant? Laurence Olivier? The king?'

'You won't believe it. The big surprise wasn't a guest.' Muriel was almost breathless and sounded like a child who had just seen her presents. 'Al asked me to marry him!'

Ann squealed.

Ma covered her ears.

'This morning. First thing. Before breakfast,' Muriel went on. 'I nearly fell over. The ring is enormous and must have cost a fortune. I wish you could see it. A big diamond with seven wee ones round it. We had champagne.'

Ann squealed again and jumped up and down as much as she could in the cramped phone box.

'Easy, love, you're on my shoes,' Ma said, grimacing.

'Sorry, Ma. Oh Mu, did you have no idea? He must have said something? When's the big day? Will it be in Omagh?'

Muriel ignored all Ann's questions. 'Ma? Are you there? Have you fainted? What do you think?'

'It's a surprise, love – no denying it – I'm very happy for you. For both of you. It's lovely. Al's such a good man.' She paused, then said, 'I hope he didn't have to.'

'Ma!' Ann and Muriel said in unison.

'Sorry, love, I know he didn't have to, but …' She trailed off and looked at Ann.

The three of them talked on for a while. Apparently, Al had got down on one knee under the Christmas tree in the library before any of the rest of his family had come down. He'd bought the ring in London – Boodles of Bond Street. She had no idea he was planning this. They had become very close, but no, they hadn't done *it* yet. He was a true gentleman. They'd been for dinner in some very posh places where there were enough knives and forks for a family of ten. They'd also been to the theatre. 'You'd love it, Ann. The theatres are beautiful.' They hadn't set a date yet, but they were in no rush. Maybe next year sometime. 'Al's just come in. Do you want a word?' Muriel asked.

Ann looked at Ma. Ma was shaking her head.

'Put him on, Mu.' Ann was beside herself with excitement.

'Hello, Ann. Good to speak to you again. Happy Christmas. Do you think I've done the right thing?' Al's voice oozed from the handset like golden syrup.

'Happy Christmas to you too, Al, and yes, you've definitely done the right thing. But I think you might have got the short end of the stick.'

'I heard that, Ann Brown,' Muriel said. Ann could hear the smile in her voice.

'What do your ma and da think of the news?' Ann asked Al. 'Did they not want you to marry a princess or something?'

Al laughed good naturedly. 'They're very happy. They're very fond of Muriel and they're not snobby. If I'm happy, they're happy and I'm very happy. In any case, most princesses aren't very bright.'

'Are you saying you think Muriel is bright? Maybe you should have got to know her first.' Ann was enjoying herself.

'You're very cheeky,' Muriel chimed in. 'I'm the brightest bauble on the tree.'

'You can come down off the tree now, my dear,' Al said, joining in the fun.

'We better go,' Ann said. 'Ma's getting cold.'

Ma looked daggers at her.

'Is Ma there?' It was Al. 'Let me say hello.'

Ma reluctantly took the handset from Ann. It might as well have been made of glass.

'Hello,' she whispered.

'Happy Christmas, Mrs Brown. Your daughter has just made me the happiest man in the world. Thank you for bringing her up so wonderfully.'

'Happy Christmas to you too, Al. I'm very happy for you both. Muriel was always my favourite.' Ma smiled at Ann as if to say *that'll teach you to drop me in it.*

Muriel came back on the line. 'Oh Ma, isn't this just the best day ever in the history of days?'

'It is, love. You go on now and enjoy the rest of it ... and don't drink too much.'

'Yes, Ma.'

They could hear Al chortling in the background. But before they hung up, Al called out 'Ann? Ann?'

'Yes, Al.'

'I wanted to ask how Walter is? Believe it or not, the last time we spoke was about a year ago when you were up in Belfast and Walter was in the Royal Victoria. I know he's back at the T&F, but how is he?'

'He's making progress. Thank you for asking. He's moving his feet and making noises like he's trying to say something. He never said anything sensible anyway, so I wouldn't worry about that bit. But yes, he's making slow but steady progress.'

Ma looked at Ann and mouthed, *does he know?*

Ann shook her head.

'Okay, Ann. Well, look after yourself and your mother, and keep working with Walter. I think you'll get there if you keep at it.'

'Thanks, Al. We better go. Happy Christmas, Mu, you lucky thing.'

'Same to you. Happy Christmas, Ma. Tell Fred I was asking for him.'

'I will, love. You go now and behave yourself.'

'Yes, Ma.'

Ann would have skipped home if she hadn't been pushing Daisy and holding on to Ma. The lights in the shops looked brighter than before, like millions of twinkling beacons of joy.

They took off their coats. Ma eased off her new shoes and rubbed her feet. In the excitement she had forgotten to change back into her other shoes.

'We need to celebrate, Ma,' Ann said, lifting Daisy out of the pram. 'Lady Muriel, eh? Is there any sherry left?'

'She'll have to tell Hilda. How will she do that?'

'She can phone her.'

'But it's the middle of the night wherever Hilda is. They don't have Christmas until at least tomorrow.'

'So they have Christmas on Boxing Day?' Ann's eyes twinkled at Ma.

'That's not what I mean. Don't confuse me.'

Ann gave her a big smile. 'I don't know. It doesn't matter, but we'll have to let Joe know somehow. Do you think we could phone the ship?'

'I shouldn't think so. We'll just have to write. He said in his card he might be home soon, but God knows when *soon* might be. It's good that they're not rushing into things.'

'You mean it's good she's not pregnant. Two of us couldn't be that stupid.'

‘I didn’t mean that, Ann. You know I didn’t. I’m just glad for them both, that’s all.’

‘I know, and I know Muriel isn’t your favourite either … because I am.’

They hugged each other, happy to be together.

‘Wait till Fred hears the news. He’ll be over the moon,’ Ma said.

They had tea and cold turkey for supper, then listened to Christmas music until the radio suddenly died.

‘I’ll do it, Ma.’

Ann took a shilling from the tin, put it in the meter and turned the knob. It clunked down into the machine and the music came back on. After a while, Ma dozed off.

Ann stared into the dying fire, dreaming about her and Walter and their fairy-tale wedding in a castle with big pointy turrets.

CHAPTER 9

In the dead time between Christmas and New Year, they wrote to Hilda and to Joe. They found Joe's letter from the navy telling him where to go for his training, so they sent his letter there. They put his letter inside a letter explaining who the letter was for and asking if they would send the second letter to Joe on his ship, wherever that was.

Both letters contained a shortened version of the story of Daisy and her adoption. They told Joe about Muriel and Al and that Hilda might get home soon and they hoped he was safe and well.

About a month later, a flimsy blue airmail envelope floated down onto the mat. Ann assumed it was from Hilda and picked it up.

'Hey Ma,' she shouted as she went towards the yard. She heard the toilet flush. 'I think it's a letter from Joe.'

Ma came back into the kitchen and looked excited as she took the letter. 'There's no stamps on it. Oh, I should have remembered – you don't need stamps to send things to the army. The navy must be the same. Stick the kettle on, love, and we'll have a read at it before you go up the town.'

Ma carefully opened the flimsy blue envelope and spread the thin paper out flat on the counter. She cleared her throat and read out loud:

> *Dear Ma and Ann, I got your letter even if it wasn't addressed to the right place. Airmail letters are known as blueys and you should address them to BF1 2HY in future.*
>
> *You have obviously all gone mad without me there to keep you right. What's wrong with Walter, apart from the obvious, that I tried to tell you about, but you wouldn't listen?*

'What's he talking about, love?'

'I've no idea, Ma. I think he's just trying to be funny.'

Ma read on.

> *Are you ok, Ma? I thought you would never stop work. You've always worked. You've never done anything else but work and now you're looking after this wean that you've adopted, or is it Ann that has adopted her, or is it both of you? Is she a United supporter?*
>
> *Great news about Muriel and Mr Plummy. I hope she's not up the duff!*
>
> *Can't wait to get home and hear all the gory details. Can't say exactly when this will be – security and all that – but soon hopefully. Get the liver and onions ready! Wouldn't it be lovely if I was home at the same time as Hilda.*

Don't tell Harry or Nigel that I'll be home soon. Best if nobody knows and I can surprise them.

I will get Hilda's and Muriel's addresses off you when I get home. Maybe we could call them. I don't suppose you have a phone in yet.

See you soon.

Love,

Joe.

'*Up the duff* indeed! He hasn't learned any manners in the navy, that's for sure,' Ma said, then she read the letter again to herself.

'He's right about the phone,' Ann said.

'He won't have to pay for it and I'll just spend all day answering calls that'll be for you,' Ma said, putting the letter down. 'I can't wait to see him. I wonder if he's got big. What if him and Hilda are home at the same time? Where will we put them? You have Daisy in with you. Joe would be okay, I suppose.'

All this was enough to send Ma into a whole new orbit of worry. Worrying had now become multi-layered and global.

'You should make a list, Ma. Write down all the things you have to worry about and then you'll not have to worry about missing anything. That'll be one less thing to worry about and you can worry about everything in turn.'

'You're very funny, my girl ... but that's not a bad idea. I'd hate for anything to go unworried about or for one of you to find out that I was worrying less about you than any of the others.'

'You don't need to worry about me, Ma. I'll be all right, and I could fill in for you sometimes so you could have a wee break from the worrying.'

'You have your own things to worry about. I'd be worried sick if I wasn't worrying about something, but random worrying might actually make things worse.'

'You're right. There's no need for both of us to worry about the same things. You take me and Daisy and Walter off your worry list. Right now, I'm going to stop worrying about worrying and make a cup of tea before I go up the town. Oh God, now I'm worried that the milk's not good.'

Ma was shaking with laughter at the stupidity of it all.

* * *

Ann still went out to see Walter every day after work, weather permitting.

'Hi Blondie, how are you today?' She kissed his forehead, sat down on the seat beside Walter's bed and took his hand in hers. 'I don't suppose you have any money? Do they pay you to lie here and get fed and watered and bed baths and all?'

Walter tapped once on the back of her hand.

'I thought not. It's just that I need a new hat for Muriel and Lord Snooty's wedding and I know for a fact that it won't match anything I've got, so I'll need a new dress and new shoes and a new handbag too. Any donations will be appreciated. If you were still driving your wee van around, firing baps at people, we'd be loaded by now. Daisy needs new stuff nearly every day. She's getting so big. It's lucky that Ma kept all our clothes from forever so there's loads of stuff for her, but she does look a bit dopey in Joe's football shirt. Don't you, love?' She pulled Daisy's pram a bit closer to the wheelchair. 'Say hello to Daddy.'

Walter was tapping his code for *happy, happy, happy*.

'I'm going to the Starr every Saturday now,' Ann went on. 'It's just dancing, honest. No shenanigans in the alleyway. I only shenaniganed once in my life and look where that got me. Anyway, I haven't found anyone nearly as good as you to dance with. No pretty blond Harpo Marx lookalikes. They're all big clumsy farmers. There's still loads of soldiers about, but you know what they're like. Having said that, your mate Robbie isn't bad looking. He's not a bad dancer either.'

Hard single taps. *No, no, no.*

'Keep your hair on. Only joking. Anyway, he's going steady with Moira Love – you know, Love's the jewellery shop. He'll be marrying into money there all right. No problem getting new hats for our Moira. He'll probably get the rings for free and all.'

She shifted on the hard hospital seat. 'Joe's coming home soon. I don't know when exactly, but even if I did and I told you, I'd have to kill you. Then who would I visit? Hilda's coming home too with wee Jimmy. Ma's had to stop taking in worrying from the neighbours, so she has.'

She put her handbag in Daisy's pram. 'It's baltic outside, so we'll have to do your exercises in here today.'

Walter gave her three taps meaning *okay*.

She stood up and pulled the curtain around the bed. Getting him up was becoming easier. Once he was on his feet, she unclasped her hands from around his back and slowly let go. He wobbled, then steadied, then wobbled a bit more, before steadying again. She moved back a foot and put her arms down by her side. He was standing still on his own.

Ann was ecstatic and jumped up and down, clapping her hands. She kissed his downy chin.

'You are my hero, Walter Green. You learned to dance, you learned to swim – sort of – and now you're going to learn to walk again. It's not like it's something you haven't done before. You just need to move your foot. Not the left one. Ma didn't like that. Your right foot. That's this one.' She tapped his right foot with hers.

Walter took a long, slow, deep breath. Sweat broke out on his forehead.

'Easy, Blondie. No need to blow a gasket. You can do it. You know you can do it,' Ann said encouragingly.

His right foot lifted off the floor and slid forward a couple of inches.

'Brilliant!' Ann said. She was concentrating as hard as Walter was, staring at his feet in their old man's slippers. 'Now the other one.'

Walter made a noise like someone getting a sticking plaster pulled off hairy skin. His left foot moved level with his right and he was still standing on his own.

Ann clapped her hands and hopped from one foot to the other in glee. 'Is that enough for today? Are you knackered?' She took his hand.

Tap, tap, tap.

A big teardrop plopped onto Walter's shirt as she clasped her hands behind him again and gently lowered him into his wheelchair. He didn't slump down like before. That was progress too. He looked exhausted, but was he smiling at her?

'Did you see that, Daisy?' Ann said, turning to her daughter. 'I thought Ma was mad, praying for a miracle. Only them uns pray for miracles and they never come true. Even if they go to somewhere like Knock and pray on their knees for a fortnight. But maybe God was listening after all. Let's hope so, eh?' She leaned over and kissed Walter's forehead again. 'I love you, Mr Green. We both do. Behave yourself and I'll see you tomorrow, unless I get a better offer.'

Tap, tap, tap.

* * *

'Look at that, Ma.' Ann held up a thick vellum certificate.

'What is it?'

'It proves I can type a million words a minute,' Ann said.

Ma smiled at her happy little girl.

'Even better, it means I go up another pay grade,' Ann added. 'Another shilling in my pocket.'

'I didn't think there was a million words,' Ma said, raising one eyebrow.

'Probably not. But it means I can get stuff done in a blur. More time to do my nails.'

'Well done, love.'

'Now that we're rich,' Ann continued, 'I was thinking we should buy that new thing for the house we talked about. Something nice.'

'Like what? We don't need anything.'

'That's the point. We should go mad and buy something we don't need. That auld thing' – Ann jerked her thumb at the coal bucket by the hearth – 'must be as old as you are. You must admit we really need a new one.'

'I think Fred bought it.'

'With his first wages?'

Ma looked confused. It didn't make sense to buy something just for the sake of it.

The following Saturday, Ann called into Crawford and Wilson's and bought a new coal scuttle. It felt good to be buying something that wasn't food or clothes. She felt pleased with herself as she counted out the money.

It took pride of place on the hearth. Reflections of the fire and the gas lamps sparkled and glinted in the gloom.

'It seems a shame to put coal in it,' Ma said. 'It'll get it all dirty.'

'It's a coal bucket, Ma. It's meant to do buckety things.'

'I thought you said it was a scuttle. That's better than a bucket. Leave it there till Fred sees it.'

Ann grinned. 'You know what comes before a fall?'

'I know it's only a bucket – scuttle – but it's lovely and shiny … and I want Fred to see it. No harm in that, is there?'

'No, Ma. No harm at all.' Ann gave Ma a squeeze.

'It's a lovely bucket, so it is,' was Fred's pronouncement. 'Health to wear, if that's the right thing to say about a coal bucket.'

'Scuttle,' Ma corrected him.

'Whatever it's called, it's lovely, so it is,' Fred said.

'Can I put coal in it now?' Ann wasn't feeling hopeful.

'We should wait till the arse falls out of the old one,' Ma said. 'Sure set it in Joe's room for now.'

Ann sighed and glanced at Fred as she carried it out. His eyes were twinkling with amusement.

CHAPTER 10

There was a loud knock at the door, loud enough to wake Ma from her afternoon nap. Her sewing scattered to the floor. She looked at the clock. It was half four. What day was it? Tuesday. Wrong day for the gas man, and the coal man – and the electric man had already been.

'Hope it's not the tinkers,' she whispered to Daisy.

The door was battered again.

'Hold your horses. No need to break the door down. I'm coming,' she called out.

Daisy was wide awake now, smiling and gurgling and looking guilty.

Ma bent over the cot and wrinkled her nose at the smell. 'I'll chase the eejit and then we'll get you cleaned up.'

There was another loud bang and a hand poked open the letterbox. 'Ma? Are you there, Ma?'

Ma's heart jumped. 'Joe? Is that you, Joe?'

She unsnibbed the door and there he was.

'Oh God, Joe.' She collapsed onto his chest, put her arms around him and squeezed.

He hugged her back. 'I can't breathe, Ma.'

'Let me look at you.' She stepped back and looked him up and down.

'Can I at least come in?' He laughed. 'C'mere, give me a kiss. How are you? What about your cough?'

'I'm all right. Ann fusses too much,' Ma said. 'She's enough to do without worrying about me. You've filled out a bit. Look at you, all grown up, in a fancy suit and all.'

'Worsted wool, Ma.' He fingered his collar and gave her a proud smile. 'Only the best.'

'Oh God!' she said and gave him another rib-crushing hug.

'You're glad to see me then?' Joe said, a broad grin splitting his face.

'Why didn't you write?' Ma asked. 'Ann told me not to worry, but you know me – I can't help it.'

'I know, Ma, I know. I'm sorry. Time just disappeared. I can't believe I've been away two years. I'll be twenty in December.'

'Let me look at you,' Ma said, standing back. 'You're very brown. Nice haircut.'

'They have proper barbers in the navy. They don't just stick a bowl on your head.'

'Sit down, sit down. I'll put the kettle on. Say hello to Daisy.' Ma nodded towards the cot and went into the kitchen to fetch the kettle.

Joe bent over the cot. 'Hello, Daisy.' He sniffed the air. 'I think you might have had a wee accident,' he said, scrunching up his face.

He spotted Ma about to head outside to fill the kettle. 'I'll do that,' he said and took the kettle from her. Ma followed him out. 'This place is looking well. New door on the bog?' he said.

'Fred's nephew, Denis, has been doing the garden for us. He's a good cub.' She followed him back into the kitchen. 'Ann's at work. She goes to see Walter every day, so she'll be home about half six.'

'There's a lot of catching up to do. One cup of tea won't be enough, by the sound of it. Is Hilda home?'

'No word of her. How long are you home for?'

Joe laughed. 'Long enough to have a proper chat. Do you want to change Daisy and I'll make the tea?'

'So you've learned how to make tea as well? Ann will be impressed.'

Joe smiled at the banter. Everything in the little kitchen was exactly where it had always been. He made the tea and Ma smiled as he brought her two digestives sandwiched together with a slab of butter.

'Good for worrying, apparently – digestives.' Joe bit into his and crumbs dropped onto his trousers. 'Do you still get snowballs?'

'Haven't had a snowball for ages. We only get them in the floods. That buck eejit Charlie Hunter still brings five every time there's a flood. Can you get them in the navy?'

'No, no snowballs. I haven't had one the whole time I've been away.' Joe put on his sulky schoolboy face.

'Oh, poor baby. No snowballs. That's awful. Do you miss your mummy?'

Joe grinned and finished his biscuits. He stood up and brushed the crumbs onto the floor.

'That's a quare mess you've made,' Ma said good-humouredly

'I'll leave them for Ann to clean up. She was always handy with a dust pan.'

'We have a sweeper thing now. A Ewbank no less.'

'Very posh.'

'Fred knew someone who was getting a new one, so he said he'd get rid of the old one for them. It's handy for Ann to run it over the mats now and again.'

'How is Fred?'

'You know Fred – always the same. Can't do enough for people.'

'Some people in particular?' Joe winked at Ma.

'I don't know what you mean,' Ma said, grinning coyly.

'So tell me all about Daisy. It sounds like typical Ann.'

They had more tea and Ma told Joe the story.

'So poor Walter is doolally in the T&F and Ann is trying to make him better,' Joe said when she finished.

'The doctors and nurses are helping as well,' Ma said. 'She says he's getting better. It's slow, but it won't be for a lack of effort – on Ann's part anyway. She loves him to bits. How she keeps so positive and cheery I'll never know.'

'I knew Ann was fond of him, but that takes some serious dedication. And she found Daisy when she was working in Belfast, and she was working in Belfast because Walter was in the Royal?'

'Yes, it was very lucky, but sad for the other family obviously.'

'The father was a policeman?'

'Yes.'

'I can see how he couldn't look after a wean on his own. He's probably happier knowing that she *is* being looked after.'

'And what about you, son? Leading Writer sounds very important. What's that when it's at home?'

'Because I'm good at sums, they put me into what's called the Supply and Secretarial Team. Office work, basically. I do the wages and stuff, and instead of being called a *seaman*, I'm called a *writer*. I got promoted to Leading Writer near the end of last year.'

'Harry said that if you were naughty, they'd make you walk the plank, but they couldn't do that to an officer, could they?'

Joe laughed. 'No, Ma, you can't be *naughty* in the navy. They don't make you walk the plank, and I'm not an officer, even though I work in the office. It just means I'm in charge of a wee team of writers and I get a bit more pay.' Joe smiled at his old ma. 'How is empty head anyway? Do you see him much?'

'Don't call him that! He's a lovely boy. I see him at church. The whole Johnston family still go every week.'

Joe knew the point Ma was making. She probably wished her own family were all still at home, safe and bored witless.

'Does Ann go to church with you?' he asked.

'No, she stays at home to look after Daisy.'

'Of course, I forgot about Daisy there for a minute.'

'Betty and I go together. We hold each other up!'

Joe pictured Ma sitting in their pew on her own and his heart melted. 'I could go with you this Sunday,' he said. 'Would you like that?'

'That would be lovely, son.'

'Mrs Bann won't be annoyed or anything?'

'No, she'll just go with her son in his fancy car like normal.'

'Was there a flood last year?'

'No, thank God. About an inch deep on the road was all there was.'

'So no snowballs?'

'No snowballs.'

'And how was stopping work? You must miss it.'

'Someone had to look after Daisy. Ann has her whole future ahead of her. She gets new certificates nearly every day.'

Joe grinned. 'But you're okay? What about your cough?'

'It's still there. Not all the time, mind. My knees are stiff and very sore at times. From all that scrubbing, I suppose.'

Ma would never have admitted to any illness or discomfort when they were children and it felt good that she could confide in him now, even just a little bit.

'You deserve a rest,' Joe said.

'This wee madam keeps me busy,' she said, picking Daisy up. 'Do you want to hold her?'

Joe held out his arms and Ma passed her over. 'She looks a bit like a baby Walter,' he observed.

'Everyone says that. It's quite a coincidence, I must say.' Ma looked at the fire rather than at Joe.

She's hiding something, Joe thought. 'What's for dinner?' he asked.

'Oh God, dinner! We only have four sausages. We didn't know you were coming.'

'Don't panic, Ma. I'll go for a dander and get a few more. Are they beef or pork?'

'Beef, I think.'

'Right, I won't be long.' Joe put on his coat and then took it off again. 'I don't need a coat on a day like that.' He draped it over the back of the armchair next to the fire.

'Don't let your man Mullan see you,' Ma warned. 'He's bound to know you joined the navy. You need to be careful.'

'I will, Ma. He thinks I'm a hero, remember.'

'That was before you joined up.'

'Don't worry, I'll be careful. I'm away.'

When Joe closed the front door behind him, Ma did a little jig.

'Well, Daisy, what do you think of your uncle?' she said. 'He's grown up into a big handsome man, hasn't he? Leading Writer no less. He'll be the captain of the ship in no time.'

She went into his room, retrieved the new coal scuttle and set it on the hearth.

Joe was back in about twenty minutes. He had to knock again; he had no key.

'Well, did you see anybody?' Ma asked as she took the brown paper parcel off him.

'No, not a soul – not one that I knew, anyway. Nothing's changed much by the look of things.'

'Nothing ever changes around here. Oh, I tell a lie. We got a new coal scuttle. See.' Ma pointed proudly at the hearth.

'That's lovely, Ma.' Joe smiled. 'And what about Mu and Mr Plummy?'

Ma hid her disappointment at Joe's dismissal of the shiny new bucket. 'She calls us at the phone box on Sunday afternoons. You can ask her yourself. She'll be surprised to hear you on the line.'

'No hope of you getting a phone in, then?'

'It costs a fiver just to get it in and then it's a pound a month to rent, whether you use it or not. That's a lot of nappies.'

'Yes, Ma,' Joe said.

They smiled at each other.

'Ann will be home soon,' Ma said. 'I'll get the spuds peeled.'

'I'll do that, Ma. You sit there and chat to Daisy,' Joe said and he disappeared. A few minutes later, Ma could hear pots banging in the kitchen and at least one swear word.

'What's wrong, son?' she shouted.

'The wee brown knife has gone mad – made me drop the big saucepan in the sink. But I've got things back under control.'

The front door banged open.

'You want to see the state of Neil Hegarty staggering out of the Bear's Paw, Ma,' Ann said. 'He could hardly stand, and he spilled his—' She nearly fell sideways into the fold-up table as Joe walked in from the kitchen. 'Jesus, Joe, where did you come from?' She dropped her bag and gave him a big hug.

Joe looked behind him. 'The kitchen. I was peeling the spuds.'

'Haha, I mean … you know what I mean. Let me get a good look at you.' She stepped back and cocked her head to one side as she took him in. 'You've filled out a bit. All brown and all. You look almost handsome … in a weird sort of way.'

'Thanks very much.' He laughed. 'You look … older. I was nearly going to say *and wiser*, but I can't tell a lie. Not in front of Ma anyway.'

Grinning, Ann slapped Joe on the arm. Nothing had changed. Ma looked happier than she had done for a very long time.

'When did you get back?' Ann asked.

'Just this afternoon. Ma has told me all about Walter and Daisy. I'd hardly been gone five minutes before you were off doing mad things.'

Ann looked over his shoulder at Ma, her eyes asking *what did you tell him?*

'I don't think Joe can believe how lucky you were to find Daisy like that,' Ma said to help Ann out. 'The fact that Mrs Evans knew the poor policeman's wife and all, and then you deciding on the spur of the moment to adopt her.'

'What will you do if Walter recovers and says he doesn't want a wean,' Joe asked. 'Maybe he'd prefer one of his own.' He was smiling mischievously.

Relieved, Ann sat down heavily on one of the dining chairs at the table. 'I'd be very happy to accommodate him!'

'Ann Brown!' Ma scolded.

'You look knackered,' Joe said to Ann as he sat down in Fred's chair beside the fire.

'I go out to see Walter nearly every day. It's quite a walk after work and all.'

'Especially at your age,' Joe said. 'You must be nearly twenty-one now.'

'How long are you home for, Mr Funnyman?' Ann asked, laughing and throwing a tea towel at Joe. It missed.

'A week. R & R they call it. Rest and recreation.'

'He's a Leading Writer, aren't you, son?'

'The cream always rises, Ma, as you know.' He pointed a finger at Ann. 'I know what you're thinking. No need to be rude in front of Ma.'

Ma looked confused. 'Right, son, no need to be rude.'

'I wasn't thinking anything,' Ann said with a poker face. 'Not about anything *floating* anyway. You've a dirty mind, that's all. You must be on good money now that you can do joined-up writing.'

'Seven bob a day and nothing to spend it on except beer and gambling.' When he caught the horrified look on Ma's face, he grinned. 'I had to open a bank account for my pay to go into. I have a cheque book and everything.'

Ma had never had a bank account. She looked so proud of her big handsome boy.

Joe got up to get some coal, making a point of admiring the new scuttle as he went.

'You told him the story?' Ann whispered.

Ma nodded.

Joe came back in and carefully placed a few lumps of coal on the fire.

'Ma was just saying she can't believe you nearly look like a grown man,' Ann said.

'I said no such thing, son. I think you look very handsome.'

'No Brussels sprouts now.' Joe flexed his arms and proper biceps bulged under his shirt.

'You look like Popeye!' Ann said, giggling.

Joe and Ann burst into the Popeye theme tune; Ma covered her ears.

They had sausages with spuds and butter for dinner and were happy to let the fire dwindle early as it wasn't that cold. Ma offered Joe a drink, but he refused.

'Don't really like spirits much.'

Ann and Ma toasted his return with a large measure of Bushmills, and Joe told them about his adventures. It was hard to tell what was true.

'An octopus!' Ann exclaimed. 'You can't eat an octopus! All those big slimy tentacles.'

'Ann Brown!'

'Tentacles, Ma. Tentacles.'

Ma was shaking with laughter.

'They'd be great at Christmas. Everyone could have a leg,' Joe added helpfully.

Ma covered her face with her hands in mock horror as Joe's stories got more and more outrageous. Ann thought she looked like the happiest woman in the world.

Eventually it got late and Ma decided to go to bed. 'Don't sit up too late,' she said to Ann. 'You have work in the morning.'

'Yes, Ma,' Joe and Ann chimed together.

Nothing had changed, *except everything has changed,* Ann thought.

'Joe?'

'Ann.'

'I need to tell you something.'

'What?'

'Not here. Can I meet you tomorrow? After work.'

'What's so secret?'

'I can't tell you now. Tomorrow.'

'It's Wednesday tomorrow, isn't it? I'll go and see Nigel in the afternoon and meet you in the Cake Shop at quarter past five. Will that do?'

'Yes, and please don't say anything to Ma.'

'I love a good secret,' Joe said. 'I'm knackered. I'm off to bed. See you tomorrow.'

'I might be away before you get up. Cake Shop.'

'Cake Shop.'

Ann scooped Daisy up out of her cot. As she disappeared up the stairs she shouted, 'I forgot to mention – we gave Harry your bike.'

CHAPTER 11

'I can't believe you gave my beautiful bike to that half-wit,' Joe said, butter dripping down his chin from the toasted soda.

'He needed a proper man's bike, God love him,' Ma said and took a sip of her tea.

'But he's not a proper man. He's a dick head and now he has my bike.'

'I think the bike is well used to dick heads,' Ann butted in, reaching to grab a piece of toast.

'Children, children!' Ma chuckled at her sparring children.

'Talking about dick heads, I'm going to see the biggest of them all this afternoon,' Joe said. 'We might go for a spin in his wee toy car, but I'll be home for dinner. Liver and onions? I'll get it.'

'That's okay, son. We can have liver and onions.'

'I'm away,' Ann said, kissing the top of Daisy's head before she headed out to work. 'See you later.'

* * *

Nigel dropped the ream of cloth he was carrying when Joe walked into the shop.

'Jesus! … Sorry, Mrs Gibson.' He gathered up the sea of green and blue paisley. 'When did you get back? … Sorry, Mrs Gibson, I'll cut this for you now.'

Nigel spread the cloth across the counter, straightened the edge along the brass ruler and, with outsize scissors, cut off four yards. 'There you are, Mrs Gibson. Diane, can you wrap this up for Mrs Gibson? The curtains will look lovely, Mrs Gibson.' He breathed out as he turned to Joe. 'So when did you get back?'

'Yesterday.'

'Your ma must have been glad to see you – when she got over the shock.' Nigel grabbed Joe's right hand in his giant paw and squeezed. Joe grimaced.

'She was. That gobshite Harry had told her that I'd probably have to walk the plank … Let go. You're breaking my fingers.'

'Sorry.' Nigel dropped Joe's hand. 'Harry's the plank for worrying your ma.'

'Ma would worry anyway. She loves it.'

'You look almost grown up. Is that stubble on your wee chin?' Nigel grabbed Joe's cheek between his thumb and forefinger.

'Piss off … Sorry, Mrs Gibson,' Joe said.

Nigel walked to the front of the shop and held the door open for Mrs Gibson.

'You've lost a lot of weight,' Joe observed as Nigel closed the door.

'About four stone since I last saw you. Still running nearly every day. Empty-head has missed you. He's started going out with girls instead.'

'And you?'

'Too busy to miss you. Didn't even know you were gone till you came back.'

'Girls, I mean, you big dope.'

'Nothing serious.'

'You mean nothing at all.'

'Haven't seen anyone I like the look of yet,' Nigel said. 'Anyway, tell me everything. Where have you been, what have you seen?'

'Have you still got the world's smallest car?'

'I have a different world's smallest car now.'

'And is Harry still on earlies?'

'He is.'

'Can we take a run out and surprise him?'

'He'll have a heart attack when he sees you.'

'Serve him right. He stole my bike.'

'He said Ann gave it to him. He thinks she fancies him, especially now he looks more like a proper man on a man's bike.'

'It would take more than a man's bike to make him look like a proper man. And Ann wouldn't fancy him if he was the last man in the world.'

'Let's have some lunch first. We can have a chat and then go and ruin Harry's day.'

'Chips in the Rex?'

'Chips in the Rex.'

At five past two, Harry came out through the factory gates wheeling a red bike. He was chatting to another man, who then got on his own bike and headed off towards the town. Harry had his left foot on the pedal and was about to throw his right leg over the saddle when he saw the green Morris Minor parked at the roadside. Joe was standing beside it.

His face split into a broad grin and, setting the bike down, he walked over. He didn't utter a word; he just put his arms around his big daft mate.

'Nice bike,' Joe said once he'd extricated himself from the bear hug.

'My girlfriend gave it to me. It was her brother's, but she said he'd got a boat so he didn't need a bike any more. Lucky or what?' Harry ran his hand through his hair. He was still smiling like mad. 'Jesus, Joe, I can't believe it. Are you still in the navy? Are you home for good? What was it like?'

'Yes, no, and they made me walk the plank for farting on the poop deck on my first day. I'm okay, by the way, thanks for asking. You look a bit – I don't know – older, thicker, if that's possible.'

'No, not possible, Joe. Stupid question, if you ask me.'

'I *was* asking you.'

'Oh! Better ask somebody else then.'

'Gimme a hug, you buck eejit,' Joe said and opened his arms.

'We've done that. People will talk.' Harry held out his hand.

Joe grinned at his favourite buffoon and shook his hand.

'When can you come for a spin?' Joe asked.

'Can't today. Things to do, people to see. Sunday afternoon?'

'What do you think, Nigel?' Joe said, peering in the open window of the car. 'Does Sunday afternoon suit you?'

'I'll call for you on Sunday … about two o'clock?' Nigel looked at Harry, who nodded.

'We call that fourteen hundred in the navy.'

'Fourteen hundred? Fourteen hundred what?' Harry asked, winking at Nigel.

'Two o'clock is fourteen hundred hours.'

'There's only twenty-four hours in a day, so how can you have fourteen hundred all of a sudden?' Harry did his Stan Laurel head scratch. 'That's about …' he started counting on his fingers.

'Fifty-eight days and eight hours,' Nigel announced.

Joe and Harry looked at him, awestruck.

'It's a way of telling the difference between before noon and after noon,' Joe said.

'Sailors in His Majesty's Naval Service can't tell the difference between day and night? How the hell did we win the war?' Nigel asked, looking flabbergasted.

'You two have got thicker without me here to keep you right. It's to avoid confusion. After twelve o'clock, it goes thirteen, fourteen, right up to twenty-four and then it's one again,' Joe explained.

Nigel turned the key in the ignition. 'Who wants to go in the back on Sunday? I'll call for you first.'

Joe and Harry raised both hands. Neither of them wanted to sit in the front with Nigel.

'That's ridiculous,' Nigel protested. 'I passed the test, eventually, and I don't think I've ever had a crash … not one that was my fault, anyway. You'll fold up better in the back,' Nigel added, looking at Harry. 'I'll see you at two o'clock-ish on Sunday afternoon.'

'Fourteen hundred hours-ish,' Joe corrected him.

Nigel rolled his eyes.

'What about the flicks some evening?' Harry suggested.

'What's on?' Joe asked.

'*Rawhide*. Goodies and baddies. Nice and simple,' Nigel said.

'I like simple,' Harry said in a little-boy voice.

'You are simple,' Nigel and Joe chimed together.

Harry beamed. 'I better go and fetch my lovely red bike that my girlfriend gave me. I'll see youse on Sunday.' He turned and was off.

'Gobshite,' Joe shouted after him.

Harry raised both arms in victory.

Nigel drove Joe back into the town and parked behind the Royal Arms.

'I'm going for a dander round the town, see what's changed. You coming?'

'Aye, why not. It'll not take long. I don't think anything's changed since you left.'

'I'm meeting Ann later in the Cake Shop. She's something very secret to tell me apparently.'

'Any ideas?'

'Not a one, Nige. That's secrets for you.'

'Maybe she's going to run away with Harry.' Nigel tried to look serious.

'Nothing's impossible, I suppose. Except that.'

They had a walk around the town – out the front of the hotel onto Market Street, down Scarffe's Entry, across the front of the Academy, then left onto the Dublin Road. Joe looked at the gasworks, remembering the endless trips for coke for the fire. Then they went left, back up Market Street. Nigel was right. Nothing had changed. They parted company outside the Cake Shop and Joe went in to meet Ann.

* * *

The next morning Joe's head was still spinning from Ann's revelations. He hadn't slept well, thinking about the enormity of what she'd told him.

Daisy was bawling, Ann was singing something about the wheel of fortune not passing her by, and Ma was coughing her lungs up. So he gave up, got up and went into the living room.

The grate was cleaned out. He could hear the kettle coming up to the boil. It was great to be home.

'I'll make the tea,' he shouted.

'You should have had a wee lie-in. You on your holidays and all,' Ann said, appearing downstairs dressed for work and looking very well.

'It would be quieter in the flippin' engine room than it is here,' Joe said, handing her a cup of tea. 'Do the McGartlands complain much?'

'Couldn't hear them if they did.' Ann grinned and took a slurp of her tea.

'Toast?' Joe asked.

'This is a rare treat. Thank you. One piece will do.'

Joe brought in a plate with a normal-looking piece of buttered toast for Ann and a thick, burnt, black heel for himself.

'You haven't changed much,' she said.

'Nothing to change,' he said, preening himself.

Ann couldn't help smiling at the wee boy in the young man's body.

'Morning, Ma. Tea?'

'Morning, son. Did you sleep well, back in your own bed?'

'Like a baby … until the baby decided otherwise.'

'Isn't she gorgeous?' Ma said.

'She is. You're very lucky to have her. A bit of a miracle, if you ask me.' Joe didn't look at Ann. 'Do you want this tea? It's getting cold.' He handed Ma her old stained mug.

Ann brought Daisy down and put her in her cradle. 'Right, I'm off.' She pulled on her cardigan and left for work.

'Any plans for today, son?' Ma asked.

'I think I might go and see Dolores – find out how her wee brother Sean's doing. Maybe take Daisy for a walk later.'

'You need to be careful, son. You know what I think of Paddy Mullan.' Ma wiped a drip of butter off her chin.

'Sure there's no IRA to worry about now, Ma.'

'They might be quiet but they haven't gone away, you know. They'll be planning something. You mark my words.'

'I'll be careful, Ma. I'll be okay.'

Joe tidied up the dishes while Ma gently rocked Daisy. They were both making incomprehensible noises as he went out to the Mullans.

* * *

'Joe Brown! How are you, boy? Long time no see. When did you get home?' The expression on Paddy Mullan's face did not match his bonhomie.

Joe was wary. 'I'm very well, Mr Mullan. Good to see you. I see batteries have gone up.'

'Everything's going up. It's the bloody British Government. Taxing people to death.'

'I don't know much about all that stuff, Mr Mullan. I was just wondering how Dolores and Sean were getting on. Has he learned to swim yet?'

'He has, Joe. Good of you to ask. Don't know if you've heard about Dolores. She's not here.'

'I heard some rumours.'

'She's joined the Sisters of Mercy in Enniskillen. It was her choice, so any gossip about why she went is just that – gossip.'

'She's going to be a nun?' Joe's eyes opened wide with disbelief.

'There are no flies on you, son. Yes, eventually she'll be a nun.'

Joe was speechless for a moment. 'I'm glad she's doing what she wants to do,' he said when he finally got his wits back. 'Following her dreams. You must be very proud of her.'

'We are indeed. Her mother thinks the gates to heaven have opened a wee bit wider.'

Joe smiled.

'I know you were very fond of her,' Paddy said. Joe blushed. 'In a different world, things might have worked out differently for both of you,' he went on, 'but we are where we are.'

'We are, Mr Mullan. We certainly are.'

'You'll have to go now, Joe. Everybody knows you've joined the British war machine. Please don't come in here again.' Paddy looked out the window of the cluttered little shop, obviously worried that someone might see him talking to a Brit. 'I can't guarantee your safety.'

Nigel had said nothing had changed, but Joe's stomach churned as he realised that everything had changed. Ann was right; life just got harder and sadder as you got older.

'I'm no threat to anyone, Mr Mullan. You know that. I joined the navy to see the world and learn things and I've learned this much – this place is pathetic. It's mad.'

Paddy Mullan just pursed his lips and shrugged his shoulders.

'Can I have four batteries before I go?' Joe said.

'C or AA?'

'C. I can't afford a new torch just yet.'

'That'll be two bob.' Paddy held out his hand.

'Good luck, Joe.'

Joe paid him and they shook hands. 'Thank you, Mr Mullan. Good luck to you too. Tell Dolores I was asking about her.'

Joe left his favourite shop, probably for the last time.

He went down to the Cake Shop and sat at the same table where he'd heard the sailor telling his tales of unimaginable adventure. He ordered a Coke and a snowball and three more to take home.

He couldn't believe what Ann and Ma had done. Such strength, courage, audacity – and boy, did she love Walter. He had told Ann that if he knew how to pray, he would pray for Walter to get better. He felt proud of her and Ma, taking on the world like that, in secret too. He knew this was a serious secret that he would have to take to his grave. Ma could never know that Ann had told him, but he was so pleased that she had. She said she was going to tell Muriel and Hilda as well, when the time was right. They agreed it was the right thing to do. They knew it would be okay. It had to be.

The following Sunday, Joe went to church with Ma. He tried hard not to stare at Doreen Johnston's bum after Harry gave him a warning glance and listened in amused awe as Harry roared his way through the hymns. The sermon was incomprehensible and went on forever. Church was another thing that hadn't changed.

The afternoon was bright and sunny.

'That's Nigel and Harry now, Ma,' Joe said when Nigel's car horn dooted. 'Will you be okay?'

'Of course. Ann will be home soon. You go and enjoy yourself. Harry's a lovely boy.'

'I'll tell him you said so. He'll be delighted.'

'Don't make fun of him now. Promise me.'

'That won't be easy, but I promise.' He kissed her on the cheek. 'See you later.'

When he got into the car, the smell inside made him gag.

'Who was that?' he said, slapping his hand over his nose and mouth.

'Welcome home, Joe. Just like old times,' Harry said. He was sitting sideways in the back, his knees up around his ears.

'Can we go out to Lough Muck?' Joe asked as he squeezed into the front seat. 'There might be some girls about on a sunny day like this.' He wriggled on the seat, trying to get comfortable in the tiny space. 'Has this thing got smaller? You'll have to talk to daddykins about getting a bigger one.'

'It's big enough. It's just you're about a foot taller.'

Joe grabbed his crotch. 'Everything's got bigger.'

'Oh God.' Nigel sighed and started the car. 'I know this is a mistake, but go on. Tell us what you've got up to.'

'One thing I can tell you – foreign girls love a sailor, especially a good-lookin' one.' Joe ran the palm of his hand across his short hair.

'I suppose you've experienced a lot of these foreign girls,' Harry piped up.

'Here, I must tell you about the one I met in Bangkok.'

'Is that a real place? Bangkok? It sounds rude,' Harry said innocently.

'It's real all right. And it's not called Bangkok for nothing, I can tell you.'

'I'm sure you're going to.' Nigel drummed his fingers on the steering wheel.

Joe warmed to his task. 'It's hot and sticky. Must be a million people running around everywhere. The smells are fantastic from all the weird food they sell in the streets.'

'Octopus?' Nigel asked as he overtook an old, rickety red tractor.

'Not just octopus. Prawns, squid, snakes, frogs, monkey's brains – you name it, they eat it.'

'You ate your own brain?' Harry sounded astounded.

'No snowballs, I suppose. I couldn't go somewhere where there were no snowballs,' Nigel said with a straight face.

'So what about the girl, Joe?' Harry reminded him.

'It was my first time in Bangkok. I met her in a bar, the kind of bar that has rooms above it, if you know what I mean.'

'So, you can stay if you get pissed?' Harry suggested.

Joe laughed. 'Not exactly, dope. You go up there … with the girls … for you know what.'

'What?'

Joe couldn't figure out if Harry really didn't know what he was talking about. 'You know … sex.'

'With a girl you've only just met?' Nigel said, glancing at Joe. 'That's not Christian, Joseph Brown.'

'That's the thing. We had a few drinks. The craic was ninety. We had a few more drinks and then she asked me if I wanted "hanky-panky" and she looked up at the ceiling. I knew what she meant. Some of the others had been in Bangkok before. I thought *why not*, and up we went. That's when things got a bit sticky.'

'You wet yourself?' Nigel kept his eyes on the road, a smile playing around the corners of his mouth.

'No, no, I mean she wanted money and I didn't have enough.'

'A prossy. You went with a prossy?' Harry's voice went up an octave. He looked genuinely impressed.

'I had to go back down and borrow a fiver from Danny.'

'So you got the money. Then what?' Harry was leaning right in between the front seats.

'She kicked her shoes off, but it was when she took her dress off that I realised things weren't quite right.'

'What do you mean *not quite right*? Go on.' Harry was gripping the backs of the front seats.

'She wasn't a real girl,' Joe said.

Nigel braked hard. For a moment no one spoke.

'What do you mean she wasn't a real girl?' he asked.

'They call them ladyboys,' Joe explained. 'He was standing there with just a tiny red silk thong thing covering his bits.'

'You mean it was a boy that looked like a girl?'

'Yep. He had lovely legs. Nicer than Dolores's. He was really pretty.'

'What happened then?' Nigel asked, looking seriously concerned.

'You didn't …?' Harry sat back in his seat in horror.

'No, I grabbed my stuff and ran.'

'Glad to hear it,' Nigel said, squeezing Joe's leg 'Has anyone told you, you have lovely legs?'

'Piss off,' Joe said, skiting Nigel's hand away and rubbing his crushed thigh. 'It was all a wind-up. I ran downstairs, my shoes in one hand and buttoning my flies with the other. The rest of the lads were waiting. They started cheering and clapping. They fired beer all over me. It turned out the ladyboy was in on it.'

'I hope he got his money.' Nigel put the car into gear and they set off again.

'He did. I think his name was Kathoey. He kept saying that. I had to buy him a beer.'

'That's the worst story ever,' Harry said quietly from the back. 'You couldn't make it up.' He shook his head.

Nigel still looked shocked.

The good weather meant that there were lots of people about at Lough Muck. Nigel had to park along the road, a few hundred yards from the swimming club. They got ice creams from the shop and sat on the jetty, their legs dangling over the water. It was muddy from all the swimmers.

'How's things in Nestle's?' Joe asked when they finished their cones. 'I'm surprised it stayed open after I left.'

'I got a promotion. I'm the deputy to the Chief Engineer now,' Harry said.

'He's got a badge and everything. Show him your badge,' Nigel said, grinning.

'Ignore the big fart, Joe. I don't have a badge. I'm not that sort of deputy.'

'How will people know you're a deputy if you don't have a badge?' Joe asked, trying to look serious.

Harry answered him seriously. 'I have white overalls instead of blue ones.'

'Good man, Harry. White overalls. That's good. And what about the football?'

'Still starring for the YMCA firsts. Giraffrey is still scoring lots of goals. We're doing okay.'

'What about you, Nige? Still running?'

'Aye, but me and a few of the others are thinking of starting a rugby team.'

'All the big donkeys that are useless at football,' Harry said, grabbing on to the jetty in case Nigel tried to push him off.

'Are you going to let him call you a big donkey?' Joe asked, looking at Nigel.

'I'm afraid he's right, Joseph. I have all the attributes of a big donkey.' Nigel grabbed himself halfway down his thigh.

Harry and Joe smiled. The huge fat Nigel they used to know would never have had the confidence to say something like that.

'Girls? Harry? Nigel?' Joe was genuinely interested. 'And I don't mean fantasy girlfriends, Harry.

'Ann isn't a fantasy. Faint heart never won fair lady.'

'She is not a *fair lady*, Harry. She drinks like a fish and swears like a trooper.'

'Sailor,' Nigel corrected him.

'Sorry, sailor. And she's seriously in love with Walter.' Joe paused. 'More than you could ever know.'

Nigel and Harry looked at him, puzzled.

'But Walter's not well,' Harry said. 'He might never get better and she might need someone.'

'She'll stick with Walter forever, Harry. No matter what happens. Trust me.'

* * *

For the rest of the week, Joe just mooched about the house, doing things that didn't need to be done. He didn't see much of Harry or Nigel and they didn't go to the pictures. Things really had changed. He spent a lot of time with Ma and Daisy, taking the baby for walks and doing the shopping.

On Friday, he went to the station on his own and went back to work.

CHAPTER 12

It was early on a Saturday morning in August and the front and back doors were already open to allow a draught through. Ann was pushing up the sash window in the living room as Ma came down.

'When was the last time this window was opened?' Ann asked, heaving with all her might.

'Twelfth of July 1912. It was a Friday if I'm not mistaken. A scorcher. The bandsmen stuck to the road.' Ma looked mischievous.

Ann flashed her a grin and grunted as she forced the window up the last few inches.

They could hear the hum of the bakery across the street. A car went past, heading towards the town.

'There's an awful lot of cars on the road these days,' Ma observed as she sat down with a cup of tea.

'You'd need eyes in the back of your head crossing the street,' Ann said. 'They come at you from all directions.' She eyed the window, checking it was staying up.

‘Who has eyes in the back of their head?’ Ma looked up at her.

‘Mrs Chesney. And she can see round corners.’

‘She can’t … can she? It wouldn’t surprise me.’

‘No, Ma. Just kidding. She can’t see past the end of her nose.’

Ma smiled. ‘It’s going to get hot.’

‘It was normal yesterday, now it’s roastin’.’

‘There’s too many cars.’

‘Yes, Ma. That’s what it is.’

‘We’ll be able to scrape the mould off the walls now it’s dried. Haven’t done that for years.’

‘I saw a mouse running *out* earlier, not in,’ Ann said.

‘Did you, right enough?’

‘I did, and the sweat was lashin’ off him.’

‘He can’t even take his coat off,’ Ma said, trying hard not to laugh. ‘Must be murder, God love him.’

* * *

Mid-afternoon, Ann came back from visiting Walter with the shopping. Her blouse was stuck to her back. Ma was dozing with her cardigan off. That’s how hot it was.

‘Fancy an ice cream?’ Ann asked her. ‘The bakery has a machine now, same as the one in the Cake Shop.’

‘Only if they have flakes. There should be enough in the tin.’

‘I have money, Ma, and yes, they have flakes.’

‘And sprinkles?’

Ann smiled at her. ‘Two ninety-nines it is, then.’

The ice cream was dripping off the ends of the cones before Ann got back across the street. ‘Had to wait for a car. Can you believe it?’ she said.

‘There’s too many cars,’ Ma said. ‘That’s two in one day. Somebody’ll get kilt, you mark my words.’

Fred looked like a soggy beetroot when he called round after dinner. He took his duncher off and wiped his forehead with a spotlessly white hanky.

Ann couldn’t remember ever seeing his head without his hat. He had a ring of steely grey hair with a tiny, shiny, baldy bit in the middle.

‘It’s very hot, Kathleen,’ he said.

‘It’s the heat and there’s too many cars.’

Fred smiled at her. ‘It is, Kathleen. And you’re right.’ He slumped into his usual chair by the empty fireplace. ‘How was Walter today?’ he asked Ann.

‘He walked a wee bit,’ she replied. ‘Just a few steps, but as soon as you let go of him, he cowps.’

‘And the talking?’

‘Getting better. He says *Ahhh* when he sees me, and *Deh* when he sees Daisy.’

‘It’s good that you can see an improvement.’

‘He’s still the same Walter. I can see it in him, but I’m beginning to think he might never be able to dance again … unless it’s a very slow shuffle’, she said with just a flicker of a smile.

Ma and Fred exchanged a look.

‘Too hot for a drink, Fred?’ Ann asked.

Fred looked at her as if she was mad.

‘Thought not,’ Ann said, laughing. ‘I’ll get the glasses.’

When Ann went out to the kitchen, Fred mouthed, *Is she okay?*

Ma shook her head.

‘Hard to believe Daisy will be one on Monday,’ Fred said, taking a tumbler from Ann’s outstretched hand.

Ann handed him the bottle of Dimple.

'Any plans?' He poured himself a small measure of the smooth blend.

'I'm going to give her back the rattle she got at Christmas.'

Ma laughed and coughed. 'You will not,' she spluttered. 'She did my head in. Worse than Joe. Didn't even make it to the King's Speech.'

Fred handed the bottle back to Ann. She poured herself and Ma a wee drop and added an even smaller drop of water. She held the jug up to Fred.

'No thanks, love. It's perfect the way it is.'

'Maybe we should give Daisy the old biscuit tin. She could whack it with her wee spoon. Wouldn't that be nice, Ma?'

Ma shook her head and took a sip of her drink. '*This* is nice,' she said.

Ann and Fred clinked glasses; Ann went over to Ma: 'Cheers!'

Frankie Laine was on the radio, singing about an untrustworthy Jezebel.

'Daisy's a lively wee thing, so she is,' Fred said, setting his glass down.

'Too lively,' Ann said. 'Like Walter on Lucozade.'

Fred blotted his forehead with his hanky. 'It's going to be hard to sleep in this heat,' he said.

'Another wee dram?' Ma asked.

'That'll help,' Fred replied. They all knew it didn't matter whether it helped or not.

As the evening settled in, the air cooled a bit.

Ann took her thoughts to bed. 'Sorry, Walter. I'm not giving up. I'll never give up. We'll dance again, I promise. Might not be a quickstep, mind, but a slow step will do. I'll see you on Monday.'

The radio was turned off downstairs and a few minutes later, she heard the front door close. The stairs creaked with each step as Ma came up to bed. It was always the last sound of every day.

'Are you okay, love?' Ma called out. 'I thought I heard you saying something.'

'Just talking to myself.'

'That's my job.'

'Yes, Ma. Goodnight, Ma.'

'Goodnight, love.'

* * *

Ann had brought a little cake and a box of small coloured candles.

'Do you know what day it is, Blondie?'

'*Ahhhh*,' Walter groaned. He looked gaunt, hollow-eyed.

'It's *Deh*'s first birthday,' Ann said.

She set the cake on the bedside locker and got the box of candles out of her handbag. She chose a pink one and stuck it into the middle of the cake. Striking a Swan Vesta, she lit the candle.

'I know you want to do it,' she said, looking at Walter, 'but it's Daisy's birthday.' She lifted Daisy out of the pram and held her face close to the tiny flame. 'Blow, Daisy. Blow out the candle and make a wish. Do you know how to make a wish? I'll make one as well and maybe your daddy could make one. Can you do wishes, Walter?'

Walter made a weird noise and tapped like a madman.

'Okay, so if we all wish for the same thing at the same time, it's bound to come true, isn't it. Go on, blow.'

Daisy started crying and wriggling uncomfortably.

'*Deh, Deh*.' Walter looked upset.

Ann blew out the candle and sang 'Happy Birthday' in a whisper. She was laughing. She set Daisy down, then she started to cry.

'We gave her a coal scuttle,' Ann said, holding Walter's hand. 'We got it ages ago because we thought the arse was about to fall out of the old one, which is older than Ma. But Ma said it was too shiny to put coal in, so we're still using the old one. Ma can't wait for Daisy to start hitting it with her rattle.' She sniffled, blew her nose and stopped crying. 'Sorry about that. Time to dance,' she announced.

They went for their short, slow shuffle. Ann sang in Walter's ear, 'The Little White Cloud That Cried'.

'I feel like a little white cloud, Walter, but the song's right – the thunder and lightning will pass. There's a good day coming.'

Back in his wheelchair, Ann kissed his cheek. Just then, Janet, the Matron, appeared with a Kodak Brownie and a wooden tripod.

'Did you believe me about the coal scuttle?' Ann said to him. 'You big eejit, I was joking. We've been using it for months. Janet here is going to take our picture. That's Daisy's real present.'

After a lot of shuffling, they found the right pose. Walter had Daisy on his lap and Ann knelt beside him so they were all roughly the same height.

Janet fiddled with the camera. 'Okay, say cheese.'

Ann *cheeeeeeesed*, Walter and Daisy gurgled. The flash went off.

'Let me try another one. Daisy wasn't looking at the camera,' Janet said. She fiddled some more and there was another flash. 'That's better.'

Daisy started to wail.

‘I’ll have this for you in a few days, Ann.’

‘Thanks, Janet. Can’t wait to see it.’ She had got up, but knelt down again. ‘That’s our first family picture, Walter. How good is that?’ She kissed the top of his head. ‘I love you, Walter Green, and I always will.’

Walter’s eyes looked misty as he said, ‘*AhhNNN.*’

She could swear he was smiling. Tears of joy poured down her face. She couldn’t help it.

CHAPTER 13

Rain was forecast for that chilly November day, but it was still dry when Ann left to go and see Walter. The post-mortem on that day's church service could wait until she got back. The rain came on just as she left the T&F and Ann was drenched by the time she got home. She felt cold, wet, tired and deflated.

She hung her soaking coat on the hook behind the door. After she had been to the toilet, she sat in the armchair beside the fire to dry herself and Daisy off, then settled Daisy in Ma's lap.

'So tell me, how was church today?' she asked.

'Stella Hudson had a new hat. A big purple thing with a ribbon on it. Ghastly.'

Ann grinned at Ma's normal, blunt opinion. 'Were the Johnstons all there?'

'Yes, all there as usual. Harry helped me out again at the end. God love him, he's loud. He hasn't a note in his head, but he's a lovely boy. He's always asking about you and Walter … and of course Joe.'

Poor Harry, Ann thought. 'I'll buck in the soup mix, then sort Daisy out,' she said as she lifted Daisy off Ma. 'She smells like the mart.'

The talk that evening with Fred was all about the weather, in particular the rain.

'It's just a question of when it'll flood, Kathleen, and I think it'll be soon,' Fred said.

'We'll need help getting all the stuff upstairs,' Ann said. 'I never thought I'd say this, but Joe was quite useful at times.'

'Aye, once a year,' Ma said with a cheeky grin.

Ann and Fred both laughed before Fred said, 'I thought he was your favourite, Kathleen.'

Ann clutched her chest theatrically, pretending to be crestfallen.

'Only when he's here. Ann's my real favourite because she's always here.'

Ma's words were supposed to comfort her and they did. I made my bed, she thought. There's no escape now.

* * *

'Worst I've ever seen,' Ma said as they finished the clean-up. She collapsed in her chair.

'I'm going to have nightmares about that poor wee fox,' Ann said.

On the afternoon of the second day of the flood, when the water had risen to the top of the downstairs windowsill, a young fox had floated past, staring up at them, its dead eyes like glass beads.

'Doesn't do to dwell on it, love,' Ma said. 'You should take Daisy out to see Walter now that it's dry. He's probably missed you. I'll try and get washed.'

'Are you sure? You look—'

‘What? Don’t be cheeky now.’

‘Tired. I was going to say you look tired.’ *Completely wrecked* was what Ann was going to say.

* * *

Walter’s face lit up like a bonfire on the eleventh of July when he saw Daisy.

‘You didn’t miss *me* at all, did you?’ Ann scolded. ‘It’s just Daisy you want.’

Walter grunted and waved his hand, shooing her off. He’d never done that before.

Ann loved it and gave him a hug. ‘Very straggly, but still unique,’ she said as she combed his hair. ‘Worst flood since Noah’s. We saw a dead fox. It was horrible … okay, time for your exercise.’ She put her arms around him and hoisted him to his feet. ‘You can nearly stand up on your own now,’ she said, delighted. ‘You just like the hug, don’t you, you dirty brute.’

Walter grunted. *Tap, tap, tap*. Was that a smile?

‘Let’s go for a wee walk. Right foot first.’

Grunt.

‘Left.’

Grunt.

‘Right.’

Grunt.

‘Heel lead.’

Walter let out a laughing grunt.

Ann wrapped her arms around him again. ‘Soon, Walter, soon. The Starr is waiting for you. I’m waiting for you and I’ll wait forever, but sooner than that would be better.’

As she left the T&F, she thought she felt content. Happy with her lot. Work was going well, Walter was getting better, even if it was slow, Daisy was thriving and full of beans, and Ma was Ma. She really had so much to be grateful for.

As Ann set her shopping down to light a fag outside Coates's shop, an onion escaped and began to roll away. However, it didn't get far. A man in a dark raincoat put his foot out to stop it. He picked it up, put the onion back on top of the shopping, flicked his lighter and held it out for her. Ann leaned forward and lit her cigarette.

'Thank you. You're very kind.'

'Minds of their own, onions. Bring tears to your eyes, they would.'

Ann smiled politely at his joke. 'I need an extra pair of hands at times.'

'Is this your wee girl?' the man asked, looking into the pram at Daisy.

'No,' Ann said. 'I'm just looking after her for a friend. I better go. Need to get home.' She felt flustered. He was sort of handsome – tall, black hair. Not her type, not her type at all.

He lit his own cigarette, took a big drag and said 'You take care now' as he exhaled a cloud of smoke.

'Thank you,' Ann muttered to his back as he wandered off down Market Street.

CHAPTER 14

The year petered out, and Christmas and the winter passed, cold and quiet like always. Ann flipped the page in the *Scenes from Northern Ireland* calendar for 1952. February's 'scene' was a clump of snowdrops and crocuses in full bloom. The page was blank. Full of promise.

Wednesday was wet and Ann didn't go out to see Walter. Instead, she hurried home after work. She knew Ma would be upset and in a complete tizzy at the news. They'd announced it at work.

As Ann opened the front door, Ma pushed herself out of her chair.

'Oh, the poor King,' she said, a tear trickling down her cheek. 'He died in his sleep, God love him.' She took off her glasses and wiped her eyes with her hanky.

Ann put her arms round her. 'It sounds like it was peaceful,' she said. 'He hadn't been well. For a long time, by the sound of it. And he would have had the best of care. It's still very sad, though. Any word of the funeral?'

'It's on Friday week, I think – the fifteenth,' Ma said.

'So, who's in charge now? We can't have no king.' Ann knew Ma would know.

'Princess Elizabeth takes over. She's in Africa somewhere. I hope she's safe. She only left a few days ago and now she has to come straight back. She's only twenty-five, dear love her.'

'Imagine being a queen at twenty-five. She's not much older than me,' Ann said. 'It's like a fairy tale.' Her wheel of fortune has turned all right, she thought.

'I feel sorry for the Queen. He wasn't old – only fifty-six.' Ma sniffled

'Sounds old to me, Ma,' Ann said, but when she saw the horrified look, she added, 'but it's not really, I suppose.' She realised for the first time that she had no idea what age Ma actually was. She was obviously old – she looked it – but how old? Ann looked inquisitively at Ma. 'I don't mean to be nosy or anything, but how old would be *really* old?'

'You won't catch me out that easily, my girl,' Ma said, one eyebrow raised. 'A lady never discusses her age. I stopped having birthdays a long time ago.'

'That Christmas when Da died – that was the last one, wasn't it? You must have been very young then.'

'That's enough.' Ma sat down and began to twirl her hanky into tight spirals. She suddenly looked distraught.

'Sorry, Ma.' Ann kissed her forehead. ' I didn't mean to upset you. I'll make the dinner. I got some kidneys on the way home. Oliver was about to throw them out, so he threw them into a bag for me instead. A shilling in your pocket and all that.'

'I hope you paid him for them,' Ma said.

'Of course I did,' Ann lied. 'Fried kidneys, onions and mashed spuds with butter. You couldn't get better in Maldonhall Manor.'

'Except Muriel probably doesn't have to hoke out all the wee tubes.'

'True, they'll have a cook to do that.'

'And someone to do the dishes.'

'And a proper mangle with proper rollers on it.'

Ma was smiling again. 'But do they have the world's shiniest coal bucket scuttle?'

'Well, they can't, can they – because we have it.'

CHAPTER 15

Time was disappearing at an alarming rate. Ann had turned twenty-two back in April. Now she was lighting the lamps earlier every night. The summer was ebbing away.

Walter was able to get up out of his wheelchair on his own. He could stand unsteadily for a few moments before crashing down again. Daisy was very boisterous, Ma less so, due to the worsening arthritis in her knees and her cough. The doctor said not to worry about it, which had the exact opposite effect.

Ann felt increasingly like she was trapped. Every day was the same: work, Daisy, Walter, Ma. There was nothing else. She hardly ever saw Iris or any of her other friends. Most of them were married now with babies and didn't go to the Starr any more. She only saw Mr and Mrs Green if she bumped into them in the street.

Then one Saturday afternoon, she bumped into someone else.

'Hello again,' said the dark-haired man in the dark coat. He was holding the door of the Reform Stores open for her as she was leaving. 'It's the lady with the obstreperous onion if I'm not mistaken.'

Ann giggled. 'I've been called worse things.'

'Can I give you a hand? Have you far to go?'

'No, I'm all right. But thank you.' She felt flustered again, uncomfortable with the attention.

'Would you like a cup of tea?' he said. 'You can get your breath back.'

Ann looked at her new watch. Plenty of time. 'That would be very nice. Thank you.' She couldn't remember the last time anyone, especially a man, had bought her a cup of tea.

The man carried her bags for her and they went to the Carlton. A girl in a black uniform took their order of tea and two fruit scones and also brought them a little glass pot of butter and another one with raspberry jam in it. The cups and saucers were fine white china, as were the milk jug and sugar bowl.

Ann poured the tea through a strainer while the man cut his scone in half vertically. How odd, thought Ann. She had cut hers crossways, like a Christian – a top half and a bottom half. And he couldn't get his finger through the handle of the tiny teacup. It nearly slipped when he picked it up.

'You're not from Omagh with that accent,' she said to him.

'No indeed, I'm from Larne,' he replied.

Ann choked on her scone and had to set it down.

'Are you alright?' he asked.

'It's just my sister was going out with a chap once. He worked for the bank and had to move to Larne when he got promoted. It seems a long time ago now. Maybe you know him? Derek Clapton was his name – probably still is.'

The man smiled at her joke. 'No, I can't say I do. Big place, Larne.'

'So what brings you to Omagh?'

'I've been coming down for training. I work for the council – in the housing dept. There was a chance of promotion, so I'll be moving down here permanently at the end of the month – a bit like your sister's ex-boyfriend in reverse.'

'Were you training today?' Ann looked at him; it was a Saturday after all.

'No,' he said, smiling. 'I went for a few drinks last night with some of the people from work and stayed over. I'll get the bus or the train later.'

'Have you family in Larne?' Ann had noticed he wasn't wearing a ring.

'My ma died a few years ago. She just keeled over in the street – brain haemorrhage, they reckon. My da's still alive, but he's doting a bit, and I have two older brothers, one married, one stuck with Da. What about you?'

'Born and raised in Omagh. Two older sisters and a wee brother. All gone.'

The man looked aghast.

Ann snorted with laughter. 'No, I don't mean gone, like dead gone. They've left, that's all.'

'That's a relief.'

'Hilda's married and lives in Canada. She moves about a lot. Muriel works in a hospital in London and if she plays her cards right, she might be marrying a real toff. And Joe just upped and joined the navy a few years ago. Oh! I shouldn't have told you that. He told us not to tell anyone.'

'Your secret's safe with me. I'm from Larne, remember.' He smiled. He had good, even teeth.

'Da died when we were all small – before the war,' Ann went on, 'so Ma had to bring us up on her own. How she did it I don't know, but she's still here to tell the tale.'

‘So you’re the only one left?’

‘Somebody needs to look after Ma. She’s still as sharp as a tack, but she has bad knees and a cough that’s beyond even the miraculous powers of Veno’s.’

‘You must have a job then.’ He smeared butter and jam on the second half of his scone.

‘Yes. Fastest shorthanderist this side of the Bann. Department of Agriculture.’

‘You must be very fast.’ He was grinning at her.

Ann and the man chatted on for a while about nothing in particular. She was starting to relax and enjoy herself when he looked at his watch.

‘I’d no idea that was the time. I’d better go. My bus.’

‘What’s your name?’ Ann asked. ‘Ma won’t believe that a man from Larne with no name bought me tea and a scone in the Carlton. She’ll want a name.’

‘Stan. Stan Webb at your service.’ He proffered his hand. Ann shook it. His hand was huge, but his grip was gentle. ‘And you are …?’

‘Ann. Ann Brown. Pleasure to meet you, Stan Webb. Thanks for the tea.’

‘The pleasure is all mine, Ann Brown. Maybe I can see you again sometime.’

‘Maybe. If you’re lucky.’ Ann flashed him her cheekiest smile.

* * *

Ann walked home in a bit of a daze. Even the shopping felt lighter.

‘Ma?’ she called out when she got in the door.

‘Yes, love?’ Ma lowered Daisy gently to the floor without letting go of her hands.

'Remember, I told you about the man who helped me with my onion?'

Ma looked confused. 'I didn't know you had bunions.'

'Onion, Ma. Onion. One fell out of my shopping. Ages ago. It doesn't matter. I met him again today. He held the door of the Reform Stores open for me. Then he bought me tea and a scone, with jam and all, in the Carlton.'

Ma sat up and pushed up her glasses. This was news, worthy of proper attention.

'Tea and scones and you don't know him from Adam?' she said suspiciously

'He's a gentleman, but wait till you hear the best bit – he's from Larne! And he cut his scone in half the wrong way.' Ann sliced down through the air with the side of her hand. 'Can you believe it?'

'He *must* be from Larne,' Ma said. 'Does he know Derek?'

'I asked him and he said Larne was a big place.'

'Cheeky brat. I still think Muriel should have stuck with Derek. He must be a manager by now. Anyway, what's this so-called gentleman doing in little Omagh?'

'He's been here a few times to do training. He starts full-time in the Housing Department in a couple of weeks – on the first of September, if that's a Monday.'

'Are you going to see him again? Do you even know his name?'

'His name's Stan. It was great, just talking to somebody my own age. Somebody different, new. A man, if you know what I mean.'

'I do, love. You're never done running from pillar to post. You need someone your own age to talk to.'

'It was great having a chat about nothing important over a nice cup of tea that somebody else made. And no dishes to do.'

'Well, I don't know how you've done what you've done over the past couple of years. All on your own, too. I haven't been much help.'

'Oh, Ma! I don't know what I'd have done without you. You've looked after Daisy for me. I know money's still a bit tight, but I'll go up another grade soon and then we'll be flyin'.'

'You deserve to have some fun. A bit of time for yourself.'

Ann looked ruefully at Daisy crawling over to the kitchen door.

'Stan, you say. Do you know his surname?' Ma asked.

'His name's Stan Webb.'

Ma looked relieved. 'Sounds Presbyterian.'

* * *

'Is that you love?' Ma shouted from the kitchen as Ann opened the front door.

Ann thought about saying something clever, but she was too tired. And it was only Monday. She nearly tripped over Daisy, who was crawling for miles every day around the living room. She picked her up, gave her a hug and a kiss and set her down again before she started bawling.

Ann went into the kitchen. 'Look what I got today, Ma.' And she unrolled a large, thick, vellum certificate.

'Another one?' Ma stopped stirring the broth, put her hands on Ann's shoulders. She looked into her eyes. 'You are the cleverest girl. Does it mean you go up *another* grade?'

'It does, Ma. Yet another shilling in my … *our* pocket.'

'You'll be the boss of the whole place in no time.'

'You always say that. I'd like to be the boss, and this is another step in the right direction.'

'You're home early. Did you not go to see Walter today?'

'I'm exhausted, Ma. I think I'll go and see him every other day for a while.'

'He'll have missed you.'

The nurses have him stumbling about the very best. He's like a Harpo Marx puppet.'

'Whatever you think's best, love. You have to look after yourself.'

'It means we can have dinner a bit earlier. You'll like that.'

'It doesn't matter to me as long as you're happy.'

'I'll explain to Walter. Tell him it's a good thing, part of his recovery plan. It means he's making progress. Doesn't need me so much. He'll understand. I know he will.'

Ann was crossing her fingers behind her back and asking for forgiveness in her head for her betrayal.

CHAPTER 16

'I swear that hill is getting steeper,' Ma said, draping her sodden coat over the back of one of the upright wooden chairs and moving it in front of the fire to dry out.

'Cup of tea?' Ann asked.

'That would be lovely.'

'Then you can tell me all the juicy scandal and gossip.'

'It's not gossip if it's true. There's a couple of rich teas in the tin.'

'Yes, Ma.'

'Has Daisy been behaving herself?' Ma cooed at the ball of energy tottering around at a hundred miles an hour. 'She's making me dizzy.'

'She'll make herself sick,' Ann said before turning to her daughter. 'Daisy! Stop running around like a mad thing. Sit up straight like a Christian and goo and gurgle like a proper wean. Like you used to, remember?'

Ma smiled as Daisy ignored her mother's advice.

'Well, tell me. What was the craic at church?' Ann asked as she set a cup of tea down in front of Ma.

'They're forming a choir apparently. Mrs Nugent's idea. At least she can sing. Even Harry can sing better than some of them that have put their names down.' Ma slurped at her tea.

'What about Harry? Is he still going out with that wee girl – whaddye call her?'

'Florence, I think he said her name is. He said he was getting engaged. He seems too young for that sort of nonsense, but he says he'll be twenty-one in January. Twenty-one! Joe'll be twenty-one at Christmas. That's only a few weeks away.' Ma looked horrified at the thought of her wee baby boy suddenly being old enough to vote.

'And Nigel?' Ann dunked her rich tea a little too long and a bit fell off into her cup. 'Shit.'

'Language! It's the sabbath.'

'Sorry, Ma. I hate it when that happens.' Ann picked up a teaspoon to try to fish out the soggy biscuit. 'Where were we? Did he say anything about Nigel? And the rugby?'

'Nigel wasn't mentioned.'

'It's just, remember I told you – must be a few months ago now … maybe longer – a few ex Academy boys – men, most of them now – were going to start a rugby club?'

'I don't remember, love. What's rugby when it's at home?'

'I'm not sure. It's a game like football, I think. Anyway, you have to be big, apparently, to be any good at it. So Nigel, being very big, should be very good at it. Anyway, he's started playing rugby – that's what I'm trying to say. And I was wondering how he was getting on.'

'Good for him,' Ma said and knocked back the rest of her tea with a loud swallow.

Ann poured more tea and they chatted on. There was no proper scandalous gossip. Muriel would have made something up, if she'd been there. Ann missed her stories.

'Are you going to tell Walter about this new man?' Ma asked Ann later.

'There's nothing to tell. He's a gentleman who helped me. We meet up and have tea and a chat. That's all there is to it.'

'Yes, dear,' Ma said.

Ann knew that what Ma really meant was *who are you trying to fool.*

* * *

'Hi, Blondie. You're looking almost human,' Ann greeted Walter as she entered the ward.

Walter stood up unaided. He held onto the wheelchair as he stood, wobbling a bit.

'Steady,' she said, giving him a hug and kissing his lips. She took off her coat and draped it over the end of the bed. 'It's bucketing as usual. Santa got me this coat the year you went up to Belfast. Do you remember?'

Tap, tap, tap. Walter made a noise like a hissing snake.

'Yes? Good, because that's two years ago now and it's still as good as new. Good make, Firestone.' She patted the dripping raincoat. 'Wee walk?' she asked.

'*Sssss.*'

'Outside?'

Tap, tap and silence.

'You're no dozer, Walter Green. It's too wet, isn't it. Well, we'll walk up the corridor a bit instead.'

Ann hooked her arm around his left arm. He had a stick in his right hand.

'Try and lift your feet up a bit higher.'

Walter gave her a frustrated grunt.

'Walk properly. Don't shuffle.'

'*Ssssss.*' He sounded like an angry snake now.

'Well, do it then and stop being such a gobshite,' Ann snapped at him.

Walter stopped and looked at her. His face was questioning. He looked confused, upset.

'Sorry, Walter.' She squeezed his hand. 'I didn't mean to sound like your ma. You're doing great. Let's go another bit.'

They shuffled on another few yards in silence. Ann kept her head turned away from him so he couldn't see the expression on her face. Back in the ward, they had a cup of tea and a custard cream.

'Not my favourites, custard creams,' Ann said. 'You like them, though, don't you?'

'*Ssssss*.' Walter bit his biscuit in half. 'Dayzzi?'

'She's getting big and boisterous. She has Ma run off her feet, which isn't hard I know, but there's not much else we can do. Not till you get home, that is – then you can look after her. That'll harden ye, so it will. I didn't bring her out today because it's too wet. Don't want her to get a cold. Then Ma would get it. Then I would get it and I'd have to stop work and then we'd have no money and then you'd get the cold. The whole hospital would have it in no time. Ma would die from pneumonia. I'd have to give Daisy away and the world would come to an end.'

Walter was smiling at her ranting.

'How's your ma and da keeping?' she asked.

'Kay.'

'That's good. I hardly ever see them now. Sometimes they're going out as I'm coming in, sort of thing … That new nurse is very pretty. Do you know her name yet?'

'AHNNNNN.'

'That explains it. Everyone called Ann is bound to be beautiful. Wouldn't you say?'

'*Ssssss.*' A smile creased his still young, smooth face.

'Just so you know, just so there's no secrets … I've met another man.'

Walter dropped the last bit of his custard cream. He waved his arm hopelessly, trying to catch it.

'Don't worry. He's not a boyfriend or anything. He's a real gentleman. He picked up my onion when it fell out on the street. He's definitely not boyfriend material. Too tall. Too handsome. Too manly-looking and his hair is dark and straight. How boring is that? I've met him a few times … in the street, I mean.'

Lies, she thought. More lies. They'd had tea almost every Saturday since September.

'To make him even less boyfriend material – and you won't believe this – he's from Larne! I must say he seems fairly normal for someone from Larne.'

Walter giggled at this. Spittle dribbled down his chin. Ann was about to get her hanky out when he wiped it himself on his sleeve.

Ann's heart leapt at another little positive sign. 'Don't do that, Walter,' she scolded, but she was smiling. 'What would your ma say?'

'*Bah-de boh.*'

'Exactly. Very bad boy. Anyway, as I was saying, imagine him being from Larne of all places. Muriel could have ended up in Larne. She escaped just in the nick of time. I have to tell you all about this chap, Walter. I will always tell you everything.' *Another lie*? she wondered.

'His name's Stan,' Ann continued, 'and he moved here in September when he started work in the Housing Department. He's staying in digs on Castle Street. He goes home sometimes to see his da. His ma died a few years ago. She just dropped dead in the street. Dangerous place, Larne. Muriel's probably safer in London. Best place in the world, London. Do you know she's been to the Ideal Home Exhibition? She said our house wasn't in it. I bet you're as surprised as I was at that news. She said there was all sorts of modern gadgets there. Refrigerators.' She glanced at Walter. 'I know, I had to ask as well. You plug them into the electric and they keep food fresh. She says milk lasts for about three days! Can you imagine? Her and Al went to see a new play by Agatha Christie. It's called *The Mousetrap*. She couldn't work out who done it at all. I'd love to go and see a play sometime. Maybe we could go to the Grand Opera House in Belfast when you're up and about again.'

'Sta?' Walter said.

'Oh yes, sorry – Stan. He's quite boring actually. He doesn't dance for a start. He thinks the flicks are too loud. I don't think he even likes music. He says he's never heard of Kay Starr! Or the best song ever.' Ann began to sing 'Wheel of Fortune'. 'Can you believe it? But as I said, he's a proper gentleman. I mean, he hasn't got me up the duff down an alleyway yet or anything. I mean how useless is that? Only a real boyfriend would do that.'

Walter squeezed her hand. He looked lost.

She patted his bony fingers. 'I know, I know, love. We'll get there. Me and you. Together.'

She did know. She knew things were changing.

CHAPTER 17

Joe's Christmas card arrived two weeks before the day itself. By coincidence, the cards from the two girls arrived on the same day as Joe's. The first one Ma opened had a picture of a polar bear on the front.

'Must be Hilda,' she said and read out the message: '*Everyone is keeping well. Jimmy is getting a train set from Santa. Happy Christmas. Love Hilda, Dan and Jimmy.* Not much news from the Page family. You open the next one, love.'

Ann opened the next envelope. 'Look, Ma. It's a picture of Maldonwood Manor in the snow, all lit up for Christmas. They have a Christmas tree in the garden! Will I read it?'

Ma nodded, smiling at Ann's excitement.

'She says *Been to the Carol Service in Westminster Abbey. Very cold. Very amazing. We will be setting a date soon. Very exciting. Al is expecting a promotion. Both still working as hard as ever. Hope you two are keeping well. Happy Christmas. Love Mu and Al.* Westminster Abbey! I'm not one bit jealous. Sure carols are carols wherever they're sung. Our service will be just as good … probably better. Date soon, eh? You'll need to get a new hat, Ma.'

'How can I traipse all the way to London? Who's going to look after Daisy?'

'They might have the wedding over here. Sure look on the bright side – you never thought Mu and Al would work out, but it looks like it is.'

'There's many a slip 'twixt cup and lip. That's all I'll say.'

'Ma!' Ann shook her head in disbelief. She eyed the third envelope. It looked like a dog had chewed it. 'This must be Joe's.'

'You open it, love. I'm exhausted thinking about what Hilda and Muriel are up to. Joe will kill me.'

Ann tore open the envelope. 'Picture of a battleship. Very Christmassy.' She held the card up to show to Ma. 'Anyway, he says *Might be getting an office job soon. Thought I might be getting married but false alarm! Happy Christmas. Joe.*'

'Joe! Getting married! He's only a wean.'

'He'll be twenty-one soon, Ma, and he's not getting married. No woman would be that stupid.'

Ma looked like she was miles away. 'Twenty-one. Imagine, old enough to vote. Can you vote in the navy if you're miles away?'

'Don't know, Ma. Can you vote if you're completely thick, is more the question.'

'He's not thick … not completely,' Ma said and they smiled at each other.

* * *

'Peter? Mrs Green? What are you doing here ?' Ann asked.

The Greens always visited during the day. To see them in the ward at half five was unusual to say the least. They looked agitated … or was it excitement?

'We wanted to tell you the news ourselves, so we stayed on.

We've been here all afternoon.' Mrs Green was definitely not herself. She looked like she'd swallowed a happy pill.

Ann was getting excited now. 'Does it concern a very handsome, young, blond chap by any chance?' She looked at Walter. She'd never seen him sitting on a hard chair in the hospital before. He looked happy; he was positively dribbling with joy.

'They say he can come home for Christmas,' Mrs Green blurted out, unable to contain herself. She was shifting from foot to foot, grinning like a Cheshire cat.

Ann was speechless. She lifted her arms to beckon the two old, worn-out figures in for a hug. Mrs Green started crying … again. They stood like that for a few minutes. Mrs Green smelled of lavender; Peter smelled of fags and Old Spice. Ann caught Walter's eye over his mother's shoulder. He gave her a crooked smile. There was still that spark between them.

'When did they tell you?' Ann asked, backing away at last. 'This is just … I don't know … just … oh!' She stopped talking and wiped her eyes.

'Today. Just this afternoon,' Peter said. 'You're the first to know. We had to wait to tell you.'

'Oh, thank you. That's so good of you.' She'd only got to know the Greens after 'the incident'. She'd had no idea what their happy faces looked like until now. 'I have to sit down,' she said, sitting on the edge of the bed. Walter reached out his hand. She clasped it in both hers, just like she'd done a million times before.

'When will he get out then?' she asked when she got her breath back.

'Friday afternoon.' Peter said, not giving Mrs Green a chance to speak. 'They said Saturday, but *Saturday flit, short sit*, so it's Friday.'

‘That’s the 19th, isn’t it? How long can he stay?’

‘At least till the Monday after Christmas – the 29th – but it might be longer,’ Peter said. He looked like a new man. ‘Maybe over New Year, they said. Depends how it goes.’

‘Maybe even permanently, they said.’ Mrs Green looked like she was about to burst.

‘Hush now.’ Peter gave his wife a little kiss on the cheek. ‘We’ll have to wait and see. If we can cope and Walter is okay, then maybe.’

‘Wait and see. Wait and see. How many times have we heard that over the past couple of years?’ Ann said, patting Walter’s bony hand and looking into his brilliant blue eyes. He was still in there.

Mr and Mrs Green both laughed.

‘It’s what they say when they haven’t a clue,’ Peter said, ‘but you couldn’t expect them to have a clue about Walter, could you.’

‘He’s unique,’ Mrs Green said, staring at her son. ’Aren’t you, love?’

‘Even Walter hasn’t a clue about Walter,’ Ann added. ‘But then he never had a clue about anything, did you, Blondie?’ She felt jubilant ‘What do you think? Home for Christmas. You’ll have to make a list.’

‘*Ssssss. Lssssst.*’

‘He hasn’t had any new clothes since the accident,’ Mrs Green said.

‘Not even knickers? Disgusting,’ Ann said. ‘I’ll get you some nice new ones. You’ll have to try them on for me.’ She gave Walter a cheeky wink.

‘Ann! You’re awful.’ Mrs Green’s face was transformed by her smile.

‘He loves it, don’t you, Blondie?’

'Ssssss.'

'This is going to be the best Christmas ever,' Ann said, leaning over to kiss his ear.

He brushed her away with his hand.

'What about you know what?' Ann pointed surreptitiously behind her hand at the po under the bed.

'I'll have to get used to that all over again, I suppose.' Mrs Green sighed, but she looked delighted at the prospect.

'You'll miss the nurses, won't you? You dirty brute,' Ann said to Walter with a smile.

Mrs Green shook her head. 'We better go, Peter, before we hear something we shouldn't.'

There were smiles and hugs and kisses all round and the Greens toddled off up the corridor, contentedly holding hands.

Ann sat alone with Walter, holding his hand for what seemed like an age.

'So if you're good, you might be home for good. How good would that be? Better than good, I think. Good isn't good enough for how good it'll be. This might be our last Monday shuffle. Are you up for it?'

'Sssss.'

He stood up by himself. Ann could hardly contain herself. They wandered slowly up the corridor, Walter clinging tightly to the stick with his right hand and Ann with his left. He was still very unsteady. They didn't talk. There was no need.

Back in the ward Ann's thoughts tumbled into a dark swirling, whirlpool of emotions that emitted erratic glimpses of brilliant, blinding light. She started to chatter to try and stop the dizzying chaos in her head.

'Not as far for me to walk if you're at home, that's for sure. Easier to bring Daisy. She's getting really heavy. I don't think your ma and da will want me calling out every day. They'll have enough to worry about. I was going to talk to you about that anyway, even before today's news. Because you have been doing so well, I was going to suggest that I only call out every other day. What do you think? Would that be okay? I'm tired, Walter, tired to the bone. Too tired to dance. A few early nights will be just the ticket.'

'*Mssssss youuuu.*'

'I know, love, but you'll be home with your ma and da. There've been times I thought you'd never get out of here. I am so happy.'

'Stahnnn?'

'He's no competition, Walter,' she whispered into his ear.

She never thought about Stan as she walked home through the cold, dark December rain. She was skipping with joy.

Ma was delighted. 'See? God was listening,' she said. 'He did a miracle for us. For you. For Walter.

'It's what we've been waiting for, Ma. He's getting out at last.'

CHAPTER 18

'Are you going to tell Stan the truth about Daisy?' Ma asked, looking up from her knitting. The shapeless jumble of pink wool gathered in her lap was on its way to becoming a new cardigan for Daisy.

'I don't know what to tell him,' Ann said, shaking her head. 'I need to think about it. If I tell him anything, it'll have to be the truth, not our made-up story. He'll find out one way or another.'

Ma grimaced. 'I hate the thought of strangers knowing our business,' she said. 'But I agree, love, you'll have to tell him the truth – if you're going to say yes, that is.'

'I hardly know him,' Ann said. 'Why the hell did he have to ask now – in the mouth of Christmas? And just as Walter is—' She buried her head in her hands. Just when she thought the wheel of fortune had finally stopped at her name, it had decided to take another turn.

'Take it from me, love, lies and deceit will wreck any relationship. If he runs a mile when he hears the truth, then you'll know. And if he doesn't run a mile, then you'll know. Even more.'

'You are the smartest Ma I've ever had,' Ann said, and she bent over Ma's wrinkled forehead and kissed it. 'But it doesn't make the decision any easier.'

'Stew?' Ma suggested.

'Stew will fix it. I'll get some more coal … in the world's shiniest coal bucket.'

'Scuttle.'

'Yes, Ma. I'll scuttle out now.' Ann gave Ma a big grin.

Just then, Fred called round to see them. He always seemed to know when wisdom and whiskey were required.

Once he had a large measure of Coleraine in his hand, he felt able to dispense his sage advice. 'You'll always love Walter, Ann. You're like Fred and Ginger. Rick and Ilsa.'

'Oh God, *Casablanca*. Such a sad story,' Ann commented.

'It was beautiful as well, love. Sad and beautiful. Rick made a big decision and it was the right one for them both.' Ma sighed.

Ann was surprised to hear that Ma had seen it. 'When did you see *Casablanca*? You never go to the pictures.'

'It was the last film I ever saw.' Ma looked at Fred.

'I agree that what Rick did was noble and beautiful, but it was very sad as well,' Ann said. 'I feel like what I'm thinking of doing is just plain selfish – sad and horrible.'

Fred took a sip of his whiskey. 'What is it Rick says at the end about not having regrets for the rest of your life? You need to live your life. You deserve to be happy.'

'With a man who doesn't dance?' Ann asked, frowning.

'Your da didn't dance,' Ma announced abruptly.

Ann looked sharply at Ma and caught Fred glancing at her too.

'Is that supposed to cheer me up?' Ann said peevishly. 'He left you. With four weans.'

'That's enough Ann, love. He died,' Fred said softly.

'Thank God,' Ma whispered, loudly enough for them to hear.

They all fell silent. Fred took another sip of his drink.

'You need to sleep on it, love,' Ma said, finishing her whiskey.

'I could sleep on it for a week and I don't think it would help.'

'Part of the problem is you don't really know this Stan, do you? He just appeared out of nowhere and now he's asked you to marry him. Do you love him?'

Ma's directness made Ann feel uncomfortable. 'I thought that didn't matter.'

'Of course it matters, love. But it doesn't matter quite so much if there's no alternative.'

'Or there's lots of money,' Ann said with a little nod.

'That too. Don't marry for money unless there's loads of it.' Ma's lips curled into a little smile.

'Be fair now,' Fred interrupted. 'Kathleen always said only marry for money if you *can't* marry for love. Isn't that right, Kathleen?'

'Absolutely. If you love him as well, then that's a bonus,' Ma said.

Ann shook her head; she was confused. 'So I can be unhappy and live a life of regrets in comfort?'

'Life isn't easy, as you now know,' Ma said. 'You have to make tough choices and then carry on and make the best of it.'

'So … marry Stan?'

'You never answered my question. Do you love him … or think you could come to love him?'

'Not like Walter.' Ann stood up. 'I need another drink.' She poured herself a large measure and wiggled the bottle in the air at Ma, but Ma shook her head. 'But maybe I could love him enough,' she went on. 'He's lovely. Gentle, kind, quiet. All those good things.'

'Does he have a bit of money saved?' Ma asked.

'He says he has enough to get the house set up. Furniture and stuff.'

'And he can get a house, but only if he's married.'

'It sounds awful when you put it like that, Ma. I hope he's asked me because we've been getting on well, not so he can get a house. He wants the same things as me – good job, nice house, four weans, phone, one of those refrigerator things. And a Dansette. A red one.'

'You used to have different dreams,' Ma observed.

'I know. But you've always said that dreams are just that – dreams. Reality is what's real.'

'You need to be careful. He might seem nice and promise you the sun and the stars, but as soon as he finds out the truth about Daisy …'

'I know, Ma. I know.'

'Only then will you know if he's up for it.'

'I hope he has no problems in that department,' Ann said, trying to lighten the mood.

'Ann Brown! You know that's not what I meant,' Ma scolded, but her eyes twinkled with mirth.

Fred wheezed and chortled, all fags and whiskey. 'You'll make the right decision, Ann,' he said once he'd caught his breath. 'But only you can make it. It'll all work out for the best. It always does.'

'Not always,' Ma whispered.

'Thanks, Fred,' Ann said. 'Right, I'm off to bed.'

But just then, Kay Starr came on the radio singing 'Wheel of Fortune'. Ann knew all the words. It could have been written for her; it was the perfect song for right now.

They all sat and listened, and after Kay sang the closing line, 'Please let it be now', Ma said to Ann, 'It will be now, love. For you. You just have to be brave again, like you were with Daisy. You'll make the right decision. I know you will. You always do.'

'There was no decision to make about Daisy, Ma. It was simple and right, but now it's not simple at all and I've no idea what's right any more.'

Ann tossed and turned all night. In fact, she hadn't slept properly since Stan dropped his atomic bombshell a week earlier. It was a waste of time praying and hoping for Walter to get better – better enough, anyway. She dreamed that they would get married, he would get a bigger van, they would have six weans (three with Walter-type hair and three normal ones) and she would become the queen of Omagh. But it wasn't going to happen. Uncle Louis, the nurses, the doctors – they all said he was being allowed home because they didn't think they could do any more for him. He *might* continue to improve, but it wasn't guaranteed and if he did, it would be very slow.

Ma was right. Dreams ended in the morning when you woke up and reality slapped you in the face. She had to make the best of what she had, even if it meant being selfish. She couldn't have left Walter if they'd been married when he got knocked down and injured. For richer or poorer; in sickness and in health. But they weren't married. Should that even matter? Love is forever; she should look after him. But she had Daisy to think about. And Ma. And what about her own needs and dreams?

Monday morning came, as dark and dismal as any Monday could ever be. She felt awful. As she splashed her face with cold water and watched Daisy holding onto the bedframe, trying to stand up, she thought, decision made. *This ends today*.

CHAPTER 19

She called Stan at his office and they arranged to meet after work in the Royal Arms.

'Not long till Christmas now,' he said as he sat down at their table with two Black Bush.

'Thanks, Stan. Good weekend?' Ann asked.

'The usual. Got my washing done. Explained to Da again that I had a job in Omagh.'

'Did you tell him about me?'

'I did, but he won't remember. I told Willy too.'

'Well, what did he think?'

'He didn't say much. He was more bothered that I didn't fight him for the last spud.'

Ann gave Stan a weak smile. 'Well, I haven't been normal either. You've turned my world upside down. I'm very flattered but—'

'I don't like the sound of that *but*,' Stan interrupted.

'Hear me out. I've thought about this a lot. There are things I need to tell you, things I wouldn't be telling you if I wasn't taking this seriously. Once you've heard what I have to say, it might be you saying *but*.'

'Uh-oh,' Stan said and took a mouthful of whiskey.

'First off, we don't seem to have much in common, but opposites attract, or so they say. I think we've got on swimmingly ever since you rescued my onion.'

'I'd say we get on more than swimmingly. I've never asked anybody to marry me before.'

'I know. I know, but there are things you should know about me before we go any further, things that very few people know. I'm in a complete tizzy about all this.'

'I didn't mean to cause tizzyness. It just felt right – asking you, I mean. I didn't need to think about it for too long. Everything seemed to be aligning, falling into place. The job, the house, meeting you.'

'Wheel of Fortune,' Ann said, nodding her head slowly.

'What?' Stan looked confused.

'It's a song by Kay Starr. Do you know it?' Ann sang the first line of the song: *The wheel of fortune goes spinning around …*

Stan shook his head. 'I don't listen to music much.'

'It's a song about luck changing. The wheel of fortune might just be turning in the right direction for both of us, is all I'm saying. If you believe in that sort of stuff, that is.'

'Can't say I do. It's another indication, I suppose, that we hardly know each other.' He picked up his empty glass, looked into it and set it down again. 'I'm not sure how I'm going to deal with a no.'

'It's not a no. It's just not a yes – not yet, anyway. Go get another drink. When you get back, I'll tell you everything, then if it's you who wants to say no, I'll completely understand.'

'Oh God.' Stan stood up and ran his fingers nervously through his black hair. 'Same again?' Ann nodded. 'I'll be back in a minute,' he said. 'Might need the toilet.' He gave her a crooked smile.

I could do worse, Ann thought as she watched him make his way to the bar. She took a deep breath and closed her eyes for a moment. Then she fished her compact out of her handbag and checked her make-up in the mirror. She had just snapped the compact shut when Stan came back to the table with two more Black Bush.

'Have you ever run a mile before?' Ann asked, swirling her drink in the glass.

He smiled. 'No, and I don't think I want to start.'

'We'll see.'

Ann took a big slug of her drink. She set her glass down, took a deep breath and told Stan everything.

He sat quietly sipping his whiskey.

'And now Walter is getting home,' Ann said, winding up her story. 'It might only be for Christmas but it may be longer. Maybe even for good.' She folded her hands in her lap. 'Well, do you need your gutties?' she asked.

Stan said nothing. He was staring into his empty glass.

'Say something, Stan,' Ann said, staring intently at him. 'I don't know what to do. My friend Iris says I should pull myself together, but I'm far too scattered. I need to stop the wheel spinning. What do you think? Has it stopped in the right place?'

'I don't know what to say,' Stan said eventually. 'That's quite a story. It's a lot to take in. You're one strong, determined lady, that's for sure. And tough – you *and* your ma. It can't have been easy for her.'

'We did it together,' Ann said. 'Fred helped a lot. Like me, he thought it was a great idea, but Ma thought we were mad. She thought the world would find out and then her world would end. But it's all worked out for the best. Until now, that is.'

'Well, I think I'll be leaving my gutties under the bed,' Stan said, the colour coming back into his cheeks. He looked straight at Ann. 'I'm going nowhere. We can sort this all out. Where there's a will there's a way and all that.'

'Oh Stan, do you mean it? Do you need time to think? You need to understand that I still love Walter. I always will. I can't help it. And what about Daisy? Ma too – she isn't getting any younger. She'll need looking after as well.'

'Whoa there, slow down. I'm sure you can love more than one person at a time,' he said.

'I love my whole family – even Joe. Is that what you mean?'

'Not exactly.' He frowned at the floor for a moment. Then he looked up and said brightly, 'We could adopt Daisy.'

Ann's eyes nearly popped out of her head. 'What? You would do that?'

'Hold on, let me finish. I understand how you feel about Walter and also why you feel you need to move on. Your wheel has turned, so to speak. Maybe you'll grow to love me the same way.'

'We want the same things, don't we?' Ann asked with hope in her voice. 'A nice house, a family, a record player …'

Stan grinned at the fierce, optimistic, beautiful lady in front of him. 'I think *my* wheel has stopped spinning,' he said. 'I didn't know you at all a few months ago. I picked up your onion and told my brothers about meeting a beautiful girl, but I never thought anything more about it. Then we met again, and again, and again. Then I realised there was something good happening here.'

'Forgive me, Stan, but before you say anything more, I have to ask,' Ann said, interrupting him. 'Is it just about the house? You know, that thing where you need to be married to get a house off the council?'

Stan laughed. 'I think that would be the worst reason in the world to get married. We'll have to live together in this house, remember. For a long time, hopefully.'

'I'm just being cautious,' Ann explained. 'Nothing much good – except Daisy – has ever happened to me before.'

'Walter was good, wasn't he?'

'Yes, he was. He is. But he really made a mess of things and he's not getting better.'

'And your ma's good too.'

'She's the best ma ever – wise, kind, positive' – Ann smiled to herself at this little white lie – 'She makes great stew. I think I'm just like her' – she tossed her hair – 'except I'm prettier.'

'She is a good bit older than you. Wait till you're her age.'

'That's not what you're supposed to say.'

'So are we agreed?' Stan asked, his eyes gleaming.

'I will if you will,' Ann said, suddenly feeling shy.

'Okay then.' Stan was beaming. He finished off his whiskey. 'When are you going to tell your ma? And Walter, for that matter?'

'I'll tell Ma straight away. I'll have to think about Walter. I'll maybe leave it till after Christmas. I don't want to spoil it for him.'

'It won't be easy. Will he even know what you're telling him?' Stan asked.

'Oh, he'll know all right. That's the worst bit – he knows what's going on. He just can't do a lot of things properly, things like walking and talking … and other things, if you know what I mean.' Ann looked down.

'It must be awful. I wonder if it would help him get over you if you stopped going to see him. It might be better for you too – so you can move on properly.'

This disturbed her. No chance, she thought. 'I know what you're saying,' she said. 'I don't know how I'll feel after I tell him. Or how he'll react. It all seems a bit cruel.'

'Just something to think about. Anyway, I'd love to meet your ma – do things properly. See what she thinks. See if I pass muster.'

That's exactly what Dan did, Ann thought, and Ma was much happier afterwards. 'She'd like that,' Ann said. 'Be prepared for an interrogation, though. She's like the Gestapo.'

'She sounds like a formidable lady. And a bit scary. I hope she likes me.'

'She is formidable. She has an opinion on everything. She doesn't like things changing, but she's seen plenty of changes. I wouldn't say she's exactly open-minded, but her brain door is slightly ajar. Play the game right and you can get in, and once you're in, you'll be in to stay. The last man to talk to her about marrying one of her daughters was allowed to whisk Hilda away to Canada at a moment's notice. So you have a hard act to follow.'

'Oh God! I'll try and do my best.'

'I guess we should leave it until after Christmas for you to meet her. Are you going home?'

'Yes, I'll get away early on Christmas Eve and be back on the 28th for work on the Monday. We can talk about a date and stuff like that when I get back, but the sooner the better as far as I'm concerned.'

For some reason Ann felt a little disturbed again. 'There's no rush, is there?' she asked.

'It's just … those new houses in Johnston Park, behind the hotel here.'

'I know where they are,' she snapped at him. 'What about them?'

'They'll be ready soon. They sound like just the ticket. Three bedrooms and a bathroom upstairs. A living room and kitchen downstairs, as well as a side passage and store room. They have a back boiler, so the fire heats the water. Two big larders, too, for all your pots and pans and stuff.'

'It sounds lovely. We don't want to miss that. A bathroom with an indoor toilet! And running hot water! I mean, how good is that?'

'I think I'm the happiest man in the world right now. It'll be great to spend a last Christmas at home, but I won't be able to wait till I get back.'

They clinked their empty glasses.

'Happy Christmas, Stan.'

'Happy Christmas to you, too.'

There was no mention of a present.

'Do you have a list – for Santa?' Ann asked.

'There's nothing I need. Honestly,' Stan said. 'We should save our money to get stuff for the house. It'll need decorating and carpets and all sorts. Sure we can get presents next year.'

'Very wise. Makes a lot of sense, I suppose. It's not like we're weans or anything,' Ann said, feeling a little crestfallen. It was dull and made no sense at all, she thought. When did sense come into Christmas?

'Exactly. A shilling in your pocket is your best friend,' Stan said and went to stand up.

Ann sat back and gawped at Stan.

'What's wrong?' Stan asked.

'Ma says that all the time.' She shook her head. 'You two are going to get on like a house on fire.'

'That's another thing. We'll have to get the house insured.'

Ann couldn't help but smile. This was seriously boring now. Like Walter said, why did life just get more complicated and boring as you got older? 'So I'll see you after Christmas then,' she said.

Stan hesitated.

'What's wrong?' Ann asked, frowning.

'As I said, I must be the happiest man alive at the moment. All my dreams are coming true, but—'

'But what? Does running a mile seem like a better option?'

'No, it's not that. It's just … is it okay to tell people – like at work – that we're engaged? I mean, are we officially engaged, do you think?'

'Oh, I see what you mean. I'd like Walter to hear it from me first, if that's okay. You know what small-town gossip is like. And you have to pass the Ma test. I'm sure you will, but you never know, and if she puts the kibosh on it, then that will be that, I'm afraid. You'll have to go back to Larne.' Ann grinned at him and, reaching across the table, put her hands on his. 'Is that okay?'

'Is it okay if I give you a wee kiss for Christmas?' Stan asked, suddenly shy.

'Why not? We've had a wee kiss before.'

'But it's different now. We've never been almost … sort of … possibly engaged before. And it's Christmas.'

'It looks like it's all I'm going to get for Christmas,' Ann said, pouting extravagantly. 'So, I suppose it'll have to do.'

'Next year I promise,' Stan said.

He came round to her side of the table, put his hands on her shoulders and planted his lips firmly onto hers. Too firm, she thought. Definite room for improvement. Suddenly she found herself thinking of Walter; she couldn't help herself. She felt guilty.

'What about Easter next year?' she blurted out. 'My birthday is the second of April. How romantic would that be?'

'Where did that come from? There was no rush a minute ago.' Stan sat down again.

'Ma might still ban it and banish you back to Larne. But let's be positive and assume she can see past any shortcomings. We should have a plan. We can bin it if we have to.'

'I like a plan, and that sounds very like one to me.'

And so, over one last drink together, they agreed on a plan.

'Happy Christmas, Stan. I better go,' Ann said as she finished off the last of her Black Bush.

'Happy Christmas, Ann, love.' The word *love* was almost a question.

They gave each other awkward pecks on the cheek and Ann set off for home.

The next morning, when Ann came downstairs, she found an envelope lying on the mat. It just said 'Miss A Brown'. There was no address on it.

It was a Christmas card from Stan! On the front was a picture of an old farmhouse and outbuildings covered in snow. A tipped-up cart, its shafts sticking up into a leaden sky, sat in the middle of an empty stone-walled yard. Inside was a verse: 'Christmas comes but once a year, But I must say adieu, While warmly wishing you were here, Or I was there with you.'

Ann showed it to Ma. 'He must have dropped it in this morning on his way to the bus,' she said.

'*Adieu*,' Ma said aloud in her best Omagh accent. 'Very romantic.'

Ann put it up with the others. Stan's first card. She would keep it forever.

Walter had come home the previous Friday as planned and Ann spent most of Christmas Eve at the Green's house; she went back late in the afternoon on Christmas Day. She sat and held Walter's hand and talked rubbish as usual. They stared at the photograph of the three of them that Matron had taken on Daisy's birthday. Ann didn't mention Stan, and on more than one occasion she had to fight back the tears. She felt like a cheat, like she'd betrayed them all. She was bewildered and completely confused, and she hated herself.

* * *

Ann and Ma had gone up to the phone box as usual to wait for Muriel to call.

'Are you all okay over there?' Ann asked her. 'We've heard about the smog on the radio. Lots of people are sick, some even dying, they say.'

'It's very bad. All the hospitals are overrun. Luckily, we're out in the country and the air is clear. What's it like over there? Are you okay, Ma?'

'It's just the same as usual here. Cold, wet, grey. None of that what-do-you-call-it, thank God.'

'Smog,' Muriel prompted her. 'A mixture of smoke and very thick fog. The smoke from people's fires gets caught in the fog and can't escape. Everyone's choking and coughing their lungs up.'

'Sounds lovely. Did you hear the Queen's Speech? We thought it was good for a first go, didn't we, Ma?' Ann said.

'It certainly was. We think she'll be a great queen. Hope so anyway. So how is everyone over there?' Muriel asked. 'What about Joe?'

'Last we heard they'd made him captain,' Ann said, relieved to change the subject.

'Of the ship?' Muriel squealed.

'No, you eejit, the football team.'

'Thank God for that. I nearly fainted when you said *captain*.'

'This is Joe we're talking about.'

'Leave Joe alone. He's doing okay,' Ma interrupted.

'Yes, Ma,' Muriel and Ann said in unison.

'What about you and Al?' Ann asked. 'When's he going to make you a lady?'

'We're not in any hurry. He's very busy with his work and I like my work.'

'You can't just be engaged forever. What about weans? You don't want to leave it too late.'

'Cheeky!' Muriel giggled. 'But I know what you mean. We were half reared when you were my age. Isn't that right, Ma?'

'Things were different then. Girls didn't have much of a say about anything.'

Ann looked at the floor. Ma patted the back of her hand.

'I have news,' Ann said quietly. 'Are you sitting down, Mu?'

'I'm in a big soft chair in the library with a glass of champagne in my hand.'

'I might be getting married,' Ann blurted out.

There was silence down the line.

'Are you still there?' Ann said.

'To Walter?' Muriel asked eventually.

'I wish. He got home by the way.'

'Oh, Ann! That's great news. It really is. Is he getting better?'

'Not really. He's better than he was, but he's not better better, if you know what I mean. The docs all say this might be as good as he'll get.'

'Oh dear! I'm so sorry, Ann. You're upset, I can tell. Poor Walter. So who is this new man in your life then?'

'His name's Stan – Stan Webb – and I bet you can't guess where he's from.'

'Ballygobackwards?'

Ann tutted and shook her head. 'No, he's from Larne. Can you believe it!'

'Oh God! ... Does he know Derek?'

'No, and he's okay ... for a Larne man. I met him quite a while ago. He picked up a runaway onion for me. Then we met again. He held a door open for me and ... well, we got chatting and got friendly and discovered that we both want the same things going forward.'

'And he can get a house,' Ma chimed in.

'Have you met this Stan man, Ma?' Muriel asked.

'Not yet, but he sounds all right. If Ann likes him, I'm sure I will.'

'And you like this Stan man, Ann?'

'I do.'

'Well, it sounds like brilliant news, then. I'm delighted for you. For both of you.' She paused. 'But what about Walter and Daisy ... and work? You love your job. There's a lot to think about.'

'There is. I know there is, but it's like I'm stuck.' Ann felt Ma squeeze her hand. 'It's hard to explain. Ma understands, don't you Ma?'

'I think so. I know you're not very happy at the minute and that's all that matters.'

'I'll always love Walter,' Ann went on. 'That will never change. I can still go and see him and talk to him. He's safe now. But I want – I need – a life of my own. Like you and Hilda and Joe.'

'And Stan definitely doesn't know Derek?' Muriel asked.

'No, I checked,' Ann said, laughing.

'Seriously, Ma, what do you think of this Stan the man thing?' Muriel asked after a moment's silence.

'Well, I can hardly say what I really think with Ann standing here beside me now, can I.' Ma flashed a naughty grin at Ann.

'Go on, make something up,' Muriel said.

'I need to meet him,' Ma said. 'See what he's made of. He sounds like he's just what Ann needs – serious and reliable. A quiet type who knows what he wants.'

'And what's that?' Muriel asked.

'A good job. Nice house. Wife. Family. Record player.'

'And happy to stay in Omagh? Sounds perfect. Is that what you want? What about the dancing and your work? You have ambitions.'

'Those dreams are long gone. I think this is what I want now, after all that's happened. I won't need to work. Stan's got a good job.'

'In the Housing Department,' Ma chipped in, clearly impressed.

Ann tutted at her and added, 'I'll be able to look after the weans.'

'Do you love him?' Muriel asked, catching Ann off guard.

She hesitated. She loved the thought of him, but out loud she said, 'Yes, I think so, but it's different. Not like Walter.'

'In what way?'

'Stan's more mature, more grown up. He's handsome. He has proper hair … And he has a job in the Housing Department!'

Muriel laughed.

'Walter might have grown up, given half a chance,' Ma muttered.

'Ma! Do you not think this is hard enough?' Ann said, exasperated.

'Sorry, love. Just sayin'.'

‘So, when’s the big day?’ Muriel asked.

‘It’s going to be all romantic, so it is,’ Ann said, perking up. ‘Good Friday is the third of April next year, so we’re aiming for the day before that – my birthday! Then Stan’s talking about going to Portrush for Easter.’

‘That is romantic. You’ll be twenty-three, won’t you?’

‘Imagine. Twenty-three and married to a man with a job in the Housing Department.’

‘When will you get into the house, then?’

‘We can get the keys on the Tuesday after we get back from Portrush. Stan already has some things bought. He’s saved quite a lot. He’s talking about a cooker and a washing machine.’

Ma snorted in disbelief.

‘He’s even said we can get a Dansette record player!’

‘You’ll love that,’ Muriel said. ‘Al has a lot of records.’

‘Have you heard “Wheel of Fortune” by Kay Starr?’

‘Yes, we bought it! It’s great.’

‘Oh, it must be great to be rich. Or in love with a rich man, at least. You never thought it would happen, did you, Ma?’

‘I never said that,’ Ma went on. ‘It just shouldn’t happen in real life, that’s all. It’s fairy-tale stuff. But it’s lovely. I’m happy for both of you.’

‘Al doesn’t need the Housing Department, I suppose.’ Ann giggled. ‘Can you let Hilda know, Mu? A phone call’s quicker than a letter, isn’t it, Ma?’

‘We’re not getting a phone in,’ Ma said with a scowl. ‘You’ll be gone and then who’s going to use it? And pay for it. I’ve no work and neither will you.’

Ann made a mental note to think about Ma and money when she didn’t live with her any more.

'But if you had a phone, we could chat every day and you wouldn't have to walk all the way to the phone box,' Ann said. 'On your own. In the howling gales and sideways snow.'

Ma smiled. 'It doesn't snow all the time. We'll see.'

Ann's heart leapt. She was sure Ma would get a phone eventually.

'How's Fred?' Muriel asked.

'Very busy being Fred, but still the same,' Ma said.

'I want Fred to give me away,' Ann said.

'Not Joe?' Muriel asked.

'It should be a mature man that does it, not a buck eejit.'

'Ann! Joe is a man,' Ma said, feigning outrage. 'At least he nearly is. I think he might have started shaving.'

'Joe can do ushing. He ushed for Hilda and Dan. It's easy. He's good at ushing. If he can make it, that is. We'll have to write to him.'

They prattled on for a while about Christmas. Muriel got a watch.

'It says Rolex on it,' Muriel said. 'It looks expensive. And it's heavy. Might be gold. Oh, and I got some fancy cigarettes as well. Sobranie, they're called. They're from Russia.'

'Better not tell Dan,' Ann said. 'Does it work? The watch, I mean, not the fags.'

'Of course. Right now it's … exactly four thirty.'

Ann looked at her Timex with its faux leather strap. It said four twenty-five. 'Correct. Well, I got a lovely umbrella. It's green and matches my Firestone coat.'

'What did you get, Ma?' Muriel asked. They heard her set her glass down.

'A big box of Milk Tray.'

'Santa will never run out of those. Anything else?'

'A Blackthorn stick with a brass handle.'

‘Stan better watch himself, eh?’ Muriel said, laughing.

‘It’s starting to sleet here, Mu,’ Ann said. ‘We better go. Happy Christmas to you both.’ She gave the handset to Ma.

‘Happy Christmas, love.’

‘Happy Christmas, Ma,’ Muriel said.

Ma set the handset back in the cradle.

Ann pushed backwards and opened the door of the phone box. Swirly sleet swept around them as they walked home arm in arm.

CHAPTER 20

Stan was given his tea in the same mug that Dan had got, the good one with the horse on it. He got the same kind of fruit cake too.

'Ann tells me you're from Larne,' Ma said as they got comfortable.

'Everyone has their cross to bear, Mrs Brown.' Stan relaxed a little as the old face in the chair opposite smiled back at him. 'My da was a postman in Malin, in Donegal. He had a cousin in Larne and they moved there in 1921. He didn't want to stay in the Free State after partition. Larne's about as far away as he could get without going across the water.'

Ann knew Ma would like this story.

Stan went on: 'Me and my two brothers were born and raised in The Roddens. It's not far from the town centre. There's a big park out the back where we used to play.'

'Do you think you'll be able to settle in Omagh?' Ma asked.

Don't underestimate this question, Stan, thought Ann.

'My plan … sorry, our plan … is to get the house in Johnston Park and make it our home. I've a good job and there's room to move up. We want a family. Ann wants about six, but maybe two will do … to start with, anyway.' He looked at Ann.

She cocked her head to one side and pursed her lips. It was a look intended to convey that they would discuss it later but the answer would still be six.

'Sorry, where was I?' Stan said, pulling his gaze away from Ann. 'Oh yes, family. They will be born in Omagh, Mrs Brown, like you and your family were. I can't see why we would want to move. I know it's important to Ann that she stays close to you and Walter.'

Good man, Stan, Ann thought. *You're saying all the right things.*

'Ann says she's told you about Walter and Daisy.'

'She has and I'm glad she did. How the two of you did what you did is amazing and … I can't think of the right word.'

'Stupid?' Ann offered.

Stan looked at her. 'No, definitely not stupid. Brave. Independent. Inspirational, I would say. Having the strength to do the right thing.'

'We haven't told anyone the truth. Not even our own family, or Walter's family, for that matter. You can understand why, can't you?' Ma was sitting forward, more animated now.

'Absolutely. No one needs to know,' Stan said, nodding. 'I promise on my life that I won't say a word to anyone.'

'Not even your brothers?' Ma looked fiercely at Stan.

'Not even my brothers,' he said solemnly.

Ma sat back in her chair and Stan let out a long sigh.

'You can relax, Stan,' Ann said, smiling at him. 'I'll get a full report from Ma later, but I think you might have passed.'

Stan grinned. 'It's important, Mrs Brown. I know that. You and Ann will be my family. I wouldn't do anything to harm any of you.'

'And Daisy?' Ma was direct as usual.

'We've talked about Daisy, haven't we, love?' Stan said to Ann.

Ann nodded.

'We're going to look into how we might adopt her,' Stan went on, 'if that's the best way forward, without too many questions being asked.'

Ma looked pleased. 'Daisy should grow up without having to deal with any of this. She's just an innocent wean who needs a proper family.'

'And that's what we intend to provide,' Stan said. 'She'll want for nothing. I promise.'

'More tea?' Ma asked, signalling the end of this part of the interrogation.

'I'll get it,' Ann said, leaping up before Stan could say yes or no.

She poured them all fresh cups.

'Sorry to hear about your ma,' Ma said as she sipped the hot tea. She didn't take her eyes off Stan.

'Thank you, Mrs Brown. I'm sure Ann has told you about it. She went out to the shops one day and didn't come back. Dropped dead in the street.'

'Was she ill or anything?' Ma asked.

'No, fit as a fiddle. Brain haemorrhage, the doctors said.'

'What's that?'

'It's a sort of bleed inside your head. They told us it would have been very quick. She wouldn't have suffered or anything.'

'Well, that's something, I suppose. It must have been a real shock for you all.'

‘I don’t think my da has ever got over it. He’s gone a bit funny.’

‘That’s just comes with old age, isn’t that right, Ma?’ Ann said with a grin.

‘No need to be so cheeky, my girl. There are people younger than me that haven’t got the brains they were born with.’

A cloud crossed Ann’s face, and Ma raised her hand by way of an apology for being so thoughtless.

Stan stepped in to ease the awkwardness. ‘Can I have another piece of cake, Mrs Brown? It’s lovely and moist, so it is. Then I’ll have to go.’

He’d remembered what to say about the cake! Ann breathed a sigh of relief. Ma smiled with pleasure.

Afterwards, outside the front door, Ann stood on her tiptoes and gave Stan a kiss on the lips. They were very dry, she noted.

‘I think she likes you,’ she said.

‘That’s a relief. She’s a lovely woman.’

‘With lovely children.’

‘They can’t all be as lovely as you.’

‘I know. That’s impossible, but Muriel and Hilda are quite pretty and they’ve done okay for themselves.’

‘What about Joe?’ Stan said. ‘He sounds like a bit of a character.’

‘Don’t tell him I said so, but Joe is quite handsome. For a big ugly lump.’

‘I can’t wait to meet him.’

‘He’s not the full shillin’, I’ll tell you now. He’s a Manchester United supporter for a start. He had a trial to play for them once. Broke his heart when they said he wasn’t good enough.’

‘I don’t really follow football,’ Stan said, ‘but I’ve heard of Man United. They’re a good team, I believe.’

'They are since they dumped Joe.'

'That's very harsh.'

'Are we officially engaged now?' Ann held out her finger and waved it around.

Stan laughed. 'You want a ring, I take it?'

'You shouldn't have to ask, you big dope. It doesn't have to be expensive. I know we need to save for stuff, but it would be nice if it was a wee bit dear.'

'Leave it with me,' Stan said, grinning from ear to ear.

He gave her a little peck on the cheek and off he went towards the town.

CHAPTER 21

By early March, Muriel, Hilda and Joe had all confirmed that they would be at the wedding. Each of them would be attending on their own. Dan couldn't say why he couldn't make it; Al had to provide cover at the hospital over Easter and his mama and papa (as he called them) were heading off on a tour of Europe, so someone had to look after the house; Joe just said he'd be there.

Ann still hadn't got up the courage to tell Walter. She was waiting for the right time, but then she realised that no time would be 'right'. One sunny Sunday afternoon, she was sitting with him at home when a nurse called to check how he was and take him out for a walk. He was now able to do that with two sticks and no chair. He was also putting on a bit of weight. He looked very happy. Ann was beside herself with self-loathing, regret, doubt and pity.

On the spur of the moment, she decided to tell Peter and Mrs Green about her news while Walter was out. A million words jumbled and tumbled out into the room.

'I love Walter, you know I do,' Ann rambled on. 'I love him more than anything or anyone else in the whole world, but ...' She ran out of words.

The Greens sat looking at her, confused and upset, but then Mrs Green set down her cup and saucer and sat up straight.

'I think you're doing the right thing, love,' Mrs Green said. 'You've got to put yourself first. Think about your future and wee Daisy. You've done more for Walter than anyone could have expected.'

'Walter looks like he's getting better, and he is. A bit. But he'll never be the same,' Peter added. 'He'll be safe and happy here with us.'

Ann was amazed and delighted. The tears rolled down her cheeks. She could do nothing to stop them.

Mrs Green reached out a hanky. 'That was my job,' she said. 'Crying. But I'm all cried out. Things are the way they are. We just have to get on.'

'I feel like I'm cheating on him,' Ann said between sobs. 'Like I'm giving up on him ... abandoning him, especially ... after all that's happened ... all we've been through.'

'You're not abandoning him, love,' Mrs Green said softly. 'I know it's tough and I know you must have thought about it over and over. You wouldn't be doing this if it wasn't right – for you, for Daisy, for Stan. Walter knows what's going on around him. He knows how he is. He'll be upset, obviously, but he'll understand. He loves you as much as you love him, so he'll know he has to let you go.'

Ann bent over and put her head in her hands; her shoulders were heaving.

Mrs Green came over and put her arms around her. 'Do you want us to tell him?'

'Oh God, no. Thank you, but I have to do it. I'm just not … Soon, I promise.' Ann knew it would be like saying goodbye and she wasn't ready.

'What about Daisy?' Mrs Green asked, sitting down again.

'Stan says we can adopt her. She'll officially become a Webb – our daughter. She'll be well looked after.'

'That's good, love. I know you adopted her in the first place so you and Walter could be a family … Oh dear, now I need a hanky.'

Peter fetched a clean one from the drawer.

Ann felt completely wretched that these good people didn't know they had a grandchild. It wasn't right, but Ma would die if she thought they knew the truth. They would die too if they knew what Walter had done.

'I've taken Walter up to the station a couple of times,' Peter said as he handed his wife the hanky. 'I wheel him up, and he has a wee walk around on his sticks. The boys look after him and chat away to him. He loves it – the trains and the noise.'

'He always did, Peter,' Ann said, relieved that the subject of conversation had shifted from Daisy. 'I'll never forget the day we went to Portrush. It was perfect. But that was like a different lifetime. So long ago.'

'You hold onto those memories, love,' Mrs Green said now she was more composed. 'They'll always be precious.'

Walter returned from his walk and Ann knew he realised something was wrong as soon as he came into the room. Something was different.

'How was he, Lucy?'

'He's doing well, Ann. We went up to the swinging bars and back. I think he's tired now.'

'You must be knackered after that, Blondie,' Ann said as cheerfully as she could. 'We'll have more of a chat the next time, before you go out with your girlfriend and get exhausted. I know you're still as thick as the day you walked into Black's office, but …'

'That's right, you can have a good chat the next time you're here, Ann,' Mrs Green said, noticing that Ann was about to start crying again.

Walter tapped his happy taps and made a sort of laughing noise. He sounded like a dying donkey.

Ann hugged Peter and Mrs Green. She kissed Walter on his forehead and left before the tears came again.

CHAPTER 22

Another week passed and Ann still hadn't told Walter. But the time had come. She couldn't put it off any longer. The wedding was in a week's time.

She called round to see him. Peter and Mrs Green went out to give them some privacy.

'I can't believe I'm doing this, Walter,' Ann began. She sniffed and took a deep breath.

They were sitting on the settee, holding hands like they'd done a million times before. Ann was perched on the edge. Walter sat up and leaned forward. He knew this was important. She'd called him Walter.

'Remember I told you about meeting Stan? Well, we've been meeting quite a lot over the last few months and … well, Oh God!' She came straight out with it: 'He's asked me to marry him.' Ann stared at the floor and then looked up at Walter.

Walter recoiled into his chair and pulled his hands away. His smooth face was creased by lines of pain and disbelief. Then he started doing his dying donkey laugh.

'Bahhd egg Ahhnn Bown!' He brayed again.

'It's not a joke, Walter – not this time,' Ann said. 'I said yes to Stan. We're getting married. In April. On my birthday.' She grabbed his hands again. 'I wish it was you. I really wish it was you.'

She lowered her chin to her chest. She couldn't look at him. It was *him* she loved – *him*. Why couldn't it be different, the way it was supposed to be?

'I don't know what else to say. I still love you, more than anyone has ever loved anybody, but I'm worn out,' she said. 'I need help – with Daisy, with Ma. I need a life of my own. I need a record player.' She tried to laugh. Walter smiled. 'I feel so awful. Am I being selfish?'

'Nohhh.' Walter sat up. 'You are boot-eh-fool.' He pointed at his chest. 'Ah'm oosless. Bain boke.' He tapped his head and tugged his hair. 'Oosless.'

Ann collapsed onto him, shaking as the tears poured down her face. Walter put his arms around her.

She didn't know how long they stayed like that before the tears stopped and she gently detached herself.

'Dayzzeee?' Walter asked.

'I'll look after her, I promise. I'll bring her to see you, if you want.' As soon as the words were out of her mouth, she wondered if they were true.

Walter nodded.

'Got to go, Blondie.'

'Bahhd egg.'

She took out the photograph of the three of them and kissed it.

'I love you, Walter Green.'

She held out the photo so Walter could kiss it too.

'Uuvvv you too Ahhnn Bown.'

She put on her coat and left.

As she walked home, she thought this must be how it felt after a funeral – empty, dark, permanent.

'I'll still see him,' she told herself through the blinding tears. 'He's safe. I'll talk to him. Tell him everything.'

CHAPTER 23

Ann stepped around Daisy's pushchair to hug her wee brother as he got off the train.

'It's good to be home,' Joe said, stepping back and looking her up and down. 'I never thought I'd say it but you're looking well!'

'What are you after?' Ann narrowed her eyes. She thought he looked very grown up, but she wasn't going to tell him that.

'You look well … for your age, I mean. Twenty-three and getting married. So who is this lunatic?'

'Stan's not a lunatic. He's anything but a lunatic. He's quiet and steady.'

'Sounds boring.'

You might be on to something there, Ann thought. Out loud, she said, 'He's lovely. We get on very well. He's my knight in shining armour. My Rick.'

'Is that yer man from *Casablanca*? That's an old one.' Joe switched his suitcase to his other hand. 'Do you still go as often?'

'No, not really. Stan doesn't like the noise, and Iris is up to her oxters in weans.'

'I bet Harry and Nigel are still going to see cowboys and Indians.'

'Ma sees Harry at church. He still sings as if he can, but he's looking well.'

'That doesn't sound like Harry. Is he sick?' Joe chuckled. 'Has he got a bird yet? And what about the big man?'

'Bird? What's a bird when it's at home? If you mean a young lady, then the answer is I think so, but I'm not sure. Don't know about Nigel. Harry says he's good at rugby.'

'You're useless. Muriel used to know all the gossip before it was even gossip. How's Ma?'

'She's doing okay. She loves … well, I *think* she loves … looking after Daisy.'

Joe leaned over the pushchair. 'She must be nearly two.'

'She'll be three in August and she's a real handful.'

'Just like her ma,' Joe said, elbowing Ann playfully in the ribs.

'Shush. Loose lips sink ships, remember,' Ann said, laughing and pushing him away.

'Poor old Ma. So what's happening? Where's the rest of them?'

'They arrive tomorrow,' Ann said as they set off towards the town centre. 'Dan and Al can't make it. Dan's working in Cheltenham and can't get away, and Al has to work too. Hilda is meeting Mu in London and they're flying over to Nutts Corner later on today. They're staying in Belfast somewhere tonight. They'll get the first train down tomorrow. We'll go and meet them, then I'm going to tell them about Daisy.'

'Good. Remind me, who all knows the truth then?'

'Me and you, Ma and Fred. And his sister and her daughter, but they're up in Belfast, out of harm's way. They won't tell anyone we know. Oh, and Stan. I had to tell Stan.'

'Does Ma know that Stan knows?'

'Yes, it was sort of her idea that I told him. She said he'd find out at some stage and secrets weren't a good thing in a marriage.'

'That must have been hard for her, but she's a wise old bird. Wise, and tough as old boots.'

'It made me think even more about what happened between her and Da. All this talk of secrets being bad and stuff.'

'Do you think Ma would die if she knew that we knew?'

'Yes! As far as she's aware, no one in Omagh knows except me and her and Fred. And Stan. And it has to stay like that.'

'You're right.' Joe nodded. 'She must have taken some persuading to go with it in the first place.'

'She did and I'll love her forever for it. I would anyway … love her forever, I mean.'

'I can't wait to see her,' Joe said. He squeezed Ann's arm. It felt like they were grown-ups.

* * *

The hug with Ma was long. Very long. Joe looked at Ann over Ma's shoulder and rolled his eyes. Ann shrugged her shoulders and grinned.

When Ma finally let go, she stepped back and took stock of the young man standing looking at her.

'I don't care what Ann says, I think you're looking well, Ma,' he said.

Ann shook her head. 'I didn't say anything, Ma.'

'That didn't take long,' Ma said, beaming at them. 'You look all grown up, son.'

'I am all grown up, that's why.'

'You know what I mean. You'll be getting married next.'

'Plenty of time for that, Ma. Haven't met the right girl yet, but it's great craic looking.'

Ma pretended to give him a clip around the ear. 'I hope you're behaving yourself.'

'No need to worry about me, Ma. By the sound of things, you've enough to worry about. Your cup must be full.'

'What do you mean?'

'Well, you've always loved a good worry, haven't you, and now this Stan man has come along out of nowhere to steal your favourite daughter.'

'I like Stan. He's steady. He has a good job,' Ma said.

'In the Housing Department,' Ann chimed in.

'Well might you laugh, but it doesn't do any harm to have connections in the right places,' Ma said. 'It's who you know that counts.'

'Yes, Ma,' Ann and Joe said in unison.

'What are you going to do with yourself when Ann moves out?' Joe asked. 'Is Daisy staying with you?'

'Don't you worry about me. I'll be all right whatever happens.'

'Can't help it, Ma. Worrying must be in the blood. Any chance of a cup of tea?'

'I'll do it,' Ann said. 'You can tell Ma all about life in the navy.' She bustled off into the kitchen to put the kettle on, one ear cocked to the conversation in the living room.

'There's not much to tell, Ma. It's freezing here compared to Hong Kong. It's very hot and sticky out there.'

'I don't think I'd like it.'

'You'd have to take your cardigan off,' Joe said.

'Oh God no!'

Ann came in from the kitchen. 'Would you like a glass of milk?'

'Have you no tea?' Joe said, surprised.

'I was talking to Daisy, you dummy.'

'Yes please, Mummy.' Even Daisy was laughing.

Joe froze and looked at Ann. Ann didn't bat an eyelid; neither did Ma.

'Do you like milk, Daisy?' Joe asked, bending over the little girl.

She nodded shyly.

'I don't suppose you have any snowballs?' Joe said.

'You could scoot across the road and get some. I haven't had a snowball in ages,' Ma said. 'Do you need money? There's some in the tin.'

'No, Ma. I have some here.' Joe patted his jacket pocket and put his coat back on.

When he returned, they had tea and snowballs. Just like old times. They chatted for ages, the conversation drifting all over the place. After a while, Joe asked, 'What's for dinner? I'm meeting Abbot and Costello later, so I'll need a good feed.'

'We have frogs' legs and jellyfish,' Ann replied. 'Mu says that's what all the toffs are eating in London. Oliver got some in fresh yesterday.'

'Ann!' Ma scolded.

'Or we could have liver and onions,' Ann added, laughing.

'Frogs' legs and jellyfish sound lovely,' Joe said, grinning. 'Nice with chips, but I had them last night, so maybe the liver and onions, if that's all right.'

After dinner, Joe said it was the best meal he'd ever eaten and offered to do the dishes.

Once Ma and Ann had got over the shock, they did a bit of walking practice with Daisy to the sound of Joe rattling the pots and pans in the kitchen. Then they turned on the radio. Ann thought of Stan as the rich baritone voice of Tony Bennett sang 'Rags to Riches'.

* * *

Joe was first at the pub. He looked at his watch. It was seven exactly, the appointed time. McAleer's was empty.

'It's quiet tonight,' he said to the barman as he got himself a pint of Harp.

'It's Tuesday,' the barman said as if Joe was stupid.

Joe sat at a table in the corner. He'd just taken his first sip of lager when Harry arrived. Joe stood up. Their grins mirrored each other and they hugged without speaking.

'Better not tell Nigel about that,' Harry said, dusting himself down after they parted. 'He gets very jealous.' He eyed Joe's beer. 'What's that?'

'Harp.'

'Can I have one of those, Charlie?' Harry indicated Joe's glass. 'In fact, you'd better make it two.'

'No problem, Harry. I'll bring them over.'

'Normous Nige will be here soon,' Harry explained to Joe.

Charlie set the two foaming pints on the table just as Nigel appeared.

'I hope those are for me?' he said.

Harry reached one across to him as he plonked himself down on the too-small chair.

'Isn't this just great? My two favourite numpties back together again,' Nigel said. 'How the hell are you doing, Captain Hornblower?'

'Talking of hornblowers, how is Mr Nesbitt?' Joe asked.

Nigel choked as he downed half his pint in one go. 'Accurate. He's very accurate, as you know.'

‘Hornblower, my arse. Captain Pugwash more like,’ Harry said, belching.

‘Are you still a deputy?’ Joe asked Harry.

‘Yessiree. Best deputy head mechanic this side of the Rio Grande.’

‘Are you still a deputy as well, Nige? Or are you in charge now?’

Nigel swallowed the rest of his pint in one. ‘Thirsty work, haberdashery. Get ’em in, Harry.’

Harry thought about saying he’d got the last round but he didn’t and went up to the bar where Charlie was slowly polishing a glass.

‘In answer to your question,’ Nigel went on, ‘my da had another heart attack.’

Joe looked shocked.

‘He’s all right,’ Nigel added, ‘but the doc told him to take it easy or he wouldn’t be. Which means I’ve inherited the ranch.’

‘Congratulations!’ Joe said.

‘Thank you. I’m thinking of putting cattle on the north pasture. Longhorns, I think.’

‘Mr Nesbitt will love that. You’ll need cowboys to look after them,’ Joe said.

‘No shortage of cowboys in Omagh,’ Nigel said.

Harry returned from the bar with three foaming pints.

‘What about the football, Harry?’ Joe asked.

‘Finished second this year. To bloody Clanabogan. Remember our first match was against them? Well, they’re even bigger now.’

‘You should get them to play rugby, Nige. Big strong farmers. Bound to be good at it.’

‘You need brains to play rugby. There’s a lot of subtlety and finesse required.’

'Looks like legalised assault and battery to me,' Joe said, picking up his pint. 'Like a fight outside a pub with uniforms on.'

'That's basically it. I love it,' Nigel said. 'I got a game for Ulster last autumn – against Munster.'

'That amazing!' Joe said, genuinely impressed. 'How did you get on?'

'They picked me. That's how I got on.'

'No, smartarse. I mean how did you get on in the match?'

'It was a very rare nil–nil draw. About as exciting as watching Harry.'

'Watching Harry do what?' Harry burped again.

'Anything.'

'Bastard.'

'So what's the craic with you? What's the navy like?' Nigel asked Joe.

'Walls have ears.' Joe put his finger to his mouth.

'Loose lips sink ships.' Nigel put his finger to his lips.

'A shilling in your pocket is your best friend,' Joe added.

'A doggy in the window means blood everywhere,' Harry said, his face the picture of innocence as he took a mouthful of beer.

Joe and Nigel looked aghast at their obviously psychotic friend and burst out laughing.

But Harry took no notice of them. 'Did you ever get to that place – the one we couldn't say? Trinko Blinko was it?'

'It's called Trincomalee, it's in Ceylon and it might be the most beautiful place I've ever been,' Joe said.

'Do you not get sick, eating all that foreign stuff?' Harry seemed genuinely concerned.

'You get used to it. Steel stomach.' Joe patted his flat belly. 'The water's the worst. You have to boil it before you drink it.'

'Does that not burn your gob?' Harry asked.

By this time, the tears were tripping Nigel and Joe.

'Are you still riding my bike?' Joe asked Harry when he got his breath back.

'Yessir, but I think you'll find it's *my* bike. Possession is ten-ninths of the law. Isn't that right, Professor Nige?'

'Your fractions are questionable, but that is a basic law of physics. Like gravity.'

'See? Anyway, it's still going strong and I'll keep it forever, because Ann' – Harry clasped his hands across his heart – 'gave it to me. I'm heartbroken. I was in with a chance there until this eejit from God knows where appeared. I can't believe she's marrying somebody from … where is it he's from?'

'Larne.'

'That says it all.'

'Apparently it's lovely.'

'Just like Ann.' Harry swooned.

'Oh God, where's the bucket?' Nigel said. He lifted the three empty glasses from the table and took them up to the bar.

'Are they going to live in Larne?' Harry asked.

'No, he has a job here,' Joe said. 'That's how they met. He was down at some training course or something.'

'Thank God for that. I'll still be able to see her up the town and I'll be there for her if it all goes tits up.'

'I thought you were engaged, or is polygyny a thing down here in the wilds of Campsie?' Nigel asked when he returned with another round.

'It's polygamy, you eejit.' Harry looked all pleased with himself for knowing the right word.

Joe ducked; challenging Nigel was usually ill-advised.

‘I think you’ll find there are four different kinds of polygamy, the most common of which is polygyny – one man, more than one wife,’ Nigel explained, looking smug.

‘So are you engaged or not? Is it Doris you call her?’ Joe asked Harry.

‘Her name’s Florence. She’s lovely, but we’re not actually engaged yet. I’m thinking about asking her. Soon. Maybe.’

‘Procrastination is the root of all evil,’ Joe offered.

‘Thief of time, dumbo,’ Nigel said.

Joe rolled his eyes. ‘What if she says no?’

‘She wouldn’t. Would she? I mean how could she?’ Harry puffed out his chest.

‘Very easily, from where I’m sitting,’ Joe said with a snigger. ‘Then when she says no, you’ll have to join the Foreign Legion like Beau Geste. That’s where broken hearts end up.’

‘Or the navy,’ Nigel observed.

‘That’s where other kinds of hearts end up,’ Harry said.

‘Ha ha. Very funny,’ Joe said, giving his friend a wry smile. ‘Here, before I forget, I must tell youse about a really spooky thing that happened to me.’

Nigel and Harry sat back and folded their arms with expectant looks on their faces.

‘It was Halloween last year,’ Joe began. ‘It was late in the day. I was just finishing the wages when the last man in the queue came up to my desk. I hardly ever look up at them. “Name?” I asked him. “Edmund Colgan,” he replied. “This is you finished, Mr Colgan,” I said, looking up at the old man. He had been in the navy a long time and was retiring. He was going home.

“‘I know you,’ Mr Colgan said, peering at me. I was pretty sure I’d never seen him before. But he insisted. “You’re Joe Brown.” I pointed to the sign on my desk with my name on it. "No, I know where you're from," he said. "I know where you were born. I know the house. I know the exact room."'

'How did he know all that?' Harry asked, his eyes out on stalks.

Joe took a swig of his beer and wiped his lips. 'Mr Colgan looked me in the eye and said, "You were born in the back room, upstairs in 12 Sedan Avenue in December 1931. Your da died six years later, nearly to the day."'

'My God!' Harry exclaimed, looking at Nigel.

Nigel shook his head.

'I asked him who he was and how he knew all this stuff,' Joe went on. '"I was born in that exact same room," the spooky old git said, leering at me across my desk. His face was like a sharpened stick and he smelled of rum.'

Even Nigel was listening properly now. 'And?' he said.

'It turned out that he was born in 12 Sedan Avenue, but left when his uncle died and left his da the farm out near Drumquin.'

'Yes, and?' Nigel was getting impatient.

'He took his pay packet and left.'

Nigel pushed his empty glass into the middle of the table. 'You never found out how he knew all that stuff?'

'Spooky or what!' Joe said.

'That's useless,' Harry said, finishing his beer. 'It's not spooky at all.'

'It is. Wait till you hear the next bit. I went to the bar after I'd finished with the wages and told a few mates what had happened. They all looked at me sort of confused. Then my mate Jack told me there was no Edmund Colgan.'

'Was he a ghost?' Harry whispered.

'We'll never know,' Joe said, giving his friends big scary eyes.

'That's too good a story for you to have made up,' Nigel said, stroking his chin. 'It's almost grown up.'

'You say the nicest things.'

'It's your round.' Nigel tapped the rim of his empty glass.

Joe staggered a bit as he went up to the bar. 'It's busy in here now,' he said to the barman.

'It's Tuesday.'

Joe just looked at him and ordered another round. He came back to the table, sloshing beer all over the place.

'What about you?' he asked Nigel. 'Any women on the go?'

'Maybe. Not sure. We go to the Tavern for a few pints after matches and I've met a girl there a couple of times. I'm a bit worried though because she looks very like a real girl.'

'She's not from Bangkok then?' Harry said, looking pleased with himself.

Joe sniggered. 'Who is this blokey girl?' he asked, gulping his beer.

'She's Willy Batty's daughter.'

'The oil typhoon?'

'That's the one. She knows her rugby too. She knows a knock-on when she sees one.'

'Definitely suspicious, I would say.'

'No seriously, she knows the rules.' Nigel was clearly impressed by this fact. 'I'm going for a piss,' he announced and elbowed his way out to the gents.

'Do you think he really likes this girl?' Joe asked Harry.

'Maybe,' Harry said, raising his eyebrows. 'Not that he'll admit it.'

'God love her,' Joe said.

Harry nodded sagely. Just then, Nigel came back, doing up his flies.

'You must have had some adventures this past couple of years, Joe,' Harry said by way of changing the subject.

'Oh God, no.' Nigel shook his head.

Joe wiggled his right ear. 'What? Sore ear. Can't hear.'

'How did you get this sore ear, Joseph?' Harry tried to look serious.

'Harry, stop it … please,' Nigel pleaded.

'Well, since you ask, I'll tell you.' Joe drank a mouthful of beer. 'I was out walking the plank one morning when this flippin' flyin' flish flew full flight into my flapper.' Joe cupped his 'sore' ear. 'Bloody sore it was.'

Harry and Nigel spluttered into their pints.

'I dropped the plank,' Joe went on. 'Nearly fell overboard. Haven't been right since.'

'You've never been right,' Harry muttered. 'Are there really flyin' fish?' he asked as more of an afterthought.

'They're a type of cod,' Nigel said with great confidence.

'Had to be a cod, didn't it!' Harry slapped Nigel on the back, pleased with his wee joke.

'Talking about fish' – Joe was on a roll now – 'We went salmon hunting in Borneo once. It was unbelievable.'

'Just like this story, no doubt. Don't you mean you went salmon *fishing*?' Nigel asked, immediately feeling he'd regret it.

'No, we went hunting. With guns. You have to go when the salmon all come back home to have weans. The rivers are wall to wall – sorry, bank to bank – fish. There are so many salmon, the locals can walk across the river on them and not get wet.'

'When does this place close?' Nigel asked, searching the pub for a clock.

'So what you do is, you wade out into the middle of the river. Then you stick the barrel of this big long gun' – Joe spread his arms out wide to indicate the enormity of the gun barrel – 'into the water. Then you pull the trigger and blast the shit out of them. You have to have someone behind you so the recoil doesn't knock you over. The river's so fast you'd get washed away.'

'And this is a traditional way to catch – hunt – salmon, is it?' Nigel said, trying hard not to grin.

'Absolutely. You get millions of them and they're already all broken up. You could put them straight in the pan … if you had a pan.'

'You didn't bring a pan!' Harry shook his head in disbelief.

'You can't hang around too long because the bank is lined with hungry bears, scooping salmon out with their paws.'

'What else would they scoop them out with?' Nigel asked.

'Good point, professor. I'll look it up.'

'I'm not sure' – Nigel stroked his chin – 'if, unlike some of your other stories, this is actually true.'

'I've never told a lie in my life and that's the truth,' Joe said, crossing his heart.

'That's a lie,' Harry said. 'Everybody tells lies.'

'You've insulted me now, Harold,' Joe said, frowning while a smile twitched at the corners of his mouth. 'We've known each other forever and now you're accusing me of lies and deceit.'

'He never mentioned deceit, and I think you'll find that twenty-one years is not *forever*, unless Newton was talking out of his arse.' Nigel stood up and scratched his own arse.

'That's true. I admit *forever* might be a bit longer than twenty-one years. But that's my first lie ever.'

'That's another lie,' Harry said, looking pleased with himself.

'The initial controversial statement is, I believe, an oxymoron,' Nigel explained.

'What sort of a moron doesn't like oxo?' Harry asked.

'How can you not like oxo! It's so easy to spell. Everything should be called oxo,' Joe said.

'Or it could be a paradox,' Nigel said, thinking out loud.

'Sounds like something you'd clean the loo with,' Harry commented before finishing his pint.

'I like that better. Paradox,' Joe said. 'I've done a paradox. Ma will be impressed.' He got up and went to the loo while Nigel fetched three more pints from the bar.

'Here, I must tell you something serious for a minute,' Joe said when he returned.

'Is that another oxo-moron?' Harry asked, by this time a little the worse for wear.

'No, seriously. I was trying to sneak past Mullan's shop on the way here when Pat roared at me. He didn't come out. He just roared my name.'

'He didn't want to be seen talking to a Brit,' Nigel said.

'Probably. Anyway, he'd seen me, so I went in.'

'What did he want?' Harry asked.

'He was as nice as ninepence. He said Dolores was asking about me and she told him that if he ever saw me, to pass on her regards and tell me she was praying for me.'

'Praying you'd become a priest and then you could get married,' Harry said.

'I don't think that's how nuns and priests work, Harry,' Nigel said. 'But things change all the time, so you never know.'

'Pat says she loves being a nun,' Joe said. 'She's found her vocation and is at peace with God. She's thinking of going out to Africa somewhere as a missionary.'

'I've never tried the missionary position,' Harry said, looking wistfully at the ceiling.

'Don't,' Joe advised. 'You'll hurt yourself.'

'You shouldn't try it either if you have a sore ear,' Nigel said.

Joe and Harry looked at Nigel, completely baffled.

'Apparently it makes your nose bleed the first time you try it,' Nigel explained.

'Have you tried this contortion with the girly boy from the rugby club?' Joe asked him.

Before Nigel could reply, Harry said, 'Maybe I *have* tried it. The first time me and Florence did … you know.' He nodded his head once. 'My nose bled. Florence had whacked it with her knee. Bloody sore it was.'

Joe and Nigel roared with laughter.

When they'd all calmed down a bit, Joe asked, 'Do youse ever see any of the others from the old gang?'

'Giraffrey is still scoring goals, as long as he's pointing the right way,' Harry said. 'And I've heard that Soup Bowles is following in his da's footsteps. He's going to be a doctor.'

'You're joking,' Joe spluttered. 'Remind me not to be wherever he is, if I get sick. How could a buck eejit like that be a doctor?'

They did lots of head-shaking, eye-rolling and beer guzzling.

'What about Eyeball? Any word of him?' Joe asked.

'Ian, as he likes to be called nowadays, is a bus driver,' Nigel said.

'Proper buses, or the excursions? Does he go to Portrush?'

'It's mostly to Bundoran, but I'm sure he does the Portrush trip as well,' Harry said. 'I met him in here not that long ago. He was asking about you. He still has the *Beano* we signed for him.'

'That seems like a lifetime ago. I know, I know, whatever it is, isn't a lifetime. It just seems like it. Things aren't the same.'

‘Thank God!’ Nigel said, finishing his pint.

‘Are you still playing football?’ Harry asked.

‘No room on the ship, you dope. The only exercise we get is walking the plank.’

‘Oh arrrgh, me hearties,’ Nigel said, doing his best Blackbeard impersonation.

‘There’s no pets allowed, so we walk the plank instead,’ Joe said. ‘We take it in turns. Twice round the deck every day.’

‘Is it on a lead?’

‘No, you just stick it under your arm.’

‘Has it got a name?’

Joe looked at Harry. ‘It has now.’ He laughed.

‘Piss off.’ Harry thumped him on the arm. ‘Where do you play, if you can’t play on the ship?’

‘Remember I said I met this gorgeous girl-boy person in Happy Valley?’

‘I thought that was in Bangkok,’ Nigel commented.

‘Was it? Anyway, Happy Valley is a huge place in the middle of Hong Kong. It has a race track and all sorts of stuff, but it also has a football pitch and that’s where we play the local teams.’ Joe squinted at his watch. ‘God, I better go.’

‘One more for the road?’ Nigel asked, lifting his empty glass and wiggling it. ‘God knows when we’ll get to do this again.’

‘Thursday night maybe,’ Harry said. ‘After the wedding.’

‘Good point, well made, Mr Johnston, but we should have another one anyway, just in case?’

So they all had one more pint … the one more they needed like a boil on the bum.

‘Cheers, Charlie,’ Harry called out to the barman as he left the pub and swerved to the left.

Nigel and Joe tried the right-turn manoeuvre and traversed Campsie Bridge without incident. They stopped outside the Café Rex, near the corner with Bridge Street.

'Can you make it to the wedding on Thursday?' Joe asked.

'There's buns, so I'll be there.'

They gave each other a manly hug and Nigel swayed off towards his house above the ranch. Joe stood still for a moment, trying to get his bearings and figuring out which foot should go first. He pointed himself down Bridge Street, then off he went.

CHAPTER 24

Ann banged Joe's door. 'How's the head?'

She heard muffled groaning and grunting from inside the room.

'Kettles on. I'll get you some of Ma's magic medicine,' she shouted. 'Trust me, it works. She hasn't had a hangover in the last hundred years.'

Ann felt like a million dollars. It was her birthday tomorrow. And she was getting married. Mu and Hilda would be on the train by now. Even Ma seemed happy. Stan was in Larne. He said it would cost a fortune for him and Spider, his younger brother, to stay in the Royal Arms, so they were driving straight to the church in the morning. It would be a long drive, but he promised they wouldn't be hungover. His married brother Jacob was staying in Larne to look after their da and Spider's wife, Charlotte, wasn't well, so there would only be the two of them. Stan had explained that he and Jacob – Cob – didn't get on that well.

Ann began singing 'Wheel of Fortune' as she put an extra spoonful of tea in the teapot. There was a clink of bottles at the front door.

'Don't worry, Joe,' she called out, 'I'll get the milk. You lie on there like a big useless lump.'

Ma came down the stairs, carefully holding Daisy's potty at arm's length. 'That wee girl needs a doctor,' she said. But she looked like she used to on Christmas morning many moons ago – happy.

Ann rushed forward. 'I'll empty it, Ma. The tea's made. Joe hasn't quite made it into the land of the living yet.'

'He was very late last night,' Ma said, scowling.

'Was he? I never heard him,' Ann said, looking all innocent.

'Twelve o'clock, the clock said.'

Ann knew it was twelve when Joe got home. She'd heard him struggling to get his key in the lock and trying to be quiet, shushing himself as he knocked into the table.

'He'll be all right,' Ann said. 'He hasn't seen Harry and Nigel for ages. It must have been great craic.'

'I hope he wasn't drunk.'

'You hope nobody *saw* him being drunk, you mean.'

Ma just grunted.

Ann went to Joe's door again. 'Are you decent?'

There was more grunting and moaning. Then she heard, 'Come in.'

'Tea and a bit of toast,' Ann said, bustling in. 'Black with lots of butter, the way you like it.'

Joe looked awful.

'Good night?' she asked.

'Brilliant. My sides are still sore.'

'Worse than your head?'

'The beer must be stronger here. We only had about a hundred pints. Must have got a bad one.' Joe took a gulp of the hot tea and grimaced. 'Are you sure this is tea?'

'Take these.' Ann held out two large blue tablets.

'Ta … I think!' Joe looked dubiously at the drugs, then swallowed them with a gulp of tea. 'Harry's thinking of proposing to what's her name,' he told Ann. 'I mean, what did she do to deserve that? Nigel told him that if he really loved her, he'd encourage her to marry somebody else.'

'That's cruel,' Ann said. 'How's Nigel?'

'He's enormous. He used to be fat enormous, now he's solid-muscle enormous. He seems to be pretty good at this rugby nonsense. He got a game for Ulster this season.'

'That sounds good. Are Ulster any good?'

'No idea. Can't be if Nigel's playing for them.'

'No girlfriend yet?'

'No … well, sort of. Maybe. He said he met a really nice girl after a match. The team go to the Tavern for pints and she was there. He's taken her to the pictures. Paid for both tickets too. He never took me and Harry to the pictures, so it must be serious.'

'Any other craic?'

'Harry's been made a deputy but he hasn't got a badge, and Nigel is putting longhorns on the top pasture.'

Ann shook her head and laughed. 'I'll fill your jug for you. You need to get up. Mu and Hilda will be at the station about half ten. I want us both to go and meet them.'

'And you're going to tell them?'

'Yes, it's the right thing to do.' She tousled Joe's already tousled short hair. 'Isn't this all just great?'

'Tell them what?' Ma asked as she sat down on Joe's bed with her tea; Ann had left Joe's door open.

Ann looked at Joe in panic.

'Harry's getting married,' Joe blurted out.

'Ach that's good. He's a lovely boy,' Ma said. 'Don't be too long, youse two. There's a lot to do.'

'Yes, Ma.' Ann and Joe grinned at each other.

'Are you bringing Daisy to the station?' Ma asked.

'Yes, it's time they met her,' Ann said. 'I'll get her sorted.'

* * *

With the screeching of metal on metal and a huge whoosh of steam, the train came to a halt at Omagh station. Windows were pushed down; hands reached out for the handles; all the doors opened at once.

Ann was standing on tiptoe, peering down the platform. 'There they are!' she shouted, pointing.

When they met up, there were hugs and kisses and tears and squeals and more hugs.

'Good day for you two to arrive!' Joe observed with a cheeky grin.

Muriel and Hilda looked confused.

'April Fool's Day,' he said.

They just tutted and laughed.

'This must be Daisy,' Muriel said, peering in at the child. 'She's beautiful.'

Daisy gurgled and gave them a big smile.

'You're as sharp as ever, Mu,' Joe said and backed away to safety.

'You look great, Ann,' Hilda said, standing back to look at her wee sister. 'You must be excited.'

'Excited isn't big enough.'

'She's been singing like a banshee since the scrake of dawn,' Joe said and covered his ears with his hands.

'Our wee Joe has a wee hangover.' Ann patted him on the shoulder.

Joe shook his head. 'Right, let's go, ladies.'

They set off for the Royal Arms, the three sisters side by side, chattering the whole way. Joe was a few steps behind, as usual, carrying the suitcases. After Mu and Hilda had checked in, they all went into the restaurant.

'You two look good, considering,' Joe said as they sat down at the table.

Ann parked Daisy's pushchair beside her. Daisy was fast asleep, thank goodness.

'Considering what?' Mu and Hilda asked together.

'Well, your age for a start, and the fact that you probably haven't had a decent meal since you left Omagh. Do they even have spuds in London? I know they don't have them in Canada.'

'And I bet they don't have liver and onions out where you are,' Hilda retorted with a grin.

'It's exactly the same, except it's octopus instead of liver.'

'Sounds exactly the same!' Muriel was laughing. 'Anyway, I'll have you know that they do a lovely liver and onions in the Ivy and it only costs fifteen and six.'

'Only? Fifteen and six! For liver and onions?' Ann couldn't believe her ears.

'Dr Al obviously has more money than sense,' Joe said. He beckoned the waiter. 'No tubes at that price, I imagine.'

'No, no tubes,' Muriel said. 'No spuds either. They're extra.'

'Good God, better not tell Ma! She's lived her entire life on less than fifteen and six,' Ann said.

'Are we having tea, ladies?' the young waiter asked, bowing imperceptibly.

Joe coughed.

'And sir, of course.'

'Do you have coffee?' Muriel asked.

'Yes, madam. Is that just one coffee?'

'I've never had coffee. I'll try one,' Ann announced.

'It's all they drink in Canada, so I'll have coffee too,' Hilda said. 'Joe?'

'Yes, let's go mad. Four coffees, my good man,' Joe said.

They chatted away about everything and nothing until the waiter brought a tray with a large silver coffee pot on it. There was also a silver bowl containing little white cubes and a jug of milk. Four tiny cups decorated with flowers on four tiny saucers completed the display.

Joe lifted one of the white cubes with his fingers. 'What are these?' He put it in his mouth. 'Sugar!' He screwed his face up in disgust.

The girls laughed at him. 'You're supposed to use these wee things, you ignoramus,' Muriel said, brandishing small silver tongs. 'Milk?' she asked him, lifting the little jug.

'Not for me,' Joe said, lifting the big silver pot. 'Is this the coffee?' He poured some into his little cup. 'It's better black.'

'Tut, tut, where are your manners,' Hilda chided. 'Ladies first.'

'Sorry, I've got out of the habit,' Joe said, looking sheepish. 'There are no ladies in the navy – no obvious ones anyway.'

'I'll try it black as well.' Ann held up her cup.

Joe poured her some coffee.

'Hilda? Milk?' Muriel was still holding the jug.

'A wee drop. Dan takes it black, but I think it's too bitter.'

'I like a wee drop as well,' Muriel said. She splashed some milk in Hilda's cup and in her own and put the jug down.

'Do you stick your wee finger out, Mu?' Joe asked, holding his cup with his little finger wiggling about in the air.

'I'll stick my finger somewhere unpleasant if you're not careful,' she replied with a good-natured growl.

'Ooooh! Very ladylike.' Joe sipped some of his coffee. It would help with his hangover. 'We should have gone to the Cake Shop,' he said. 'Do they still have them big white mugs?'

'Some of them aren't as white as they used to be, but yes, they still have them.' Ann sat forward on the edge of her seat. 'We couldn't go there. Not today. Too many people could listen. Here is more private.'

'Walls have ears, remember.' Joe grinned.

Startled, Hilda and Muriel looked at each other.

'Sounds ominous,' Muriel said. 'Don't tell me the wedding's off?'

'No, the wedding's not off. And no, I'm not pregnant. I'll explain later. There's a lot of catching up to do first.'

The next hour passed in a flash as they each shared what had been happening in their neck of the woods. All was well in Hilda's world. Dan would be in Cheltenham for a while. He couldn't or wouldn't say exactly how long. Somebody looked after Jimmy for them during the day. Joe was now land-based in Hong Kong. He loved being in the navy. There were lots of girls, but nothing serious apart from that one scare. He was captain of the navy football team. He loved it.

Muriel was spending more and more time at Maldonwood Manor. Al was very driven and ambitious at work. Yes, they had set a date, definitely later this year. She wanted Ma to be there when she told them. Yes, Al was well; yes, his parents were lovely – sort of snobby, but it wasn't their fault.

Ann was jealous of Muriel's fairy-tale world and Hilda's family bliss. They were both wearing dresses that looked expensive – from shops, not home-made.

'Your bag's lovely, Mu,' she observed when Muriel lifted it to move her feet.

'Al bought it for me for Christmas. It's a new make.' She read the badge on the bag: 'Givenchy. Never heard of them, but it's lovely, isn't it?'

'It's better than some of the bags I've had, that's for sure,' Joe said, leaning back out of reach.

'We don't want to hear about your sordid secrets, thank you.' Hilda went to take a sip of coffee. Her cup was empty.

'Order more coffee, Joe, would you,' Muriel asked.

'Why do I have to do it? You're not in Madinthehead Manor now, you know,' he complained.

Muriel ignored his jibe and shot back, 'Cos you're the nearest thing we have to a man, that's why.'

Joe put his arm up.

The waiter was beside him in a flash.

'Can we have more coffee, please?' Joe said in his poshest accent.

Muriel mouthed *can we have more coffee, please* in an exaggerated way, her lips twisting and turning all over the place. Joe pointed his finger at her.

They didn't have to wait long for the waiter to bring them another tray of cups, saucers, fresh coffee and milk, and sugar cubes.

'You do it this time, Mrs Bossy Boots,' Joe said to Muriel and folded his arms.

Muriel did the honours and passed the filled cups around.

'Right,' Ann said, looking at Muriel and Hilda. She had their complete attention. 'Joe already knows this. I told him the last time he was home. I couldn't tell you over the phone, Mu, and I couldn't put it in a letter to you, Hilda. I have to tell youse face to face. I think you'll understand when I'm finished.'

Muriel and Hilda set their cups down on the saucers. Joe sat back and stared at his shoes.

Ann left nothing out as she told them the truth about Daisy and how Ma and Fred had helped to concoct the story about adopting her. 'And that's where we are now,' she concluded.

'Jeeze!' Hilda exclaimed, sounding very Canadian.

Muriel didn't say anything for a moment. Then she got up, came round the table and gave Ann a big hug and a kiss. 'How did you do that? Juggling work, Walter, Daisy, Ma. How did you do all that on your own? You are … I don't know. Words fail me.'

'I wasn't on my own,' Ann said, blushing a little at such effusive praise. 'Ma has been amazing, and Fred knows – we couldn't have done it without him. He always seems to know when to say the right things. There's no way I've done it on my own. As Ma says, you just get on with things, don't you? Nothing else for it.'

'Until now,' Joe said quietly.

'Until now.' Ann smiled at him.

'So Stan is your fairy-tale prince, at last,' Hilda said.

'Yes, sort of. Maybe the wheel of fortune has finally stopped.'

'What about poor old Walter?' Muriel asked. 'You can't just dump him, can you?'

'It took me ages to tell Walter, but he seems to understand. He tried to be brave. He said he was sorry for being so useless. It was awful. He's not useless.'

'What about his ma and da? What do they make of all this?' Muriel asked in her talking-to-a-patient voice.

'Mrs Green said I was doing the right thing, for both me and Walter. I think she wants to mummy him again. Peter takes him up to the station sometimes. He's always loved the trains and the craic. He'll be well looked after.' Ann looked down at her hands, gripped in her lap. 'I'm being selfish, aren't I? It's me who's useless.'

'Oh Ann, this is all so sad.' Hilda patted Ann's tightly clenched hands.

'You're definitely not selfish,' Muriel said softly. 'Sometimes you have to think of yourself.'

'That's a bit of a contradiction,' Joe said, again moving out of range. But his sisters ignored him.

'I have to think of Daisy and Ma, not me,' Ann said, on the brink of tears.

'You need *you* to be happy and not knackered all the time. Then you'll be able to look after them and yourself.' Muriel was back in sister mode.

'Look at the torture Cinderella had to go through before her Stan appeared. Think of the happy ever after bit.' Joe held out a hanky.

'I'm getting worried now,' Ann said, trying to smile.

'Walter's not going to get better, is he?' Hilda said.

Ann shook her head.

'He can't look after himself. You can't be there all day every day,' Hilda went on. 'He needs his ma. You need to get married – tomorrow, to Stan. So get your big knickers on and crack on with it.' Hilda beamed at Ann.

Ann gave them a weak smile. 'I wish it was Walter I was marrying.'

'Come on now, pull yourself together,' Muriel said. 'You have everything to look forward to – a new house, with taps and hot water and a bath. What more could you want?'

'I've told him I want a record player,' Ann said, starting to get her sense of humour back. 'I told him I'm not marrying him if he doesn't buy one, and it has to be a red Dansette.'

'That's the girl. Blackmail is always a good tactic,' Joe said, draining his coffee cup.

'Does Ma know you've told us the truth?' Muriel asked.

'Nope, the only person she knows I've told is Stan. She can't know I've told youse lot. It'll kill her. I promised her. But I couldn't not tell you.'

'That was another hard decision you had to make, but it's the right one. Don't worry, we'll get through this together,' Hilda said. She put an arm around Ann's shoulders and gave her a squeeze.

'Let's go and see her. She'll be wondering where we've got to. No idea why, but she's just a wee bit excited to see you both.' Joe pushed his chair back and stood up. The waiter appeared like magic again.

'Can we have the bill, please?' Joe said, slowly reaching for his wallet.

'Can you put it on my tab?' Muriel said quickly. 'Room 4.'

'Certainly, madam. No problem.' The waiter bowed and retreated.

'Obsequious little toad,' Muriel whispered.

'He's only a baby. He can't be much older than Joe. And he didn't break anything. We should leave him a wee tip.' Ann watched Joe's face ease into a smile.

Muriel and Hilda went up to their rooms to get their coats.

'That was good,' Joe said, helping Ann on with her coat. 'Definitely the right thing to do.'

'Oh God, Joe. I don't know what the right thing is any more. I really don't.'

Muriel and Hilda soon reappeared in their expensive-looking coats.

'Thanks for getting the coffees, Mu,' Ann said. 'Ma can't wait to see youse.'

'Well, she's already seen her favourite,' Joe said, running his fingers through his hair. 'Seeing you two will be a big anticlimax for her.'

'Her favourite never left,' Ann muttered under her breath as she reached for her handbag.

No one contradicted her.

As they made their way to Sedan Avenue, Muriel said, 'Tell us more about Stan.'

'Big nose?' Joe asked, gently elbowing Hilda.

'You need to get your mind out of the gutter, Joseph Brown,' Muriel scolded, but laughter bubbled through.

'Yes, Ma, but I'm looking at the stars.' Joe preened.

'Oh God, I'm going to be sick,' Hilda said, pretending to gag.

'You're not up the duff again, are you?' Joe asked, stepping back out of reach again.

'Who said that "in the gutter, looking at the stars" thing?' Ann asked.

'Me. There now,' Joe said.

'Dope.'

Looking at the stars, Ann thought. Out loud, she said, 'You all looked at the stars and *your* dreams all came true. Maybe it's my turn now.' Her siblings all nodded. They were in perfect agreement for once.

When they reached the door of No. 12, Joe rapped on the door. 'Mrs Brown?' he said in a deep voice, trying to sound like Orson Welles.

'Who is it? Go away. I don't want any, whatever it is,' Ma said. Then she opened the door and her face exploded with joy!

CHAPTER 25

For a few moments, Ma couldn't speak. Muriel and Hilda took it in turns to give her big long hugs. Ann lifted Daisy and stood back to let them get on with it.

'Look at you two, dressed to the nines,' Ma said, her eyes sparkling. 'You look gorgeous. Beautiful. Both of you.'

Joe coughed.

'You look gorgeous too, son.'

Joe pushed his shoulders back.

'You look great, Ma,' Hilda said.

'How are you? How's your cough? Are your knees still giving you jip?' Muriel asked.

'I'm grand. I don't go out too much. Ann does the shopping.'

'You look great for an auld doll,' Joe said.

'Joe!' Hilda scolded.

'Well, she does. It's no wonder we're all so gorgeous, is all I'm saying.'

'You've filled out a bit.' Hilda poked Joe in the belly. It was rock hard.

'Solid muscle,' he said.

'From the neck up,' Muriel tittered.

'Leave the cub alone. You're only in the door.'

'Yes, Ma,' all four of them said at once.

'Sit down, sit down. Bring over one of them chairs, Joe.'

'Yes, Ma. I'll sit on the hard wooden one.'

'Biggest arse,' Muriel said.

'Solid muscle.'

'Girls, girls!'

'Sorry, Ma.' Muriel looked at the floor, but couldn't stop her lips from twitching with a smile.

They had egg and onion sandwiches for lunch. Ma had made them. 'They're Ann's favourites, aren't they, love.' Ma was in mischievous form and it delighted them all to see the new woman in the old chair. The craic went on all afternoon.

'Do we need to light a wee fire or is it just me?' Joe asked. 'I think it's getting chilly. My arse is frozen solid, that's for sure.' He stood up and massaged his backside.

'Will you do it, Joe?' Ann asked. 'I need to see to Daisy.' She was happy to milk the mothering situation for all it was worth.

'Certainly, madam. You're wish is my command. Cinderella shall go to the ball and I will send the bill to Room 4.'

Ann grinned at her big, dopey wee brother and looked around at Muriel, Hilda and Ma as they chattered away. I couldn't be happier, she thought as she picked Daisy up. Then an image of Walter, his head wrapped in bandages, flashed before her.

'Are you okay, love?' Ma asked. 'You look like you're miles away.'

'Just dreaming, Ma. I'll go and heat up the stew.'

'Oh Ma, stew.' Hilda licked her lips.

'Mmmmmmmm. Yours is the best stew in the world, Ma,' Muriel said.

Ann didn't bother to tell them that she'd made the stew.

* * *

Later, Fred arrived with a bottle of Black Bush. Muriel and Hilda delved into their bags and produced two bottles of Mateus Rosé. There was still a lot of catching up to do.

'Have you got a corkscrew?' Muriel asked as she tore the cover off the top of her bottle.

'Joe, go and see if you can find a corkscrew. I can't remember us ever having one, can you, Ann?'

'No, Ma. I don't think we have one.'

Joe came back from the kitchen empty-handed.

'Sure go next door, son. Jean's bound to have one.'

Joe sighed and went out. Two minutes later he was back, brandishing a rusty wooden-handled corkscrew. It looked like it might have been the first one ever made.

'Jean's looking well. Says she can't wait to see you all.'

'Here, open that.' Muriel handed Joe her bottle. 'I'm sure we'll see Jean and the rest of them tomorrow.'

'I'm not one of your servants.'

'And this one.' Hilda held hers out.

'Now I know how that bloody waiter must feel,' Joe muttered.

He sat down, clamped a bottle between his knees and screwed the corkscrew in. When he pulled it back up, there was a satisfying sound as nearly all the cork popped out.

They didn't have any proper wine glasses either. Ma held out her tumbler and Joe poured.

'STOP! That'll do, son.' The glass was half full. 'Never had much wine before. You don't like it, do you, Fred?'

Fred had poured some whiskey into his favourite chunky tumbler. 'I prefer a drop of this,' he said, holding his glass up to the light. 'And maybe the odd wee bottle of porter, if my tubes need cleaned out.'

'Fred! That's disgusting,' Hilda said, grimacing.

'Nothing like it for cleaning your tubes.'

'I'll take your word for it.'

Fred raised his glass again. 'I must say, you two have grown into beautiful young ladies. You should be proud of them, Kathleen.' He took a mouthful of whiskey.

Hilda held out her glass and Joe filled it nearly to the top.

'Joe! That's too much!'

'You never told me to stop.'

'Dope.'

'Ann … wine?' Joe held the bottle out to her.

'I'll try a wee drop. It looks a bit fizzy.'

'The Queen drinks this. It's all the rage in London, so it is,' Muriel said, taking a swig.

'*So it is.*' Joe laughed. 'You can take the girl out of Omagh, but you can't get Omagh out of the girl.'

'Did you make that up?' Ann asked, seriously impressed.

'No, apparently the Queen said it to Lord Gobshite at the palace the other day.'

When he'd stopped spluttering with laughter, Fred said, 'You're looking well too, Joe.'

'Thank you, Fred. I'm glad somebody's noticed that I'm even here.'

'Awww diddums.' Ann patted Joe on the head. 'There's no way any of us is going to tell you that you've become really good-looking. Or that you'd be a great catch for any woman. Are we?' She looked at the others. Ma took a drink. Muriel and Hilda shook their heads.

'Why not?' Joe asked. 'If it's true.' He pushed his shoulders back and sat up straight.

'Cos we stopped doing April Fool's years ago,' Ann replied.

'Don't listen to them, son. I think you're the best-looking man in the room by a mile.'

'Thanks, Ma,' Joe said, grinning.

Fred gasped in mock horror.

Ma gave Fred a sideways look. 'He's a lot younger than you, Fred,' she said. 'You were just as good-looking when you were twenty-one.'

'Better looking than Da?' Ann asked. She couldn't help herself, but Ma ignored the question.

'So you two flew over on an aeroplane yesterday. What was that like?' Ma asked. 'Why didn't you come here straight away?'

'I met Muriel at the airport in London,' Hilda said. 'We flew to Nutts Corner and then got a taxi into Belfast. It was tea time by then, so we stayed in the Royal Avenue Hotel and took the train down to Omagh today. The flight was very noisy and very bumpy. You'd need good clear tubes, Fred.'

'That must have cost a bob or two,' Joe observed. 'What kind of plane was it?'

'That's rich husbands for you,' Muriel said, giving her sister a friendly nudge with her elbow. 'Any idea about the plane, Hilda?'

'It was white with propellers. Said BEA on the big thing at the back.'

Joe shook his head in disgust.

'Well, smarty pants, how did you get back from wherever you were?' Hilda asked him.

'Troop carrier from Hong Kong. That took two days. We stopped twice – at Bombay and Cyprus – to refuel. Then I got an RAF plane from London to Sydenham, army lorry into Belfast and the train to Omagh.'

'That's quite the journey,' Ann said, genuinely impressed by the effort he'd made to get back for her wedding. 'And you did this all on your own?'

'No, the troop carrier was full of troops, surprisingly.'

'Haha! You know what I mean.'

'I knew some of the others. It was a long journey but good craic.'

Rich husbands, Ann thought. Her sisters were living her dreams for her. She couldn't get enough of hearing about the people and the places, the food and the music. Shoes and handbags, theatres and art galleries, things they took for granted in their worlds.

The noise at No. 12 went up as the wine and the whiskey went down. Sometimes the girls were all talking at the same time.

Joe covered his ears. 'How do you put up with this, Fred? Just two of them must be bad enough.'

Fred pulled two plugs of cotton wool out of his ears. 'Eh?'

When the laughter subsided, the chatter erupted again.

'I can't believe Stan's from Larne,' Muriel said. She was starting to slur her words. 'What are the chances!'

'He says Larne's a lovely place,' Ann said. 'And before anyone asks, he doesn't know Derek.'

'Derek had a nice car,' Joe commented.

'Not as nice as Al's,' Muriel said.

'*Not as nice as Al's*,' Joe said, mimicking her hint of an English accent.

Ann went on: 'He lives in a place called The Roddens. It's near the town. There's a park behind them where they used to play when they were wee.'

'Did you say he has two brothers?' Hilda said, looking a bit bleary-eyed.

'Yes. One's married – Jacob. Stan calls him Cob. Cob Webb. Get it?'

'Yes, Ann, we get it.' Muriel rolled her eyes.

'Well, Stan and Cob don't get on. Cob is married. His younger brother, Willy, is at home with their da. Everybody calls Willy Spider.'

'Why?' Joe asked.

'Oh God, Joe, don't encourage her,' Hilda said with a weary sigh.

'Why what?' Ann asked.

'Why do they call Willy Spider?'

'Cos their last name's Webb. Dough head.'

'You never told us that.'

'I did, but you weren't here at the time.'

'Ah, that's all right then.'

They were all giggling.

'No word of a ma in all this,' Joe asked before reaching for a refill.

'She went shopping one day and dropped dead in the street. Very sad. Spuds everywhere,' Ann explained.

'Not onions then?' Joe asked.

Ann laughed. 'No, not onions.'

'It's lovely you're wearing Ma's dress at your wedding, just like I did,' Hilda said with a dreamy look on her face.

'I had to get it taken in.' Ann put her hands on her hips.

'Haha, very funny,' Hilda said. 'Anyway, it's beautiful. I suppose this will be its last outing.' She glanced at Muriel.

'You hope,' Joe said with a grin.

'Joe!'

'Well, anything could happen. Just saying.'

Ann thought Joe had his doubts about Stan, but Ma liked him, or so she said. She wouldn't lie. Would she? She never lied.

'Have you and Al set a date for your big day then, love?' Ma asked Muriel.

'Thought you'd never ask. I was going to make a big announcement, but it's Christmas Eve,' Muriel said, her eyes shining with excitement. 'I mean, how romantic is that? He proposed on Christmas Eve, so it seems perfect.'

Fairy-tale perfect, Ann thought.

'Getting married on your birthday is every bit as romantic, love,' Ma said, noticing something flicker across Ann's face.

'London or here?' Joe asked Muriel.

'Neither. The service will be in the local village church and the reception will be at the house. There'll be plenty of room for you all.'

'How many rooms did you say there were?' Joe couldn't take it all in.

'Hundreds. No seriously, I think there are fourteen guest rooms.'

'Bloody hell.'

Ann was happy, excited and jealous all at the same time. 'It'll be fancy then?'

'I imagine so.' Muriel looked dreamily at the ceiling.

'Fancy cars and all?' Joe was dreaming too. 'Can't wait.'

'We have a fancy car,' Ann said, needled a bit by Joe's comment.

'Uncle Louis's old wreck of a thing doesn't count,' Joe said.

'No, he has a new one, so there. It's red.'

'Oh wow, a red car!' Joe said sarcastically.

'It's a Riley RM,' Fred said. 'And it's a cracker.'

‘Ahhh, thank you, Fred. That is a cracker of a car. Any wine left? Tell us about the polar bears, Hilda.’ Joe was a bit tipsy again.

‘There aren’t any in Cheltenham.’ Hilda said. ‘Nobody told me that before we traipsed halfway around the world. We went to see one in London Zoo, but it made me cry. It was too sad for words.’

A gloomy silence descended for a moment until Joe held up an almost empty wine bottle. ‘Last wee drop anyone?’

Ma was having trouble keeping her eyes open. ‘Look at the time,’ she said. She struggled to sit up.

‘Yes, Ma,’ they all said in unison and turned to stare at the clock.

‘There’s no need to be so funny,’ she said. She looked bleary, weary, but very happy.

‘No, Ma.’

‘It’s long past your bedtimes. Big day tomorrow.’

‘Yes, Ma.’

‘That’s my last wee drop for tonight, Kathleen,’ Fred said, setting down his glass. ‘The rest will do another day.’

‘Fred will escort you ladies back to the Royal Arms, won’t you, Fred?’ Ma said.

‘Yes, Ma,’ Fred said, standing up and saluting.

They all stood up and saluted back.

CHAPTER 26

That night, Ann slept like her baby. The next morning, she was wakened by a gentle knocking at her door.

'I've made you a cup of tea,' Joe whispered.

'What are you after?' Ann asked. 'Come in.'

'I'm not after anything. It's your wedding day. You're my sister and I love you.'

'Oh God! Daisy, get me a bucket.'

'It's true. Happy birthday, by the way. Twenty-three, eh?'

'Yes, getting old. I feel old.' Ann sat up and took the steaming mug of tea from Joe. 'This is lovely. Thank you.'

'You look happy.'

'I am happy.'

'Good. You deserve to be happy.'

'What are you two whispering about?' Ma appeared at the bedroom door looking like a wraith in her tattered old dressing gown.

'Happiness and optimism, Ma,' Joe said. 'Strange ideas, I know but—'

'There's no need to be so cheeky.' Ma gave Joe a playful slap on the ear. 'Go and get dressed.'

'Yes, Ma.'

'Did you sleep well, love?' Ma asked Ann when Joe had left. 'Happy birthday.' She held out a small red envelope.

'Best sleep I've had in ages.' Ann took the envelope.

'Good. I'll go and make the porridge. It'll set you up for the day. Then we'll get started on your hair. Louis will be here at quarter past eleven.'

'Yes, Ma.'

Ann didn't have much of an appetite, but she managed to eat enough to put Ma's mind at ease. She had a good wash and Ma helped her to fix her hair. Then she put on Ma's dress, added the finishing touches and gave Joe and Ma a twirl. They both agreed that she looked sensational. Stan was a very lucky man.

Uncle Louis arrived dead on time. 'You look beautiful, Ann,' he said. 'Like that actress. What's her name? She was in that comedy film with Bob Hope.'

'*My Favourite Spy*?'

'Yes, that's it, I think. Very funny. Who was the woman in it?'

'Hedy Lamarr.'

'That's her. You look just like Hedy Lamarr.'

'Fred thinks she looks like her too,' Ma said proudly.

'Well then, it must be true. Fred's no dozer. Does Stan look like Bob Hope, by any chance?' Uncle Louis asked.

'I think he looks like Stewart Granger,' Ann said, looking like the cat that got the cream. 'Oh, Uncle Louis. I can't believe it!' She gave him a big hug.

'Watch the dress, love.' Ma had started worrying early.

'It still looks beautiful after all these years, Kathleen,' Uncle Louis said with a beaming smile.

'Third outing for it,' Ma said, wistfully fingering the cuff of a sleeve.

'All lucky,' Ann commented.

'Well, two out of three isn't bad, I suppose.' Ma picked a thread off Ann's shoulder.

'New hat, Kathleen?'

'New ribbon. New bow. It would take something special for me to get a new hat.'

Ann and Louis shook their heads and smiled. Just then, Joe came in from the yard.

'Good God, Joe,' Uncle Louis exclaimed. 'You've fairly shot up. New suit?'

'Worsted wool. Only the best, isn't that right, Ma?'

'Yes, son. Right, we need to get going.'

'Yes, Ma', they chorused as they left the house, Ann pulling the door closed behind them.

'This is some motor, Uncle Louis. Is it the RME?' Joe ran his hand lovingly along the front wheel arch.

'Yes, I'm very pleased with it.'

'It's a nice colour,' Ann said, opening one of the back doors.

'Can you get in there, Kathleen?' Louis held open the other back door.

'I'm in. Joe, help Ann with her dress.'

'Yes, Ma.'

'You need to get to the church,' she said. 'Get a move on.'

'Yes, Ma, I'm gone. See you there.'

'Don't get your shoes dirty.'

'No, Ma.' Joe was shaking his head as he set off on foot.

The service was due to start at eleven thirty, so they left the house at eleven thirty. No self-respecting bride was ever on time.

The neighbours came out to see Ann leave the house. Then they'd rush up to the church and squeeze in at the back.

The car pulled up outside the church and Ann smiled radiantly at the people waiting outside. Uncle Louis helped her out of the car. She gathered her dress and her flowers, ready to make her big entrance. What she didn't see was Peter, with Walter in his wheelchair, on the opposite side of the road. Uncle Louis saw them and waved, but said nothing.

Ann felt like she was floating. Muriel and Hilda, waiting at the door of the church, sorted out her dress. Her sisters looked magnificent in matching pale blue dresses that looked expensive. Ma handed Ann over to Fred and gave her a wee kiss on the cheek before going into the church with Louis.

Fred had made a monumental effort wearing a smart suit and waistcoat. 'You look beautiful,' he whispered, tucking Ann's hand over his arm.

'You're not so bad yourself,' she said. 'You clean up rightly.'

Ushering duties over, Joe had come out to see her arrive. He gave her a wee pat on the bum. 'Go for it.'

'Can I just stand here forever?' she asked.

'No, the scones will go hard. Get in there,' he said and disappeared into the gloom.

'Right, let's go,' Ann whispered to Fred. He nodded to the Reverend Goodman, who nodded to Mrs Nugent, the organist, and something that sounded like Wagner started up.

Ann saw Stan standing near the top of the church. He looked handsome in his dark blue suit. The tall man beside him must be Spider.

Is this really happening? she wondered as she glided up the aisle. *What on earth am I doing?*

The McGartlands and other neighbours were near the back. Harry and Nigel were on the outside of a pew halfway down. Two rows in front of them was Iris and her husband. She saw the girls from work. They'd told her they were very happy for her but sad to see her go. Her jaw was getting sore from smiling.

Then she was there beside him. *Don't cry*, she told herself. *Just don't cry.*

'You look stunning,' Stan whispered.

The service was a blur. Hymns, readings, Fred saying 'I do', then leaving her. Daisy started to fidget. Stan glanced at her, a flicker of agitation crossing his face. There were more hymns, followed by the vows, then the ring – a simple, single diamond. She shivered as he slipped it onto her finger. *Don't cry*. His ring was a plain gold band. His fingers were long and bony.

'I now pronounce you man and wife. You may kiss the bride,' Reverend Goodman said, looking beatific.

Ann glanced at Ma, who looked tearfully ecstatic.

Stan and Ann exchanged a hesitant little kiss. The congregation erupted in applause. The happy couple went off to sign the registry. Then Mrs Nugent treated them to a rendition of 'Happy Birthday' as they walked down the aisle together.

They were greeted by warm sunshine outside, where more onlookers had gathered. Holding hands, posing for photographs, flash bulbs going off. Ann's bouquet was caught by Harry's girlfriend, Florence.

Then they went into the church hall for the reception – sandwiches, cakes and gallons of tea. Fred had come prepared. Ann had a wee nip of brandy from his hip flask. Lovely.

Then it was time to go. There were hugs and kisses and handshakes all round while Spider brought the car, decorated with white ribbons, round to the front of the hall. The tin cans tied to the back bumper made an awful racket as they drove off.

What they didn't notice was the man rushing over to the church, the startled faces of the wedding guests. Hands raised to gaping mouths, hankies fluttering like little white flags.

CHAPTER 27

They got the early train back from Portrush the Tuesday after Easter. Stan had to get to the housing office to fetch the keys to their new house in Johnston Park. He had ordered a bed, a three-piece suite and a sideboard, all to be delivered in the afternoon. Ann appeared delighted, but she worried about what monstrosities might appear. She'd never seen new furniture. So they talked about furniture, the future and red Dansettes the whole way home. Ann was in heaven. This is nearly too good to be true, she thought.

While Stan was getting the keys, Ann rushed round to see Daisy and tell Ma as much about the honeymoon as decency would allow.

'Jesus, Ma, what's wrong?' she said as soon as Ma opened the door. 'Are you alright?' Ma was crying. 'Come on, sit down. Tell me all about it. Is it Daisy? What's happened?'

'It's you who needs to sit down, love,' Ma said between sniffles.

Ann's heart was racing. She'd never seen Ma in such a state. She helped her over to her chair.

'What's happened? Is it Fred?'

'You need to sit down, love.'

'I'm alright. Tell me what's happened.' Ann was scared now.

'It's Walter.'

Ann's heart froze. 'What about him? What's happened?'

'He's dead.'

Ann collapsed back into the other chair. The next thing she knew, she could hear Stan talking. And another man who sounded like Dr Bowles. She couldn't make out what they were saying. She could hear Daisy crying. She felt sick.

'You've had a shock, Ann,' Dr Bowles was saying. He held out a little glass vial. 'Take a sniff of this.'

It had a nasty, sharp smell, like cat pee, but it cleared her head a little.

'How do you feel?' Stan asked, putting his arm around her. 'Can you sit up?'

She straightened herself up. The world whirled for a bit, then settled. She was in the chair opposite Ma's. There was a blanket over her knees. Dr Bowles and Stan were standing in the middle of the room. Ma had Daisy on her knee. Everyone looked very worried.

'What happened?' Ann asked.

'You fainted, love. I got Jean next door to go and get Dr Bowles. Then Stan appeared, looking for you. You should have been at your new house.'

Stan jangled a set of keys.

Ann stared at her lap for a moment, trying to recall what had happened. It was something bad, something … 'Walter! Oh God! Tell me what happened.'

'Peter was bringing him up to the station last Thursday, just like he often did. They stopped at the church to see you getting out of the car. Louis even waved at him. Walter said you looked beautiful. Then they went on. Everything seemed normal. Peter was busy as usual. The next thing he knew, someone was running down the tracks, waving and shouting.' Ma paused and dabbed her mouth and eyes. 'Walter had gone off up the line towards Londonderry like he used to do with Peter years ago. He could walk a good bit on his sticks. They don't know if he fell or what. The train hit him on a bend …' Ma ran out of words.

Daisy was crying 'Mummmeee' and reaching out for Ann. Ma set her down.

'Can you give her to me, Stan?' Ann said.

Stan picked her up awkwardly. Daisy screeched.

'I better go,' Dr Bowles said, putting on his coat. 'I'll call in tomorrow and see how you are.'

Ann swayed back and forward with Daisy in her lap; the motion soothed her as much as Daisy. No one spoke. After what seemed like an age Ma said, 'The funeral was last Saturday. Joe and the girls went.'

Ann sat silent as the tears rolled down her face. Stan knelt in front of her and took her hands in his strange bony hands. Time stopped.

'Will you be okay if I go back up and sort this furniture out?' he asked her awkwardly.

Ann didn't answer.

'Ann?'

'Oh God, Stan, it's the first day in our new house and I haven't even seen it yet.' Ann felt sorry for him. 'A new Chesterfield and everything.'

'Don't worry. It's not a real Chesterfield, it just looks like one. It's covered in blue velvety material. You stay here and rest a wee while. You can come *home* later. We'll get chips.'

'There's a brown envelope for you, love.' Ma pointed at the mantelpiece.

'It'll be my wedding gratuity. They told me I would be getting it. One hundred and fifty-six pounds, nine shillings and fourpence.'

Ma reached the letter over to Ann.

Ann took it and put it in her handbag. 'I'll sort this out later. I have to go and see them.'

'Who? You need to rest!' Ma was grey with worry.

'Peter and Mrs Green. I need to see them.'

'You can go tomorrow, love.' Stan held her shoulders.

'I'm going today. I have to go. Right now.'

'Have a cup of tea first, love. I have digestives.'

'Tea would be good,' Ann admitted. She was nodding her head like a zombie. 'Do we have butter?'

'We do. I'll put the kettle on. Will you stay for a cup, Stan?' Ma asked.

'No, I'll not, Mrs Brown, thanks all the same. I need to get on.'

'Kathleen. Please call me Kathleen.'

'Thank you, Kathleen. I'll head on here. Are you sure you're okay?' he asked Ann.

But she wasn't really listening to him. 'Yes, I'll be fine. I'll see you later.'

'Don't be too long. You've had a shock. You need to keep warm.' Stan sounded concerned.

'Yes, doctor,' she said, trying to smile.

After the hot tea and biscuits, Ann felt a bit better. A proper cuddle with Daisy helped too. Then she put on her coat and went to see the Greens.

She remembered nothing of the familiar journey. All of a sudden she was knocking their door.

They looked old and worn out, but they seemed pleased to see her.

'I don't know what to say. I'm so sorry. I can't—' Ann let Mrs Green's arms enfold her.

'Some are saying he committed suicide,' Mrs Green said. She was as distraught as Ann.

Peter didn't speak. Walter's wheelchair was in the corner. Ann went over and ran her fingers over the handles.

'I'll take that back to the hospital,' Peter said. 'I'm sure someone else could use it.'

'What happened, Peter? I know what you told Ma, but—'

Peter ran through it again: Walter had seemed okay, chittering away as usual, until they stopped at the church. He never spoke after that.

Ann started to bawl again; the anguish was unbearable. 'I caused this. If I'd stayed with him, this would never have happened.' She could hardly get the words out.

'It's *not* your fault, love,' Mrs Green said, trying to comfort her. 'We'd talked to him about you getting married. He understood. He was upset, but he understood. Or he said he did.'

'He was putting a brave face on it,' Ann said. 'We were a team and I abandoned him.'

'You shouldn't think like that, Ann.'

'But you know it's true.'

Mrs Green looked at Peter. 'No, love, it's not true. I think that you getting married to Stan brought home to him the reality of his situation. He knew he wasn't going to get better.'

'Oh God.' Ann sniffled. Her eyes were red and raw. She had no tears left.

'Is he in the Dublin Road Cemetery?'

'He is, love – away over near the wall on the left as you go in.'

'I'll go now, if that's all right. I need to see him.'

'Do you want me to come with you?' Peter asked.

'No, it's okay, Peter. I want to go on my own. I need to speak to him.'

It started to drizzle as she reached the gates of the cemetery. She saw the mound of fresh earth where five wreaths had been laid. She read the notes on them. They were from the Greens, the Brown family, the staff at the station, the staff at the T&F and from Ann.

That set her off again. They'd sent a wreath from her. It was beautiful. She blew her nose and straightened her coat.

'Bloody hell, Walter. I leave you for a couple of days and look what happens. I hope it was an accident.' She paused. 'It wasn't an accident, was it? …

'I was going to come and see you today with Daisy. She's getting very boisterous. She knows something bad has happened. I was going to bring you egg and onion sandwiches. The weather's lovely. We could have eaten them outside.

'Poor old Stan doesn't know where to put himself or what to say. I suppose you don't care about Stan, though. Why should you? But he's a good man, Walter. We had ice cream in Portrush down at the harbour, just like *we* did that day. Do you remember? Stan doesn't like sprinkles. Can you believe it! He says they stick in his teeth. One probably stuck in his teeth when he was a baby and now he thinks it's going to happen every time. No sprinkles! And he wouldn't have a beer outside the Harbour Bar either. He said it was uncouth to drink outdoors like a lout. We had to squeeze inside. Couldn't even get a seat …

'We have a new house that I haven't even seen yet. Stan's got new furniture for it. It has a bathroom upstairs with a bath in it. And a toilet. And a basin and taps. If you light a fire, it heats up a big tank of water and you get hot water from the taps. Imagine!

'Oh God, love, are you at peace? Can you walk properly up there? And dance? And talk like a Christian? Can they comb your hair properly? You are in heaven, aren't you? Ma said God would forgive you. I hope he has. Not much use if he hasn't. I mean, how will I ever find you if you're not? I'm definitely going to heaven, God or no God.

'Right, I better go and see this new house. Stan is getting us chips for tea. I hope he means fish as well. We could have had a better first day in our new house, I suppose, but it's not your fault. Don't ever think that. I can't believe you're gone. Please forgive me, Walter.' She kissed the tips of her fingers and touched the wooden cross where the headstone was to go.

She took the photo of the three of them out of her handbag. She showed it to Walter and kissed it. 'I love you, Walter Green,' she whispered. She could have sworn Walter whispered back, 'I love you too, Ann Brown.'

She cried all the way home and was nearly at Ma's front door before she realised she was at the wrong house. She turned and walked back up the town, down Scarffe's Entry, past the green wooden huts of the clinic and up around the bend into Johnston Park.

Stan took her wet coat and draped it over the back of a dining chair in front of a lit fire.

'I got Scarffe's to deliver some coal,' he explained. 'Are you okay?' He steered her towards a comfy-looking armchair on one side of the fireplace.

'It's lovely, Stan,' Ann said, running her hands over the back of what was obviously her chair. Stan's pipes were in a rack at the other end of the mantelpiece. His armchair was on the far side of the fireplace. The settee was along the back wall. The sideboard was between the settee and the big front window.

Ann felt nothing. She felt numb – to the new house, to Stan and to his new furniture. Yet this was the day she had been looking forward to for so long. So much for her new start.

Stan went out for the fish suppers and she went upstairs to have a look around. Their bedroom was at the front. There was also a smaller L-shaped room at the front. The bathroom and another bedroom were at the back and there was a hot press on the landing. It was a palace.

The grey plastered walls were ready to paper or paint. She realised she didn't know what Stan preferred or what colours he liked. Walter would have pretended to have an opinion and suggested mad colours, but then left it up to her.

She went back down and poked the fire. She wondered how long it took to heat the water. She could have a bath! Right now, maybe. But she decided to wait until Stan got back.

They didn't have any plates or cutlery, so they ate out of the greasy newspaper. 'It's just like being in Portrush,' Ann said, blowing on the steaming hot food.

'We need to be careful not to get grease all over the chairs,' Stan mumbled through a mouthful of chips. 'How are you feeling now, love? It should have been a wonderful day for you … for both of us … but it's been a bit of a disaster.'

'Not your fault, Stan. We didn't know what Walter was going to do.' *Don't cry,* she told herself.

‘What did he think he was playing at?’ Stan said. ‘And on your wedding day of all days.’

‘I think it was his way of ending it.’

‘It? What it? There was no it. It was over.’

Ann held her counsel. It would never be over between them. She knew that, now more than ever.

‘I think he did it for me,’ she said. ‘To let me go, set me free.’

‘From him? But you are free. You’re with me.’

‘I know, Stan. I’ll be okay in a day or two. You go back to work and I’ll get the house sorted. It’ll be good to be busy.’

‘That’s the girl. Finished?’ He gathered up the greasy newspaper. ‘There’s a bin out the back. Have you seen the back garden yet? Room to grow some stuff if we want.’

‘Sounds lovely, Stan. Could I have a bath, do you think?’

‘We don’t have any towels. I meant to go down the town and get stuff like that today. What a start, eh?’ He was smiling.

‘We won’t forget day one, that’s for sure. I’ll go shopping tomorrow.’

‘You’ll need a list. I like a good list.’

Why does that not surprise me? Ann thought.

They went to bed early that night. Ann didn’t have to feign exhaustion as she turned away from Stan. She wondered how Ma was getting on, just her and Daisy. She wondered if Mu, Hilda and Joe all got away okay. The wheel had turned the world on its head again.

Bloody Walter! Bloody dopey, blond, gorgeous Walter! She cried silent tears until sleep rescued her.

CHAPTER 28

Nearly two glorious years of the monotony of marriage to a good steady man had dulled Ann's expectations, dulled the pain, dulled everything.

She put the brake on the pram.

'Happy birthday, Walter Green,' she said. 'You'd be twenty-five today if you'd been smarter. Sorry I haven't been up to see you since … well, you know. I just couldn't. Stan told me not to. He said it wasn't healthy. I have tried. I really have, but I never listened to you and there's no need to listen to him either. What he doesn't know won't hurt him, eh?

'So much has happened.' She folded down the hood of the pram. 'This is Mary. I wanted to call her Kathleen after Ma, but Stan wanted to call her Mary after his ma and she's dead, so it seemed like the right thing to do. So, she's Mary Kathleen Webb. Sounds all right, doesn't it? She was one there last month. Everyone says she looks like me. Lucky her, eh?

'Daisy starts school in September. Can you believe it? She'll be five in August. She's still living with Ma. Stan promised to adopt her when we got married, but then he reneged on it. I was ragin' with him – couldn't believe it. I swore I'd never forgive him. But he said Daisy was good company for Ma. He might be right – she'd be lonely without her – but he promised.

'There's room for her in our house, but Stan says there'll be no room when we have three or four weans of our own. Daisy's very lively. She's getting to be too much for Ma. I bet you were like that when you were wee. You wouldn't know this, but Ma nearly had to take her out of the church during the wedding. Stan wasn't best pleased, I can tell you, but she settled down. She looks just like you – except she has proper hair. Ma's glad she has proper hair.'

Ann started to cry a little. She took the dog-eared photograph of her, Walter and Daisy out of her handbag and rubbed a thumb across Walter's face.

'I still have it. Look.' She waved the photograph at the sky.

'The wedding was great, thanks for asking,' she went on. 'Pity you missed it … Oh! Sorry. That didn't sound right.' She wiped her eyes. 'Mu and Hilda flew over in an aeroplane. Hard to fly over in anything else, I suppose. Dan and Al missed it too, so you weren't the only one. Hilda's wean wasn't there either. Bloody hell, who *was* at it?

'Dan is definitely a spy! He's working in Cheltenham in England. There's a big spy place there. He won't even tell Hilda what he does there, so he must be a spy. Maybe he's a real-life James Bond. You'd like James Bond. I hope he writes more stories about him. Forgotten his name now – not James Bond, obviously – the man who wrote the book. *Casino Royale* it's called. Dan's probably training the trainee spies. How do you become a spy, do you think? I'd love to be a spy. You'd have been useless. You have to be smart to be a spy.

'Mu and Al finally got married. A year ago at Christmas. I was really looking forward to it – big posh wedding in their big fancy house – but Stan said I was too far gone with Mary to risk going over. I sometimes think he did it on purpose so I couldn't go. Or is that just me being paranoid? He was right as usual, but that was another dream gone. I've never been to London. Hilda says the wedding was like something from a fairy tale. There were two hundred people at it. Two hundred! That's a lot of cake. No sign of any weans yet. Al's very slow. He's smarter than you but just as slow.

'How's Joe, did you say? Nearly forgot about him. Good job you're here … He's having the time of his life. He's on dry land now in Hong Kong. In a proper office like where I used to work, remember? He's still playing football. Still telling wild stories. Mostly about girls. Mostly made up, I imagine. It's hard to tell with Joe. Apparently he told Harry and Nigel that he chatted up a very pretty girl once, only to find out she was a boy.' Ann leaned in to whisper: 'I can't tell you how he found out – not in front of Mary.

'Stan's been saving for a television. He says we should be able to get one to rent by the summer. Imagine, a TV! Muriel got us a Dansette for our wedding. A red one. I only have six records. Kay Starr's my favourite. I play them over and over when Stan's at work. He says his office is very noisy and he needs peace and quiet when he gets home, which is fair enough, I suppose. I just think he doesn't like music. How can you not like music? He'd let me buy more records, but he says that saving for the TV is more important.

'Ma's keeping very well, thank you. She gave us a clock for a wedding present. She got three when she retired, so she gave us one of those. Mu and Hilda were raging cos they never got a clock. They send her money every month for

Daisy. Daisy keeps her on her toes. The flood last year was pretty bad, so Stan let Ma and Daisy come and stay with us. Ma liked the inside toilet. She even had a bath, God love her.

'I don't see your ma and da too often now, not after your shenanigans. Your ma doesn't seem to have changed much. She still loves a good cry. I have to put my brolly up every time I see her. She'll never get over what happened. She says it wasn't my fault, but I think she thinks it was. And she'd be right.

'If I hadn't have overreacted the night of the party, even though you behaved like a pig on heat, you wouldn't have gone off in a huff. And you wouldn't have got knocked down. And I'd still have you, and Daisy would have a da.

'It wasn't easy getting married, I can tell you. It wasn't fair on Stan either. I pretended it was you, but it wasn't. I think Stan knows somehow. Anyway, we are where we are.

'What's it like where you are? Are you dancing with the angels? They're all men, though – Gabriel and all – so how does that work? Must be the best music up there and the best dance floors. And endless egg and onion sandwiches. Do they stink to high heaven? Get it?' Ann smiled at her wee joke.

'You probably already know everything I've just told you … or is it just God who knows everything? It must be boring knowing everything. Nothing to learn about anything. Does he pass all the gossip on to everybody? That would keep him busy. Maybe he has too much else to do.

'If you do know what's going on, you'll know that Stan's a good man. He's kind and … well, he's kind, but between you and me, he's a bit boring. He takes things awfully seriously, especially money things. He put my wedding gratuity in the bank for a rainy day! I wanted to buy stuff. And he doesn't like music, but I've told you that already. He doesn't dance and doesn't think I should go dancing on my own. He doesn't like the flicks either. The last time I was at the pictures was with Iris. We saw *Seven Brides for Seven Brothers.* Great musical! You'd love it. But it was ages ago.'

Ann sighed loudly. 'Anyway, as I say, we are where we are. I'd be lost without Stan. He's my here and now and my future. But you will always be my forever.' Her eyes filled up again. 'Please don't tell anyone I was here today,' she whispered.

Ann stood up, kissed her fingers and touched the cold marble headstone with them.

'I'll be back soon, I promise. I won't leave it so long. I miss our wee chats and I know you like to listen to me rabbiting on. Right, I better go. Stan likes his dinner ready when he gets in. I love you, Walter Green.'

She listened to him whisper in the breeze.

She kissed the photo and put it back in her bag, then dried her eyes and set off back down the path.

When Ann got to Ma's, she could hear Daisy playing in Joe's old room. Ma was slumped in a chair in the living room; she looked exhausted.

'How's she been today, Ma?' Ann asked.

'Oh, just the same. I don't know where she gets the energy from. I can't keep up.' Ma went to get up from her chair but slumped back down again. 'It's too cold to play outside, so I've been deafened in here all day.'

'Mummy, Mummy,' Daisy screamed when Ann stuck her head round the door of Joe's room. She got up and threw herself at Ann.

'Slow down a bit, love. You nearly knocked me over. Let me see your doll?'

Daisy held up her new Bakelite doll. Both its arms were outstretched. 'Kiss Dolly, Mummy. Kiss Dolly.'

Ann bent down and kissed the doll on the lips. 'What are you going to call her? You'll have to give her a name.'

'She's Dolly. That's her name.'

'Well, hello Dolly. Is Daisy looking after you? She is? That's good.'

'Mummy?'

'Yes, love?'

'Can we take Dolly for a walk?'

'Of course we can. Put Dolly in the pram beside Mary. You can help me push.'

'Take as long as you like,' Ma said, giving them a little wave of her hand.

She was coughing as Ann closed the door.

CHAPTER 29

Stan wheeled his bike through the gate and down the front path, past a narrow row of daffodils that Ann had planted. She'd always liked the heroic, raggedy few that had grown in Sedan Avenue.

'Hello, love. It's me,' he shouted as he parked the bike in the passageway. He came in and took off his overcoat.

'Dinner's ready. Mince and onions.'

'Lovely. I'm starving. Did you get Bisto?'

'Yes, I remembered when I was in the Home and Colonial.'

'What do I always say about lists? Can't forget if you have a list.'

Ann rolled her eyes. 'Busy day?' she asked as she spooned the brown gloop out onto the plates. She carried them over to the table and sat down.

'Just the usual.' Stan put a spud in the middle of his plate and began to mash it into the stew. 'That wee girl Evelyn that I was telling you about – she's going to have to go. She's useless.'

'She's only young, Stan. How long has she been there?'

'Doesn't matter. She's useless.' He forked a dollop of gravied mash into his mouth. 'Any more spuds?'

'Course there is.' Ann had learned that he didn't like too many spuds on his plate at one time; he preferred to ask for more. 'One?'

'Two. They're not that big. Did you get them in Coates?'

'No, he's charging tuppence a stone more than the Home and Colonial.'

'Eejit.'

After dinner, Stan sat down in the living room, lit his pipe and opened the paper.

'What sort of day did you have then?' he asked as Ann came and sat opposite him in her armchair.

'Oh, just the usual. Took Mary shopping. Went to see Ma and Daisy. Cleaned the bathroom. I got Ajax. It's good stuff.'

Stan grunted and puffed on his pipe.

Ann set the receipts for the groceries on the small table beside Stan. He got out his little notebook and entered the amounts in his tiny neat writing.

'Bacon's gone up a bit,' he commented.

'Everything's going up. Oliver blames Churchill.'

'Eejit. We'd have lost the war only for Churchill.'

'He knows that, but he says he's too old now and it's different in peacetime. No excuses.'

'Brain of Britain, our Oliver. Still, I think we might have enough for that TV next month, or April at the latest.'

'Oh Stan, a TV! It's so exciting. Can we buy another record soon as well?'

Stan smiled at her. 'How many records do you need? You have six. You can only listen to one at a time.'

Ann pouted.

Stan shook his head in amusement. 'Of course you can. Sure we'll go to Woolworths on Saturday.'

Ann beamed at him and got up to check on Mary. She was a very quiet child compared to Daisy. They were both like their das, she thought as she kissed the sleeping beauty's forehead.

She came back into the living room. 'The water should be hot now. I'll do the dishes.'

Stan grunted. Puffing away on his pipe, he rustled his paper and folded it to another page.

Even after nearly two years in their new house, Ann still thought it a miracle that hot water came out of the tap just minutes after lighting the fire. As she washed up the pots and pans, she tried to dream about the future, but nothing came. The past was always vividly right there. She gave herself a shake. Things could be worse.

'Can I put on the radio?' she asked Stan when she came back into the living room. 'The Forces Show is on at half seven.'

'If it's not too loud.'

Ann turned the knob on the big Bush radio that Spider had given them as a wedding present and the radio slowly came to life. Frankie Vaughan was singing 'Something's Gotta Give'. Ann closed her eyes and the world disappeared.

She listened to the radio all day when she was in the house. She liked *Mrs Dale's Diary*. Mary Dale's life with her doctor husband, Jim, seemed like the life Ann had dreamed of, after all her younger, bigger dreams had died. When classical music came on, she didn't turn it off. Her mind drifted. She felt happy in her make-believe world.

Monday was washing day. She never told Stan that she did the washing for Ma and Daisy along with their own. She had a washing machine that made it a lot easier. It even had a mangle attached to the top of it. Stan took no interest in what was hanging on the line.

On Wednesday morning she wrapped Ma's washing in a sheet and took it back to Sedan Avenue.

'Your washing, madam,' she said, dumping it on Fred's chair.

'Don't leave it there.'

'I'll put it away after we have a wee cup of tea. I got some digestives.'

'Is it dry?'

'No, it's not. I never even washed it. I just bring it up to Johnston Park every week for the craic and then bring it back down again.'

'No need to be so cheeky,' Ma scolded.

'Sorry, Ma. It's dry as a bone.'

'That'll have to do, I suppose.' Ma laughed, which turned into a cough and then a wheeze. 'Tea would be lovely,' she eventually said. 'Not too much butter on the digestives, mind.'

'No, Ma.'

CHAPTER 30

Ann stood back and admired her beautiful daughter. 'Look at you, all ready for your first day at school. Are you all excited? Got your sandwich and your apple?'

Daisy nodded. There were curls everywhere. Walter's curls; Ann's colour.

'You look a picture.' Ma pressed a shilling into her little hand. 'A shilling in your pocket is your best friend. Always remember that and you'll be okay.'

Ann gave Ma a broad happy smile.

'I went to the same school many moons ago.' Ann retied Daisy's laces for the umpteenth time. 'There aren't many of the old teachers left now. Mr Marks is still there. He teaches sums. You'll like sums. Mr Lee is still the headmaster. He must be a hundred if he's a day.'

Daisy's face was glowing. 'My shoes hurt.'

'It'll take a wee while for them to soften up. Take them off when you get into school, if your feet get really sore. Now say bye-bye to Nana.'

'I want Nana to come.'

‘I’ll get my coat,’ Ma said. ‘We both need to see her off on her first day.’

Ann looked up and sighed. You should be here to see this, Blondie, she thought. ‘Right, let’s go,’ she said aloud and opened the door.

Daisy dragged them across the road and up to the main doors of the school. Ann shivered as the memories washed over her. Then Daisy let go of their hands and darted inside. Ann and Ma went in to make sure the teachers knew who she was, but Daisy didn’t need any help.

* * *

At two o’clock, Ann and Ma were anxiously waiting for Daisy to come out.

‘Well, how was it?’ Ann asked.

‘We had to sit up straight and fold our arms like this.’ Daisy demonstrated perfect arm folding.

‘And what else did you do?’

‘We had to say our names. Then our mummy’s and daddy’s names. I said I didn’t have a daddy. Mr Stewit came over and told me that my mummy was married to my daddy. I said Daddy wasn’t my real daddy cos he told me so.’

Ann fell to bits inside. She felt real anger. ‘Your daddy shouldn’t have said that, Daisy. He is your daddy and he loves you very much.’ She wrapped her arms around her serious, sad, confused daughter. ‘What did you say your teacher’s name was?’

‘Stewit. Mr Stewit. He’s funny-looking.’

‘It’s Stew–art.’

‘Stew Art.’

‘There you go. Good girl. Why is he funny-looking?’

'He has a big beard like Santa, only it's ginger and so's his hair. It sticks out all over the place. He mustn't have a brush.'

'And what else did you do?'

'We did letters. A B C' – Daisy counted them out on her fingers – 'D. And numbers. I can count up to ten,' she said and she did. 'Can I go back tomorrow? Mr Stew Art said "see you all tomorrow", then we had to leave our jotters and our pencils on his desk.'

'Yes, love, you can go again tomorrow,' Ann said, exchanging an amused glance with Ma. I need to have a quiet word with Mr Stewart, she thought. She knew this was just the beginning for wee Daisy. 'Let's go and get an ice cream.'

Daisy danced ahead of them up the street.

CHAPTER 31

Another year later and life continued much as it had always done. Stan went to work, came home, ate his dinner, examined the day's receipts, entered the figures in his little notebook, made a remark about prices going up, lit his pipe and read the paper. Life was so normal Ann had no need to think about the fateful vagaries of the wheel of fortune. It had stopped spinning.

Ma's health got a bit better and she ventured out occasionally, now that Daisy was in school. She even made it as far as Johnston Park a few times, although she had to stop in Bob Campbell's wee shop at the top of Scarffe's Entry for a breather and a fag and a chat. Ma was intrigued by the washing machine, and fascinated by the taps, the bath and the electric lights. Even the street lights were electric now and came on by themselves when it was getting dark.

'How do they know when to come on?' Ma asked.

'No idea,' Ann said. 'There must be a man who sits and waits beside a big giant knob. When he can't see his paper, he puts ten bob in the meter and turns on the lights.'

'It can't be ten bob. Can it? Every day?'

'Maybe not in the summer, when he doesn't need to turn them on till about ten.'

Fred still called with Ma most evenings for a drink, a chat and a wee dance. Often, they just listened to the radio.

Joe had got married in Hong Kong, but it didn't last very long when he discovered the baby wasn't his.

Hilda and Dan had settled back in Vancouver.

Ann met Iris for coffee now and again. They joined the Women's Institute and made cakes. Ann bought a sewing machine and mended things.

It was February 1956 and the day of Muriel and Al's wee girl's first birthday. Ann called Muriel to wish baby Kathleen a happy birthday.

'Are you having any more?' Ann asked. 'One doesn't seem right. Who are they going to fight with?'

'I think we're going to have more, but Al's not in any rush, as usual. I'd rather have them all together and get the bawling and screaming and the nappies over as quickly as possible. What about you and steady Stan?'

'Well, now you mention it …'

'Seriously? Are you?'

'I think so. You sort of know, don't you? I haven't even told Stan yet. I just feel different. I'll know for definite soon enough.'

'Oh, that's great, Ann. It really is. Things are looking up for you. Maybe you'll get over to see us sometime?'

'Stan says he doesn't like the thought of flying. He's never done it. Neither have I, but I'd love to give it a go. It'll not be anytime soon, I don't think, what with the weans and Ma and all.'

'You're still looking after everyone else. What about you?'

'I'm grand. Iris and I have great craic. There's dancing in the Legion on Wednesday afternoons. The band are useless and the floor's all sticky, but it's better than nothing. Some of the auld boys aren't bad dancers as long as the music's slow. Jives are illegal – too dangerous.'

'Listen, Ann, I've got to go. Kathleen's busting a lung here. But she told me to tell you thank you, Auntie Ann.'

'I didn't get her anything.'

'But you phoned. It's the thought that counts. She can't wait to meet you.'

'I'll just keep on dreaming,' Ann said. Just like always, she thought.

The following week, Ann patted her belly and smiled at Stan. 'I've some good news for you.' Stan grunted without looking up. Ann continued, 'I'm pregnant again, love.'

This was important enough for Stan to set his paper down and put his pipe in the rack. He smiled back at his beaming wife. 'Are you sure?'

'Yes, absolutely.'

'Oh love, that's brilliant news. Do you want a boy this time?'

'That would be nice after two girls, but I don't really mind.' She caught a flicker of confusion crossing Stan's face when she said 'two girls'. 'What about you?' she asked.

'A boy would be good. One of each and all that.'

'I think two of each would be even better.'

'Well, we'll see. It's great news, it really is.' He stood up and gave her a big hug, lifting her off her feet. Then he kissed her on the cheek and sat down.

He was about to pick up his paper again when Ann said, 'Why can't we adopt Daisy like you promised? She's growing into a beautiful little girl, but she needs her daddy.'

'But I'm not her daddy, am I? We have our own family and soon we'll have no room. Daisy loves her nana. And you must admit your ma would be lonely without her.'

Ann was torn. There was no point arguing with Stan. He couldn't be a da to Daisy, she knew that now. The coldness had begun the day they got back from their honeymoon in Portrush. Her reaction to Walter's death had left him in no doubt where he stood. She remembered the look he gave Daisy when she started fidgeting in the church. She wasn't his and she was a constant reminder of Walter. But Ann was her ma and she wanted to be a proper mother, not just popping in to see how she was. Ma loved her to bits and Stan was right – Sedan Avenue would be quiet without her – but Daisy was already asking difficult questions. Nobody had said it was going to be easy, but they'd never said it would be this hard either. *We'll get there*, Ann thought, but she had no idea how.

A baby boy appeared in September that year. 'Que sera sera' by Doris Day was on the radio when Ann brought him home in the afternoon. As so often happened, the song matched her mood perfectly. Stan wanted to call him Arthur after his own da. Ann agreed. She thought it was a lovely name.

Muriel knew that Stan held the purse strings tightly and told Ann, when she phoned to congratulate her, that she thought it was awful that he gave her 'pocket money' every week. Ann said £2 was plenty. It was on top of the housekeeping money he gave her. She could buy whatever she wanted with it – make-up, perfume, records. Clothes were negotiated separately. Stan didn't include Daisy and Ma in his calculations.

'Not because he's nasty,' Ann hastened to add. 'He's just careful.'

'Miserable, I'd say. Does he know about Hilda and me sending money?' Muriel asked.

'I don't think so. He's never asked and I've never said anything.'

More secrets, Ann thought. She'd tried to get rid of them, but Walter was right – life did get more complicated and a lot less fun as you got older. She cashed her sisters' cheques for Ma and said nothing.

On Saturday evening, when Arthur and Mary were in bed, Ann asked Stan if she could put the radio on.

'If it's quiet,' he said. 'Most of the new stuff that's on nowadays is just noise.'

You never liked any of the old stuff either, Ann thought, but she said, 'I think some of it's brilliant – Eddie Cochran, Elvis, Lonnie Donegan. It's different.'

'You can say that again!'

'It's different.'

'I didn't mean ...' Stan shook his head and buried it back in the sports pages. 'Not too loud now,' he said without looking up.

Ann turned the dial to 208 – Radio Luxembourg. The best music she'd ever heard crackled out of the tiny speaker, and she gently danced to it as she did the ironing behind Stan's chair.

* * *

Daisy was being obstreperous at school. Noisy, disruptive and inattentive, according to Mr Stewart. Hardly a week passed without her bringing home a letter from her teacher or Mr Lee, the headmaster. She wouldn't do her homework for Ma either. She lied about even having homework. Ann had to stand over her and make her do it. Then there were tears, tantrums and stress.

Mary was placid by comparison, and Arthur just ate, slept and filled his nappy. Ann somehow seemed to sleepwalk through all this. She dealt with the everyday things without making any plans, without daydreaming, except when her rock and roll records were on the Dansette. That was her time – hers and Walters. She wasn't sad, or lonely. She had Walter to talk to.

In November 1957, they had another wee boy who they called Willy, after Stan's brother Spider. Meanwhile, everything else continued on as usual. Stan went to work, came home, ate his dinner, filled out the ledger, smoked his pipe, read the paper and went to bed. Then one day he shocked Ann.

'I think we should redecorate the living room,' he announced.

'Why? Why now?'

'The wallpaper's on over four years. It's black above the fireplace. It would brighten the place up. You can pick the paper.'

'And the paint?'

'That'll need done too, I suppose.'

This was exciting. New wallpaper! She would have to go and hoke through those big sample books. She felt a meeting with Iris coming on. They could chat about patterns, paint, pelmets. It would need wine.

'I'd love that, Stan. When were you thinking of doing it?'

'As soon as you like. We'll measure up at the weekend – work out how many rolls we'll need.'

Two weeks later, and after two days of chaos with paste and paint everywhere, the walls were covered with yellow, green and blue geometric shapes. White gloss gleamed on the woodwork.

Stan had been growing spuds and other vegetables in the back garden, but as the children got older, they needed somewhere to play and the little square of grass at the front was useless. So the vegetable plot at the back was turned into a big lawn, creating a new problem. Their wee lawnmower couldn't cope.

'It just doesn't cut it, Stan,' Ann joked.

Stan laughed and had to admit she was right. 'So we need a new lawnmower as well.'

'It's a good job you're so good at saving. Have we enough?'

'Leave it with me.'

Stan came home a few days later with a second-hand Atco push mower. He'd had to carry it home and push his bike as well.

'Have we any beer?' he gasped as he collapsed into his chair.

Their neighbours had all moved in at near enough the same time as they had. There was plenty of friendly conversation and gossip as they passed each other going in or out. Tim, who lived in the next house up, worked for the *Conn*, while Frank in the next house down worked in the Royal Arms. He organised all their functions, weddings and wakes. Above Tim was Aiden. He was a car mechanic and had a garage behind one of the posh three-storey houses in Campsie. In the first house, as you came up round the corner into Johnston Park, was Cecil. He was a mechanic, too, but worked in Nestle's fixing their lorries and vans. He knew Harry to see.

They didn't see as much of the people that lived in the terrace of single-storey houses opposite them. Stan was keeping his eyes and ears open for one for Ma. Ann thought it would be brilliant to have her and Daisy living just across the road.

'I've lived here all my life. Why would I want to move somewhere else?' Ma said when Ann broached the subject with her.

'Were you born here then?'

'I know your game, young lady.' She sighed and put her knitting down. 'If you promise not to tell anyone, even Stan, I'll tell you.'

'Tell me what?'

'I was fifty last month.'

Ann's mouth fell open. Why was Ma telling her this now? 'Why didn't you say anything? We could have had a party – with cake. Mind you, it might be hard to get one big enough. I'd have had to buy five of those wee boxes of candles! Mrs Devlin probably wouldn't have that many.'

'That's exactly why I've never said anything. No need for parties. I've never had one. And Fred is the only person to buy me a present. Good excuse, he reckons, to buy Black Bush.'

'So Fred knows?'

'Fred knows everything.'

'You mean about Da as well?'

'That's enough now. No party, no new house. That's the end of it.'

Ann brushed digestive crumbs off her skirt into her cupped hand and tipped them into her empty mug. 'How is Fred?' she asked. 'I haven't seen him for ages.'

'Just the same – drinks too much, smokes too much, falls asleep in the chair. Can't thread a needle any more.'

'Same as ever then?'

'Indestructible. I'll never get rid of him.'

You don't want to get rid of him, Ann thought.

'And how's Stan?' Ma asked. 'He never comes round. Does he ever see Daisy?'

'Stan's okay. Always busy. He makes sure Daisy wants for nothing.'

'Him and Muriel and Hilda. She's spoilt rotten.'

'Mu sounds like she's doing well. Off to Paris for a holiday. Imagine that!'

'She won't like it.'

'Why do you think she won't like it, Ma? It's supposed to be all rebuilt and beautiful again.'

'They all speak foreign and Joe says they eat snails – on toast – for breakfast.' Ma pulled a face.

'Joe says a lot of things. Mostly they're not true, even in his own head.'

'His head is very odd, I must say.' Ma had a wee laugh. 'Is he still married?'

'No, he left … Angela, was it? … ages ago. Found out the baby she was pregnant with couldn't have been his.'

'Now that's a surprise,' Ma said sarcastically.

'Ma! That's your favourite son you're talking about.'

'I know. He's a good boy really. Just a bit—'

'Thick?'

Ma said nothing. She set her empty cup and plate on the hearth.

'He says he's had dinner with a Rear Admiral,' Ann said.

'Oh, I don't like the sound of that.' Ma pulled another face.

Ann burst into a fit of laughter. They sat silent for a minute, each of them in their own thoughts. Daisy was sitting at the table doing her homework and all they could hear were her loud sighs and the scratching of her pencil as she tried to do her sums.

'Oh, I nearly forgot – Daisy needs new shoes again,' Ma said. 'She's shooting up like a nettle.'

'I'm not a nettle,' Daisy shouted.

'No, you're not, love. Nana just means you're getting very big, very fast,' Ann said. She got up and went over to her daughter.

Daisy's tongue was sticking out at the side of her mouth. She was concentrating hard.

'Mummy, what do you get when you add fifteen and seventeen?' she asked.

'Have you written them down one on top of the other?' Ann asked, peering at Daisy's jotter.

Daisy nodded.

'Good girl. So what is five added to seven?'

Daisy stuck her pencil in her mouth and thought very hard. Then she counted it out on her fingers: 'Eight, nine, ten, eleven, twelve. TWELVE.' She flashed her killer smile at Ann.

'That's right. So put a two under the line, under the five and the seven. That's it. Now carry over your ten to here.' Ann pointed to the spot. 'So now you have three ones here, one above the other. See?' Daisy nodded. 'So put a three under the line beside the two.' Daisy scrawled the number. 'Now what's that number you have here under the line?'

Daisy tapped the pencil against her teeth. 'Thirty-two,' she said eventually. She dropped the pencil on the jotter and sighed.

'It's easy when you know how,' Ann said. 'Have you more to do?'

'No, that was the last one.'

'Okay, sharpen your pencil and put it away in your pencil case.' Ann turned to Ma. 'I'd better go.' She kissed the top of Daisy's head and put on her coat. 'No need to worry about Johnston Park until a house actually comes up, I suppose. That could be a long time.'

'I hope it never comes up,' Ma said. 'And how can I not worry about it? It's now on the "worry about this when I remember" list.' Ma gave Ann a cheeky grin and waved her off.

* * *

Ann knelt down at the grave.

'I've only got a couple of minutes today, love. I think your daughter might be as thick as you are – sorry, were – if that's possible? She's a bit slow at her sums. You were good at sums, though – I'll give you that. Five baps at a penny ha'penny each? You had the answer in no time. She must take after me then. She looks like you, though – more and more every day. Maybe she could become the first bread woman in Omagh. Imagine that? If only she could add.

'I've got four weans now. Can you believe it? Two of each, as planned. And they all have normal hair. Imagine if you were the da of all of them. There'd be hair everywhere. Stan has normal hair. Stan has normal everything.

'How's things with you? I hope you're behaving yourself. You don't want to get kicked out. Have you met God yet? You've been there long enough. Maybe he doesn't bother with the dopey angels, the ones that were lucky to get in in the first place. Humphrey Bogart is up there now … and Oliver Hardy. Have you met them yet? Mind you, it must be a big place. Millions of people. Where do they all go? And what do you do all day? Maybe there are no days. Just one big long … thing. Is there dancing? Can you get Radio Luxembourg?

'I bumped into your ma and da a few weeks ago. Your ma started crying as soon as she saw me. Your da looks really old. They miss you. I miss going to work. It was easier than looking after three – sorry, four weans. No, four weans and a ma. Wrong again, four weans and a ma and a husband. *And a partridge in a pear tree.*' Ann sang the last bit. 'Better go. Stan still doesn't know I come out here for a wee chat now and again. He wouldn't understand. Don't worry, I'll be back soon.'

Ann took the old photograph of the three of them out of her handbag, kissed it and zipped it back in the inside pocket. She wiped her eyes. She always had to wipe her eyes. It wasn't getting any easier.

'I love you, Walter Green.' She paused for a minute. 'I know, love. I know,' she whispered. She straightened her dress, touched his headstone and left the cemetery.

CHAPTER 32

'Happy birthday, love,' Ma said and handed Ann a small parcel. It was wrapped in brown paper and tied with white string.

'Oh Ma, you shouldn't have! ... don't know why people say that. *Of course* you should have. What is it?'

'You'll have to open it to find out.'

'Open it, Mummy.' Daisy was hopping from one foot to another with excitement.

Ann carefully undid the string and let it drop to the floor along with the paper. They would be put away to be reused. In her hand she held a small red box with 'LOVES. THE JEWELLERS' embossed in gold on the top.

Ann gasped and gently lifted the lid. Nestled on a bed of black velvet was a gold cameo brooch.

'Oh Ma, it's beautiful. I've always wanted one of these.' She held the brooch up against her chest.

'Me and Nana went. I helped buy it.'

'Nana and I,' Ann corrected her, but Daisy wasn't listening.

'Put it on, Mummy. Put it on.' She jumped up and down.

Ann pinned the brooch to her blouse and looked at herself in the old stained mirror above the mantelpiece.

'Nothing from Stan, I suppose,' Ma said. She was standing behind Ann, admiring the reflection.

'I don't think he knows it's my birthday, much less our anniversary. I don't think he even knows we're in a new decade,' Ann said. 'He just went off to the market as he usually does on a Saturday.'

'You know the way I've always said "a shilling in your pocket is your best friend"?'

'I've never heard you say that.'

Ma slapped her daughter playfully on the shoulder. 'I was going to go on to say "but sometimes it's good to let the odd one escape".'

'Do mummies always tell people off?' Daisy asked. She flashed her killer smile at them both.

'Yes, dear. They never stop,' Ann said. She turned back from the mirror. 'You *know* he's never bought presents or sent cards, even at Christmas,' she said to Ma. 'Well, there was that one, before we got married. He's hardly going to start now.'

'I hope you still get him things.'

'He really means it when he says *you shouldn't have*.'

'Will I put the kettle on?' Ma asked.

'Absolutely. I brought snowballs. I think they've got smaller.' She lifted one out of the paper bag 'Do you think they're smaller?'

'Snowballs!' Daisy grabbed the bag.

'Go and get some plates, love. There's a good girl. I'll make the tea.' Ann was about to get up.

'You sit there. It's your birthday. *I'll* make the tea,' Ma said and she shuffled out.

Ann sat fidgeting. She wasn't used to not doing things.

Over tea and snowballs, they chatted and read the birthday cards from the others. When the tea was finished, Daisy hoked around in her school bag, pulled something out and hid it behind her back.

'What have you got there?' Ann asked, poking her daughter in the stomach.

With a flourish, Daisy produced a card. 'Mr Stewart helped me make this at school. It's for you, Mummy.'

Ann studied the picture on the outside and opened the card; inside it simply said 'Love Daisy'. 'It's lovely. Thank you, sweetheart.'

'I was doing the drawing – me and you and Nana holding hands. Look! – and Mr Stewart asked if I wasn't going to draw my daddy. I said I didn't have a daddy. Not a proper one anyway. So I didn't draw one.'

Ann drew her little girl into a tight embrace. 'You do have a daddy. You know you do, but it's complicated. I'll tell you all about it when you're older.' She caught Ma's worried look. 'For now, you have me and Nana and that's all you need. Your card is beautiful. Thank you. Give your mummy a kiss.'

'Can we sing?' Daisy asked and without waiting for an answer she burst into a full operatic, out-of-tune rendition of 'Happy Birthday'. Ann and Ma covered their ears as the pitch peaked at 'dear mummy' and they patiently waited for her to finish.

'Nothing wrong with your lungs, love,' Ann said, laughing and shaking her head. 'Now tidy up the cups and plates, there's a good girl. I have to go.'

Back at home Ann thought over the conversation she'd had with Daisy. Her daughter knew things weren't normal. Every wee girl should have a daddy, shouldn't they? She didn't show

Stan the card that Daisy had made her. She didn't show him any of the cards. She left them in Sedan Avenue.

When Stan came home from the market later that day, Ann handed him a little package.

'Happy anniversary, love,' she said.

'You shouldn't have,' he said, ripping open the paper. Ann had bought him a new pipe. 'I already have two pipes,' he said. 'You can only smoke one at a time.'

'I know, but it's seven years,' she said. It seemed longer, she thought, and then scolded herself for being unkind. 'This one is curvy. It's called a Rhodesian shape. Your other ones are all straight. You could take this fancier one to the pub maybe.'

'It's very nice. Thank you, love.' He gave her a peck on the cheek. 'Is that ...?' He sniffed the air hard.

Ann nodded. 'Steak and kidney? Yes, I've made a pie.'

'Smells lovely.' He handed her his coat. 'Hang that up for me, love. I need the loo.'

Mary was upstairs reading. Arthur and Willy were spreadeagled on the living room floor. Arthur was playing with a cardboard box fort, three plastic Indians and a couple of cowboys. Willy was chewing the other cowboy.

Ann finished preparing dinner while Stan read the paper. When they had all gathered around the dining table, Ann lifted the golden, steaming pie out of the oven. Stan liked the pie so much he had a second piece, and he helped himself to more spuds, as usual. It made Ann feel good that he enjoyed her cooking so much. She did the washing up and then got the children ready for bed.

Mary was in the L-shaped room at the front of the house; the two boys shared the small room at the back. Mary read her own book while Ann read to the boys. It only took a couple of pages of *Half Magic* before Arthur and Willy were asleep. She looked in on Mary. She had fallen asleep with *Charlotte's Web* lying open on the bedspread. She kissed her on the forehead and turned her light out. For Ann, this was heaven, tucking in her three angels. It should be four, but she wasn't going to complain. She couldn't have everything; she knew that now.

Finally, she sat down. Stan was smoking one of his old pipes and reading the paper. Connie Francis was on the radio.

Ann lit a cigarette. 'Should we have a wee drink to celebrate?' she asked. 'What do you think? It's my birthday as well, remember?'

'Right enough. What age are you?'

'Thirty.'

'Happy birthday, love. You look as gorgeous as the day I met you,' he said and blew her a kiss. 'A wee drink wouldn't do any harm, and sure it's Sunday tomorrow. I'll have a wee Jameson.'

He wasn't going to move, so Ann got up and poured two whiskeys. She took a large glug out of her glass and filled it up again before she brought his over to him.

They clinked glasses.

'Happy anniversary, love,' Stan said. 'And happy birthday.'

'Happy anniversary, Stan.' She took a sip of her drink. 'The weans are asleep. It's just perfect, isn't it? Here's to the next seven years.'

'Absolutely. Cheers!' he said and he picked up his paper.

CHAPTER 33

Daisy wasn't ready. Ann didn't need Mr Stewart to sugarcoat it. He was trying to be kind. Daisy had an engaging personality, he said; she was lively and inquisitive, funny and kind. What he meant was, she was fidgety, noisy and disruptive. But when she flashed that killer smile, it was impossible to be angry with her.

The eleven plus exam consisted of four papers: General English, General Knowledge, Comprehension and Arithmetic. Daisy was quite good at all of them, but just not good enough. She would not be going to Omagh Academy, the grammar school, when she left primary school; she'd be going to the new Omagh County Secondary Intermediate School. It was less academic and more practical. Ann wished she'd had this eleven-plus thing to do.

'Don't worry, Daisy. You've done plenty of practice papers. You know you can do them,' Ann reassured her. 'Anyway, it doesn't matter which school you end up going to. You'll still learn a lot more than I ever did. Just do your best. The world isn't going to end. Nobody will die and it'll be wet again tomorrow.'

A very agitated Daisy stood in the living room in her school uniform. 'Fiona'll get a hundred. And so will Alastair. They always get a hundred.'

'Don't worry about Fiona and Alastair. Everybody's different. I bet they can't make a cup of tea like you can. We can't all be eggheads.' Ann brushed non-existent threads off Daisy's shoulders. 'It takes all sorts to make things work. Look at your Uncle Fred. He's as thick as champ, but he can make a suit out of a piece of cloth. Not everybody can do that.'

Ma chimed in. 'He *used* to be able to make a suit out of a piece of cloth. Now he's just as thick as champ.'

That got a laugh out of Daisy. 'I'm going to tell Uncle Fred what you said about him.'

Ma pretended to panic. 'Oh no, Daisy, please. Please don't say anything. I'll get into trouble.'

Daisy looked confused at the thought of her nana being in trouble. She gave her a hug. 'I won't say anything, Nana. I promise.'

'Good girl. Now, have you got everything?'

Daisy quickly rummaged through her little cloth bag. 'Yes.'

'Right, let's go,' Ann said, opening the front door.

Together, the three of them marched across the street. Ann and Ma watched Daisy disappear into the old stone school. Ann's heart melted for her wee girl. She was as bright as a button, with energy to burn, but as thick as her da.

The results arrived a few weeks later. Daisy cried for about two minutes. Then she heard the other children playing outside, and with a shriek and a scream she ran out to join them.

'She'll be fine, love,' Ma said to Ann. 'It's just a pity she doesn't take after her ma in the brains department.'

'Well, I suppose she can't have looks *and* brains.'

'You have.' Ma gave her daughter a little smile.

'Oh Ma, you say the nicest things … I suppose you want a cup of tea now?'

'You don't think I was being nice for nothing, do you? … And a piece of that apple tart you made would be good. Not too big a bit, mind.'

'Yes, Ma.'

* * *

Time did its thing, never stopping for breath. Before they knew it, it was 1962 and Jimmy Young was on the radio. *Animal Magic*, *Boss Cat* and *Blue Peter* on the TV kept the children quiet for minutes at a time.

It was also time for Willy to start school.

'Ready, love?' Ann asked him. They were standing outside the primary school gates.

He didn't look ready. He started to cry. 'Don't wanna go,' he said in between sobs.

'You have to go, Willy. Mary and Arthur go to school. They love it and so will you. You'll learn all sorts of new things and you'll make lots of new friends. You have to be brave.'

'Like a soldier?'

'Yes, love, like a soldier. And you know what brave soldiers get when they get home?'

'What Mummy?' He looked up at her, his wee face a shining picture of innocence.

'A snowball and lemonade, that's what.' Ann chucked him under the chin

He gave her a timid smile. 'I'm a soldier,' he said and puffed out his skinny chest.

'You're a *brave* soldier.'

'I'm a brave soldier,' he repeated and beamed at her.

'That's the boy. Now go on in. There's the teacher.' Mr Stewart was waiting at the front door. Ann waved at him and he waved back. 'I'll come and fetch you later and you can tell me all about it.'

'And I can have a snowball and lemonade?' Willy said.

'Yes, love.' She kissed him on the top of his head and gently ushered him through the gate.

Off he walked, his little satchel at his side. By the time he'd taken Mr Stewart's hand, he'd forgotten all about her.

So with Willy now at school, all four of Ann's children had gone to the Model, and Mr Stewart had taught all four in P1. God love him.

* * *

'Quiet!' Ann roared. 'My head's comin' off my shoulders.'

The TV was on and Valerie Singleton was making a model of Buckingham Palace out of a cornflakes box.

The two boys were squabbling over a colouring book and Mary was making it ten times worse by not letting them have the crayons – at least, not the ones they wanted.

'There's crayons there,' she said, pointing to a couple of stubby bits lying on the carpet.

'Gimme it.'

Willy made a grab for the red crayon but couldn't reach because Mary was holding it above her head. Arthur saw his chance and dived on the blue one that lay at Mary's feet.

'Give your brother the crayon. What age are you now? … Arthur! Stop it.'

By this time, Arthur was attempting to apply a hint of blue to Mary's grey school socks.

Mary kicked him away. 'That'll not come out.'

Ann turned off the TV.

'I was watching that,' Mary complained.

'You were not,' Ann said with a snort.

Willy grabbed the red crayon from Mary's hand.

'Let me tell you three hooligans something,' Ann shouted. 'Willy! Arthur! Listen. This is important.' She paused to make sure she had their full attention and put on her serious face.

They were standing in a line. 'We do not have any cornflakes, the scissors are blunt, the glue is all gunked up and it's dinner time.' The weans sniggered, trying hard not to laugh. Ann smiled at them. 'Come on, tidy up this mess, at least a wee bit. Then go and wash your hands. Be back down here looking like Christians in ten minutes or I'll—'

'What, Mummy?' Willy said.

'If you don't look like Christians in ten minutes, and I know that won't be easy, I'll ... sell one of you to Fred.'

'Which one?' Arthur asked, hopping about like an eejit.

'Me, me!' Willy had his hand up as if he was in school.

'I'll decide later,' Ann said. 'After inspection. Go. Quickly. Your da'll be home soon.'

Ann knew that the threat of being sold to Fred was not the most effective deterrent; he always carried an endless supply of sweets and chocolate.

'What's for dinner?' Arthur asked.

'Liver and onions.'

Mary grimaced and stuck her fingers in her mouth. 'I hate liver and onions.'

'You liked it last week. It's your Uncle Joe's favourite. And it's your daddy's favourite – well, one of them anyway.'

'Daddy likes everything,' Arthur pointed out.

'Still don't like it,' Mary said, pouting.

'It's either that or a slice of raw turnip,' Ann said.

Mary grinned.

'Go. I won't tell youse all again.'

'You will, Mummy.'

'Go!'

'See!'

'Scat! Now!'

They disappeared and Ann tidied up the marginally less messy mess they'd left behind.

'Only me,' Stan announced from the passageway about half an hour later. 'Something smells good.'

He handed his overcoat to Ann. She hung it on the hook behind the kitchen door. It was heavy with ice.

'Good day?' she asked.

'Just the usual,' he said. He sat down and took off his shoes. Ann handed him his slippers. She put the shoes out in the passageway to dry.

'Dinner will be ready in about five minutes. The weans are just getting washed.'

'Good. I'm starving.' Stan sniffed the air. 'Liver and onions?'

'No flies on you, Stanley Webb. I'll get some more coal. Is it still freezing out there?'

'They say it's going to last till Easter.'

'April? My God, it's never been this cold for this long.'

'Just have to stay warm. Keep the fire lit.'

Ann went back to the kitchen to finish making the dinner. She kept an eye on the onions to stop them burning and watched carefully as the thin liver slivers curled and shrank on the pan. When the edges blackened, they were ready. Then she tipped the boiled potatoes into a bowl, grabbed the butter and set it all out on the kitchen table.

She went to the bottom of the stairs and shouted: 'Dinner's ready … It's your favourite, Mary.'

She could hear Mary making gagging noises and the boys giggling as they tumbled down the stairs. Then she pretended to inspect them as they filed into the kitchen. She pointed at Willy as they sat down.

'What?' he asked, looking down at himself.

'You look perfect, son.'

Willy looked pleased with himself. Then he realised his mistake.

'So you're all safe from Fred,' Ann said. 'He'll just have to eat all his chocolate himself.'

'He'll be sick, Mummy. It would be Christian of us if we helped him not get sick,' Willy said.

'Dinner first … Come on, Mary! Don't turn your nose up. You used to like liver and onions.'

'This is a good piece of liver, Ann. Kenwall's, no doubt.' To show his appreciation, Stan shovelled a forkful into his mouth.

'Yes, I called in earlier. I wasn't going to get liver. I was thinking of tripe or kidneys.' Ann knew the reaction this would get. All three weans groaned and gagged, then giggled.

Stan smiled, enjoying the effortless banter between Ann and the children.

'I got a star today, Daddy,' Arthur announced, looking pleased as punch.

'Don't speak with your mouth full,' Stan said sternly. 'Finish your dinner. Have you got homework?'

A pat on the back wouldn't have gone amiss, Ann thought. 'All done. Isn't that right?' she said aloud. 'Sure you're the smartest weans in this house by a mile.'

'We're the only weans in this house,' Willy said.

Mary rolled her eyes at her ma's wee joke that still caught Willy out.

'See, I told you,' Ann said, giving them all a beaming smile. 'Now, tidy up your plates. You can either watch the news, read or play … quietly' – they burst out laughing – 'or go to bed with a dollop of cod liver oil. Good for your tubes.'

Mary curled up in a chair with her book, *The Wolves of Willoughby Chase*, and Arthur sprawled on the floor with *William's Treasure Trove.* Willy got out the crayons again, determined to finish colouring the clown.

An hour or so passed in relative tranquillity, Arthur and Willy silently squabbling every now and again until a glare from their father put an end to it.

'Right, it's eight o'clock. Time for bed,' Ann said eventually and she got up to turn off the TV.

'Hey, I was watching that,' Stan complained.

'And there's me thinking you were reading the paper,' Ann said.

'I was. I am. I can listen to the TV at the same time.'

Ann shook her head. Young weans were hard enough to deal with; old ones were ridiculous.

'Got your comic, Willy?' she asked.

Willy held up an old scrunched-up *Dandy.*

'Good boy. Jammies cleaned, teeth on and I'll be up in a minute with the hot water bottles.' Her new electric kettle made filling the bottles much easier – hardly a job at all.

'Mummy, that's silly! You can't put our teeth on,' Willy said with a giggle.

'Bed!' Ann shooshed them all up the stairs.

All the blankets they had were on the beds. It was hard to wriggle under the weight of them. Ten minutes later, hot water bottles were pushed in at their feet. Then Ann settled down with Arthur and Willy to read *Dr Seuss's Sleep Book*.

'It's a funny name, Mummy. How do you say it?' Arthur asked.

'Dr J*uuuu*ice,' Ann said.

'Like orange juice?' Willy mumbled, half asleep.

'Is he an orange man?' Arthur said mischievously.

'He might be, but he's an American, so he probably isn't,' Ann said.

'It would be good if he was,' Arthur said. 'He could come and march up and down and bang a big drum and then write a funny book about it.'

'He could. We'll write to him and ask him,' Ann said.

'Where would we write to?' Arthur asked.

'America, silly,' Willy said, looking pleased with himself.

'Go to sleep now.' She kissed their foreheads and turned off the light.

Then she looked in on Mary. 'You okay, love?'

'Yes, Ma.'

Ann smiled at her beautiful, cheeky daughter. 'Don't be staying up too late now.' She knew Mary would be sensible and turn off her light when she was ready. 'Night night.' She bent down to kiss the top of Mary's head.

'Night night.'

Ann went back downstairs and settled into her armchair. She lit a cigarette. Stan still had his nose in the paper.

'Oliver had some very sad news today when I was in the shop,' Ann said.

'What's that, love?' Stan muttered from behind the newspaper.

'He's leaving the band. Too old, he reckons.'

'It comes to us all. He's not sick, is he?'

'No. Just had enough of the late nights and trying to run the shop as well.'

Ann thought about Oliver and her mind drifted back to when she used to dance to his music in the Starr Ballroom. She hadn't been there for about ten years. Where had all that time gone?

'How was your ma today, love?' Stan folded up his *Daily Express* and set it on the floor at his feet. 'She must be feeling the cold.'

Ann was taken aback by his sudden concern for her mother. Stan rarely showed any interest in anything other than his own routine world.

'She's okay, I think. Her cough is definitely getting worse.'

'That house can't be healthy. It's as damp inside as it is out.'

'I mentioned it again to her about moving, but she won't hear of it. She's going out feet first, she says.'

'There's no houses coming up soon anyway, but that can change very quick.'

'Granny Smith in number three looks like she's on her last legs,' Ann said with a cheeky smile.

'Ann! That's an awful thing to say.' Stan grinned back at her. 'But you're right. I'll keep an eye out. It's all we can do.' He never asked about Daisy.

Ann had been a bit worried about Daisy. Now in her second year at the Intermediate, her daughter had been staying out a lot and Ma never knew where she was. She never seemed to have any homework and she was failing every test. Ma was at her wit's end.

'It's my fault, Ma,' Ann had said when they talked about it. 'I should have put my foot down with Stan – made him keep his promise. She needs discipline. She needs a da.'

'You can't go blaming yourself for everything that isn't perfect,' Ma had said. 'Or blame other people. Things are what they are. Daisy's young. She'll find her way. We just have to be there for her as best we can.'

'I know you're right. When are you ever wrong?'

'I've made plenty of mistakes, don't you worry.'

'We all do, but it's hard to watch her not caring about herself – about anything.'

That conversation had been a few weeks ago. Since then, Ann had tried speaking to Daisy. She'd thought her daughter wasn't listening – she'd just nodded her head – but now Daisy seemed to be stepping up and helping. She was making meals, washing up, fetching coal.

'Daisy's a great help to Ma these days,' Ann said to Stan now. 'She even goes out to break the ice in the toilet in the mornings. Then she gets angry when it freezes up again. She's learning the hard way that nothing's ever easy.'

'Just like you and I did,' Stan said, puffing on his pipe.

Always full of sympathy, Ann thought, but she said nothing.

CHAPTER 34

It was autumn and the pavements had become carpeted in slippery orange, red and gold leaves. Ma didn't go out; much too dangerous.

Daisy was hardly ever in; much too boring. But she was in bed now; much too cold.

Ma bent down and lifted a lump of coal out of the not-so-new, not-so-shiny coal scuttle. Daisy had made sure it was full for her. Ma set the large lump in at the back of the fire. She gave it a bit of a prod with the poker to try and liven it up a bit. Fred would be cold when he called round.

'Well, Kathleen, a man would need a wee dram on a night like that to warm the cockles of his heart,' Fred said when he arrived. He bent over in front of the fire and rubbed his hands together.

'Your heart's cockles are never warm,' Ma said. 'Never seen such cold cockles.'

'They're warm enough in the mornin'. They only get cold at night,' he said and he hung his coat on the hook at the back of the door like he always did.

He opened the cupboard beside *his* chair, lifted out the bottle of Bush, set two glasses on top and poured two generous measures for himself and Ma. He sat down, took a sip and let out a deep sigh. The two old friends raised their glasses and talked about their day and the latest gossip.

'There's a serious shortage of scandal at the moment, Kathleen. Mrs Chesney's husband died. Of shame probably. The funeral's tomorrow, if you fancy going. Hard to beat a good funeral.'

'That's true, but I have to finish this cardigan for Daisy. Won't be long till it's winter again.'

'Is it my imagination or does time go quicker as you get older? A week's still a week, but it only seems to last about three days.' Fred turned on the radio.

The Beatles were singing 'She loves you, yeah, yeah, yeah'.

'They play some awful stuff nowadays,' Ma said, nodding at the radio. 'Whatever happened to Kay Starr? She was a proper singer.'

'She was Ann's favourite, wasn't she?'

As if by magic, a slow waltz came on. Fred stood up and reached down to grab Ma's hand. She took it and he helped her to her feet. They danced in the flickering light of the gas lamps and the glow of the fire.

'Thank you, madam,' Fred said when the last bars of 'Moon River' had faded. He gave her a little bow.

'My pleasure, sir.'

They sat in silence for a while, puffing and wheezing, getting their breath back. Then they had another wee Bush.

'That Christine Keeler one's a right piece of work,' Fred said out of nowhere.

'I don't know much about it. Innocent till proven guilty, I say.'

‘I bet Hilda’s man, Dan, the man, knows all about it, what with them Russians up to their oxters in the middle of it.’

‘Typical toffs. Looking after their own.’

Fred set his empty glass down. ‘Right, I better go, Kathleen. It’s freezing out there. They say it’s going to be the coldest winter since last year.’

Ma smiled at the old dope. ‘And that was a cold one. It lasted right through till the summer.’

‘And now it’s winter again. Told you time was getting faster. I blame the Russians.’

‘Here, before you go, I need to go to the loo. Will you wait for me?’ Ma pulled her cardigan tightly around her shoulders.

‘Of course. Do you want me to stand guard at the door?’ Fred asked, his eyes twinkling with good humour.

‘And whistle “It’s six miles from Bangor to Donaghadee”, like you did when the weans were wee?’

‘Ahh, those were the days, Kathleen. Life was simple and a week lasted a week.’

‘It’s still simple. You get up, do what needs to be done, worry a bit and go back to bed.’

‘It is when you put it like that,’ Fred said, smiling at her.

Ma put on her coat and shoes and went out to the toilet. She wasn’t long; it was too cold to linger.

‘You’re right, Fred, it’s freezing out there,’ Ma said when she came back in, rubbing her hands together to warm them.

Fred was sitting in his chair. His pipe had slipped out of his mouth and was lying in his lap.

‘Are you asleep?’ Ma went over and lifted his pipe, tapped it out against the side of the grate and set it up in the rack.

Fred didn’t move.

‘Fred?’ She nudged him gently.

‘Nooooo!’ A high-pitched keening sound whistled out from the bottom of her soul. She shook him; his head fell to one side. ‘Fred, Fred, wake up,’ she begged. ‘Please, Fred.’

But Fred was never going to wake up again.

She kissed his forehead, then knelt beside him, put her head in his lap and cried with him for the first time in over twenty-five years, only stopping when her knees screamed at her to get up. ‘If only things had been different,’ she whispered as she gently touched his lips.

She set more coal on the fire, put her coat and woolly hat back on and sat with him all night. As the sun rose the next morning, the fire died and she woke to the sound of a wood pigeon hooting in the trees across the road at the school. She could hear Daisy moving about upstairs. Ma got Fred’s coat, kissed his forehead again and whispered ‘Goodbye, Fred.’ Then taking a deep breath, she draped his coat over him, covering his head.

From the bottom of the stairs, she called out, ‘Daisy? I need you to do something for me, love.’

Daisy came down looking bleary-eyed. It was only six o’clock. ‘Have you been down here all night, Nana?’ She spotted Fred sitting in his chair. ‘Did Uncle Fred fall asleep? Is he alright?’

Ma put her hands on Daisy’s shoulders.

Fear, doubt and panic scuttled across the girl’s face.

‘I need you to get dressed, love,’ Ma said, looking Daisy straight in the eye. ‘Make sure you put on an extra jumper. Then I want you to go up to your mummy’s house and tell her to come down here as fast as she can. Can you do that for me?’

Daisy nodded. ‘Why is Uncle Fred covered up? Will I still have to go to school?’

'Your Uncle Fred was very old, Daisy. He had a big heart, but it must have been worn out. Last night it stopped.'

'What does that mean? Will it start again?'

'No, it won't start again, love. Your Uncle Fred is dead. I need your mummy to help me now. Can you get her for me? Please?'

'Yes, I'll put on my good jumper and my school one.'

'And your woolly hat.'

'My woolly hat. Yes. Woolly hat.'

'Good girl.'

'Will I still get my chocolate?'

Ma smiled at the confused and frightened child. 'Yes, love, when you get back you can have chocolate for breakfast. What about that?'

Daisy's eyes lit up, then a cloud crossed them. 'Are you sad, Nana? Uncle Fred was your best friend.'

'Yes, Daisy. I'm sad – very sad.' Ma stifled a sob. 'I was lucky. Fred was the best friend anyone could ever have had. Now go and get dressed.'

* * *

Ann threw the front door open. 'Ma! Ma! What's happened? Are you all right? Daisy said Fred was dead.'

'I've boiled the kettle,' Ma called out from the kitchen. 'A cup of tea'll warm you up.'

'What?' Ann was initially nonplussed by Ma's calmness, but then she thought, typical Ma.

'Get me a fag, there's a good girl,' Ma said to Daisy. 'Your chocolate's on the table.'

'Found it already, Nana.' She had chocolate lipstick to prove it. She handed her nana a half-empty pack of Embassy and a box of matches.

Ann made tea. Ma looked exhausted; old and ashen-faced.

'We were just chatting,' Ma explained once she had another hot cup of tea in her hand. 'Just stuff and nonsense as usual. He said he thought he should go, even if it was a bit early, cos it was so cold and slippy. I went out to the loo. When I came back, his pipe was in his lap.' She sat there for a moment, deep in thought. 'I thought he had fallen asleep,' she said quietly. Tears trickled down her face. 'I put my coat on and sat with him all night. Then Daisy got up and went and got you.'

'You're a good girl, Daisy,' Ann said. She was proud of her. 'No need to be scared.'

'I'm not scared, Mummy. Uncle Fred is in heaven. But I am sad. He was Nana's best friend and he brought chocolate. He was nice.'

'Here, listen, you need to get ready for school. Have you any room for porridge after all that chocolate?'

Daisy shook her head. Ann was glad she wouldn't have to make it.

'Are you all right, Ma?' she asked.

Ma nodded, but she looked shell-shocked.

'I need to go and get the weans off to school,' Ann said. 'Then I'll go and tell Fred's brothers. I imagine they'll go to Porter's.'

Ma was silent.

'Is that okay, Ma?'

Ma nodded.

Ann lifted Fred's duncher and kissed his baldy head. She couldn't stop the tears. 'Oh Ma.'

Ma stood up and they hugged and cried together.

'We'll be all right, love. Go and do what you have to do. I'll stay with him.'

CHAPTER 35

'She's had to grow up very quickly. I think she's surprised even herself,' Ann said.

'That's good.' Stan finished his tea. 'I always said they got on like a house on fire. It's good to see Daisy helping out.'

'Are you going to the mart?' Ann asked, knowing rightly he was going. He always went on a Saturday morning.

'Yes, I'm meeting a chap called Jack Boyce. He's from Donegal, up near Malin. He says he knows my da.'

'Plenty to chat about then. I'll walk down with you, if that's all right.' Ann went to the bottom of the stairs. 'Mary?'

'Yes, Ma?'

'I want you up by the time I get back. Make sure those other two eejits put their trousers on the right way up. And knickers on the *inside*, please.' She could hear the boys giggling.

'Yes, Ma. Can Daisy come up to listen to records? Can we do some more tests?' Mary asked. She had the eleven-plus coming up the following year and she loved doing the practice tests.

'Yes and yes. Make sure you all clean your teeth. No donkey-breath allowed.'

'Yes, Ma,' chorused all three.

'And toothbrushes are for your teeth. Don't stick them anywhere else.'

'Yes, Ma,' they chorused.

'And socks before shoes, remember.'

'Yes, Ma,' they chorused again, laughing this time.

Ann heard the bathroom door close and the bolt click into place. Good girl, she thought to herself.

* * *

Daisy made the tea and brought in digestives with the regulation thick layer of butter sandwiched between them.

'Is it okay if I go up to see Mary?' she asked her ma.

'Yes, she's expecting you. I know music's better loud, but don't deafen the neighbours.'

'No, Ma,' she said, giving her a cheeky grin.

'Do you fancy going out for a wee walk?' Ann asked Ma. 'Get some air about ye.'

'Daisy and I went out this morning, didn't we, love?'

Daisy nodded and sucked on the straw in her bottle of Coke. 'They've started knocking down the shops for the new bridge,' she said. 'Slevin's is gone already.'

'There's four of them going, isn't there?' Ann said.

'Anderson's, Adrian's and Nora Mullan's are all roped off. We got some sausages off Oliver on the way back. Then Cokes in Devlin's and then two snowballs.' Daisy looked pleased with herself.

'Two snowballs? Where's my snowball?' Ann feigned outrage.

'They're for later, when there's just me and Nana. We listen to the radio. Nana doesn't like a lot of the new stuff, but there's some good ones, isn't there, Nana?'

'I like that one – "The Chapel of Love",' Ma said.

'You've never been in a chapel in your life!'

'It's not a proper chapel,' Daisy said. 'Nana says it's American, so it doesn't count.'

'Are you going to get ready to go up to Johnston Park?' Ann asked, wondering why Daisy wasn't getting a move on.

'She has something to tell you first, haven't you, Daisy,' Ma said.

'Don't be cross, Mummy ... but you know how I'm no good at school and I hate it?'

Ann nodded. 'Go on.'

'Well, I'm leaving. I'm leaving as soon as I can. I'm going to get a job and look after Nana.'

Ann wasn't surprised. In fact, she was delighted, but she didn't want Daisy to see that – not just yet.

'You've obviously thought about this,' Ann said solemnly.

'Yes, I hate school. I can't wait to leave.'

'Well, you'll have to wait till the end of this school year. Fifteen next August! Hard to believe. What do you think, Ma?'

'You were working when you were fifteen and so was I,' Ma said.

'You told me you started work when you were five.' Ann smiled.

Daisy laughed. 'What age *were* you when you started work, Nana?'

'Ten. I worked in a laundry.'

'That must have been hard.' Daisy sounded really grown up.

Ann was full of renewed admiration for the old worn-out woman in the old worn-out cardigan.

'We didn't know any different then,' Ma went on. 'I worked there till I got married.' She stopped and looked away. The shutters had come down again.

'Any idea what you might want to do for a job?' Ann asked Daisy.

'I want to be a pop star like Dusty Springfield. I want to be on *Top of the Pops*.'

'Top of the what? What's that when it's at home?' Ma asked, looking mischievous.

'It's on TV. All the singers and groups go on it. The Beatles are on it and even Elvis sometimes.'

Ann wondered if it was only the music her daughter liked. 'Right, so pop star it is then, but you might need something to tide you over in the meantime. I'll start asking around.'

'Will you, Ma? That would be great.' Daisy gave Ann a quick hug.

'We'll get you sorted out, won't we, Ma.'

'There's always work for those that want it.' Ma pointed a finger at Ann and nodded. Ann took the cue.

'And you'll soon find out that a shilling in your pocket is your best friend. Now go. Mary's waiting for you. She has that new record by the Honeycombs.'

'Their drummer is a girl. I could be a drummer,' Daisy said, her face lighting up.

'You could, dear. Anything is possible. It's good to have dreams. Now go.'

Ann stayed with Ma until nearly lunchtime. She thought she might pass Daisy on the way home, but she didn't. There was vegetable broth for lunch, so it didn't take long to get ready when Stan arrived about ten minutes after she did.

In the afternoon, the boys watched whatever sport was on TV, just so long as it wasn't horse racing. Stan put his paper down when the wrestling came on. They all booed at Mick McManus and cheered on Big Daddy.

Ann and Mary were out in the kitchen doing more practice tests. Just as the football scores were being announced, somebody knocked the door. Stan got up and, with a smile on his face, put his fingers to his lips. The boys' faces gleamed with excitement. A secret!

Stan spoke to a man at the door but didn't invite him in. After a few minutes the door closed, and Stan came back in and sat down.

Ann heard the front door close and came out to ask who had been at the door.

'It was Jack … Jack Boyce,' Stan said. 'Remember I told you I was meeting him this morning?'

'What did he want?'

'He wanted a hundred pounds.'

Ann looked at Stan, a man she sometimes thought she didn't know at all. He didn't do jokes. And he was careful with money. 'Why would he—'

'He wants a hundred pounds for the car I've just bought off him,' Stan announced, looking jubilant.

The noise that ensued went beyond what three small humans could possibly be expected to make as the children screamed and danced around the room. Stan covered his ears. Ann did the same. She had never seen Stan look so happy, other than maybe on their wedding day and the days the children were born.

It was nice of him to discuss it with her first, she thought, and then scolded herself for being churlish. Cars are men's things and Stan looked after the money. He wouldn't have bought it if he couldn't afford it. One hundred pounds was a lot of money though.

'You never said you were buying a car,' Ann said.

'I didn't know until there now. We talked about lots of things down the mart and it just sort of came up. I went to have a look at it. He wanted a hundred and fifty. I said I only had a hundred and he said he needed to think about it and would let me know. That was him letting me know. You didn't think I did *spur of the moment*, did you?'

'No, I must admit, it's a surprise. A big surprise ... a good surprise. A great surprise. What sort of car is it?'

'It's a Borgward Isabella.'

Ann and the children looked completely bewildered.

'A what? A buggered Isabella?' Arthur said, giggling.

'Don't swear at your father,' Ann chided him, smiling.

'It's German. It's second-hand, of course, but it's only just about run-in. Only four thousand miles on the clock. It's like new. A real new one would cost over five hundred quid, so it's a bit of a bargain.'

'When are you getting it?' Ann asked, genuinely thrilled. 'More importantly, what colour is it?'

'It's black with red seats. It's got a cigarette lighter and a clock. Not many cars have those. It's only got two doors. Four would have been better, but it can do up to eighty miles per hour! Jack's going to clean it. He says I can pick it up tomorrow after church. What do youse think?'

'Can we, Mummy? Can we?'

They were all hopping round her. It was like a school for whirling dervishes.

She put a finger to her chin and frowned. 'I don't know now. There's the washing and I have all that ironing to finish. And I want to wash my hair.' But her face cracked into a big grin when she saw the children's disappointment. 'Of course we can,' she said and the noise went through the roof again.

Stan was beaming.

* * *

After church the next day, Ann shepherded the children outside. They looked like angels in their Sunday best. *It was a pity there was only one Sunday in a week,* Ann thought. Stan didn't do church. He would be waiting for them to get back so they could all go and get the new car. Winter was keeping its powder dry, and all the chat after church was about how the good weather wasn't going to last. The previous year, Ann wouldn't have been surprised to see a polar bear walking up Sedan Avenue, but today was beautiful.

'Come on, my little treasures,' she said. 'The sooner we get home, the sooner we can go and get the new car.'

They trooped home along Fairmount Road, down the Kevlin Road, then left up a little hill into the top end of Johnston Park. Gracy's egg factory was below them on the left. A wee right turn and their house came into view. Outside, a beautiful black car was gleaming in the winter sun. The children took off like the Lone Ranger chasing baddies on a Saturday morning.

Stan heard the banshees and came out of the house. He looked like all his Christmases had come at once.

'Jack brought it round. Saves us all walking down to Campsie. I thought it would be a nice surprise.'

'You're getting good at surprises, Stanley Webb. Should I be worried?' Ann nudged him. 'We agreed that three was enough.'

Stan laughed, not something he did often. It was a grunting, hacking sort of noise.

He unlocked the doors and tipped the passenger seat forward. It was hard to tell one child from the other as they wriggled in, a tangle of limbs and heads that somehow ended up facing in the right direction in a neat row in the back.

Stan pushed the front seat back in place and held the passenger door for Ann.

'Thank you, sir.'

'You're welcome, madam.' The door clunked shut.

'Can we go for a spin, Daddy?'

'Please, Daddy.'

'Pleeeeese.' Willy had leaned forward. He was half an inch from Stan's ear.

'What will the neighbours think, us out enjoying ourselves on the sabbath,' Stan said, trying to suppress a smile.

'They'll be thinking, I wish we had a buggered Isabella,' Ann said, watching out for twitching curtains.

'Borgward. It's a Borgward.' But Stan couldn't help laughing.

He pulled out the choke and turned the key. There was a deep satisfying rumble as the engine fired. Then he pushed the choke back in and they were off. The car was facing down the park, so that's the way they went, towards Scarffe's Entry.

'Will it fit up the entry?' Ann asked as they passed the clinic.

Arthur waved at a group of boys playing football in front of the Academy. 'I hope they saw it was me,' he said.

'Squeeze in, weans. This'll be a tight fit,' Ann called out as they approached the narrow entry.

The three of them squeezed into the middle of the back seat. Willy disappeared, but they could hear him squealing with joy – at least, Ann hoped it was joy and not suffocation.

The car glided up the steep little hill with an inch to spare on each side. The coal and timber yards were shut. Bob Campbell's shop was shut. Stan edged the bonnet of the car out into Market Street, turned left and then right into Bridge Street.

'We're going to see Nana and Daisy,' Mary shrieked.

'Whoever's first to learn to speak quietly will get a prize,' Ann said.

'What's the prize, Mummy?' Willy whispered.

'What? You'll have to speak up, love. It's very noisy.'

'Mummy! What's the prize?'

'The prize is … no toenail cutting for a week.'

'That's not a prize!'

'It's better than a poke in the eye with a burnt stick.'

'You'll need a better prize, Mummy,' Willy shouted and the noise got worse.

They crossed Bell's Bridge and turned left down Sedan Avenue.

'Doot the horn, Daddy,' Willy demanded.

As he tooted the horn, the door of No. 12 opened and Daisy raced out. Ma stood in the doorway. Ann got out of the car and the children fell out in a pile.

Ann looked at Daisy. She looked amazed that this shiny machine was theirs. Then she thought, it won't take her long to work out there's only room in the back for three.

'Do you want to go for a spin?' Ann asked Ma and Daisy. 'Daisy, you get in the back. Let Ma go in the front. Mary, do you want to go in the back with Daisy? … You two heathens can wait here with me.' The boys groaned their disappointment. 'You'll have plenty of goes.'

Ma closed the front door of No. 12. 'I hope the neighbours are watching,' she whispered proudly to Ann.

‘Of course, they’re watching,’ Ann said. As if their ears were burning, Mrs McGartland appeared and three other front doors opened. Perfect, Ann thought with a smile. Ma straightened her back and tidied her hair.

‘You look like the Queen of Sheba, Kathleen,’ Jean McGartland said with a smirk.

‘Lovely car!’ Pat came over for a closer look. ‘Borgward’ – he read the word off the boot. He nodded knowingly as if he knew what this was and approved.

Ma struggled to get in, but with a little gentle poking and prodding, she got settled in her seat and the door was closed. Everyone waved as the car drove off. It was like a wedding, only cheaper.

CHAPTER 36

'SANTA!'

The shriek from the boys' room woke Ann. She sighed and rolled over. Stan snored on, oblivious. She could hear the whispered noises of the children, now trying to be quiet. She put on her slippers and dressing gown and went to see what was going on.

'There must be somewhere in the world where Santa comes *after* breakfast. He can't be everywhere at half three in the morning,' Ann said, still bleary-eyed.

'He can, Mummy, cos he's magic. He has to come when you're asleep.' Willy was ripping green holly-patterned paper off a box.

'It would be a bit odd if he appeared down the chimney when you're having your toast,' Mary said. 'The fire would be lit. He'd burn his bum.'

'Exactly,' Arthur said emphatically.

Mary brought her presents into the boys' room, which was now full of shredded wrapping paper. There was Santa and snowmen confetti everywhere.

'A cowboy outfit!' Willy yelled in delight.

'Is your gun the same as mine?' Arthur asked, pulling his trigger. There was a loud click.

They had both got exactly the same – sheriff badges and holsters; cap guns with strips of blue caps that popped loudly; white hats. They were goodies, after all.

Mary had got a small transistor radio. It cost about ten times as much as the boys' stuff put together. Now she could listen to what *she* wanted. She turned it on. Thoughtful old Santa had even put batteries in. It hissed static.

'Nothing on yet, love. The wee men in the radio aren't awake at this hour.' Ann caught Willy's eye; he looked as if he was about to ask about the wee men, but then understanding cleared the question off his face. He smiled at his ma. Ann smiled back.

She escaped the whirlwind and went downstairs to make a cup of tea. As the kettle boiled, she hoked in a cupboard and pulled out her present for Stan. It wasn't very well hidden. He never looked in the kitchen cupboards. She tucked it under one arm and carried up mugs of tea for them both.

Stan was awake by the time she got upstairs. 'What time is it?' he mumbled.

'Half four. Santa came about an hour ago.'

'That was good of him.'

'Tea?' She set his tea down on the locker on his side of the bed and handed him the small flat present. It was wrapped neatly in grown-up black and gold paper. 'I hope you like it,' she said.

He turned it around in his hands and gave it a good feel.

Ann got back into bed. 'Open it.'

Stan neatly opened one end and slipped the contents out.

'Driving gloves!'

'Do you like them?' she asked. She knew what was coming next.

'You shouldn't have,' Stan said. 'We agreed. Only the weans.'

You agreed, she thought. 'I know, but what with the new car and all. That steering wheel must be freezing. They're real leather.'

'They're lovely.'

'They only had black or red. I didn't think you were a red-gloves type of man.'

'Thank you. Happy Christmas, Mrs Webb,' Stan said.

'Happy Christmas, Mr Webb,' she said and leaned over and kissed him.

Stan set down the gloves and reached for Ann under the blankets.

'Stan! Not now,' she said, giggling.

'Why not? It's Christmas.'

She couldn't stop him, not that she really wanted to. His grunts and groans were drowned out by the cacophony of the gunfight at the O.K. Corral. It sounded like Mary was the damsel in distress.

Afterwards, Ann tidied herself up and went in to see if there were any survivors. The scene before her eyes was magical, full of joyful wonder and excitement.

'Try and quieten down a bit,' Ann said. 'Take a book back to bed for a while.'

They looked at her as if she was mad.

'Can we open a selection box?'

'You're pushing it, Arthur Webb. Chocolate at this hour? Unheard of. Probably illegal.'

They looked theatrically glum.

'Until now,' she added, knowing she'd been outmanoeuvred. But she loved it.

They roared their approval.

'One piece each. I have them counted.'

'They're not even opened yet.'

'Doesn't matter. I'll know. I know everything, don't I?'

'Yes, Mummy.'

'Right, a bit of peace and quiet for about five hours and then we'll have toast.'

The weans all giggled.

Stan lit the fire. The grill went on after the shortest five hours on record. They all loved Marmite except Stan. He was a thick-cut marmalade man. *Very appropriate,* Ann thought. The toast was served on plates in the living room because every surface in the kitchen and the dining table was laden with dinner stuff.

'Put on your Christmas record, Mummy.' Willy's face was covered in chocolate and Marmite.

Ann turned the Dansette on, slipped the LP out of its glossy outer sleeve, then the inner paper one and, holding the edges of the disc between the palms of her hands, she carefully put it on the spindle. She clicked the switch, the record dropped down and began to spin. Then the arm lifted and moved across, and the needle settled on the disc.

The honeyed tones of Jim Reeves singing 'Silver Bells' filled the room. They were transfixed. They played both sides of the LP.

'I like the Christmas card one,' Arthur said, reading the sleeve notes. 'It says "An old Christmas Card" and then in brackets "Horton". What does that mean, Mummy?'

'It means the song was written by a man called Horton.'

'You really do know everything, Mummy,' Mary said.

Ann nodded and smiled. 'Correct.'

She got up and put on her coat, gloves, shoes and woolly hat.

'I'm going down to get Daisy and your nana. Be good and take it in turns to shout, rather than doing it all at once. Your daddy's in charge. Isn't that right, Daddy?'

Stan grunted, poked the fire and puffed his pipe.

Ma and Daisy were ready by the time Ann got there. Daisy had got new sensible shoes for work.

'Nana says not to wear them today, which is fair enough. But I will eventually need to wear them a wee bit every day till they soften up.'

'Bring your selection box,' Ann said. 'And Mary will love to read that *Jackie* annual.'

But before they set off for Johnston Park, Ma and Ann wanted to go to the phone box. Speaking to Muriel was still a big part of their Christmas ritual. Daisy waited for them outside.

Muriel, now a full-time mother and a socialite, brought them up to speed. Everyone's cards had arrived in time, even Joe's. He was now working in London, at the new Admiralty Board in Whitehall no less. Hilda and Dan were in Vancouver. Hilda thought they'd be staying there permanently, but who knew. Jimmy was playing the guitar and seemed to be very good at it. Al was head man in the Maudsley Hospital now.

'You can tell Al that your Uncle Louis isn't very well,' Ma said. 'He's going to have to retire soon. His tubes are blocked. His cub Jim is out in Rhodesia in the Department of Agriculture. He says they grow a lot of tobacco. Fags must be about a penny a packet out there.'

'Al will be sorry to hear that – about Uncle Louis, I mean, not about Jim. He was always a clever cub. Mine must take after Al, cos she knows about things that I didn't even know were things. She was talking to her da the other day about a spaceship that's going to take pictures of Mars. Mars! I mean.'

'The only thing my weans know about Mars is that one a day helps you work, rest and play,' Ann chipped in.

'They forget about the rest bit very easily,' Ma said with a smile.

They filled the time with happy chatter, sending season's greetings to everyone. When the operator asked for more money, it was time to go.

'Ho! Ho! Ho! Let's go,' Ann said, letting the phone box door swing shut behind them.

Daisy bounced up off the bench she'd been sitting on. 'At last! My bum's frozen solid.'

'Good, that'll keep it quiet for a while.'

'Mummy!' Daisy rolled her eyes.

Ann put an arm around her daughter's shoulders and the three of them walked slowly through the quiet streets to Johnston Park.

When she got home, Ann thought she'd walked into the wrong house. The two boys were quietly playing a game on the back of a selection box, Mary was reading her *Bunty* annual and Stan was dozing in his chair. The fire was a low glow in the grate.

'What happened here?' Ann asked. 'I can see the carpet. Did the Christmas angels call round?'

'I tidied up,' Mary said, looking up.

Arthur squirmed round onto his back. 'We helped too,' he said.

'I'm sure you did, love. What did you do?' Ann looked at Willy who was still moving his counter on the game.

'Mary said the best way I could help was to stay out of the way. So I did.'

'Well, son, you did it really well.'

'Yes. I'm good at it.'

'Course you are, love.'

Stan roused himself. 'Hello, Kathleen. Happy Christmas! Did Santa come to Sedan Avenue then?'

'Happy Christmas to you too, Stan,' Ma said. 'Santa brought me a box of Milk Tray, which was a real surprise. Just like it is every year. And new slippers. Very cosy. Fags, of course. And a bottle of Bristol Cream.' She patted the bag she was holding. 'Was he good to you?'

Stan laughed, a real pipe-smoker's chortle. 'He was indeed. A year's supply of pipe cleaners and a lovely pair of driving gloves.' He reached down beside his chair and held the gloves up for inspection.

'It's a lovely car, so it is,' Ma said.

Daisy was standing quietly near the door. 'I got new shoes,' she said.

Mary and the boys looked at her feet.

'Not these. I'm not wearing them cos they need to be worn in and they're for work.'

'But you can't start work till the summer,' Mary pointed out.

'They'll be well broken in by that time,' Daisy said with a smile. 'I got the *Jackie* annual too.'

Mary held up her *Bunty*.

'Are "The Four Marys" in it?' Daisy asked.

'They're the first story.' Mary loved 'The Four Marys'. She imagined she was Mary Simpson, the poor but clever girl at the posh school.

Daisy and Mary started to talk enthusiastically about the story and the two of them disappeared upstairs.

'You could have said something to Daisy,' Ann said, staring at Stan. 'You could at least have asked her what Santa brought.'

'She told us what Santa brought. Shoes and a book. What more do we need to know?'

Ann caught Ma's eye as she sat down. She thought Ma looked diminished somehow, tired and sad. It had been over a year since Fred died and although Ma never said as much, Ann knew she missed him like mad. This was the first time ever that she hadn't spent Christmas Day in Sedan Avenue. Last year, after Fred's death, Ma had wanted to stay at home, where all her memories were, but she couldn't face it this year. It was also the first time Daisy had spent more than a short time with her brothers and sister.

Stan was under strict orders never to say the word 'half-sister'. His disinterest was bad enough, but he was left in no doubt that referring to her as a half-sister would be crossing a serious line.

'Is it too early for a wee sherry?' Ann asked, trying to lift the mood. The children were too quiet, too calm. She preferred the whirlwind and the noise.

Ma's eyes twinkled. 'Never too early, Fred always said.'

'Fred was a wise old owl. I'll get the glasses. Stan?'

'It's only half ten,' Stan said, looking at the clock on the mantelpiece.

'But it feels like half six!' Ann said.

'Go on then. It's Xmas after all,' Stan conceded.

Ann went out to get the drinks. She thought it was very posh that they had proper little sherry glasses.

She handed one to Ma and one to Stan. 'I've put the oven on,' she announced as she sat down with her own.

'What time will the dinner be ready then?' Stan asked and took a sip.

'About two-ish.'

'The Queen's on at three,' Ma said, licking her lips. She'd finished her sherry.

'We can have the plum duff after the Queen. If we have it in here, we can watch the circus.'

Ann put Jim Reeves on again. It was the best Christmas record ever, she thought to herself. As Jim started into 'Blue Christmas', her thoughts drifted, as they often did when she listened to music. The Christmas dance in the Courthouse – had it really been fifteen years ago?

They had a choice of Mateus Rosé or Black Tower wine with their dinner; the children had Ribena.

'They're lovely bottles,' Ann commented. 'I'll maybe stick candles in them afterwards.'

There wasn't enough room for them all at the dining table, so Daisy and Mary had their dinner on trays in the living room. The boys stayed with the grown-ups. Ma sat beside Willy and Arthur was opposite, nearly but not quite out of kicking reach.

Ann got up to go and see if the girls were all right and listened in to their chatter from the doorway. It brought back memories of her and Iris in the Cake Shop a lifetime ago.

After dinner, Daisy volunteered to help with the dishes. The fire had been lit for ages and there would be plenty of hot water.

'We'll soak the pans and stuff first,' Ann said. 'Just stack the plates and cutlery on the table. Let's go and listen to the Queen.'

Once the speech was over, Daisy followed Ann back out to the kitchen.

'Do you not want to watch the circus?' Ann asked.

'I don't like clowns,' she said. 'They're for babies.'

'Your nana thinks they're funny.'

'That's different.'

'Why?'

'She's Nana. She's special.'

Ann looked at the serious teenager trying to be a grown-up and laughed.

'What are you laughing at?' Daisy asked, not sure whether to be offended or not.

Ann wiped a pink Brillo Pad sud off Daisy's cheek. 'I'm just proud of you, that's all. All grown up – doing the dishes, going to work. It's great.'

'What was in this? It's mingin'.' Daisy held a small pan out at arm's length.

'Let me see? ... That would be the cranberry sauce. It caught a wee bit on the bottom. Just let it soak again – for a day or two.'

Daisy smiled. 'A year or two maybe.'

'I have to go to the loo.' Ann set her lit cigarette down in the ashtray. 'I'll not be long.' When she came back, she caught Daisy glugging the dregs of the Black Tower.

'Have you finished?' Ann asked, not letting on she had seen anything.

'Yep.' Daisy looked proud of herself as she spread a damp drying cloth over the back of a chair to dry.

'Good girl. The plates and all will be a doddle after that. Let's have a wee break first.'

Ann picked up her cigarette. It looked a good two drags shorter. She said nothing, but Daisy's eyes flicked away and she knew that Daisy knew she knew.

Foreign-looking madmen were leaping about on the backs of white horses when Ann and Daisy went back into the living room. The boys were lying on the floor on their bellies staring at the TV as if hypnotised. Their *Dandy* and *Victor* annuals lay beside them. Mary was glued to the telly as well and Stan was puffing his pipe. Ma was dipping into the Milk Tray. Daisy went over to her and lifted a chocolate out of the box.

'I know you don't like the coffee ones, Nana,' she said and flashed her killer smile.

Ann didn't like the fudge ones in her Black Magic, but Willy, the weirdo, seemed to love them. He liked everything.

The noises, the smells, the togetherness. Ann couldn't help reminiscing, as Jim Reeves would say. It reminded her of Christmas when she was wee, but it wasn't the same. She missed Fred, with his chocolate decorations and secret sixpences. They had a TV now, she thought, yet she knew she'd swap it for Fred any day. She wondered if Fred had ever seen a TV.

With Daisy's help, she finished the dishes. She was careful to leave almost a whole cigarette burning in the ashtray when she nipped out of the kitchen for a moment. When she came back, she put her arm around Daisy's shoulder as the girl stood drying the gravy jug.

'What's that for?' Daisy asked. 'What are you after?' She sounded spookily like Ann when Walter had been nice to her.

'Nothing. It's been a lovely day, that's all, and you've been a great help. We're a good team.'

There was cold turkey, ham and stuffing for supper with lots of salt, accompanied by Christmas songs on the radio. Stan and Ma were competing to see who could snore the loudest. The children were reading their annuals, Willy giggling at something in the *Dandy*. The Rolling Stones came on – Mick Jagger was singing about being a little red rooster. Arthur pricked up his ears, put his annual down and stuck his ear to the radio. He'd have turned the volume up if he could have got away with it.

Ann, meanwhile, knew how the rooster felt. She couldn't have crowed right now even if she'd been paid to. But somehow she stirred herself.

'Right, we better think about heading. Ma! Ma!' She went over and gently touched her on the shoulder. Ma snorted. The children all burst out laughing.

'We better go, Ma. It looks like it's bucketing out there. Coats, hats, gloves.' Daisy pretended to pick up Stan's new driving gloves. Ann grinned at her cheeky daughter.

'Can you little Christmas angels go and get your jammies on? I want you ready for bed by the time I get back or else.'

'Or else what, Mummy?' Willy asked innocently.

'Or else I'll pull your ears off and dip them in my tea.'

The boys scattered, giggling.

'You can have a bit of peace and quiet for a while now, love,' Ann said to Stan.

Stan grunted. 'Chance would be a fine thing.'

Ann shook her head. Tough life being the man of the house, she thought. She lifted his empty glass. 'Refill?'

'Why not.'

Daisy chattered the whole way to Sedan Avenue. Ann tried to listen. It was stuff about work and having a shilling in her pocket and Elvis Presley. But Ma was quiet, and Ann wondered what she was thinking about.

At No. 12, the fire was out, of course, and the house was cold.

'I'll get the kettle on for hot water bottles,' Daisy said, running out to the kitchen.

'Will you be okay, Ma?' Ann asked. 'Will you be warm enough?'

'Don't worry about me, love. You shouldn't worry at all at Christmas. I've had enough Bristol Cream to knock me out. It was lovely, wasn't it?'

'It was, Ma. The whole day was lovely.' Ann kissed her on the forehead.

Daisy came back with the jars filled. Ann couldn't have been prouder.

Back home in Johnston Park, Ann slumped into her chair. 'I hope Ma had a good day … She was exhausted when she got home. They were going straight to bed … I thought she was a bit sad. Bound to be, I suppose. Bound to still miss Fred. *I* still miss Fred … It was great craic all the same, wasn't it? And them acrobats acrobating like lunatics. Rather them than me, is all I can say … Dinner was good. Not much left over, which is a good sign.'

Stan grunted. 'Yes, love. You must be exhausted yourself.'

'I'm okay,' she said, amazed that he had noticed.

She put the telly back on. *Xmas with the Stars* was on, but the Black and White Minstrels were drowned out by record-breaking snoring. Ma could never have beaten that, Ann thought, smiling. So she sat there on her own, listening to Stan's snores over the top of the TV. She lit a cigarette and had another wee drink.

'Happy Christmas, Blondie,' she whispered, toasting the air.

CHAPTER 37

'Happy Birthday, Blondie. Thirty-five today. Never thought you'd make it, but here we are. Do you get old up there, or are you always the age you were when you went in? I've probably asked that before, but I've forgotten. So what have you been up to?'

Ann knelt down at the side of the grave. She'd brought an old towel, so she wouldn't get her knees dirty. 'Did you know the trains have stopped? I know they always stopped at the station. That's not what I mean. I wish they'd stopped that day you decided to walk into one … No, this is different. They're stopped for good. Forever. No more trains to Omagh. Can you believe it? Some eejit over in London decided that stopping the trains would save them a few bob. The last one was yesterday. Good job you're not up in the Royal now. There's the bus, I suppose, but it stops at every hole in the hedge. And how do you get all them people onto a bus?

'I met your da the other week. He looks old, but I suppose he is old, so that's all right. He said he was doing okay. He said your ma is too, but she gets confused easily nowadays and doesn't go out much. Your da is going to retire. No option really. He's going to look after your ma. It's all very sad.

'Daisy is leaving school this year. She'll be fifteen in August. It's the right thing for her. She's not thick or anything – not as thick as you, anyway – she just finds it hard to concentrate. She's started asking questions about why she has no da. Having no da is the problem. Stan's a good man, you know he is, and he's great with the other three, but he doesn't seem to know what to say to Daisy. He's a man – hard and tough and stupid … I love you and I love that we had Daisy, but why did you walk into that van? Even worse, why did you walk into that train? I mean, there's thick and there's thick, but walking into big hard things – twice! That takes the biscuit.

'Christmas was good except Ma is still missing Fred. I'm sure I told you, he died just sitting in his chair. Good way to go, I suppose. Better than walking into a train anyway. Do you have Christmas? Must be a big thing up there, I'd have thought – for the Christians anyway. Don't know what the others all do. Maybe they're not even there, or they're in a separate room or something.

'I'm keeping well, thanks for asking. I get the odd dance down at the Legion. Some are a lot odder than others. Remember your old mate John? Used to go out with Doreen? He goes to the Legion now and again. He used to be a half-decent dancer. In fact, I nearly dumped you for him, but he was too clever and far too good-looking. Anyway, he can't put one foot in front of the other now. He's not as bad as you were after your accident, but nearly. He's been flirting with me, trying to chat me up. Can't blame him, I suppose. I'm still as gorgeous as ever, aren't I? Say yes or I won't come back.

'Joe is married ... again. I know it's hard to keep up. Second time lucky, eh? Hilda has a pet polar bear that speaks Russian, and Muriel and Al have bought a flat in St John's Wood ... I had to ask as well: it's a very posh part of London. No, I'm not jealous. Why would I be? We have a new telly. So there. What more could you want!

'How's Daisy? You might well ask. Well, she's beautiful, like her ma. She might be useless at school, but she's good at helping her nana and doing stuff around the house. She's such a kind soul. She's a bit wild. She sneaks a wee drink and a smoke now and again, but didn't we all at her age. And I think she's seeing boys – older boys. Ugly ones with black hair. It's not good. What should I do, eh?' Ann grabbed the top of the headstone.

'I have to stand up, Walter. My knees are busted.' She pushed herself up and leaned against the stone. 'What's that? Just be her ma? You're right. I'll be her ma, no matter what, like my ma did for me. That's all I can do. Good man, Walter. I knew you'd have the answer. I think you might have got a bit smarter since you died. Wouldn't be hard, would it?'

Ann shook the dirt from the towel.

'Anyway, I've got to go. Husband to wash, weans to cook. Never a dull moment.'

She kissed her fingers and touched the headstone with them. Then she fumbled in her handbag and took out the crumpled photograph. 'I love you, Walter Green,' she said and kissed it.

Walter whispered in the breeze.

'Go on, you dipstick,' she said. 'I'll be back soon.'

CHAPTER 38

Stan took his pipe out of his mouth and sat up. Ann knew that something serious was coming.

'Don't tell the weans just yet, but I was thinking that maybe we could go for a wee run in the car at Easter. What do you think?'

Ann spluttered into her tea. She set the mug down on the hearth. This really *was* serious. And very rare, on two counts. Firstly, Stan hardly ever spoke after he'd had his dinner, and secondly, he hardly ever had ideas. He must have thoughts, Ann surmised. He probably just never let them out. They maybe spun around in his head until he thought of something else, and then that spun around for a while until it disappeared.

'Where did this lovely idea come from, Stanley Webb?' Ann asked. 'Is it a birthday present?'

Stan blushed and Ann realised he'd forgotten again. 'No,' he said. 'Willy called me at work the other day. Da's had to go into hospital and I thought we could go up and see him and stay for a couple of days. Make a weekend of it.'

'You never said about your da. Why didn't you tell me?'

'I was waiting to see if he was going to be in for long, but Spider says he might have to stay in. For good maybe.' Stan set his pipe down. 'He's in a geriatric ward for the bewildered. He was forever wanting to leave the house to go and see his ma in Malin. I mean, she died years ago. They couldn't leave him in the house.'

'Oh Stan, that's desperate. You should have said.'

'I just did.'

'I know, but you should have said earlier. A problem shared and all that. I could have got Ma to do extra worrying. That always helps.'

Stan smiled. 'Willy says we could go and stay with them in The Roddens. It's a lovely big house and we could take the weans to Drains Bay and go on the wee ferry to Islandmagee. Dixon Park is just out the back. It has a roundabout and swings and all for them to play on.'

'And you could go and see your da,' Ann added.

'You'd have to come with me. I wouldn't know what to say to him.'

'You big eejit! You just talk to him. I've had a bit of practice talking to the bewildered. Of course I'll come with you. That's what wives are for.'

'Talking of wives, Charlotte, Spider's wife, can look after the weans. And they have a dog.'

'Oh, they'll love that.'

'It's just a puppy. An Alsatian, I think. They call him Lassie.'

'Very imaginative.' Ann grinned at Stan who was clearly struggling with it all. 'It sounds like a plan,' she said reassuringly.

In the twelve years since their honeymoon, they had never been away anywhere. This was exciting.

* * *

'Right, weans, and I mean all of youse … Willy, stand up straight and look at me.'

Arthur and Mary faced their mother; Willy turned round to look out the window. Mary manoeuvred Willy into line.

'But I'm not a wean, Mummy. I'm nearly eight,' Willy said, standing as tall as he could.

'You remain a wean until you can do the dishes,' Ann said. 'I caught Mary rinsing out a cup the other day, so she's officially not a wean any more. This is important and you all need to pay attention.'

Arthur and Willy put their hands up to speak, but Ann covered her ears. 'I'm not listening. Lalalalala.' When the noise simmered down, she began again. 'Okay, I … sorry, *we*' – she looked at Stan – 'have an announcement to make, and after this announcement, you'll need buckets and spades, so listen carefully.'

Mary, Arthur and Willy looked bewildered.

Ann cleared her throat. 'We are going to the seaside.'

The three children exploded, transforming into three dancing monkeys. Eventually, they started asking for details. Arthur wanted to know if they were going in the car, Willy asked if they'd be able to go swimming, and Mary wanted to know when this was happening.

'We're going at Easter,' Ann said. 'The only problem is, because it's such a long journey, we can only comfortably fit four of us in the car. That means one of you will have to walk.'

Stan was enjoying this.

'Not me. I'm still a wean,' Willy insisted, doing his best to make himself look really small.

'Whoever is the most baddest behaved before we go will have to walk behind the car. You might have to run a wee bit at times cos the car can go very fast down hills.'

'Don't be cruel, Mummy,' Stan said, laughing. 'No one has to walk. It's far too far. We'll tie one of you to the roof.'

'That's a good idea, Daddy.' Willy looked at his brother. 'If you put your hat on your ears, you won't get cold or anything.'

Initial doubt soon turned to giggles. Then the noisy monkeys were back.

'We can take questions now,' Ann said and she sat back.

Arthur put his hand up. 'Can we bring toys?'

'One – between you. I'm joking. One each. Next.'

'Will we miss school?' Willy had both hands up.

'No, you won't miss school. We're going at Easter, during the school holidays.'

'Maybe we'll miss church,' Mary suggested. They all looked happy at this possibility.

'Yes, we will miss church, unfortunately. So you'll all have to go twice tomorrow to make up for it.'

'You're very silly, Mummy.'

'Don't you call me silly, Willy Webb.' Ann went to chase him. Willy dived in behind the settee, shrieking and giggling.

'What seaside are we going to, Ma?' Mary asked.

'We're going to a place called Larne. It's where Daddy's from. His family lives there. His daddy, your granda, is in hospital. So, we – me and your daddy – are going to visit him. There's a park with a roundabout and swings near your aunt and uncle's, and we can go to the beach as well. They even have a dog. It's a wee puppy called Lassie. It'll be a great adventure.'

'Like the Famous Five?'

'Exactly. Just like the Famous Five … but without the ginger beer.'

'Awwwww!' They all groaned.

'It makes you fart something desperate,' Ann added. 'We'll have milk instead.'

They all shook their heads at their very silly Mummy.

'Will your daddy get better soon?' Mary asked her da.

'Let's hope so,' Stan said, taken aback by Mary's concern. He wasn't used to the children asking him questions. 'He's being well looked after.'

'We'll know more when we see him,' Ann said. 'Now go and get cleaned up. Sausages for dinner.' Ann peered behind the sofa. 'Willy, come out of there. You're scaring the spiders.'

* * *

On Easter Saturday, they packed their two old battered suitcases. Stan's was about to fall apart and one of the locks didn't work. They filled a cardboard box with toys, teddies and books.

'What's that you're reading now, love?' Ann asked Mary as she set a book and her radio carefully on top of the pile of stuff in the box.

'It's called *Lord of the Flies*. It's by William Golding. It's brilliant, but it's a bit scary.'

'Just remember, it's only a story,' Ann said reassuringly.

'Yes, Ma,' Mary said with a smile.

'Right. Have you all got clean knickers on?'

'Mine were clean when I put them on,' Willy said, looking mighty pleased with himself.

'I'm not wearing any, so's to keep them clean for the seaside.' Arthur patted his backside.

'Good thinking, Arthur Webb. Just watch your whatsit doesn't get caught in the zip.'

'Mummy!' Arthur looked horrified at the thought.

Stan had washed the car and filled it with petrol at Torney's. Willy spotted him coming up Johnston Park.

'There's Daddy now. Let's go!' He was beside himself with excitement.

'Who's going in the middle?' Ann asked and they all looked at each other.

'The middle is the best seat cos you can see out the front,' Ann pointed out.

'Me. Me.' Willy was waving his arm about like a bullrush in a breeze. 'I wanna sit in the middle.'

This was the result Ann wanted: Willy was the smallest and they would all fit in better.

'Okay then, pile in,' she said. She tipped the front seat forward and had a lovely view of three bony backsides as Arthur, Willy and Mary squeezed into the back. Willy immediately leaned forward between the front seats to watch Stan click the gear lever on the steering column.

It was a beautiful day for the trip. They stopped for lunch at the side of the road – cheese and ham sandwiches, crisps with a wee blue bag of salt inside and tea from a flask. Ann thought it was the best tea she'd ever had.

Mary looked mischievous when she announced that she preferred egg and onion sandwiches. She knew her mother hated egg and onion, but she didn't know why.

'When you're making the sandwiches, you can have egg and onion,' Ann said. 'Cheese is better for you. It's good for your bones.'

They packed up and got going again. Willy felt sick and they all got restless as the journey wore on. Ann made a suggestion that she quickly regretted.

'Why don't we sing something? It'll pass the time.'

'What'll we sing?' Arthur asked.

'*All things bright and beautiful*', Mary began. They'd sung it in church the previous Sunday. When Arthur joined in, Ann was reminded of Harry, Joe's friend – plenty of volume, not so much tune. Willy had to shriek to be heard. Ann covered her ears. Stan gripped the steering wheel, his knuckles turning white.

They reached Larne in the middle of the afternoon and made their way to Uncle Willy and Auntie Charlotte's house. They were brilliant hosts. Their house was big and spacious. The three floors were a great novelty for the children, who imagined being in a castle or a haunted mansion. They played in Dixon Park with Lassie, while Stan, Ann and Spider visited Willy Senior.

Ann thought it was sad to see Stan not knowing what to say or do with his da. Mostly they just sat with the confused old man. It was sad, too, that Jacob and his wife weren't there.

'Tell him about work,' Ann suggested. 'Or the price of houses. Or tell him about Isabella. He'll be all excited about the car.'

But Stan stared straight ahead and said nothing.

Memories came flooding back for Ann. They should have brought him an egg and onion sandwich, she thought.

'Tell him about the weans,' Ann whispered. 'Tell him how well they're doing at school.'

Exasperated, Stan got up and left the room. Ann followed him out and could hear Spider start chatting to his da as she left.

The next day was Easter Sunday and they drove down the coast a wee bit to Drains Bay. Stan and Ann walked along the beach while the children built sandcastles. Then they ventured into the water and screamed as the freezing cold waves broke over them. Again, Ann had flashbacks to the

East Strand at Portrush. She squeezed Stan's hand. They motored on and had tea in Ballygally Castle Hotel. It was a real haunted castle, and the children lapped up the scary stories the waitress told them.

But all too soon it was time to come home again.

Ann wasn't sure if Stan had got anything at all from the trip.

CHAPTER 39

Saturday mornings were taken up with the timeless pilgrimage to the County Cinema for the children's matinee. Six pence in and six pence for sweets in Bob Campbell's tiny gold mine at the top of Scarffe's Entry. If Bob was tired of being asked 'How much are the penny chews?' he never showed it. 'Two for tuppence,' he always replied. At the pictures, it was the Keystone Cops, Bugs Bunny, the Three Stooges and Laurel and Hardy, and cowboy and adventure films of all sorts that filled the cinema, along with the deafening noise of laughter and shrieks as the kids fired sugary missiles everywhere.

On Saturday afternoons, youngsters came down from Cannondale and Festival Park for football kickabouts. Arthur had started playing football at school and there were enough children in Johnston Park to make a game, just like Joe had done.

In May, Arthur sat down with Stan to watch his first ever game on TV. It was the FA Cup final. The build-up went on for hours and the new telly needed endless adjustments.

The vertical and horizontal hold knobs at the back required delicate twiddling.

'That's it now. No, it's gone again. That's it. Try the vertical one now.'

Stan made Arthur walk around the room with the aerial, turning it in all directions for the best picture. Eventually it all settled. The crowd sang 'Abide with me', the Queen appeared in the Royal Box, the National Anthem was played by the big army band and then they were off.

'I want the team in white to win, Daddy,' Arthur said.

'Good team, Leeds. No reason why they can't.'

Arthur was glued to it, roaring at the telly and at the referee, groaning at every foul and every near miss. Leeds United lost 2–1 to Liverpool, but they had a new fan for life. Stan later admitted to Ann that he thought it was boring.

Spring turned to summer, the heat began to rise and Stan surprised them all with an idea again.

'You know yer man Jack Boyce that I bought the car off?' he said to Ann one day. 'Well, he's from Donegal?'

'Aye, I remember you said. He's from near Malin, isn't he?'

'He's actually from a wee place called Portsalon, if you've heard of that.'

'Can't say I have. Did he just say he was from Malin cos he knew you were from there and he wanted to sell you the car?'

'You're very cynical, Mrs Webb. He never said he was from Malin. He said he knew my da, who *is* from Malin.'

'So what's this all about then, now that we've sorted out where Jack *isn't* from?'

'He says that Portsalon has the most beautiful beach you've ever seen and nobody goes there.'

Ann guessed what was coming next. 'So we're going there?'

'Jack's family have built a new bungalow right opposite the beach. You have to go across a field first, but he says it's not far. They're renting out the bungalow for holidays. Jack says we can stay whenever we want.'

'For free?'

Stan laughed at Ann's optimism. 'I think he said it was only twenty quid.'

'A week?'

'No, a fortnight. We could go to celebrate Mary passing the eleven-plus.'

Ann was as excited as the children by the prospect of a proper holiday. A whole two weeks away at the seaside, and in another country too. Exciting foreign money to deal with. They booked the first fortnight in August.

Time crawled by like a snail racing up a plank. The July parades came and went; then at last it was August.

It was self-catering and they had to bring everything with them – pots and pans, the bread bin, cutting board, cutlery, plates and cups, sheets and pillowcases, towels. Stan borrowed a roof rack and a tarpaulin to cover their boxes of stuff. They squeezed as much as they could into the boot, and everything else was packed into the back of the car alongside the children.

Ann went down to see Ma and Daisy the evening before they left. Daisy had started work in Love's jewellery shop at the end of June.

'How's it going, love?' Ann asked as she took off her coat. She sat down at the table.

'I love Love's,' Daisy said, giving her mother her big beaming smile. She was sitting in Fred's chair.

'I love it that you love Love's, love. It's lovely,' Ann said, hugging her nearly grown-up child. 'And you're not annoyed about not coming on holiday with us?'

Daisy shrugged. Ann could see the resigned acceptance.

'There's no room for me in the car, sure. Just like when youse went to Larne. I have a job now anyway. And Nana needs somebody to look after and worry about, don't you, Nana?'

Ma nodded. 'There's plenty to worry about, I can tell you.'

'That's the girl,' Ann said. 'You're too old for sandcastles anyway.'

'It sounds boring. Buckets and spades are for weans.'

Ann realised that Daisy had never been on a beach; she wasn't sure if Ma had either. 'It'll be boring if it rains,' she said, doing her best to play it down. She was about to point out that there would be no TV, but stopped herself just in time – Ma and Daisy had no telly either. 'Here's a spare key so you can look after Johnston Park – lift the letters and make sure everything's okay.'

Daisy perked up at this. Ann could almost read her mind: the whole house, empty for two weeks!

'I want you to be good,' Ann said.

'Of course, Mummy,' Daisy said, beaming at her as if butter wouldn't melt. Ann made a mental note: *best not tell Stan about this arrangement*.

'Will you be okay, Ma?' Ann asked.

'Of course. Me and Daisy'll be just grand. Youse go and enjoy yourselves.'

After dinner that night, Stan stopped puffing on his pipe and turned to Ann. 'It'd be a good idea to leave a key next door when we're away,' he said. 'They can lift the letters and put the bin out. Keep an eye on the place.'

Ann almost groaned out loud. 'Good idea, love.' Good job there was a *spare* spare key, she thought.

Barry McGuire was on the radio, rasping out 'Eve of Destruction'. Ann smiled at the song's hopeless desolation. I hope he's wrong, she thought as she dried the dishes.

* * *

When they got back from Donegal, Ann went straight round to Sedan Avenue.

'The kettle's boiled,' Ma said. 'Tell me all about your holiday.'

Ann brought in tea and a plate of digestives, stuck together as always with an unhealthy amount of butter.

'It was brilliant,' she said. 'We only had two wet days. The rest of the time we were on the beach nearly all day. The weans loved it. There's an old aeroplane half buried on the beach. It crashed during the war. They spent hours trying to dig down to see more of it. The beach is miles and miles long with a beautiful mountain at one end – Knockalla, I think it's called – and Portsalon itself at the other end. The village is just a pub, a pier, a wee café and a grand hotel. Stan preferred the Guinness in Rita's pub. Thank God. It was about half the price. I got a bit of a tan.'

'I can see that. Did Stan like it?'

'You know what he's like. Doesn't say much. He was happy just watching the weans play in the sand and paddle in the sea. He didn't join in much. It's not very manly making sandcastles. He liked the peace and quiet. We went for walks along the beach and round the wee country roads. It's a beautiful place. We're going back again next year. How did you and Daisy get on?'

She saw from Ma's face that all was not as it should be. 'Come on. What's happened? Has she been going to work?'

'It's not that,' Ma said, brushing crumbs off her skirt. 'She hasn't missed a day, as far as I know. It's just that sometimes she doesn't come home and I don't know where she goes. When I ask her, she says she was at a friend's house listening to records.'

She was probably in our house listening to records, Ann thought. 'She doesn't stay out all night, does she?' she asked.

'No, she always comes home eventually, but sometimes it's very late. She tries to sneak in, just like you used to.'

Ann smiled at the memories.

'Sometimes she comes home for her dinner and then goes out again. Sometimes she goes for chips with her friends. I didn't see her at all for a couple of days last week. I've been worrying as hard as I can. I've nearly made myself sick.'

'Oh, Ma! Where is she now?'

'Up the town somewhere. She said she'd be back for dinner. She knows you're coming home today.'

'Have you anything in for dinner?'

'There's a few spuds. They're sprouting, but they'll be all right.'

'And that's all?'

'Daisy's doing the shopping. She'll be back. She said she'll be back.'

'Does she lie to you, Ma?'

'No, she doesn't. At least, I don't think so. She always comes home when she says she will and she always makes sure the chores are done. She's been really good. It's just I don't know where she goes or what she's up to.'

'Maybe she doesn't want to worry you.'

They both burst out laughing.

‘I’ll make more tea and wait for her,’ Ann said.

Ann and Ma chatted away as the afternoon wore on, but there was still no sign of Daisy. Ann was worried now. Daisy had a shilling in her pocket that maybe wasn’t her best friend.

‘I’ll have to go soon, Ma,’ she said. ‘The weans’ll need their dinner. They were unpacking the car when I left. They’ll be hungry.’

‘You go on, love. She’ll be home soon.’

‘I’ll see you tomorrow.’ She bent over and gave Ma a wee kiss goodbye.

As Ann turned left out of Bridge Street, she glanced to her right to see if it was safe to cross the road and saw Daisy standing outside the Central Bar with three other girls. When Daisy spotted her, she immediately dropped her fag and stubbed it out with her foot. She said something to the other girls and started walking towards her mother.

‘You need to get home, young lady,’ Ann said to her. ‘Your nana is worried sick about you.’

‘Nana worries about everything,’ Daisy said dismissively. ‘She was worried when you were away because you were in the Free State. She thought you might be kidnapped or arrested or something.’

‘Don’t try to change the subject,’ Ann said. ‘She told me you stay out late. A lot.’

‘We just go to the Golden Griddle and listen to the juke box until they throw us out for not buying anything. We share a chip and have a Coke each.’

That’s my girl, Ann thought, but she needed to be firm with her … strict. ‘Have you got all your shopping?’ she asked.

‘Yes, Mummy,’ Daisy said, whining like a spoilt child.

Ann imitated her daughter's little-girl voice. 'Well, go on home then and look after your nana.' But she added in a normal voice, 'I missed you.'

'I missed you too. Did you have a good holiday?'

'We did, love. I'll tell you all about it when your nana's calmed down and stopped worrying.'

'I'll never hear about it then,' Daisy said, smiling at her ma.

'Maybe you can come with us next year.'

Daisy looked sceptical. Ann went to give her a kiss.

'Ma! Not here – in the street! I'm not a baby!'

'You'll always be my little baby, my little diddums,' Ann said, chucking the panic-stricken Daisy under the chin.

'Oh God,' Daisy said, smiling and wriggling away. 'I'm away. Nana will be worrying about me.'

CHAPTER 40

The glorious blue of summer was fading into the gold of autumn.

Mary had passed the eleven-plus. She would be going to Omagh Academy. Ann and Stan were beside themselves with pride. She was the first person in either family to go to a grammar school. She was their daughter, she was smart, and she was gorgeous – just like her mother, Ann thought. On her first day, she looked just like a wee girl should on her first day. The uniform had cost a fortune. She had a new schoolbag and pencil case. Ann had been nervous and emotional. Mary was just excited.

Even though the school was less than a hundred yards away from their house, Ann went to meet her.

'Well?' Ann said.

'It was good. They divide everybody up into three groups – houses, they call them – named after the three rivers. I'm in Drumragh.'

'Why?'

'No idea.'

'Did you learn anything?'

'Not really. It was all about timetables and where the dining room is and all the rules. You're not allowed to run or hop or smoke or talk or fart or chew gum or eat sweets or read comics or wear brown shoes.'

'That's a lot of rules. Did you write them all down?'

Mary smiled.

'Do you think you'll go back?' Ann asked.

'Probably.'

Daisy had worked all summer in Love's. She drove Ma and Ann to distraction. Ann heard rumours about boys, so she sent her extensive spy network of friends into action.

'I think she's going out with Alvin Lee,' Iris told her.

'I saw her in the Rex with Tony McPhee,' Jean said.

'She went to the pictures with Roy Buchanan. They went to see *The Cincinnati Kid*,' Maud reported in hushed tones.

'Just be careful, love, that's all I'm saying. I did exactly what you're doing when I was your age, but …' Ann realised she couldn't finish the sentence.

'But what, Ma? You had me and wished you hadn't?'

Ann winced. 'No! No, absolutely not. I fought against the world to have you. Don't ever think that.'

'Sorry, Ma, but what happened? Who *is* my da? Where is he? Is he still alive?'

'I can't tell you. Not yet.'

'Why not?'

'I just can't. I promised Ma. Other people will get hurt too. I'll tell you as soon as I can. But not now.'

'Nana knows?'

'I'm telling you now, do NOT talk to her about this. She doesn't deserve to be upset and she will be very upset, and I mean VERY upset.'

'But what about me? I'm upset. Do I not count?'

'Of course you do, love. You're more precious to me than you can possibly know. I'll tell you everything one day. I promise. As soon as I can.' Ann was close to tears.

'Just not as precious as Nana and whoever else you think will be upset.'

'It's difficult, love. Please, you've got to trust me on this, Daisy,' Ann said, imploring her confused and angry child. 'I love you, but I need you to help me. Please.'

Daisy studied her ma for a few moments, then came over and gave her a huge bear hug. 'I love you too, Ma. This sounds big, so make sure to give me plenty of warning before you tell me everything. I think we might need a large bottle of Blue Nun.'

'Each,' Ann said with a weak smile. She puffed her cheeks out and exhaled noisily with relief. 'You won't mention any of this to Nana? Promise me.'

'I promise. I'm going away soon anyway.'

'What do you mean *going away*? Where are you going? When?'

'I want to be a nurse. I've filled the forms in. I'm going to the Erne Hospital at the end of the month to start my training.'

'But that's in Enniskillen.'

'You're smarter than you look,' Daisy said, making big eyes at her ma.

'Don't be cheeky. You never said.'

'You never asked.'

'How could I know to ask? Does Nana know?'

'She will as soon as I get home. I only found out this morning. I didn't want her worrying all on her own, all day, so I didn't say anything … I think I'll make a good nurse.'

'I think so too. You're good with people. You care about them.'

'I care about you, Ma. I'm not sure that you're always as happy as you make out to be.'

Ann was stunned at her daughter's insight. 'Rubbish! I'm the queen of Happyland.'

* * *

Daisy left on the Sunday morning bus. Ann made all the weans come to say goodbye. Stan stayed in the house; he wanted to wash the car before taking them to church. They all squeezed into the living room in Sedan Avenue.

'It's like a wake,' Ma observed. 'The house hasn't been this packed since, well …' She looked distant as she remembered. '… since a long time ago.'

Arthur picked up the old cardboard suitcase. 'It's not very heavy,' he said, jiggling it about.

'That's because it's empty,' Daisy replied.

'Is it?' Arthur shook it again. 'Why?'

'You're not allowed to go away without a suitcase. It's the law,' Daisy said.

'Even if it's empty?'

'Especially if it's empty.'

Arthur looked at Ann, confused.

'She's winding you up, dopey,' Mary said, coming to the rescue. 'It just feels empty cos you're so strong.'

Arthur beamed.

They all walked over to the bus station together. Mary and Daisy embraced at the steps of the bus. Like proper sisters, Ann thought. Arthur and Willy got a perfunctory hug, like proper brothers. They never thought much about the fact that the big sister they hadn't had a chance to get to know very well was moving further away. There were kisses, hugs and tears from her ma and her nana.

'I'll be back soon,' she said and she disappeared into the bowels of the bus.

They all waved as the bus pulled out and then stood quietly, not quite knowing what to do. It felt like things had changed and would never be the same again.

Ann hummed 'Wheel of Fortune' in her head.

'We need to get a move on,' she said, glancing at her watch. 'Your da will be in the car looking at his watch and drumming his fingers on the steering wheel.'

Ma came back to Johnston Park after church. In the afternoon, Mary insisted on walking her back to Sedan Avenue. Ann half-heartedly protested.

'I'm nearly twelve, I know how to walk and I know where to go,' Mary argued. 'What's the problem?'

Ann was proud of her. It meant she would be able to get on with the ironing. 'Are you sure, love? Just be careful crossing the roads.'

'Yes, Ma.'

Ann knew they would be okay. But would Daisy be okay? How would she cope out in the real world on her own? More importantly, how would Ma cope, living on her own for the first time since Da died? Even when she'd been in Belfast having Daisy, Fred had been around to help.

Oh God, Ann thought, it was time for some serious worrying.

* * *

The flood that year wasn't the worst there had ever been, but it was bad enough. Stan and Arthur helped get all the stuff upstairs in Sedan Avenue. Ma came and stayed with them in

Johnston Park. She had to share with Mary. It wasn't ideal, and after three days, she was itching to get home.

Afterwards, Mary helped Ann clean the place up. Even then, it was against her better judgement to let Ma go back to Sedan Avenue.

'You can't stay here on your own, Ma,' she said when Ma was safely ensconced in her own chair. Ann had done what little shopping Ma needed. She went out to put the kettle on and put the shopping away.

She came back into the living room and sat down. Ma was staring into space. Ann looked around at the sticks of furniture, the mouldy mat in front of the fire, the damp patches and the mould. She forced herself to say nothing. They were Ma's sticks, Ma's mat, Ma's damp patches. It was Ma's house.

'I'm tired, Ann,' Ma said. 'I've never felt so tired.'

'You were born tired. You've always said so. A good night's sleep and you'll be as right as rain.'

'I can't sleep. It's too quiet without Daisy. Every creak and rattle wakes me, even though I've heard them all a million times. Then I wriggle about and can't get back over.'

'When Daisy was here, all you wanted was peace and quiet. Why don't you stay with us?'

'Too much of anything isn't good for you, and I can't stay with you. There's no room. It's not fair on Mary, two of us wriggling around. I don't think she slept the whole time I was there.'

'If Stan hears of a house in Johnston Park, will you take it? He'll need to know.'

'We'll see. I've never lived anywhere else,' Ma said forlornly.

Ann stood up and gave her a peck on the cheek. 'Finish your tea. Have you any washing that needs done?'

'It's in Joe's room.'

'I haven't heard from Joe for ages. Is he still married? Maybe you could start worrying about him again for a while,' Ann suggested. 'It might help you sleep.'

'That's true. A good worry at bedtime always does the trick.'

'Maybe that's the problem. You don't have anything to properly worry about any more.'

Ma snorted. 'There're loads of things to worry about. I just have to think of them and get them in the right order.'

'You do that. And you'll think about Johnston Park? That'll be something new to worry about.'

'I said I'll see.'

That was as close to a yes as Ann could hope for.

* * *

Daisy came home on Christmas Eve. She got off the bus in her nurse's uniform. She looked very grown up. Ann met her and started an interrogation, but Daisy was in no mood.

'I'm very tired, Ma. Is it okay if I tell youse everything tomorrow? I need a wee sleep. Is Nana okay?'

'I know you'll find this hard to believe but she misses you. She says the house is too quiet.'

Daisy smiled. 'Did you miss me too?'

'Of course I did. I've had to do all the things you used to do. I'm exhausted.'

'So you didn't miss *me*?'

Ann stopped. 'I can't tell you how much I missed you. You were … are …' Ann dabbed her eyes with her hanky.

Daisy set her suitcase down and they hugged there in the street, oblivious to the stares of passers-by.

Ma was delighted to have her back. She had sausages in for dinner, and the fire was sending flames up the chimney; the house was almost dry again.

Daisy went to bed for a while, but after dinner she went out. 'Christmas party, Nana. I won't be late.'

Later, Ma heard her, muttering and swearing, trying to get her key in the lock. She stumbled on the stairs. It was three in the morning.

'Are you okay, love?' Ma called out.

'Toilet' was all Daisy said.

Downstairs doors banged and the banister creaked.

'Sorry, Nana,' Daisy said in a loud whisper as she walked past her nana's bedroom. 'Great party.'

Then Daisy's bedroom door slammed and within seconds, all Ma could hear was snoring.

Ma smiled. 'I can't have it both ways,' she said to herself and fell asleep.

The next day, Christmas Day, Ma and Daisy met Ann at the phone box.

'We had Lord and Lady Lucan over for drinks last night,' Muriel said, sounding more than ever like she was on a different planet. 'The canapés were out of this world.'

Ann and Ma looked at each other, trying hard not to laugh.

There wasn't much news from Hilda in her cards; Jimmy had now started a band, a loud rock band apparently called 'The Black Dogs'. She couldn't say where Dan was. Joe was still in London and might be in Omagh soon for Nigel's wedding. Ann was amazed. Nigel getting married at thirty-six! Wonders would never cease. They nattered on until the money ran out. They never put more in after the first few bob.

Ann vowed to bring up the phone question with Stan again. They had everything else – except a spin dryer. She wanted one of those as well.

Back at Johnston Park, Daisy disappeared upstairs with Mary as they waited for the dinner to be ready. The boys played with the Scalextric set that Santa had brought, making unnecessarily loud car noises, especially when they went round bends. Stan puffed away on his pipe and nibbled at a box of dates.

During the meal, Daisy was very quiet and didn't eat much, but Ann noticed that she had three glasses of wine. After the Queen's Speech, she said she was going out for a walk.

'Can I come with you?' Ann asked.

Daisy nodded.

They got wrapped up in their winter coats, scarves and mittens and set off down the park.

'Are you all right, love?' Ann began.

'I'm feeling a bit sick. I was at a party in Lorna's house last night.'

'Who's Lorna?'

'She's a nurse. We started at the Erne on the same day. She was actually on the same bus as me that day I left Omagh.'

'So it was a good party, I take it.'

'Too good.'

'Any boys at it?'

'Mostly ugly. Black hair and hairy faces. There was one good-lookin' one. Wally, his name is. He works in the bakery.'

Ann was stunned. Was Daisy making this up? Did she know? How could she know? She kept her cool. 'What does this Wally look like?' she asked. She wasn't sure she wanted to know.

'Blondy hair, skinny. Good-looking in a soft sort of way. He was funny.'

Ann shivered. The gods were playing games.

'No funny business, I hope,' Ann said, crossing her fingers inside her mitten.

'No, Ma. I'm not stupid.' A quick glance said all there was to say.

'Are you planning on seeing him again?'

'I doubt it. He was a bit thick. He probably won't even remember me being there.'

Thank God, Ann thought, that would be too weird. History repeating itself. 'As long as you had a good time,' she said aloud. 'Let's get back. It's too cold to stay out.' She shivered again and it wasn't just because of the cold.

CHAPTER 41

Ma opened the rickety old toilet door. When she'd finished, she pulled the rusty chain and wrapped her cardigan tightly across her chest. Treading carefully so as not to slip on the slimy green concrete, she went out of the yard and into the garden beyond.

The scattered clatter of daffodils shone out amongst the weeds and nodded at her as she wandered up the path. The pole for the washing line was lying on the ground. It looked like it couldn't hold itself up, much less a line of clothes.

Fred's nephew, Denis, had stopped coming to look after the garden some time ago. Must be at least a couple of years, she thought, but she couldn't be sure. She did remember that he'd got married and moved to Sixmilecross. What was there in Sixmilecross? she wondered. Fred would have got somebody else to come, but Fred was gone too.

The flower beds were a ragged, tangled mess of nettles, dandelions and couch grass. She bent down to try and pull out a piece of grass, but it refused to come and she straightened up, wheezing with the effort.

The old mangle stared at her, rusted and covered in glistening cobwebs. She touched the hard, cracked rollers that had served her so well over the years.

It might be spring, but it was still cold outside and she went back into the house. It was no warmer there. It was still damp from last year's flood. It was empty, quiet. Even the clock had stopped. 'Nobody to wind you up any more, Mr Clock,' Ma muttered. Nobody winds anybody up any more, she thought.

She knelt down to clean out the grate, her knees screaming at her, and started to cry. They were silent tears of defeat, tears no one else would ever see.

Once the ashes were in the bucket, she set the fire and tried to light it. Then she realised she'd forgotten to fill the coal scuttle, the scuttle that had once been the newest, shiniest thing in the house now looked as if it had sat on the hearth forever. The fire flickered and went out.

She reached up and, holding onto the mantelpiece, hauled herself up. She hoped there were tablets in the cupboard.

There was some water in the kettle, so she lit the gas cooker. A cup of tea always made things better. But the water only got as far as lukewarm when the gas ran out. She trudged into the living room and got some coins from the tin. She put them in her pocket and patted them. It's still true, she thought. Best friends.

Once the coins were in the slot and the gas was back on, she made a mug of tea, put her coat on and sat down to wait for Ann. She'll be here soon.

* * *

'Ma! Ma!' Ann shook the bundle huddled in the chair. 'Wake up, Ma.'

'What? What time is it?' Ma asked, squinting as she struggled to waken up. 'I must have dozed off.'

'Thank God! You had me worried there. It's half nine. Are you all right?' Ann looked at the unlit fire.

'Couldn't get it to go at all, love,' Ma said.

'It needs some big lumps. Where's Joe when you need him, eh?'

Ma smiled. She missed the banter.

Ann lifted the coal scuttle and filled it with proper-sized chunks in the back yard. Then she reset the fire and put a match to it. Within a few minutes, flames were flickering and the coal was catching.

'That's it lit now,' Ann said. 'I'll put this stuff away.' She lifted the shopping bag. 'Have you had any breakfast?' she shouted from the kitchen.

'The bread was a bit mouldy. I'll have a bit of that fresh stuff. There's marmalade.'

'The *Woman's Own*'s on the table. It's gone up to eight pence,' Ann said as she came in with the tea and toast.

'Everything's going up.'

'Still only four pence each. And you get Green Shield Stamps!' Ann said cheerfully.

'I've been thinking,' Ma said, licking a blob of golden shred off her thumb.

'Oh dear, should I get the doctor?'

'Very funny. Listen, I think it's time to go,' Ma said, looking at Ann, a mixture of dread and relief in her eyes.

'You mean … to leave here?'

'What did you think I meant?'

Ann nodded. She put one hand on top of Ma's. 'Good.'

'It makes me sad, but I think the house is telling me it's time to go. Even the clock has stopped.'

'You must be a bit lonely as well.'

'I still miss him.' Ma's eyes were glistening.

'Fred?'

Ma nodded.

'So it's all Fred's fault. How very dare he go and die on you like that! He knew you'd be left on your own. Selfish git.'

Ma chuckled. 'Daisy too. She's as much to blame. Galivanting off to Enniskillen of all places.'

Ann was relieved to see Ma smiling again. 'Exactly. She could do nursing a bit closer to home.'

'Right here.' Ma waved her arm around the little room. 'There can't be many in the hospital as sick as me.'

'She'll be a great nurse.' Ann looked into her mother's eyes and rubbed the back of her hand. 'Are you ready to tell me about Fred? And Da? What happened, cos it's obvious something happened.'

Ma sighed. 'Fred was the only one who knew.'

'Knew what?' Ann was on edge now.

Ma set her empty mug on the hearth. 'Well, Fred and John were best friends – had been since they were wee. John was the most handsome man you've ever seen.' Ma stared wistfully into the distance. 'I met him in the laundry. He came in one day with a big load of band uniforms. I went out to help him bring them in from the van.'

'What age were you then?'

'Fifteen. He was sixteen. He was tall with jet black hair. Could have been a film star. And he was funny. A real gentleman, he was. We hit it off straight away.'

'What about Fred?'

'Fred was always there with him. They worked together for the council and played together in the band. John wanted to join the army. I was besotted with him and he seemed besotted with me. He joined the Royal Inniskilling Fusiliers and a couple of years later, when he was home on leave, we got married.'

'What year was that?'

'I had just turned eighteen – 1925.'

'He must have been away a lot.'

'He was home on leave exactly four times.' Ma giggled and looked like a mischievous child.

'And Fred?'

'Fred's family were tailors. He started working there as soon as they needed him. Fred missed John as much as I did.'

'So what happened?'

'John was away all over the place and I was on my own with you lot.'

'Oh Ma, not you and Fred. You didn't, did you?'

'No! Absolutely not! Fred wasn't a ladies' man, if you get my drift. He looked after me. He would do anything for me. He'd have done anything for John. I think he was a wee bit jealous cos he could never get as close to John as I was.'

'So Fred was a … you know?'

'If he was, he never let on and I didn't care. He was just Fred. John told him everything. Then one day, John told him something and made Fred promise not to tell anyone ever. But Fred was shocked by what he told him. It was a promise he couldn't keep. What he'd heard was too awful to keep to himself. It was a choice between his friendship with John and common decency.' Ma shook her head and continued. 'Fred, being the man he was, felt he had no choice and he told me what John had told him.'

'And?' Ann was leaning forward. This was like a movie.

'He told Fred that he had met a woman in Gloucester – he was with the Gloucestershire Regiment at the time – and he'd fallen in love with her. In fact, he'd more than fallen in love. He'd married her. They had three weans by the time he told Fred.'

'What?' Ann couldn't believe her ears. 'But he was married to you.'

Ma looked like all the wind had gone out of her. She took a deep breath and went on. 'He said he was going to leave me and all of you and go and live with this other floozy.'

'Oh Ma!' Ann groaned. 'Did he go? Is that why we don't remember him?'

'No, he never got the chance. He got sick and died. There was a lady at his funeral. She stood at the back. She looked at me as we walked past on the way out. I knew it was her and she knew that I knew. Never saw her again.'

Tears trickled down Ma's wrinkled old face and the sight broke Ann's heart. She was about to say something, but Ma carried on talking.

'I loved him, Ann. I loved him so much. I thought he loved me. He did love me, I know he did … for a while anyway. I'd never felt so alone. There was no time to wallow, though. After the funeral, I came home and made the dinner and life went on.'

'Fred must have felt awful.'

'He didn't know what to do. He didn't want to betray John, but he couldn't let him betray me either. He thought I might have been able to change John's mind – convince him to stay in Omagh with us. Fred knew it would be the end of their friendship. But I'm not sure I would have tried to persuade John to stay, even if I'd had the chance. I told him I knew about the other woman on the day he died. You should have seen the old bastard's face.'

'And you and Fred have been best friends ever since.'

Ma nodded.

'Just friends?'

'As I said, Fred was a gentleman. I'll never speak ill of him. He probably loved John more than John ever loved me, and he knew that I knew that.'

'Oh Ma! That's the most awful thing I've ever heard. How did you ever get over it?'

'Just had to get on with things. I had the four of you to look after. Not much time for dwelling.' Ma looked straight at Ann and grabbed her hand. 'There's no need for anyone else to know about this.'

'No, Ma, no need.' Ann's mind was racing at a hundred miles an hour, going back over everything she could remember, seeing it all in a new light. 'I remember the wee chocolate ornaments that Fred used to bring at Christmas. And him standing whistling outside the toilet door.'

'And the tanners that he gave you all, thinking it was a big secret I knew nothing about.'

'So the love of your life left you on your own, just like mine,' Ann said.

'Except Walter didn't mean to leave you. He was taken from you.'

'Result's the same, though. And you had Fred, and I found Stan.'

'What about you and Stan?'

'What do you mean?'

'It's just something Daisy said a while ago.'

'Daisy should mind her own business.'

'She would say you *are* her business. She thinks you mightn't be quite as happy as you let on.'

'If ifs and ands were pots and pans …' Ann began

'… there'd be no need for tinkers,' Ma added.

They smiled at each other.

'We are where we are, Ma. It could be worse.'

'What should I bring with me?' Ma asked, looking round the little room.

Ann looked at her Ma with new, awestruck admiration.

* * *

'How did you get her to move?' Daisy asked her ma, taking a bite off her Marathon.

They were watching the dignitaries opening the new Drumragh Avenue bridge. It was December and it was freezing.

'I didn't. She made her own mind up,' Ann replied. 'The house held too many memories she said.'

'Too many mice, rattles, draughts and damp patches more like,' Daisy said through a mouthful of chocolate and nougat.

'True. Then we got a phone in! That clinched the deal.' Ann smiled. 'Now she only has to cross the road to use it and she can sit in the warmth of our house and talk to Muriel with a cup of tea.'

'At last!'

'Stan might be slow, but he gets there in the end. Seriously, love, she misses Fred so much. She's lonely and lost without him.'

'And then I went and left her as well.'

'Different thing completely, although she did say.'

'Say what! I'll have a word with her when I get in.' Daisy grinned. She looked all grown up and beautiful.

'I hope it stays up,' Ann said, nodding at the new bridge. 'Let's go and get warmed up.'

They walked up to the Cake Shop.

'What are you having, love?'

‘I’m getting it. What are *you* having?’

Ann felt chuffed – her daughter treating her. ‘A milky coffee and a piece of Christmas cake would be lovely.’

‘I’ll have that as well, please,’ Daisy said to the waitress.

‘So what’s this all about? Cake and fancy coffee in the Cake Shop? What’s the big secret?’ Just as she said it, Ann’s heart sank. Please no, she prayed.

‘No, I’m not pregnant, Ma,’ Daisy said as if she’d read her mind. ‘I know someone who got pregnant by some mystery man. Led to all sorts of problems.’

Ann smiled at the sassy woman opposite her. ‘I can’t believe anyone could be that stupid, but I hear it can lead to all sorts of beautiful things too.’

Daisy tucked a strand of hair behind her ear and pouted her bright red lips. ‘You always say the right things, Ma.’

‘So … come on, what’s the secret?’

‘Well, I’ve been thinking. When my training’s over – and I know that’s another couple of years away yet – but when it’s over, I’m going to join the QAs.’

‘What’s the QAs when they’re at home?’

‘The Queen Alexandra’s Royal Army Nursing Corps.’

‘The army?’

‘But as a nurse.’

‘Why?’

Daisy was sitting forward, animated, excited. It reminded Ann of the time Joe came home after hearing the sailor talk about his adventures in the navy. That was in the bloody Cake Shop as well, she thought. She’d have to start going to the Carlisle.

‘I’ve read all about it,’ Daisy went on enthusiastically. ‘They can send you anywhere. I could end up … well, anywhere and I’d learn so much.’

'Look at you, all grown up and all. I knew you'd be a great nurse.'

'So what do you think?'

'You'll probably go no matter what I think …' Daisy was smiling and nodding, willing her to say yes. '… but I think it's a great idea. It'll be a great adventure. I assume you have to be fully trained to get in.'

'Yes, and you have to be single. No old married sisters in the QAs.'

'Sounds like great craic! You'll have to be careful though – all them handsome soldier boys.'

'Was Da a handsome soldier boy?'

Ann looked down and was about to speak when Daisy said, 'Sorry, Ma, I know – wind my neck in.'

They got up to leave. Daisy paid the bill.

'You're the only one who knows about my plans to join the army,' Daisy said.

'No need to tell anyone else if you don't want to. Plenty of time.'

'We can tell Nana if she starts to run out of other things to worry about.'

'She'll never know, in other words,' Ann said. More secrets, she thought, but this was a good one.

They linked arms and set off up Market Street together.

CHAPTER 42

Four years later and The Kinks were on the radio. It was a bright Saturday afternoon in March and Ann was looking forward to Daisy getting home from Germany. Maybe she'd get a job back here, she thought. Then she realised she sounded just like Ma when Hilda, Mu and Joe had decided to escape.

Mary, Arthur and Willy would be home soon after their respective hockey and rugby matches. They hardly ever seemed to win, but they loved it. Ma would be over soon to 'help' with the dinner and the housework. Actually, it was more of a chat and a few cups of tea. The house move had done Ma good. Her cough had improved a bit – the doctor said it was because she wasn't sitting in the damp any more – but her arthritis was getting worse. Stan, the creature of habit, was down at the mart.

Ann turned the music up. She liked The Kinks.

She'd bumped into Mrs Crammond, her old boss, outside Wellworths earlier. They were chatting about this and that when Mrs Crammond asked, 'Have you ever thought about going back to work?'

'I'd love to, but I might be too old now.'

'Not old – experienced, Ann. Experienced. People like experience. Takes ages to get it.' She said that a Miss Rock had taken over in the Department of Education from her old friend Mr Nugent. 'But that's not the important bit,' she went on. 'She needs someone to take over as the head of the typing pool. The lady doing it had to leave. Seriously ill, apparently. Very sad, but every cloud and all that.'

Mrs Crammond offered to give her a reference. That sealed the deal.

Ann had dreamed of going back to work ever since she thought the weans were old enough to know what murder and arson were and had the wit to avoid both.

She decided she would tell Stan after dinner, after he'd had a wee drink. Maybe she'd make it a wee bit bigger than a wee one. She wasn't sure how he'd react. He probably wouldn't care that much. He might care more when I tell him I'm getting driving lessons, she thought. They were a birthday present to herself for her big birthday.

She was right on both counts. Stan thought that her going back to work was a good thing. Especially when she told him she would be head of the typing pool and would be starting on £1,869 a year. More money coming in, less time for it to go out. Good idea. Driving was a whole other thing.

'I can share the driving when we go on longer trips,' Ann argued. 'It means you can relax. You won't get so tired and grumpy, and your back won't seize up so much.'

'How could I relax? Sure I'd be up to high doh with you driving.'

'Why?'

'Because you're nearly forty and women can't drive, it's a well-known fact. They can't park properly or do three-point turns … or work the petrol pumps or put air in the tyres. I'm happy to do the driving.'

'Is three points all you can do?' Ann asked, the picture of innocence. 'I can do a seven-point turn, no bother.' She laughed. 'And I've learned to reverse park. It's easy once you find the right gear. What if you're sick and we have to rush Ma to the hospital?'

Stan narrowed his eyes at her and then smiled. 'It doesn't matter what I say, does it. You've probably passed your test already.'

'I'm doing it next month. I'll have been paid by then.' She held her empty glass up. 'Another one?'

* * *

'April showers bring May flowers,' Ann muttered to herself as she put her coat back on and buttoned it up to her neck. She was only going across the street to Ma's, but it had rained the whole way home from work and she didn't expect it to stop any time soon. The children went to Ma's after school. Mary would be doing her homework; she hoped the boys would be doing theirs; Ma would probably be asleep. She opened the front door.

'That's her now,' came Willy's voice from the scullery.

They looked unnervingly like angels when she walked in. Ma opened one eye and then closed it again.

'Happy birthday, Mummy,' they shouted in unison and jumped out at her.

'Close your eyes, Mummy.' Willy was hopping from foot to foot.

Ann did as she was told. There was much giggling and whispering. She heard a match flaring.

'Okay, you can open them now,' Mary said.

There was a cake on the table with four flickering candles on top.

'There's only four candles, Mummy, cos we couldn't afford forty,' Willy explained.

'It's beautiful,' Ann said, beaming from ear to ear. 'Did you make it?'

Their faces said *don't be silly.*

'We saved our pocket money,' Willy said.

'*Some* of our pocket money,' Arthur corrected him.

But Willy paid no attention. 'Mary went to the Cake Shop.'

'Cut it, Mummy. Cut it.' Willy held out the bread knife. 'It's a jammy spongy one with cream. Your favourite.'

'It's a Victoria sponge,' Mary informed them in an *I-know-everything* voice.

'Victoria sponge. Sounds like somebody from Willy Wonka,' Arthur said, holding out his plate.

Ann cut the spongy sponge. Cream and jam oozed out everywhere. Meanwhile, Mary poured out some lemonade.

'Not too much now. You'll not eat your dinner.'

'Yes, Ma.'

'Now?' Willy whispered theatrically behind his hand to Mary.

Mary nodded and he reached behind the curtain. With a flourish he produced a small red parcel.

'We got this for you as well, Mummy.' He held it out towards her.

Ann was starting to feel a bit overwhelmed. She hadn't been expecting any of this. She carefully opened the shiny red paper (Ma would keep it), and inside was a blue box with 'Parker Pens' embossed on the lid.

'We know how much you like to write to people – Auntie Hilda and Muriel and Uncle Joe,' Mary said.

Arthur took the box as Ann examined the shiny silver pen.

'It doesn't need ink or anything,' Willy said. 'There's a thing inside that has ink in it and when it's done, you get another one.'

'Another pen?' Ann winked at Ma.

'No, silly. Another ink thingy to go inside it.'

'It's called a cartridge,' Mary said, sounding more and more like a school teacher.

'A cartilage,' Willy repeated. 'You get a new cartilage.'

Ann took her hanky out of her pocket and dabbed her eyes. She never got presents, not special ones like this anyway.

'We know Daddy doesn't buy presents, but it's a special birthday, so we thought *we* would buy you one,' Arthur explained.

'What's so special about being forty?' Ann tried to look sad.

'Life begins at forty,' Ma said, reaching for her daughter's hand.

'Does it indeed? Sounds wonderful. I've been waiting for it to begin for ages.'

She kissed them all, deliberately slobbering over the boys until they could take no more. She kissed Ma and mouthed a 'thank you'.

She held up the pen. 'It's lovely. You're all lovely. Your daddy's going to be home soon. So, dinner. Come on, get your coats.'

The children looked pleased with themselves. As they should, Ann thought as she took Ma's arm and watched them cross the street in a windmilling flurry of arms and legs.

'Happy anniversary as well, love,' Ma said, giving Ann's arm a squeeze.

CHAPTER 43

Ann was never so glad to get in the door after work. It was March, but it had just started to snow, horrible wet sleety stuff. She found Arthur sprawled on his belly in the living room, doing his homework. The Dansette was playing at full volume.

'Why are you not over at your nana's?' she asked him.

'What did you say, Ma?'

'Nothing. Who's that?' She took off her coat.

'Ten Years After. It's brilliant.'

Alvin Lee was telling everyone to 'Love Like A Man'.

'Not Leonard Cohen then.' Ann went over and turned it down.

'Sorry, Ma. I didn't realise what time it was.'

'Is it this Friday you're going to see Led Zeppelin?'

Arthur got up. His face was bursting with excitement. 'Yes. Can't wait!'

'Well, get tidied up. I'll go and get your nana. Then we'll get the dinner on.'

'Nana needed a wee sleep, so we left her in peace. I've peeled the spuds,' he added.

‘Good man. You know you’re my favourite don’t you?’ She squeezed his cheek between her thumb and forefinger. He pulled away, smiling. ‘Where’s my other two favourites?’

‘Mary’s not home yet. Willy’s upstairs, arguing with his slide rule. I don’t think maths is his best subject somehow. He makes a wile racket when he gets frustrated.’

‘What *is* his best subject?’

‘I don’t think they teach it at the Academy,’ Arthur said with a grin.

‘That’s cruel.’

‘Sorry, Ma. I know everybody can’t be as clever as me.’

‘Why don’t you go and help your brother, if you can get your big head through the door.’

Stan got home before Mary. Coat hung up. Slippers on.

‘Just going up to the wee boy’s room.’

Just then, Mary came flying through the door. She was flushed and out of breath.

‘Hockey practice went on a bit late today, love,’ Ann said, smiling at her daughter.

‘Aye, it did,’ Mary said, panting. Her cheeks were flushed.

‘So how is Charlie then?’ Ann asked, watching Mary out of the corner of her eye.

‘Ma!’

Ann laughed. ‘It’s okay, love. Your secret’s safe with me.’

‘It’s not a secret. Not now anyway. Not that it ever was in the first place.’ She stormed upstairs.

Stan met her on the landing. ‘Are you okay, love?’

‘Yes, Da. It’s just Ma being Ma.’

Stan laughed. ‘I know what you mean. I gave up years ago.’

* * *

On Saturday, Arthur got up very late. Stan had left for the mart.

'How was the concert?' Ann asked him when he finally appeared.

'Deafening. You could feel the bass in your chest. My ears are still ringing. Can't hear a thing. It was amazing. They played everything. "Dazed and Confused" went on for about half an hour. Then Robert Plant announced they were going to play a new song. It was the first time they'd ever played it live and it was incredible! Big long song called "Stairway to Heaven". It was amazing. Jimmy Page was on fire! It'll be on the fourth album. Can't wait for it.'

Can't wait either, Ann thought as she made tea and toast for her happy, deaf son.

'So Jimmy Page plays the guitar, just like your cousin?'

'Never really thought of that. Same name and all,' Arthur said.

Ann mouthed 'amazing' at him.

On Sunday after dinner the phone rang.

Stan took his pipe out of his mouth. 'I wonder who that could be?'

Ann stroked her chin. 'I wonder how we could find out?'

Stan rolled his eyes. 'Very funny. Just answer the bloody thing. Can you not turn the ringer on it down a bit?'

Ann picked up the green Bakelite handset and said 'Hello?'

She listened for a moment, then put her hand over the mouthpiece. 'It's Daisy,' she told him.

'Surprise, surprise.' Stan stuck his pipe back in his mouth, puffed a bit and realised it had gone out.

'Seriously, love? … Oh, that's brilliant … You're right. It's flown in … Stoke what? … Mandeville? … Sister? That's good.'

'Do you have to repeat everything she says?' Stan asked grumpily as he pulled a pipe cleaner through the stem of his pipe.

Ann ignored him. 'Oh, are you now? … Have you learned any German? Mary can speak German … No, she's not smarter than you. It's just she learned it at school.'

'She bloody is.' Stan muttered as he packed a wad of Black Cat tobacco into the bowl of his pipe. 'Smarter than everyone that girl.'

'I am here, Da,' Mary piped up.

Stan struck a Swan Vesta, set it to his pipe and started puffing, filling the room with fragrant smoke.

Ann chatted and listened for a while, her face animated by frowns and smiles as Daisy spoke.

'It's hard to believe her three years in the QAs is nearly up,' she said after she'd hung up. 'She's got a job lined up in a big hospital in England. Stoke something. I've forgotten.'

'Mandeville,' Arthur grunted from his prone position on the sofa. *Rugby World* was spread out in front of him.

'That's it – Stoke Mandeville. She'll be a sister. How good is that?'

'She's already a sister,' Willy said, looking confused.

'This is a different kind of sister, love. In a hospital, a sister is like a boss nurse.'

'She'll be good at that,' Mary said.

'But wait till you hear this' – Ann tucked her feet under her in the armchair and sat forward – 'She's met a chap out there.'

'A German?' Willy looked horrified.

'No, he's English. Alan, he's called. He's from a place called Aylesbury. It's near Stoke Mandeville and that's why she got a job there … because they're getting married!' That got their attention. They all stared open-mouthed. Stan took his pipe out of his mouth and glowered over the rim of his glasses. His face asked the question.

'No, she's not pregnant,' Ann said indignantly.

'So she says.'

'Da, that's a horrible thing to say. She's fallen in love with an Aylesbury Al.' Mary swooned and clutched her heart.

Arthur and Willy pretended to be sick.

'Is he a soldier?' Mary asked.

'No, she said he has a proper job at a school, but he's also a musician,' Ann said. 'He was over in Germany playing with a band. Guitar, I think.'

'What's his surname, this mad musician?' Mary wanted to know everything.

'Fulton. She'll be Mrs Fulton.'

'That's Blind Boy Fuller's real name,' Arthur said.

'What is?' Now Ann was confused.

'Fulton Allen. Blind Boy Fuller. It's not *him*, is it? Big influence on Led Zeppelin. Not as direct as Willy Dixon, mind you.'

'Is Daisy's boyfriend blind?' Willy piped up.

'No. At least she didn't mention it. Anyway, his name's Alan Fulton, not Fulton Allen.

'He must be blind if he's marrying Daisy.' Willy giggled at his joke.

'Willy! That's cruel. He might not be blind, but he must be desperate.' Arthur started giggling too.

'Well, I think it's great news,' Mary said, mature and sensible as usual. 'Daisy deserves to be happy.'

Stan grunted. 'That thing from the London Palladium's on soon. Who's on it tonight? Would you have a look at the paper, Mary?'

* * *

Stan planted two rows of spuds in the back garden. The boys weren't best pleased as this took away a significant chunk of their football pitch.

'St Patrick's Day. Best time to get them in,' Stan said, straightening up and stretching his back. 'You two can cover them over.'

'When will they be ready, Da?' Willy asked, flinging soil all over the place.

'September sometime.'

'How do you *know* when they're ready?' Arthur said.

'When the boys at the mart tell me,' Stan said with a smile. 'Right, don't be all day at that. You've studying to do.'

'Yes, Da.'

In the house, studying was getting intense. Mary studied quietly in her room while Arthur liked to listen to music. He said it helped him concentrate. He listened to the oddest stuff though, Ann thought. Most of the musicians seemed to be blind. Willy used the table in the kitchen. Ann tried to help him with his sums. Sums were easy until they started putting letters in them, she thought.

Mary was doing her A-levels in May and had only two months left to revise. She was very calm about it, but Ann was worried because Mary obviously wasn't worrying enough.

'No point both of us worrying,' Mary said when Ann asked her about it. 'Let me know if you come across something more important to worry about. Then I might give it a go.'

'We could get your nana to do a bit.'

'Good idea. She's quite good at multi-worrying. In fact, I think the more worry balls she has in the air, the happier she is.'

'What are you revising today?'

'French grammar. Boring stuff.'

'Well, as long as you know what you're doing.'

'Yes, it's French grammar.'

'Very funny. Egg and chips for dinner.'

'Did you get some Angel Delight?'

'I did.'

'What flavour?'

'Pink.'

Mary looked up from her book and smiled. 'My favourite.'

* * *

Mary's A-level results were better than any of them, except Mary, could have hoped for – three A grades in French, German and English Language. Ann and Stan were bursting with pride. Mary would be going to university!

'Bristol looks like it has the best course, Ma,' Mary said, flicking through brochures.

'Where's Bristol?'

Mary opened the atlas. It was dog-eared and the spine was cracked. All of them denied that it had been them who had scribbled over the graphs and bar charts at the front.

'There.' Mary pointed at a spot halfway down the map of England. 'And we are here.' She turned the page to the map of Ireland.

'Do you want to go and see the place before you make your mind up?' Ann asked.

'No need, Ma. Sure you and Da have Daisy's wedding to go to. That'll cost a lot.' Ann could hardly believe that this beautiful, intelligent, thoughtful young lady was her daughter. 'I'll be able to sort everything out over the phone. They have places for students to stay. Halls of Residence, they're called.'

‘You’ll be staying in a hall? Very posh.’

‘No, Ma.’ Mary frowned. ‘The hall just joins the rooms up – like it does in a hotel.’

‘I’ve never stayed in a hotel,’ Ann said. ‘Apparently they’re like Halls of Residence.’

Mary shook her head and smiled.

Ann gave her a hug. ‘I’m so proud of you, love. We both are.’

‘Getting there is only the start, Ma. It’s what you end up with that matters.’

‘You sound very grown up. Have you been taking tablets?’

Mary laughed. ‘No, Ma.’

‘What will *you* end up with?’

‘A Bachelor of Arts degree in Modern Languages.’

‘Olden languages aren’t much use, I suppose,’ Ann said, a mischievous twinkle in her eye. ‘Seriously though, then what? After you get this degree?’

‘I want a job at the United Nations in New York.’

‘Oh, excuse me! You’re not coming back to Omagh then.’ Ann laughed. She was impressed with her daughter’s ambition, but dreaded the thought of having to let her go. What she said was, ‘Good for you, love. New York, eh? Why not. The sky’s your limit.’

‘Or maybe I could do something that involves travelling. Be a tour guide. You get to travel the world and get paid for it.’

‘That sounds exciting. You could be a tour guide in Canada and go and see Auntie Hilda. I think she has polar bears in her garden.’

‘I’d need to be able to speak Canadian.’

‘True,’ Ann said, laughing.

‘But they speak a lot of French in Canada.’

'Dan speaks French. And he could teach you Russian.'

'Russian would be rushin' it.' Mary giggled.

How this could be the same Mary who had put lipstick on five-year-old Arthur's face just as they were about to go to church, Ann wondered, or who had hidden Willy's shoes as they were getting ready to go in the car to Portsalon, only relenting when a nervous breakdown looked imminent.

'We should go and see Bristol.'

'No, Ma. No need. If I don't like it, I'll come home. I can get my old Saturday job back in Bogue's and we'll all live happily ever after.'

'That's my girl. Too much ambition isn't good for you. Know your place. That's what I say. You should stay at home like me and look after somebody.'

'Who?'

'Anybody. Whoever needs looking after.'

'Sounds like we have a plan.'

Ann felt a pang of jealousy.

'I'll try and call every Sunday,' Mary added, 'if I'm not at church or in the pub, that is.'

'Jesus, Muriel and Daisy already call every Sunday,' Ann said. 'Three calls in one day – your da won't be able to get his nap.'

CHAPTER 44

Later in August, they went to Portsalon again. The sun shone gloriously nearly every other day.

On one of those glorious blue days, Ann and Stan were sunbathing on the beach. Ann was already a golden brown; Stan was molten red. The three children announced they were going to walk over to the aeroplane. Without lifting her head, Ann warned them to put sunscreen on.

Mary put on a long loose blouse over the top of her red bikini and flicked her long blond hair out over her shoulders. She was tanned. She looked like a model. Arthur pulled on his white Leeds United shirt. For reasons known only to himself, Willy was now a Manchester City fan, but his sky-blue shirt was miles too big for his skinny frame and he tucked it into his shorts.

Knockalla Mountain loomed large to their right; the new road up it was like a silver necklace of hairpins. To their left was the partially buried American plane. It was just a short walk past the plane to Portsalon itself. They paddled across the freezing river that created a kind of mini estuary in the sand on its way down to the sea. The rivulets shone golden in the sun. At the end of the beach, they walked up a few stone steps and across a lawn that ran all the way down from the dark, imposing hotel. Then they went past the golf club towards Rita's. They went in past the sweets and the buckets and spades, the little fishing nets and the plastic footballs hanging in string bags, to the back bar with its view of the pier and the beach stretching away to the mountain in the distance. They could see the tiny dot that was Ma's red sunshade.

Mary went out to the front bar. She was the oldest and looked nearly grown up. She came back with a pint of Woodpecker cider for herself, a pint of Guinness for Arthur and a Football Special for Willy. It was a sweet, fizzy, brown drink that looked a bit like beer. It even had a head on it; children thought it was very grown up.

Rita followed Mary into the back bar. 'Do your ma and da know you're here?'

'They sent us,' Mary said, looking as innocent as her virgin namesake. 'They said they wanted some peace and quiet.'

'What they're doing on their own in the sand dunes is anybody's guess, but they told us not to hurry back,' Arthur said and he tried to wink. He had a creamy moustache he was totally unaware of.

Rita lifted a few empty glasses off the table next to theirs.

'We think this might be our last summer here, Rita,' Mary said, taking a sip of her cider.

Rita set the glasses down. 'Why's that? You've been coming for years. Must be ten … fifteen.'

'I'm off to university in England in September and they won't come without me. It just wouldn't be the same, Ma says.' Mary ran her hand through her hair.

‘It’d be far better.’ Willy wiped foam off his nose. ‘We could have a room each.’

‘Who would show you two dopes how to make a proper sandcastle?’ Mary asked.

‘Big round piles are the best,’ Arthur said, almost eating the head of his Guinness. He felt very grown up. ‘Buckets are for weans.’

‘I still like a bucket, I must say.’ Willy looked comically thoughtful as he stroked his chin.

‘Exactly my point,’ Arthur quipped.

‘Maybe you’ll get back someday, Mary. You won’t be at university for ever,’ Rita said.

‘Maybe. We’ll see. I’m sure I will.’

After they’d finished their drinks, they wandered back to the spot where they’d left their ma and da on the beach.

‘Where did you lot get to?’ Ann asked, knowing exactly where they’d been. Ann thought Mary looked gorgeous – *just like me when I was her age*.

‘We went to Rita’s to say goodbye. I had a Fanta and the boys had Football Specials,’ Mary said.

The boys nodded. Ann narrowed her eyes at them, then looked at Mary. But she said nothing; they were on their holidays.

They trudged back across the field to the bungalow. Then they got washed and dressed and went out to the little wooden restaurant beside Rita’s for their last holiday dinner: fish and chips times five.

CHAPTER 45

The rest of the year passed almost without notice. Arthur went to see Rory Gallagher in the Ulster Hall just before Christmas. Ann made the mistake, at some stage, of saying that she actually quite liked 'Tangerine' by Led Zeppelin. So the boys got her *Led Zeppelin 4* for Christmas. She laughed when she saw it.

'Do you not want it, Ma?' Arthur asked, almost before she'd finished unwrapping it.

'Can we have it?' Willy grabbed it.

As 1972 began, Arthur began serious studying.

'How can you study with that racket?' Ann asked him.

'What racket?'

'Put on J.J. Cale. I like him.'

'Crazy Mama.'

'That'll do.'

'It was meant to be a comment.'

'Very funny. Turn it down and do your sums, like a good boy.'

'Yes, Ma.'

Eventually he took to disappearing to his bedroom with a radio.

He sat his last O-level on Thursday 25th May and went to Bogan's afterwards to celebrate with a few mates. They took their school ties off and went in by the side door to the back room. Arthur had two half pints of Guinness. The boys were noisy and boisterous. A summer of freedom, flirting and football lay ahead.

Their other classmates had gathered in the Golden Griddle, so Arthur and his pals joined them. They made a plate of chips last for hours. Arthur didn't get home until after eight o'clock and he went straight to his bedroom.

Ann thought he seemed a bit agitated and decided to check that he was all right. She knocked and popped her head around his bedroom door. 'Is everything all right, son? How do you think you've done?'

Arthur looked up. 'Everything's fine, Ma. I don't know how I've done, but it should be okay. The subjects I want to do for A-level – Biology, Geography and English Lit – should all be okay. I'm just tired, that's all.'

'Of course they'll be okay. Sure you're nearly as smart as me. You'll be fine.'

Arthur smiled at her. 'Nobody's as smart as you, Ma.'

Ann leaned down and hugged him. 'You say all the right things.'

'I know. I wonder where I get that from.'

'When do you go to see what's-his-name – the new headmaster – about A-levels and stuff?'

'He's called Mr Hooper and I've no idea.'

'Go to sleep. Is there rugby tomorrow?'

'No. It's Friday tomorrow. But there's no more anyway, even on Saturday. It's the summer holidays.'

‘Thank God. The washing machine will be very happy. Goodnight, son.’ She kissed his forehead.

‘Night, Ma.’

At work the next morning, Ann had hardly got her coat off when Miss Rock, her boss, called her into her office. Her normally friendly face looked set and serious.

‘Sit down, Ann.’

Ann sat down. ‘What’s wrong? You look … upset.’

‘It’s Arthur.’

‘Arthur?’ Ann was puzzled. She’d left him still in bed just half an hour ago.

Miss Rock held up her hands, palms out. ‘Don’t worry, he’s not hurt or anything, but—’

‘But what? What’s happened?’

‘Mr Hooper called me first thing. He said he was going to phone you here, but I said I’d rather it came from me. There’s no easy way to say this, Ann. Arthur’s been expelled.’

‘Exp— What? What for?’ Ann didn’t understand. Her mind was reeling.

‘The walls of the Academy are covered in graffiti. It’s mostly infantile and poorly spelled, but some of it is very rude towards Mr Hooper.’

‘How do you know it was Arthur?’

‘You know Mr James, the caretaker?’

Ann nodded. Elmore James lived in the grounds of the school.

‘Well, his daughter Eleanor was going out for the night about quarter to eight. She recognised Arthur and Gary Moore walking towards the gates at Johnston Park. There was another boy with them whom she didn’t know. It was only this morning when Mr James was going to start his summer cleaning that he saw the graffiti.’

'That doesn't prove it was Arthur who wrote on the walls,' Ann said indignantly. She was shaking and dropped her pen. She bent down and struggled to pick it up. Don't cry, she told herself as she sat back up.

'I'll get you a glass of water,' Miss Rock said and got up from behind her desk.

'Can't be Arthur,' Ann mumbled to herself. 'He's too smart to be that stupid. Must be a mistake.'

Miss Rock came back and handed Ann a glass of cold water.

'Thank you,' Ann said. 'Does anyone else know about this?'

'No, no one else knows anything about it, but news travels fast around here, as you know, and Eleanor is not the most discreet person I've ever met.'

'She must have made a mistake. Arthur wouldn't do a thing like that.' Ann couldn't think straight. 'He's a smart boy. Why would he—' She set the glass of water on the desk and got out her hanky. 'This is madness.' She shook her head in disbelief. 'Sorry, Miss Rock. I … I don't know …'

'Where's Arthur now?'

'He's at home. Probably not up yet.'

'You need to go home and talk to him.'

'Is there anything I can do? Will Mr Hooper change his mind? Maybe if Arthur apologises and cleans it all off?'

'That's up to Mr Hooper. It's worth a try, but as things stand, Arthur has no school to go to in September. I know he's a clever boy. It's a real pity.'

Ann stood up, steadying herself with the desk.

'Do you know how he did in his exams?'

'It's too early to say yet, but from his previous results, I imagine he's done really well.'

'Even though he can't spell?'

Miss Rock smiled. 'Go home and look after him.'

'I have that report to do for you. I was going to finish it this morning.'

'Don't worry about the report. I'll get someone else to finish it. I'll just have to check it more rigorously, that's all.'

Ann tried to smile. 'Thank you, Miss Rock.'

'Eileen. Please.'

This really is serious, Ann thought. Nobody calls Miss Rock Eileen.

Ann set off for home. It had started to rain, and she looked up at the heavens and shook her head. The wheel of fortune had turned again. The walking helped to calm her down. Nobody had died; it wasn't that serious. She'd sort it out. Arthur was going to be the best marine biologist the world had ever seen – apart from Jacques Cousteau, of course. Still, he needed his arse kicked.

As Ann passed Taggart's at the bottom of Scarffe's Entry, she could see the field in front of the Academy. No one was playing football. She looked at her watch. It was only half nine.

When she got home, Arthur was sitting on the settee, his head in his hands. He was listening to 'Sinner Boy'. Ann scratched the record as she lifted the stylus off.

'Ma! What are you doing here?'

'You know fine rightly why I'm here. Miss Rock called me into her office first thing. Never even got my arse in my seat ... You're in serious trouble, Arthur Webb.'

'Yeah, Gary phoned.'

'So you know you've been expelled. Expelled, Arthur ... It's nothing to smile about! You've no school to go to in September. Do you know what that means? What happened? Tell me it's all a mistake.'

'It was just supposed to be a bit of craic, Ma. We hadn't planned it or anything. Paddy Lock was in the Griddle. We call him Pad. Get it?'

Ann wasn't amused. 'This is serious, Arthur. Who the hell's Paddy Lock?'

'He goes to the Sacred Heart. We know him from football. He's good craic.'

'And?'

'And … well, Pad had some cans of paint with him. He was going to spray his bike. Gary and him walked up past the clinic with me. They were going to cut across the school to get home. Suddenly Pad stops and says he has this idea. "Come on, it'll be great craic," he says. "Five minutes. Then you can go home to your mummy and tell her how smart you are." I told him you already knew how smart I was, but he kept insisting. "Wait'll you see," he says, "it'll be great." Pad gave me and Gary a can and the next thing, we were writing all sorts of stuff on the walls. It was like we'd gone mad.'

'So it's this Pad Lock's fault? We can blame him for this?' Ann felt the stress flow out of her.

'No, Ma, no. Pad had the paint, but I didn't have to take it. I could have said no and just come home. I didn't have to write on the walls. I was two minutes from the house and could have come home, but I didn't.'

Ann felt strangely proud of her son, taking responsibility, not blaming his friends. He still needed his arse kicked though.

'I'm sorry, Ma. It was a moment of madness. I'm an idiot. I'm sorry. I'm sorry you're upset and I'm sorry I've let you down.' He put his head in his hands. His shoulders were shaking.

'You think I'm upset? Wait till your father gets home,' Ann said quietly.

'What do we do now?' Arthur said, still sniffling.

'You're going to ring the school.'

Arthur looked horrified.

Ann held her hand up to stop him speaking. 'You're going to ring the school and ask if you can go in and see Mr Hooper. Today. You're going to apologise, beg for forgiveness and offer to clean the walls. You're going to ask him to change his mind.'

'Oh God, Ma.'

'Yes, Oh God.'

'Will you come with me?'

'No, I think it needs to be just you – man-to-man sort of thing.'

'Maaaa!'

'*Maaaa.*' Ann echoed his pleading squeak. 'Just tell him what you told me and that you're sorry, really sorry, and hope he changes his mind.'

They heard the front gate slam against the fence.

'There's your da,' Ann said. 'He must have heard in work.'

'Oh shit.'

The front door slammed shut. Stan didn't even take his coat off.

'What the fuck have you done? Bloody smart alec. Too bloody smart for your own good.' He slapped Arthur hard on the side of his head, knocking him sideways on the settee. Ann saw Arthur clench his fists for a split second, but he covered his head instead and stayed down.

Stan's right hand was still raised.

'Stan! Stop it!' She grabbed his arm. 'Smacking him on the head isn't going to help.'

'He didn't get smacked enough, that's the problem. It's your bloody fault. You're far too soft with them.'

Ann stared at the angry stranger in front of her. 'I'm their mother and they are good weans,' she said calmly. 'Arthur is a good boy.'

'*Good boys* don't get expelled from school. The whole town knows. I found out in my tea break.'

Ann realised this was probably the real reason for Stan's anger – big strong Stan with the delinquent son and everyone knowing his business.

She knelt down beside Arthur. 'Stop crying, love,' she whispered. 'Go up to your room.'

'*Stop crying, love!*' Stan mimicked Ann. 'Bloody hell, he's not a baby.'

Ann ignored Stan. 'Get your jammies and toothbrush and stuff. You can stay at your Nana's tonight.'

'No bloody way. He'll do no such—'

Ann pushed Stan away. 'Shush. You need to calm down. We all need to calm down. Go on, Arthur.'

Arthur crept out of the room.

'I'll get you a wee whiskey,' Ann said, watching Stan slump into his chair. 'We need to work this out. Together.'

Just like Ann, his Nana took the news in her stride. 'How could you be so stupid?'

'I've never been stupid before. Maybe you get stupider as you get older.'

'I must be very stupid then.' Ma winked at Ann.

'I didn't mean that, Nana.'

'I know you didn't, love.'

'I don't know what I mean any more.' Arthur sounded exhausted.

'Is Stan really angry?' Ma looked at Ann.

Ann nodded. 'He hit him, Ma. Hard. On the head.'

'Oh dear. No need for that. Are you all right, love?'

'It was only a slap. On my head, so it didn't hurt.' Arthur tried to smile. His head was splitting though.

Ann stayed at Ma's until Arthur seemed settled.

'You can call the school on Monday when your da's at work. I'll bring some stew over later.'

'Thanks, Ma.' Arthur stood up and mouthed *love you* as she was about to leave.

'I love you too,' Ann said, 'but sometimes you don't make it easy.'

At dinner that night, Ann sat Willy down and explained what had happened.

'He'll be a hero!' Willy said, excited to have a hero for a brother.

'He's a disgrace,' Stan butted in. 'That's what he is. A bloody disgrace.'

Ann ignored him. 'He's not a hero, Willy. He's in a lot of trouble. So please don't wind Arthur up when you see him. He feels bad enough as it is.'

Willy nodded sombrely.

Ann sat down opposite Stan. 'He'll never become a marine biologist without any A-levels. We need to work out what to do.'

'He'll be in jail if he carries on like this.' Stan puffed hard on his pipe and sipped another whiskey.

'Can I go and see him?' Willy asked.

'You're not going anywhere,' Stan barked, still in *I'm-the-boss* mode.

Ann ignored him. 'That would be good, Willy. He needs his brother. Don't stay too long though.'

'I'll not ask him if I can have his football boots if he has to go to jail,' Willy said with a grin.

'Yes, better not. Talk about Leeds and Led Zeppelin.'

'Yes, Ma,' Willy said.

He got up from the table and ran out the front door. An hour later, he was back.

'Well?' Ann asked.

'He's okay. Quiet. Feeling sorry for himself.'

'Bloody right, he's feeling sorry for himself,' Stan muttered.

Ann ignored Stan's less-than-helpful commentary.

Willy eyed up his father. 'I think I'll go up to bed. I'm nearly finished *The Devil Rides Out*.'

'What the hell kind of a book is that?' Stan asked gruffly.

'It's by Dennis Wheatley. It's scary.'

'You let them read rubbish like that?'

Ann ignored this as well. 'Go on, son. You can take it back tomorrow, then?'

'All three books, Ma.'

'Good boy. Sleep tight.'

'Night, Ma, Da.'

'Good night, son,' Ann responded.

Stan grunted.

Ann and Stan sat on in silence, Stan pretending he was watching TV, Ann staring into the fire.

After an hour or so, Ann said, 'I'm going to bed. Are you coming?'

But Stan just grunted and puffed on his pipe.

'It'll all look different in the morning. Nobody died,' Ann said.

Stan gave his pipe another puff.

On Saturday, Ann went down the town early to do the shopping; she didn't want to bump into anyone. Stan didn't go to the mart. They didn't go to church on Sunday.

First thing Monday morning, Arthur rang Omagh Academy. Ann was standing beside him for moral support.

'It's Arthur Webb here.'

Ann could hear the receptionist gasp. 'Oh.'

'Can I come in this morning and speak to Mr Hooper, please?' Arthur asked.

'I'll need to ask him. Hold on a minute.'

While they waited, all they could hear was the clock ticking on the mantelpiece. Neither of them dared speak. Eventually, the receptionist came back.

'He says you can come in if you want. He's here all day.'

'I'll be there in fifteen minutes,' Arthur said and he hung up.

He put on his uniform, making sure it was clean and neat, and went to the school. He knew some of the teachers were watching him out of the staffroom window as he walked past. He straightened his back.

He thought he was calm, but his stomach was churning. He tried to think about what he should say. Plead insanity? Beg for mercy? No, he wouldn't beg. No need to beg. He'd speak to Mr Hooper man-to-man. He'd understand it was just a moment of madness. He'd offer to clean it off. Damn it, he'd beg for mercy.

He knocked firmly on the door.

'Come in.'

He turned the handle. His heart was pumping.

'Webb! You've a nerve, I'll give you that.'

'Please, sir, I want to apologise and explain what happened. I don't know what got into me. You know it's not like me.'

'I'm listening.'

Arthur told him what he'd told his ma.

'Very good. Apology accepted. We'll not be pressing charges. Now get out.'

'But …'

‘Get out now!’ Mr Hooper stood up and pointed at the door. He was a glowering, quivering mass of rage.

‘Please, sir …’

‘Out! Now!’ he shrieked.

Well, fuck you, Arthur thought as he turned and left. He was shaking. ‘Not pressing charges! Jesus!’ he muttered to himself as he walked away. Teachers were supposed to understand. They were supposed to help people when they made mistakes. Fat lot of use this lot were.

Arthur walked slowly past the staff room, holding his head high. He felt like crying.

CHAPTER 46

While her son was with the headmaster, Ann was sipping tea in Eileen Rock's office.

'Let's assume that Mr Hooper won't agree to take Arthur back. The options are Dungannon Royal or Portora in Enniskillen. Strabane is a good school too, but they don't have an A-level English teacher,' Eileen said.

'They're both miles away,' Ann said in despair.

'They're both about an hour by bus. You'd have to pay for the bus. Or he could become a boarder at Portora, but that would be expensive.'

'Oh God, I don't know what to do for the best.'

'You'd need to go and see Mr Blackmore at Dungannon and Mr Richards at Portora and see if they'd be willing to take Arthur.'

'And what if they don't? Then what do we do?'

'We'll cross that bridge when we come to it,' Eileen said. 'Anyway, you don't know yet. Maybe Mr Hooper will take him back. Go home and see how Arthur got on and take it from there. He needs you more than we do at the moment.'

'Thanks, Eileen.'

'Well, how did it go?' Ann asked the sullen boy on the settee when she got home.

'He listened but he didn't listen, if you know what I mean. He accepted my apology, then told me to get out. Said he wasn't pressing charges.'

'Charges? What charges?' Ann hadn't been expecting that.

'Gary says we did criminal damage to the school.'

'Oh God, Arthur! … Don't tell your da.'

'I don't think he'll ever speak to me again.'

'He'll come round. He's a good man. He just finds it hard to show his emotions.'

'He can show anger pretty well.' Arthur shrugged.

'Aye, he has that one sorted out all right. It's disappointing that Mr Hooper wasn't in more of a forgiving mood.'

'He's like Da. The world says he should be angry, so he's angry. No alternative reaction is possible. Well, good riddance, I say. It's a shitty school. Half the teachers are violent bullies who like caning people – bloody perverts – half of them are senile and well past it, and the other half are both. They're all useless. I'm surprised anybody ever passes their exams. Mary must be a genius.'

Ann was quietly amused by Arthur's rant – and his appalling maths.

'You had three halves in there,' she said with a smile, trying to diffuse his anger.

Without missing a beat he said, 'Three halves don't make a right.' A smile twitched at the corners of his mouth.

'Try not to be unkind, son. Rise above it. Be strong. We'll sort it out … somehow.'

'Yeah, somehow.' Arthur sighed heavily. 'Five minutes of madness and everything is gone.'

'I know what you mean, son,' The night at the Starr Ballroom flashed in her mind. 'You have to remember the rest of the time, not just those five minutes. It's what you do afterwards that counts. Think of all the good things – good marks in everything, captain of the rugby team, top scorer, smart, good-looking.'

Arthur blushed. 'I'm only the top scorer cos I kick all the penalties.'

'You kick all the penalties because you're the best at it.'

'I'm the captain, that's why. And I'm the out-half.' He paused for a moment. 'And I'm the best at it.' He was smiling again.

'Good man. So now that you're not going to jail, the question is, what do we do with you?'

'I could forget about school. Get a job – maybe with the council.'

'You wouldn't last a day!'

'Ma! You're supposed to be on my side. I'm fit. I could dig sheughs all day if I had to. Look at these for sheugh-digging arms.' He flexed his biceps.

Ann squeezed them and nodded solemnly. 'Not bad, not bad, but you're a bit skinny.'

'I'm an athlete.'

She laughed. 'I didn't mean you couldn't do the work. I meant you'd be bored to tears in no time. You need a job that'll stretch your enormous intellect.'

Arthur pushed his shoulders back and puffed out his chest. Ann grabbed his ears.

'Ow! That's sore.'

Laughing, Ann let go. 'We need to think properly,' she said. 'You need to do your A-levels. You can't go to university without A-levels and you can't be the next Jacques Cousteau without a degree in fish.'

'I'll kill her,' Arthur mumbled.

'Who?' Ann already knew who.

'Mary. She's obviously blabbed. I told her it was only a notion. I'll never be like Jacques Cousteau.'

'She didn't blab. I tortured her until she told me.' Arthur smiled at her. 'I made her listen to Ken Dodd until she cracked. And she didn't say "notion", she said "dream".'

'Same thing. They never come true.'

Ann secretly agreed, but out loud she said, 'They do sometimes. Look at your Auntie Muriel. Living the dream in a castle with servants and fountains and proper glasses. And Auntie Hilda – she's in her dreamland as well, surrounded by polar bears and multilingual spies.'

'What about your dreams, Ma? Did they come true?'

'My dream was to have you – captain of the team, kicker of penalties, best marine biologist ever.'

'Just me?'

'Yep. You're my favourite.'

Arthur laughed again. 'Nothing else? No other dreams?'

'No, nothing. I have simple needs.'

Arthur didn't believe her, but he smiled at her. 'The Undersea World of Arthur Webb,' he said.

'That's the spirit! Anyway, all this dreaming isn't solving the question of what happens next. The options are Dungannon or Portora. What do you think? Who has the best rugby team?'

'They both have good teams, but is that it? What about my mates?'

'You can't take them with you.'

'I know. It's just—'

'Better without your mates, if they just get you into trouble. Anyway, you'll make new ones. No one said it was going to be easy.'

'Gary says he's going to the tech. He wants to be joiner.'

'But you can't do A-level biology at the tech.'

'I know, but it made me think.'

'Oh God no, not more thinking.'

'Seriously, this is proper thinking.'

'Go on then. Do I need a drink?'

Arthur shook his head. 'You said nobody said it was going to be easy. Well, what about this for a *not easy* option? What about this for a *very not easy* option?' He glanced at his ma to gauge her initial reaction.

'Go on.'

'You know how there's some of them uns that play football with us?'

Ann nodded.

'Well, some of them are almost human.'

Ann pretended to look shocked.

'They are, Ma. They're normal – nearly – and the smarter ones go to the Christian Brothers School. Maybe I could go there.'

Ann was stunned. She couldn't speak. Then she shook her head. 'No chance, son. You're not going to the CBS. You must be mad. Desperate and mad. Your da would have a fit. He wouldn't allow it, and as for Ma – she would have to disown you.'

'When did you ever worry about what he says? Can we at least talk to them? Pleeease, Mummy.' Arthur put the palms of his hands together like he was praying and looked at her with big pleading eyes.

'Stop looking at me like that,' Ann said. 'You know I can't resist it.'

'We could go and talk to the head buck cat brother and see what he says. If it looks like I'll have to become an altar boy or learn Irish or play Gaelic football, then so be it. I'll even sit on his knee if they have a good biology teacher.'

'Arthur Webb! That's probably blasphemy or something.' Then Ann remembered Sinead, the brilliant nurse in the Royal all those years ago, her friend. 'But nothing beats a try, I guess,' she said.

'What's the worst that can happen?' Arthur asked.

'The head brother could wave that smoky thing at you and hypnotise you into becoming one of them.'

'I never thought of that. I'll close my eyes and hold my breath.'

'Ma will never speak to you or me ever again,' Ann said.

'I know Nana will hate it, but she'll be okay. She always knows what the right thing to do is, even if it's not the easiest.'

How true is that, Ann thought.

'But your da won't hear tell of it. He'll go mad.'

'I'll wear a crash helmet when we tell him.'

'*Ask* him, you mean …' Ann paused. 'No, you're right – we'll *tell* him. I'll tell him Miss Rock suggested it as an "out there" option, so we can't just ignore it.'

'See? I knew you were the smartest ma ever … Will we give it a go then?'

'Yes, son, we'll try. It's completely mad, and the Troubles don't make it any easier. But if they don't want to beat you up all the time or teach you how to light candles and count to twelve, then it's worth a go.'

Arthur looked puzzled. 'Eh?'

'There're twelve stations of the cross. You'll have to get up to speed with all this stuff. You'll have to know your Ash Wednesday from your Advent calendar.'

'Homework for the summer, eh? Maybe they'll all become

Prods when they see how happy and smart you can be without knowing all that stuff.'

Ann shook her head and laughed. 'Aye, well don't count on it. Let's go and see them first.'

'You might just be the best ma ever, Ma.' Arthur reached over and gave her a wee kiss.

'No might about it,' Ann said, trying to look stern.

* * *

'He is *not* going to the Christian Brothers. That's the stupidest thing I've ever heard.' Stan sat down and reached for his pipe, indicating that that was the end of the discussion.

'Stan, listen – it might be the best option. They have the best teachers. Miss Rock thinks we should at least talk to them – find out if they really have horns and eat their children.'

'The brothers are celibate, Ma,' Arthur interjected. 'Maybe they eat other people's children. Keeps the place tidy.'

'See! Too bloody smart for his own good,' Stan growled. 'He should join the army. Learn some discipline.'

'What he needs is to do his A-levels,' Ann said emphatically.

'He's only in this mess cos you let him run wild, galivanting off to concerts and all sorts. You don't even know where he is half the time.'

Ann was getting angry. 'So I should have left it all up to you? Is that what you're saying? You've never shown the slightest bit of interest. I agree that everything is my fault because I'm the only one who has done anything. I've brought them up. But weans need their da as well. I know what it's like not to have one.'

Stan clenched his fists. His eyes were slits. 'I am their da. They've never wanted for anything.'

'And they're very grateful – *we're* very grateful – but this isn't about money or things, even though sending Arthur to the Christian Brothers would be the cheapest option' – Ann hoped her inspired reference to 'cheap' would have an impact – 'It's about Arthur's future.'

'He made a mistake and he should pay for it, not told *there, there, poor baby.*'

He looks lost, Ann thought. *And angry, because that's how he's supposed to feel. He's out of his depth. The poor man has no idea how to deal with this. It's like there's a heart of gold beating inside a big stone statue.*

'Everybody makes mistakes, Stan.' Again, Ann found herself being reeled back to that night outside the Starr. 'But you shouldn't have to pay for them for the rest of your life. Five minutes was all it was – out of sixteen years. He's suffered enough.' Ann was in full flow. 'We need to do the right thing for him and not worry about what anybody else thinks. He's *our* son, not theirs. He doesn't need smacked on the head or sent off to join the army. He's smart. He knows what he's done and he's learned from it.'

'Has he? He seems to have got over it pretty quick if you ask me.'

Arthur was sitting with his head in his hands.

'He hasn't "got over it". Can you not see how he feels? He wants to move on – not forget it, but move on. He knows it was stupid. He's not denying that, but he needs to look forward now, not back. What's done is done. All we can do is help him find the best way to move forward. He's our son.'

Arthur didn't move, except to tap his hands against his head in applause.

Stan puffed on his pipe as if he'd heard none of what she'd said.

‘Have you never made a mistake?’ she asked him.

Stan glowered at her over his glasses.

‘I hope that look doesn’t mean what it looks like it means,’ Ann hissed at him.

‘Do what you like. You always do,’ he eventually said.

And always will, she thought. What she said was, ‘Well, somebody has to do something. It might not work out, but we won’t know unless we try.’

Stan just puffed away on his pipe, sinking further into his chair and looking more and more like an old man.

A couple of days later, Arthur and Ann braced themselves for a visit to Omagh Christian Brothers.

‘Are you okay?’ Ann asked Arthur, brushing his hair back from his face with her hand. He was wearing his going-to-church clothes and looked very dapper.

‘Yes, I think so. Nervous, but up for it, if you know what I mean. Like going to the dentist, only more important. What if he says no?’

‘He won’t say no. You do your butter-wouldn’t-melt thing and I’ll do my concerned-Ma thing. He’ll do his good-Christian thing and we’ll all be okay.’

‘Why are you always so positive about everything? I wish I was as optimistic. What if he’s spoken to Mr Hooper?’

‘Of course he’s spoken to Mr Hooper. Eileen Rock has spoken to Mr Hooper and to Brother McGlynn. She says he’s a lovely man and he’ll do the right thing. He knows how smart you are and he likes his rugby apparently.’ Ann knew that not being able to play rugby was a big thing for Arthur. ‘Maybe you could start a team.’

‘Yes, Ma. And there will be peace on earth.’

‘Don’t mention *peace* or Bloody Sunday or anything to do with the Troubles.’

'Pretend nothing's happening you mean?'

'Exactly. Everybody else does.'

Arthur pulled a face.

'Don't do that. You'll hurt yourself,' Ann said.

'What if he asks me what I think?'

'Well, then you'll have to gauge what the right answer is at the time.'

'Would the truth not be the right answer?'

'No … maybe … not always. What you say and what you think can be very different. You can tell him what you think when you're leaving.'

'Today?'

'No – God, for somebody so smart, you can be very thick at times. When you're leaving to go to university. He won't want to talk about the Troubles either. This is about school stuff.'

'Yes, Ma.'

'I met a really nice Catholic once. We became friends. Haven't seen her for a long time though. Sinead, her name was – still is, probably.'

Arthur grinned. 'Where did you meet her?'

'She was a nurse in the Royal up in Belfast.'

'What were you doing in the Royal?'

All the old secrets flooded back. And all the old lies. 'I was visiting a sick friend.'

'Did they get better?'

'No, he died. Come on. Let's go.'

CHAPTER 47

Deep breaths. Ann mouthed *Are you okay* at Arthur. He nodded and straightened his tie.

Ann knocked the door.

'Come in,' said a deep, warm voice inside.

As it turned out, Brother McGlynn was a delight. His office was big, with leather armchairs and a large mahogany desk. There were religious pictures on the walls, but there was also one of him holding a guitar and another of him standing beside Mike Gibson, the famous rugby player, whom Arthur recognised immediately.

'Good morning, Mrs Webb.' Brother McGlynn stood up as they walked in. He was large in every direction. He came round the desk and held out his hand. 'And you must be Arthur.'

Arthur's hand was crushed in a huge paw. Jesus, Arthur thought, taken aback by the strength of the man's grip, and immediately felt guilty for blaspheming.

Ann got a gentle, fingers-only handshake.

'Sit down. Please.' Brother McGlynn indicated an armchair to Ann. 'You sit here, Arthur.' He pulled out a straight-backed chair on the other side of his desk.

'Yes, sir.'

'I'm not a sir. I'm a brother.' He beamed at Arthur benignly.

'Yes, Brother.'

'Good man.' He scooped his cassock under his bum and sat down behind his desk.

'You've got yourself into a bit of bother, I believe,' he began, looking directly at Arthur. His voice was warm and gentle.

'Yes, Brother, I—'

Brother McGlynn held up a large hand. 'Miss Rock has told me what your mother told her. I've also spoken to Mr Hooper, who obviously saw the results of your' – he coughed into his hand – 'youthful antics. He told me you'd come in to see him to apologise. That was a brave thing to do. Shows maturity. No, what I would like to know is why you want to come here? You can speak your mind. There are obvious issues. At the moment we have no Protestant pupils in the school – I hate the word "Prod", don't you? – and we've never had any. So tell me, why should that change?'

He waved his hand to indicate that Arthur could speak.

Arthur cleared his throat. 'I want to be a marine biologist, if and when I ever grow up.' He glanced at his mother. She nodded.

Brother McGlynn smiled at this exchange.

'And in order to become a marine biologist, I need good A-levels,' Arthur went on. 'And then I need a good degree. I've put myself and my ma in a very difficult situation. The only Prod – sorry, Protestant options' – Brother McGlynn smiled again – 'are Dungannon or Portora. Both are awkward and costly, not just in bus fares, but time-wise as well. They're good schools, I know that. I've played rugby against both of them.'

Good man, getting the rugby bit in early, Ann thought.

'I don't know anybody at either of those schools, but I do know some boys who go here. We've played football together in the summer for years. I'd consider some of them to be good friends – as much as that's possible given the circumstances.'

Stay away from the Troubles, son.

'They've only good things to say about this school, and I need to be somewhere where I can respect the teachers and feel that that's a mutual thing. I need to knuckle down – work hard, harder than I have so far. I need good teachers. I need your help, Brother.'

Arthur exhaled loudly.

Brother McGlynn sat back and clasped his hands across his not insignificant belly. 'That's quite a speech, Arthur.' His large face looked serene.

'I've been practising,' Arthur said, flashing his best angelic smile.

'You mentioned rugby.'

'Yes, I've been captain of the school team since the under-fourteens. We're useless, but I love it.'

'A leader of men,' Brother McGlynn said with a beaming smile.

'I doubt it. No one else would do it.'

'You're too modest. Where do you play?'

'Campsie mostly.'

'No, I mean what position?'

Arthur went bright red, embarrassed at his misunderstanding.

Stay calm, son.

'Sorry, Brother. Out-half.'

'So, you *are* a leader of men. I played a bit at Trinity. Second row mostly. What A-levels do you want to do?'

This sounds hopeful. Ann looked at Arthur, but Arthur didn't take his eyes off Brother McGlynn.

'English literature, geography and biology.'

'The all-important biology. Can't be a marine biologist without biology, and you'll need geography so you'll know where you are, but why English lit?'

'I like reading. I read a lot. All sorts of stuff. I like Beckett and Wilde.

'We are all born mad, some remain so.' Brother McGlynn was grinning at Arthur.

Oh God. Ann was panicking. She'd no idea what he was talking about.

'*Waiting for Godot*?' Arthur hazarded.

Ann held her breath. Was he right?

'It is indeed, Arthur. We have an excellent English teacher here – Brother McFarland. He's a big Shakespeare man. Have you done any Shakespeare?'

Oh shit, Ann thought.

'Just *Hamlet* and *Macbeth*. I like *Titus Andronicus* but. It's completely mad. I can understand why it's not on the curriculum.'

'Can you, indeed.' Brother McGlynn raised one eyebrow. 'Have you read it?'

'Only a synopsis. But it tells you enough to drop it into intelligent conversations.'

The big man snorted with delight. 'I've actually read *Ulysses* – all of it – and I strongly recommend that you don't.' When he laughed, his whole body wobbled. 'Back to biology. We don't have an A-level biology teacher at present. We're looking for one. In the meantime, any of our pupils doing biology at A-level have to go up to the Loretto Convent. How would you feel about that? Would that be a problem?'

'Don't see why. I'm used to girls being in class.'

'They won't distract you?'

'Not in class anyway.'

Ann closed her eyes in a long, slow blink.

Brother McGlynn smiled. 'The teacher is a man. Mr Vaughn. Steven Vaughn.' He shifted in his chair. 'What other interests do you have, apart from rugby?'

'I like music. All sorts of stuff. As long as it's good. Mostly Blues. I like good guitar players.'

'Do you play anything?'

'No, unfortunately. I've just about mastered the record player … I noticed the picture of you with a guitar.'

'I've played a bit in my time. Traditional Irish, folk, that sort of stuff.' Brother McGlynn turned to Ann. 'Have you any questions, Mrs Webb? You've been very quiet.'

'I realise that it's Arthur you need to talk to, not me.'

'But you're his mother. You're very brave to even consider letting him come here. What does Mr Webb think? Maybe I could meet him.'

'He's a bit less enthusiastic, shall we say.'

'I understand. It can't be easy. It's an unusual thing, especially here' – he waved his arms to indicate outside – 'especially now. You must have concerns.'

'Will he be safe?'

'I and my staff will do everything in our power to ensure Arthur is treated with dignity, kindness and respect. As long as he doesn't walk up and down the corridors singing "The Sash", he should be okay. We'll tell the school at assembly before he comes and put the fear of God into any naysayers.'

'I won't be singing anything … unless it's by a blind black Blues singer,' Arthur butted in.

Arthur! Ann was mortified and changed the subject quickly. 'Thank you, Brother. Will he have to go to prayers or confession or anything?'

But Brother McGlynn was beaming. 'No, not unless he wants to.'

'It's just we need to keep his da as happy with this as we can.'

'I understand completely. Do you want to have a look around before you make up your minds?'

'That would be lovely, Brother.' Ann's eyes met Arthur's. *Yeee haaa.*

The school surprised Arthur. The lockers in the cloakrooms were all intact. No doors were hanging off. The paint wasn't peeling. It was quiet. It felt like a place of learning.

On the way back to his office, Brother McGlynn broached the sports issue. 'So, we've established that you're a keen rugby player.'

'Yes, Brother.'

'I think you're aware that we don't play rugby here. Will that be difficult for you? We have a reasonable Gaelic team with some good players. One or two could go all the way to county level.'

'If that's the price I have to pay, then so be it. I intend to concentrate on my studies. Maybe I'll get a game on a Saturday with the Accies. It's not a big deal. Or I might try Gaelic.'

Ann's sharp intake of breath was audible.

Arthur smiled. 'Although I don't think my da would be too happy about that.'

Ann breathed out again.

'It's not an easy game to pick up from scratch, but that's for another day.' Brother McGlynn turned to face Ann. 'You should be proud of your son, Mrs Webb. It's a credit to you that he's so self-aware. Mistakes should create opportunities. Arthur seems to have learned that some actions have unpleasant consequences, but he's not sulking or blaming others or raging at how unfair the world is.'

'Thank you, Brother,' Ann said, waves of relief washing over her. 'My ma always taught us that the world wasn't fair, that it owes you nothing. All you can do is your best. Just do the right thing and get on with it. He's definitely learned from this.'

Brother McGlynn opened the door of his office. The meeting was over.

'I'll contact Miss Rock. We'd be delighted to have you here in September, Arthur, if you decide this is where you want to be. It might not be the easiest option, but I'll do my best to make it as pleasant as possible.'

'And I'll try and stay out of trouble, Brother. Seven hundred pupils against one aren't good odds.' Arthur gave him that angelic smile again.

Brother McGlynn reached out his hand. Arthur braced and tried to squeeze back this time, but the big man got the better of him again.

As they left the grounds, Ann said, 'Well, that was easier than I thought it was going to be. Where did all that stuff come from that you came out with?'

'I guessed it would be useful to know some stuff, so I sat up all night studying.'

'You did not! I heard you snoring.'

'So *you* were up all night.' Arthur laughed.

'I was worrying. Good quality worrying at that … and it worked.'

'He seems like a nice man … for one of them.' Arthur grinned at his ma.

They walked on for a while in silence.

'You'll need a new uniform,' Ann said eventually. 'Do weans your age have school bags?'

'No, Ma. No school bag.'

They stopped at Gracy's to let out a lorry laden with eggs. Arthur reached for Ann's hand and she turned to look at him. She was about to ask, 'Are you crying?' but instead, she just squeezed his hand. As she smiled at him, the sun came out.

* * *

'Willy!'

'Yes, Ma. I know. I was waiting till you got home. I'll do them now. How did it go?'

'It went well,' Ann said.

'I was brilliant, even if I do say so myself,' Arthur said.

'Don't be too cocky, Arthur,' Ann said. 'It'll come back to bite you.'

'But it did go well?'

'It did, son. Brother McGlynn seems like a good man and it looks like a good school.'

'It's not wrecked inside or anything,' Arthur said.

Willy looked amazed. 'Will you have to light candles?' he asked.

'No, no candles.'

'Get the spuds peeled, Willy. Your da will be home soon and he'll have enough to contend with without his dinner not being ready.'

'Yes, Ma. They're very big. Nearly as big as Arthur's head,' Willy said. 'But I'll give them a good slap. That'll sort them out.'

'Willy! Don't let your da hear you saying stuff like that,' Ann scolded.

'Or I'll be next?'

'No, you won't. That'll never happen again,' Ann said, ruffling Willy's hair. *I promise*, she vowed to herself.

'We need to go and see Ma.' Ann looked at Arthur.

'We do. She'll be okay – I hope.'

* * *

'Will you have to go to Mass and do confessions and light candles and all that other stuff they do?' Ma looked confused and frightened.

'No, Nana. I won't have to do anything like that. No RE classes. No prayers. Nothing. I just have to go to my classes, spend time in the library in between and come home again.'

'Will you have to learn Irish and play garlic?'

Arthur and Ann grinned at the old lady whose world was shifting beneath her.

'No, Nana. They speak English, believe it or not, and I don't think they let Prods play Gaelic. So there'll be no indoctrination. I'll sing "The Sash" on the way home every day to ward off the evil spirits.'

His nana smiled. 'You're a brave boy. That's all I can say.'

'So you're okay with it? I can go?'

'I don't like it, not one bit. But you wouldn't be going anywhere near the CBS if there was any alternative. You might have to deal with some dopes making dopey comments, but sticks and stones and all that.'

'Oh Nana!' Arthur hugged the thin woman in the cardigan.

Ann stood and watched, her fingers crossed, happily hoping.

CHAPTER 48

In the summer of 1972, Daisy married Alan Fulton in Aylesbury registry office. Ann and Stan flew to Luton and got a bus to Aylesbury; Mary made her way from Bristol. Alan's mother and sister were there, and Stan gave her away. There was no one else. Afterwards, they went to The Duck for sandwiches and wine, although Alan preferred pints of bitter.

Ann thought Daisy looked stunning in a simple white dress and told her so when they got some time to themselves later. 'Alan seems like a nice fella,' Ann added.

'He is, Ma. He's lovely.'

'I'm so proud of you. All grown up and married and all. I can't believe it.' Daisy beamed. 'So how are you finding Aylesbury?'

'I haven't got to know many of the locals yet, but this is a good pub. They're all dead friendly. One of the girls from the hospital comes here with her hubby. I've met loads of other people too. I'm in the women's darts team. Alan's in the men's team. He's very good.'

'Darts! You've never darted in your life.' Ann put her hand to Daisy's forehead as if she was checking her temperature.

'Very funny, Ma.' Daisy smiled. 'I used to dart behind the bicycle shed for a quick fag.' Ann rolled her eyes. 'Another drink?'

'I'm okay, love. I've had three already,' Ann said. 'You're going very fast. Don't get drunk and ruin your big day.'

'I won't, Ma. I learned to drink properly in the army.'

Daisy stood up and put her hand on Ann's shoulder to steady herself. She went off to the bar. She came back with another glass of white wine.

'So Alan's the caretaker at the local school?' Ann asked.

'Yeah, Aylesbury Grammar. Job for life as long as he keeps the toilets dunged out. He still plays in the band, but only now and again. They're pretty useless!'

'Don't be so cruel. What's the house like?'

'It's a bungalow. It's in the school grounds. It's lovely. Sure call round tomorrow before you go home.'

'I'm not sure if we have time. I'll speak to Stan. You're all set then. Good job. Good man. Free house.'

Daisy looked at her lap and pursed her lips.

'What?' Ann narrowed her eyes for a moment, concentrating, as if she were tuning in to her daughter's mind. 'You're not? Are you?'

Daisy's body relaxed and she smiled coyly. 'We only just found out. That's why things went so fast.'

'Oh Daisy! That's fantastic. I will have that drink after all.' Like mother like daughter, Ann thought, only Daisy's wean would have a da. *I know you're watching, Walter. You're going to be a granda! Isn't it fabulous*?

'You're going to be a granny,' Daisy said, clutching Ann's hand. 'And Nana—'

'She'll be a great granny. Stan! Mary!' Ann shouted across the room. 'Wait'll you hear this.'

Alan was standing at the bar with his best man. He turned round to look at Daisy. He knew from Ann's reaction that she'd told her ma the news. He looked like he was the happiest man in the world.

Mary hugged Daisy when she heard. 'You lucky thing. Everything's worked out, eh? I'm so happy for you both.'

'Congratulations,' Stan said, all stiff and awkward as usual. 'I'll go and buy Alan a pint. So what relation will this child be to me?'

Daisy closed her eyes and looked down at the floor. Mary stared at her da in disbelief.

'It'll be your grandson or granddaughter,' Ann said, shaking her head.

'Right, right. That's good,' Stan said and he was gone.

The next morning, they all had serious hangovers. Stan and Ann went to see the bungalow for a few minutes before catching the bus to the airport. Mary stayed with Daisy a bit longer before she needed to get back to Bristol.

The journey home seemed to take forever. Ann could barely look at Stan, never mind speak to him. She couldn't forget what he'd said at the wedding reception.

Stan eventually found the car in the airport car park.

'I was looking for the old one,' he said as they got into the new red Allegro.

They drove to Omagh in silence.

CHAPTER 49

Ann put the old flowers in the bin and replaced them with fresh ones.

'How's things, Blondie?' she said. The ground was too wet to kneel on, so she leaned against the headstone.

'Good job your birthday wasn't yesterday. Bloody bomb scares everywhere. Never a dull moment down here. No time to sit around playing a harp, that's for sure! Muriel's been invited to a garden party at Buckingham Palace. Al, too, of course. I think it's more to do with Al than Muriel, but that's by the by. Can you believe it? Buckingham Palace! Ma's beside herself. There'll be movie stars and all sorts at it.' Ann looked around the cemetery. It was deserted. 'Do they have garden parties up there?' she continued. 'I bet it's just one big party, eh? And no hangovers! You probably get tired of it after a while and just want a bit of peace and quiet. I know I would.

'Muriel's weans are both at Cambridge! If it wasn't Muriel, I'd be jealous. She sounds just the same. Hilda seems a bit lonely at times. Jimmy travels all over the place with his group, and Dan is still sneaking about doing spy stuff. He must be getting a bit old for it now. Maybe he's training the new spies, but he's still away a lot.

'Joe's married again. He seems happy. Arlene, her name is. She works in Lloyds Bank in London. That's where he met her. He works there too now. He likes London. Not sure how many weans he has now. Probably doesn't know himself.' Ann rooted around in her handbag, took out an apple and bit into it.

'Daisy's had two boys,' she said, still chewing. 'I know it was quick, and they were so close together as well. Matthew and Luke they're called. Very biblical. There must be loads of Matthews and Lukes up where you are.'

Ann finished eating her apple and, without moving from her spot, threw the core at the bin. Bullseye! *I could have been good at darts.* She leaned both elbows on the headstone. 'Daisy seems a bit at odds with herself. She often sounds drunk on the phone. She still asks about her real da. I just keep telling her that I'll tell her as soon as I can. She'll just have to wait. I still see your da up the town. Your ma's in the T&F now, but you probably knew that, didn't you?

'Daisy talks a lot about Father this and Father that. They seem to be in the hospital all the time, and she says our lot – the Prods – are useless. All the Christianity in the hospital seems to come from them uns. They're very dependable apparently. I've told her I already have a son who's half Catholic. Have you heard of Horslips? Irish rock! Mad, I know. That's what Arthur was playing the other day when I got home. His da would go mad if he heard him listening to that sort of stuff. Anyway, I told Daisy it sounded like she was going to turn, and do you know what she said? No? Well, I'll tell you. She said, "It doesn't matter over here, Ma. Nobody knows what you are and nobody cares either." Can you believe it? I'd care.

'I must admit, going to the Christian Brothers was the best thing Arthur ever did. He settled down, worked hard – well, hard*er*, which wouldn't be hard. He had to go to the convent for his biology classes. He seemed to like that for some reason. He fell in love with Shakespeare – not literally … you know what I mean. He made some really good friends. And now he's off to the New University of Ulster at Coleraine. I know it's not Cambridge, but it'll have to do. He's studying Environmental Science. Don't ask me what that means, but I think he's given up his dream of becoming a marine biologist. Not many people get to do their dream job. You were one of the lucky ones. You dreamt of driving a bread van and that's what you did for your entire life. Lucky man, I say.'

Ann stared out over the graveyard to the hills beyond. 'Willy has his A-levels next year. God love him. He's too tall to be really clever. Six foot six! How can you be smart at that height. He spends his whole life in his friend Peter's house. They listen to music, so he says.

'Stan's just the same as ever. My knight in shining armour. The problem is he never takes his armour off. I'm not sure I know who's inside it any more. Don't get me wrong – we still have a laugh and go to the Legion. We never want for anything. I just wish he would loosen up a bit. I know he won't now. Too set in his ways. I just ignore him most of the time. Still hasn't let me drive the car. Never will. I've probably forgotten how to, anyway.

'I've joined the church choir, by the way. Did I tell you? Rehearsals are on Thursday nights. Great craic. Mrs Nugent had to tell Harry that enthusiasm and volume weren't enough. Poor Harry! He was devastated. It's Women's Institute on Tuesdays.'

Ann stood on for another few minutes saying nothing. She liked the peace and quiet of the place. She could think better.

'Right, better go,' she said eventually. 'Bangers and mash tonight and the spuds aren't even peeled yet.'

She took the old, tattered photograph out of her bag. She kissed it and hugged it to her chest. It still made her cry. 'Love you, Walter Green,' she whispered.

The leaves rustled his reply.

CHAPTER 50

'Can you and Da come over for the graduation, Ma?' Mary asked on the phone.

'Of course we can, can't we, Stan?' Ann relayed the information to him.

'Try and stop me!' Stan said loudly, hoping Mary could hear. 'First class honours! We're dead proud of you, so we are.'

A few weeks later, when Mary stepped onto the stage at Bristol University, Ann cried tears of pure joy. She looked magnificent in her gown and mortar board. She looked at Stan. His eyes were glistening. Those tears have travelled a long way, she thought to herself. She fumbled for his hand and gave it a squeeze. He squeezed back. He was human after all.

After the ceremony, they all got uproariously drunk. Then Ann and Stan went to their hotel and Mary and Daisy carried on partying. The next day, Mary travelled back to Omagh with them, although they all looked like they should be in hospital.

Over the summer Mary caught up with her school friends. They went to the Lovers Retreat and Lough Muck and drank cider. She had registered with an employment agency before she came home, and she bought *The Times* and *The Telegraph* every day.

'That's where all the jobs for smart arse's like me are advertised,' she said as she asked for a few more bob to pay for them. 'I'll pay you back when I'm rich and famous. I promise.'

Ann believed her; anything was possible. 'Nothing in the *Conn* then for a multilingualist?' she asked her daughter.

'Multilinguist.'

'That's what I said. It must be hard to listen in all them different languages.'

Mary just smiled and shook her head.

The summer was warm, slow and glorious. In the middle of August, the phone rang.

Ann was just in from work. 'Hello, Omagh 44857,' she said in her best telephone voice.

'Hello. Could I speak to Miss Mary Webb, please?'

Ann put her hand over the mouthpiece and roared, 'Mary! It's for you. Sounds very posh.'

Mary came bounding down the stairs, two at a time, and grabbed the phone. 'Hello … Yes, that's me.' There was a long silence. 'Geneva? … Next week.' Mary did a lot of nodding, then mimed writing with a pen. Ann hoked around in a drawer and set a pen and notepad in front of her.

'Yes, yes, I'm writing it down,' Mary said, switching the telephone receiver to her other hand. 'Yes … Yes … Yes … Tickets? Yes … Good … Great! Thank you … Okay, yes, thank you. Goodbye. Bye.' Mary set the handset down and, flinging her arms around Ann's neck, began jumping up and down and squealing.

‘Whoa! Calm down. You’ll hurt yourself … or me! Who was it?’

‘Miles somebody or other. He works for’ – Mary consulted her scribbled notes – ‘the Afro Swiss Shipping Company. He wants me to go to Geneva for an interview next week!’ Mary was bouncing on the spot. ‘They’re sending me tickets and hotel bookings and everything. Oh God. Ma, what do I do?’

Here was another daughter living Ann’s dreams for her. It was as good as she was going to get, she thought, and she was delighted.

‘First thing you need to do is calm down,’ Ann said. ‘I’ll make a cup of tea. Put on that new Rod Stewart record. You’ll need to change the speed. Then we’ll go and tell your nana.’

‘Some singles sound better at thirty-three,’ Mary said with a giggle.

And so they had tea and hugged and cried as ‘Sailing’ blared out of the new stereo.

* * *

Mary got the job as Personal Assistant to the Chief Executive Officer of the Afro Swiss Shipping Company. It meant she would have to spend two weeks in Geneva and two weeks in Lagos every month.

Arthur had gone to Aylesbury to work for the summer; Willy was working in the American Folk Park, pointing people at the toilets. Ann and Mary started intense atlas searches to find Lagos and Geneva. Ann was ecstatic and even started thinking about visits there herself.

‘Lagos might be a bit of a stretch,’ she said. ‘I’ve asked in Wattersons and there’s no flights from Belfast. They had no idea how to get there, but nothing’s impossible.’

'There must be a flight from Geneva,' Mary pointed out.

'Good thinking, love. Not only gorgeous, but smart as well. Just like your mother.'

'Yes, Ma.'

Stan was so proud of Mary that he almost said so out loud. He'd said as much to Ann. She'd told him to say it to Mary, not her. 'Tell her you love her, for God's sake. Maybe even give her a kiss.'

She'd thought he was going to, but all he did was cough and shuffle his feet and say, 'Well done, girl. Just be careful, that's all. Don't get carried away.'

'No, Da.'

Ann shook her head and rolled her eyes at him. But then she put her hands on Mary's shoulders. 'Your da's right, sort of. You do need to be careful. But you know that. You're a sensible girl, but you need to enjoy life too. You need to live it, love it.' Ann started to sing: '*Living, loving …*'

'*She's just a woman*,' Mary joined in. They laughed. 'You love Led Zep really, don't you? I bet you listen when there's nobody else here.'

'That would be telling,' Ann said with a wink.

* * *

Mary came home for Christmas, but Ann saw very little of any of the weans – it was all pubs, parties and hangovers now.

Christmas dinner was as noisy as ever. Mary took centre stage with her tales of life with the jet set. Ann was reminded of Joe's wild stories, only there was more chance that Mary's were true.

'They eat warthogs,' Mary said.

There were looks of disgust all round.

'They taste amazing – like pork. They are a sort of pig after all, only nicer. Impala's good too. They cook them over an open fire called a barbecue. They shorten it to BBQ.'

'Are there cannonballs?' Ma asked, a bit glassy-eyed.

'It's Joe who has the cannonballs.' Ann couldn't help herself. 'Or so he says.'

Arthur choked on a carrot.

'On his ship, I mean,' Ann added, slapping Arthur on the arm.

Mary laughed. 'No, Nana. I don't think there are any cannibals any more, and Lagos is a big city. We stay in the Hilton Hotel. It's on an island, so it's very safe.'

'That's good, love. It's just you hear all these stories about the jungle.'

Willy suddenly exploded into Tarzan's jungle yodel. He'd had a few glasses of red.

Everyone burst out laughing at him.

'It's bad manners to yodel with your mouth full,' Ann said. 'Do they speak English?' she asked, popping a sprout into her mouth.

'Who?'

'The Lagossers?'

'The city-based Nigerians speak mostly English, but they have a very strong accent. The business people are from all over the world. It's often three or four languages in the same meeting.'

'How do you keep track of who's saying what?' Willy asked, pouring himself some more wine.

'I have to take control. Get them to speak one language at a time. Then it's easy.'

'Does your boss speak English?' Stan asked. There was a split second of stunned silence. Stan hardly ever joined in.

He looked a bit uncomfortable being the centre of attention. But Mary didn't bat an eyelid.

'Yes, English and German.'

He must be a bit tipsy, Ann thought as Stan asked, 'And they own ships?'

'Yes, we have fifty-six ships.'

'And they go all over?'

This is like a conversation. Ann smiled with delight.

'Mostly between Nigeria and Europe, but sometimes other places.'

'Will *you* be able to go to these other places sometime?' Ann asked, now more interested in Mary's answers than in Stan's unprecedented questioning.

'I hope so. Jack – Mr Baumgarten, my boss – is talking about some big conference in Rio next year.'

'Rio? Rio de Janeiro?' Ann smiled dreamily. 'That's where they have those big beaches that go on forever, isn't it.'

'I'll bet they're not as good as Portsalon,' Willy said.

'What sort of cattle do they have?' Stan asked.

What an odd question, Ann thought. She was convinced he was drunk.

'Skinny ones, with big horns. They wander all over the place.'

'Do they not have farms?'

'I don't know, Da. We never leave the hotel. It's just what I can see from my balcony.'

'*My balcony*. Oooooooh,' Arthur said. 'How very grand. All you need now is a Romeo.'

'Is there one?' Ann asked, suddenly very interested.

'No, Ma. No Romeo.' Mary laughed.

'That's probably a good thing. It didn't end well for them,' Arthur pointed out.

'It is very grand though. It's a different world. Coke costs one pound a bottle in the hotel. It's mad.'

'You're joking!' Arthur gasped. 'A quid for a Coke.'

'Bob Campbell would be a millionaire if he could charge a quid a bottle,' Willy said, looking shocked.

'He's probably a millionaire anyway, the number of sweets you lot have bought off him over the years,' Stan quipped.

Ann stared at him. Maybe he was coming down with something.

'Millions well spent, Da,' Mary said. 'Imagine having loads of money but you'd never tried a gobstopper.'

While they were all chatting, Willy had been counting on his fingers. 'That's exactly ten times as much as a Coke costs in Wellworths.'

They all applauded and burst out laughing.

Ann brought out the plum pudding and brandy butter, and afterwards they all settled down to watch the Queen. The snoring started before she was finished.

CHAPTER 51

Ann set the little posy of flowers down on Walter's grave and tidied it up a little.

'Why did you have to be born in February, you eejit. It's freezing.' Ann pulled her coat tightly around her. 'Anyway, happy birthday. Forty-seven! I can't believe it's twenty-four years since I saw your wee face. Have you started shaving yet? Only joking. There's nobody left at home to wind up, so you'll have to do. Mary's away galivanting around the world speaking ten different languages at once. She says she's learning Chinese – Mandarin, she calls it. I told her, the only Chinese she needs is "Number 37 please".

'I don't hear much from Arthur. He never comes home. It's his last year at Coleraine. I've no idea what he's going to do next. He's not going to be a marine biologist, that's for sure. Another pipe dream that was never going to come true.

'Willy did well enough in his A-levels to go to the Ulster Polytechnic at Jordanstown, but he's decided to join the police now. Imagine! He says the Troubles will be over soon, but Ma has gone into super-worrying mode and I'm not far behind her. I try and fit an extra worry in on the way to church. It's a good way to pass ten minutes. We've tried to talk him out of it, but he won't listen. Big money apparently, but … I don't know.' She took off her woolly hat, scratched her head and put the hat back on.

'The rest of them seem to be getting on with life. Muriel and Al have been invited to St Paul's Cathedral in June for the Queen's Jubilee thing. It's like she's in a different world to the rest of us. How the other half live, eh?

'I know you don't *live* as such, but I do and I'm still your other half and I never get invited anywhere. Do you ever wonder what we'd be doing now if you hadn't tried to stop that train with your forehead? I do, all the time.'

Ann fell silent for a few moments. She still felt a deep sadness when she thought about what might have been.

'Daisy's doing well. Her boys – our grandsons – are very clever apparently – just like their granny. I can't picture you as a granda. You were never old enough. At least, you never *looked* old enough. She's still in Stoke Mandeville. She says Jimmy Saville's never out of the place. Do you have TV up there? *Top of the Pops*? He's on it all the time. Daisy says he's a bit weird.

'Hilda sent us some photos. She's getting old and fat. Her boy Jimmy is making a real name for himself now – playing loud stuff on the guitar at a hundred miles an hour. Goes all over the world. He's making a fortune, she says.

'Joe's still in London working in Lloyds Bank. He won't come home cos of the Troubles. Did you know Paddy Mullan's in jail? Ma always said he was a bad egg. Dolores is still in Africa, converting the heathens. Plenty of work for her here, if you ask me.

'What about me? … Thanks for asking. I'm all right, I suppose. More than all right. I've everything I've ever dreamt of. Okay, I know that's a wee lie, but seeing your weans growing up and doing well is the best thing ever. I know your ma and da never got to do that, but that's not your fault, Walter, it's mine. There's never a day when I don't wish it could have been different. I wish we'd *won* just one competition. Just *entered* one competition. That would have been good.

'I never see your ma now and the odd time I see your da, he just looks lost. I think he goes to McAleer's a lot. Daisy still pesters me to tell her the truth about her da and I will, as soon as my ma and your ma and da have passed. It's all still awful and it's all still my fault.'

Ann wiped away a tear that was running down her cheek. She blew her nose and took a deep breath.

'My ma isn't as bad as yours, but she's getting there. Doesn't know what day it is half the time, but then I could say the same about myself. Do you have days? They must all be the same. Sounds very boring if you ask me … Oh, you're not asking me. That's all right then. You run on and count the clouds. I'll go and buy some spuds. We only need two now.

'Oh here, I nearly forgot why I came out to see you. Apart from your birthday, of course. Mary has got engaged! To some fella called Chris. She met him at a party in the hotel in Lagos. That's in Nigeria, by the way. Anyway, you won't believe this, but Chris's da is the Honorary British Consul in Dunkirk. That's in France. Try and keep up. Chris works at the British Embassy in Lagos. You're right – maybe he is a spy like Dan, but he's not old enough to be a proper spy. He's only twenty-three, the same age as Mary. The same age you were when you walked into the train. The same age I was when I married Stan. Spooky or what?'

Ann started to sob; she couldn't help herself.

'Are you all right, love?' An old man walking past came over to her and put a kindly hand on her arm.

'Yes, yes, thank you. I'm okay. Too many memories, that's all.'

'Oh, I know, love. It doesn't get any easier, does it,' he said and trudged on his way.

Ann took the battered photograph out of her handbag and gave it a little kiss. She could barely make anything out in the image any more. Her tears flowed uncontrollably.

'Sorry, Walter. It's just ... it's just everything. I'm so happy and it's just not fair.'

She put the photo back in her bag.

'I love you, Walter Green.'

A crow squawked in the trees.

'All right, all right, I'm going,' she muttered, smiling.

CHAPTER 52

Birthdays came and went, just like any other day, and Ann assumed this one would be no different. She put on her new green dress and sang 'Happy birthday to me' as she left the house.

Stan, still a man of very fixed habits, was at the mart. She had a pair of his shoes to leave in to Taggart's. They needed new heels. The shoes were as old as he was, she reckoned.

'They'll probably be ready on Monday, Ann. But it may be best to leave it until Tuesday.'

'No rush, Paddy.'

She went on up Scarffe's Entry. She had to stop to let a lorry loaded with scaffolding planks reverse slowly out before it edged its way into the street. Then she nipped into Bob Campbell's.

'Hi, Bob.'

'Good morning, Ann. You look full of the joys.'

'It's my birthday. Could I have twenty Embassy Regal please?'

'Happy birthday. Is it a big one?'

'No, nothing special. And one of these.' She picked up a Marathon bar.

'That'll be sixty-five pence please, Mrs Webb.'

'Thank you, Mr Campbell.' She smiled at the cheerful red-faced man she'd known her entire life. She counted out the coins. 'I'll have enough coupons soon to get a new teapot.'

'You'll need a van for them then.'

'Just about. I must have a million of them. Thanks, Bob.'

'Have a nice day.'

Outside, she opened the Marathon, took a bite and closed her eyes. Bliss. She knew the toffee would stick in her teeth, but she didn't care. She was forty-seven and could do what she liked.

She whizzed round Wellworths and, as they were having gammon for dinner that night, she bought a cabbage. It always had to be cabbage with gammon.

Mary phoned most Sundays, but she said she would call today to wish her happy birthday. Arthur would call before he went off to play rugby for the university. Daisy would call from Aylesbury later on. Willy was studying for the police exams. He was at his nana's today to get some peace and quiet.

Ann got home and opened the letters. There were cards from Muriel, Hilda, Joe, Daisy, Arthur and Iris. She'd have to meet up with Iris again sometime soon. She hadn't seen her in ages. She switched the kettle on and put the shopping away. Ma would probably bring her card over later. Willy will have signed it just so he wouldn't have to buy one himself. She sat down with her tea in her 'Best Ma in the World' mug. Stan would be home soon. Lunch was salad and leftover chicken. She thought about having a drink, but decided it was too early. They had a nice bottle of Shiraz for later that night.

The phone rang. She looked at her watch. It was only eleven; too early for Mary, although it was a different time where she was. She answered it.

'Omagh 44857.'

'Is that Mrs Webb?' a posh English voice said.

'Yes, I'm Mrs Webb. Who's calling?'

'My name is Horace Walpole. I'm calling from the British Embassy in Lagos, Nigeria.'

Ann started to laugh. 'Has Chris put you up to this?' She could imagine Mary asking Chris to get someone to call and wind her up on her birthday.

'No, Mrs Webb. Is there someone there with you?'

'No.' Just then, Stan came through the door. 'Yes,' she said. 'My husband's just come in. What's this about?'

'It's getting warm out there,' Stan said, but he froze when he saw she was on the phone. She was holding her hand up and frowning.

'I'm sorry, Mrs Webb. I'm afraid I have some bad news for you. It's about your daughter.'

'Mary? What's happened?' Blind panic swept through Ann and she started flapping her free hand.

'I'm afraid—'

'Just tell me. What's happened?'

'Mary went swimming this morning. She got caught in a rip tide. There was nothing anyone could do.'

Ann fell silent. Stunned. She could hear the clock ticking. She tried to process what she was hearing. Stan came towards her, but she held him back with her hand.

'You must be mistaken. Mary loves swimming. She's good at it.'

'I'm sorry, Mrs Webb. Her fiancé was there, but there was nothing he could do.

'Chris was with her?' Ann felt dizzy and sick. She had broken out in a sweat.

'Yes, Mr Babbington was with her. Unfortunately, he got to her too late.'

'What do you mean *too late*?' Ann's heart was bursting.

'I'm afraid she's dead, Mrs Webb.'

Mary dropped the phone. She could hear Mr Walpole's tinny voice talking on the floor. Time stopped. The room spun.

'Ann! Ann! What is it?' Stan looked scared. He picked up the phone.

'Mrs Webb? Mrs Webb? Are you still there?'

'Hello? This is Mr Webb. Who is this?'

'I explained to Mrs Webb. My name's Horace Walpole. I'm calling from the British Embassy in Lagos. I can't tell you how sorry I am. We all are. It's an awful shock.'

'What happened?' Stan said through clenched teeth.

Ann was like a statue. Her hand was still up by her ear where she'd been holding the phone.

'Your daughter Mary. She died this morning, Mr Webb. She drowned in the sea near her hotel.'

'I don't understand,' Stan said. All the colour had drained from his face. He listened as Mr Walpole spoke.

Meanwhile, Ann had collapsed into the nearest chair. Her mouth was still open; her mind was shut.

'Yes. Okay. Thank you.' Stan set the handset back down; his hand was shaking. 'He says he'll call back later, when they know more.'

'More? More about what? ... Maybe it isn't true,' Ann said, a flicker of hope in her voice.

'She's in hospital apparently. It's on the island near the hotel.'

Ann brightened up and blew her nose. 'She must be all right then, if she's in hospital. Maybe they made a mistake. Oh Stan!' A big tear ran down her cheek.

Stan knelt beside her and took her hand in his. They sat like that for what seemed like a long time, neither of them speaking. But then Ann started rocking and wailing. The sound she made was primeval. Stan sat on the arm of the chair and put his arms around her shoulders, intending to comfort her, but then he started to sob too, his shoulders heaving. They cried together as they clung to one another. Their world stopped.

After a while, Stan sat back, sniffing. 'Look at me. Look at me, Ann.' He shook her gently.

Ann raised her head. Her eyes were red pools of tears, and snot was hanging from her nose.

'That man's going to call back when he knows more. You're right. Maybe they made a mistake.'

'Oh, please God.' Ann closed her eyes, sending up a silent prayer.

'I'll get you a drink,' Stan said, getting up. He spotted Kathleen coming in through the gate. 'There's your ma.'

'Oh shit! What do we tell her?'

Ma opened the front door, came into the living room and held out a red envelope. 'Happy birthday, love.'

CHAPTER 53

Mr Walpole did call back. There had not been a mistake. Mr Chris Babbington identified the body; the post-mortem would be on Monday. They would sort out the paperwork to allow Mary's body to be released from the hospital and arrange for her to be flown home. The repatriation process could take a few days: 'The bureaucracy in these places … blah, blah. We'll keep you informed.' Chris would be travelling with the coffin.

Ann thanked Mr Walpole and hung up. Numbness had replaced shock. The wheel of fortune was lying shattered in a hospital morgue in Nigeria. The world was dreamy and unreal.

Stan called his brothers. Ann had calls to make too, all very difficult, all very short. No one had any words; just tears, bewilderment and disbelief. Everyone would make arrangements to come home; Joe was advised not to, but he insisted on coming anyway.

Ma made tea.

Willy had to go into the training depot on Monday. He said he wanted to stay at home, but Ann knew he was glad to escape the suffocating gloom.

The house filled with people and stayed filled all day, every day. Shadowy figures offered sandwiches and cups of tea and spoke in muffled whispers. Ann couldn't keep track of it all. One minute she was listening to someone. She would nod and look up and it would be someone else.

There were silent tears and hugs as each of them arrived: Arthur first, then Daisy and Alan, followed by Muriel and Al, and then Joe. Hilda arrived from Canada on the Thursday.

'I wonder what the rest of the world is doing for bread,' Arthur said to Daisy in the kitchen.

'Eh?' Daisy looked up from a sink full of mugs.

'It looks like we have it all here.' Arthur indicated the pile of sliced pans stacked on top of the washing machine.

'The world's supply of biscuits as well.' Daisy nodded at the pillar of biscuit tins in the passageway. 'The world will have to come here for their custard creams.'

'I think they already have.'

The kitchen had turned into a well-oiled production line. A second kettle had appeared from somewhere and the three teapots never cooled. As day turned to evening, tea turned to wine, whiskey and beer. There was an unconscious knowing as to when this should happen. It got earlier and earlier as the week wore remorselessly on.

Ma was in her element, mixing, mingling, moaning, gasping at the gossip. What a hero, Ann thought more than once as she watched her mother intercept people who were bringing her plates of egg and onion sandwiches. At the start of the week, the sandwiches were cut into neat little triangles; by Wednesday they were lucky to be cut at all.

Ann looked across the hearth at Stan. He had his full suit of armour on. He cried at night, in bed.

Harry, Nigel, and Arthur and Willy's school friends all weighed in. Mary's friends were almost hysterical. Funerals were for old people.

Mr Walpole called again: Mary had left Lagos and would be on the first flight from London on Friday morning.

Ann suddenly remembered Stan's good shoes were still in Taggart's. She felt overwhelmed. Incapable of thought.

'I'll get them, Ma,' Arthur offered. 'Breath of air would be good.'

Ann gave him a kiss and a quid. 'Keep the change. For going.'

Arthur smiled at her. She was broken.

When the day arrived, Willy was still in the training depot. Ma held the fort at home. The rest of them went to Aldergrove in two large black limousines, along with an empty hearse, to meet Mary's coffin off the plane.

They were allowed onto the tarmac and waited beside the plane. The rain was coming down in sheets. The passengers all disembarked. Mr Baumgarten, Mary's boss, and Chris and his parents were last off.

Chris was tall and handsome; fine-featured and tanned with short light brown hair. *Good catch, Mary,* Ann thought. He was inconsolable, a boy without armour. They hugged and he apologised through a raft of tears for not looking after Mary.

The one and only time I get to meet my Mary's fiancé is at her funeral, Ann thought. *Thank you, God!*

His parents were tall, elegant and aristocratic. They looked lost, out of place. They exchanged polite handshakes and expressed their condolences. They seemed genuinely shocked and upset at the confused, intense grief they were faced with on the tarmac.

Mr Baumgarten was lost for meaningful words too. Ann thanked him for everything he'd done. She knew he'd paid for all this.

Mary's coffin emerged from the back of the plane. Ann moaned and collapsed into Stan. He wrapped his arm around her waist. She buried her head in the wet tweed of his coat. She felt physical pain. She thought her heart would burst.

As the undertakers were about to lift the coffin off the trolley into the hearse, Chris went over. Joe and Arthur followed. Then Stan and Alan. They all helped to lift it. It was heavy, lead-lined to preserve the body, important when travelling such a distance. The coffin could not be opened.

They drove to Omagh in silence, the swish of the windscreen wipers providing a hypnotic, white noise soundtrack.

* * *

The Reverend Goodman was waiting at the church. Stan, Joe, Arthur and Chris took up position to carry Mary in, but they struggled under the weight. Al and the undertaker had to step in and help. Ann could see tears on all their faces. She hadn't cried for days, but this was too much. She felt lost.

Reverend Goodman prayed and talked about God's great plan. *Glad to be part of it*, Ann thought as his words blurred into a baritone drone. Joe had his arm round her. Daisy was between Alan and Arthur, their arms wrapped round each other. Willy was holding onto his nana. Stan stared at the organ pipes. Chris was being supported by his ma and da, one on either side. Al stood solid between Muriel and Hilda.

Ann was brought back from the black when the Reverend Goodman stopped talking. He said the church would remain open for as long as they needed. The verger would come to lock up later on. They all sat on, almost silent sobbing and sniffing the only sounds.

Chris got up and laid his head on the coffin, spreading his arms out along the shiny oak. His chest was heaving.

It got dark. The church got cold.

Ann realised her bum was numb and she stood up. 'I could murder a fish supper,' she said to the holy space.

Everyone agreed that food would be a good idea. She assumed that Mr Baumgarten, Chris and his parents would go back to the Silverbirch Hotel. But Chris said he wasn't leaving; they could lock him in. Daisy volunteered to stay with him.

Eventually the verger convinced them that he had to lock up – insurance and security and all that.

The big wooden doors slammed shut behind them.

* * *

The world and the crows were packed into the church for the funeral. Everyone else stood outside. It was still raining.

Ann listened to the blur of comforting Christian cliches. The Reverend Goodman was saying all the usual things, except he missed out the bit about how bloody cruel and unfair it all was. Obviously, some things had escaped the notice of the celestial planning department.

Ann bowed her head at the appropriate moments. She noticed little specks of dust and the knots and imperfections in the wooden floor.

When the organist struck up 'Abide with me', the floodgates opened again. Her mind was a black, bottomless void.

She needed to be supported as Mary's coffin was lifted onto the men's shoulders, the effort etched onto their faces, their wet eyes staring straight ahead.

Harry and Nigel took over from Arthur and Willy at the church door for the last short lift to the hearse.

The police ensured their cortege didn't have to stop anywhere, with officers at every junction keeping traffic at bay, and they saluted the coffin as it passed.

By the time they got to the Dublin Road Cemetery, the storm had picked up and the rain showed no sign of stopping. The biting wind whistled through the hole in Ann's soul. It was as if she was floating, looking down on the desolate scene. All feelings, all thoughts had stopped.

At the graveside, Daisy held on to Ma on one side and Alan, the other; Al was between Mu and Hilda. Willy and Arthur stood tall beside Joe. Chris was being held up by his parents.

Ann noticed Stan standing beside her. He was hunched with the weight of his armour, tears streaming from glassy eyes.

'Earth to earth. Ashes to ashes …'

Ann looked around at everyone. Love was holding them all up. On this day, in this moment, love was all they had. It was all they needed.

She looked over towards Walter's headstone. *Look after her for me, Blondie.*

The leaves rustled in the wind, and she swore she heard him whisper back, 'I promise. I love you, Ann Brown.'

About the author

Sam Young was born and raised in Omagh. He went to both Protestant and Catholic schools before university. He worked in financial services before retiring in 2021.

He and his wife, Mae, have travelled extensively, but long haul has become shorter haul following Mae's MS diagnosis.

Sam's other loves are gardening, rugby (Ulster and Ireland), football (Leeds United) and the blues. He reckons these last two are made for each other!

The Cruellest Month is the sequel to the well-received *Dancehall Days* (2024) and the second novel in the Ann Brown trilogy, a story inspired by the life and times of Sam's late mother.

@SamYoungAuthor

@samyoung_author

Printed in Dunstable, United Kingdom

71009554R00231